FALCONI'S GIFT

FALCONI'S GIFT

First Book In The Viking Saga Series

GARY DOC NELSON

Waterside Productions

First Printing, 2021

ISBN-13: 978-1-939116-78-9 print edition
ISBN-13: 978-1-941768-25-9 ebook edition

Waterside Productions
2055 Oxford Ave
Cardiff, CA 92007
www.waterside.com

For my children, Matt, Adrienne, Gary II, and Whitney

TABLE OF CONTENTS

Prologue

THE BEGINNING 941 AD

Three longboats rowed west around the toe of land to the north. Each side of the lead ship had twenty-five oars, half of them manned by two men. The two ships following each had twenty oars both larboard and starboard. Somewhat faster than their leader, they were single stroked, but with extra men in the hold, sitting below the rowing thwarts. At a signal from the lead boat, they came along side and the captain of each climbed on the larger vessel.

The three captains were dressed in the same long woolen tunics and sealskin boots with wrappings around wool leggings. Around their shoulders, extending to their waists, were cloaks of animal fur, one of wolf, one of sewn pelts of Arctic fox. The leader who welcomed them preferred wolverine, as it never froze, no matter how low the temperature or ferocious the wind. All three wore beards, with various strains of blond and red mixing in profusion. The only thing that distinguished them from each other was their shoulder covering and the style of their helmets. In all other ways, they were identical—so much so that in a hall, when they had discarded their cloaks, their own men could not tell them apart.

They were triplets, identical in all aspects—size, strength, and courage—and inseparable since their birth, which had caused their mother's death. They grew up until they were eleven in a small, isolated village, three wet nurses giving them nourishment without caring which child they suckled. The village offered no other children their age to play with. Their father was conflicted, proud of his three male offspring yet blaming them for the death of his wife. He resolved his dilemma by providing for them from a distance: he retained the three wet nurses, and when the boys were three, he sent one of his men to the village to begin instructing them in the manly arts. When the triplets were eleven, he brought them to his own stead and soon wished he had not.

The boys were strange. They could speak the Nordic tongue, but when they conversed with each other, they used their own private language. Most of the time, though, they would not even speak. They simply looked at each other and then got up at the same time, or nodded to each other, as if they had spoken out loud. Each had an affinity for a specific skill. One was becoming a fine sailor, seemingly one with the small boat that he sailed in the bay. Another would sail as well, but always had an eye toward the horizon with an affinity for sensing what weather was approaching. The third, Jarl, who their father suspected had been the first born, spent more time learning weapons and asking the older warriors about battles, both at sea and on land, his questions penetrating and insightful. The other boys, although identical, looked up to Jarl as their leader, following his actions with a unity of purpose. The three had quickly dominated the other children, even older boys, by providing a united front. The nurse maids had done their job well and each was large for his age, looking to take on the strength and grace of his father. At twelve he took them a-Viking, raiding south across the inland sea. Seven years later they had their own longboat. Two years after that they had three longboats, but rather than raid independently, they always operated in concert.

Standing in the stern, the longboat rising and falling in the swell of the rising tide, they discussed the final preparations for their attack. It was a conflict they had not wanted but now felt was inevitable. Despite their successes in the past year, the three had been shunned by other Vikings, unable to join the fleets which were raiding to the south or across the North Sea to the island of the Angles. They had sent a messenger to the chief of this land, asking for a meeting to resolve whatever the dispute might be, but the request was not answered, and the messenger had not returned.

They had decided to beach their ships on a small rocky spit and march inland to the chief's stead rather than row the two kilometers up the small inlet. They feared that the banks of the inlet would allow for an ambush by archers and not permit their craft to turn around if a quick withdrawal was necessary. Redhand, was a powerful chief, able to call at least twenty remaining longboats to his leadership, but his men were spread wide, and it was their hope to strike quickly before help could arrive.

As they moved across the boulder-strewn landscape and into the rich cultivated ground that fronted Redhand's stead, a group of armed men appeared from the village nestled in the hollow at the end of the inlet. Jarl noted that the numbers were equal to his own band, but the quality of the weapons and armor was not. With a silent command to his brothers, they moved at a run toward Redhand's warriors.

Only a few weapons had clashed when a grey-bearded giant with fine armor stepped forward and yelled, "Stop!" in a voice so deep and powerful that both sides hesitated. Jarl quickly bellowed, "Falkhand, hold!" Only a few clashes of sword, axe, and shield followed, and then those arms fell quiet as well.

"Jarl Falkhand, I would speak with you." The giant held his sword level with the ground in the palms of both hands.

The leader of the attacking force stood forward, his brothers moving to both the right and left of their line without a spoken word. "I am Falkhand."

An uneasy truce was quickly agreed upon, and the leaders sat in chairs hurried from the adjacent longhouse. "Why have you attacked me?" Redhand asked sternly. "I have ever been on good terms with your father."

"You and other Vikings have shunned us during the last raiding season and this. You have killed our messenger. An attack by you and others was expected."

"I have not killed your messenger. He is in my home." Redhand jerked his head toward the longhouse that had produced the chairs. "You really have no idea why you are scorned by all? Two seasons ago did you not raid with the chief Blood Axe to the island?"

"We did. We had three ships. We joined his eight. It was successful."

"Not so for Blood Axe. He lost many men and gained little. It is said that you betrayed him, left him to perish."

"That is a lie. Before we attacked the village he had selected, we could see that they were prepared and had many men to repel our landing. There were too many men to have come from that small town. I realized that they must have brought the entire defenses from the larger settlement to the north. I spoke to Blood Axe, telling him this. We could row there faster than the defenders could travel by land. Blood Axe is a stupid brute. He would not listen. He had eight ships; I had three. We left him to his folly and attacked the northern town. If he lost men, it is his fault, not mine."

"This is not what the skalds sing in their saga," said Redhand, leaning forward.

"What saga?"

"You really don't know? You have never heard it told? Of course you wouldn't. No skald would risk his life telling it to you or your men."

Jarl heard the sound of muffled weapons and turned as one with his brothers. Between his men and the sea they saw advancing an equal number of warriors as protected Redhand's stead, but these were fully armed, most with mail and shield.

"Ease, Falkhand. I have no desire to kill you or your men, but only a fool would not ensure peace at a council."

"If that is true," answered Jarl, realizing that a fight would no longer be in his favor, "then I ask you to bring a skald who can sing me this false saga."

"That will offer no problem," said Redhand, motioning a man from the third rank of the men behind him to the front. "It is not a long saga."

The skald began nervously, but after a few sentences, his deep, resonant voice caught the cadence of the tale, and seeing no reaction from either Falkhand or his men, he grew in confidence. He sang about Blood Axe's heroics and fighting prowess, and of the Falkhands' treachery and use of black magic to conjure up more enemies to face Blood Axe's men. At the end, Jarl stood, his body rigid. The skald backed quickly away through the ranks of warriors.

"I mis-spoke about Blood Axe. He is a stupid brute who lies and would lay the blame on others for his own stupidity. He was warned before the raid, both of the danger and that I was leaving."

Suddenly, words flashed through Jarl's head: *To your back.* He couldn't tell which of his brothers had sent the warning, but he moved quickly to the side, drawing his sword, swinging it over his head toward the spot where he had just been standing. Behind him a youth was trying to redirect his sword from the path that seconds before would have hit Jarl Falkhand. It slammed down onto his chair as Jarl's blade took the boy's hand at the wrist, slicing cleanly through it. The hand, still gripping the sword that would have taken Jarl's life, fell to the grass of the meadow as the boy was grabbed by two of Redhand's warriors and one of Falkhand's.

Thank you, brother, Jarl answered as his breathing again slowed. He did not lower his sword but turned toward Redhand, who he now realized had also shouted a warning.

"That was not my doing. I am never foresworn. You will not be harmed here."

Falkhand was loath to show fear or even concern in front of the old chief, particularly as he was surrounded by his warriors. He nodded as he slid his sword back in its scabbard. However, a group of his warriors circled around him, facing the rear ranks from where the youth had come. "I have been told that of you, which is why I sent my man to ask for a council."

"He came, but a delegation from Blood Axe came three days before, asking for my boats to join him in this year's raids and warning me that an attack from you was imminent. That was a moon ago. Your man told me that if he did not return, you would consider me of the same mind as the others. I was reluctant to let him to return to you, as I thought he might be a spy. Your man was right. Blood Axe was wrong. What would you have of me?"

"The saga explains much. It worries me that so many believe the lie. I would ask two things of you."

"What are they?"

"I would ask your advice on how to deal with this saga—how to get the other tribes to trust us again."

Redhand laughed, a deep roar of a laugh moving up through his chest and throat, crinkling his eyes and spurting saliva into the air in front of him. "To think we almost came to blows. I have been thinking on that very thing since I first heard the saga and considered the source. You and your brothers have a good name. All that have sailed with you praise your ability and your trustworthiness. However, they also all suspect dark magic in your success.'

"The saga has two messages: first, that you deceived and broke your oath to Blood Axe. This, most that know you or Blood Axe do not believe. The second part, about black magic, is the more dangerous. Even watching your response here today, I am inclined to believe it. How did you know the youth was about to kill you?"

"My brother warned me. You did not hear him. It was not black magic. We are brothers born together. Our mother died during our birth and our father left us alone with our nurses. Growing up, we developed our own language that only we use. It is not magic. It is simply the circumstance of our birth. The same is true of our luck. Kjell has great ways with ships, Jan has great weather luck and skill with crops, and I have great luck in battle. All these are things that other Vikings have, but we use them together, and it is perceived as magic." Jarl kept from the older chief that they each could speak to each other's minds. It was something that even their father had not known, only suspected.

"There is a simple solution, one that I recognized when your messenger first arrived. You must separate, at least until you each have your own reputation. I suggest that one of you go south and join the Danes under my banner. Another I will take with me as my second in command. You, Jarl Falkhand, I would have stay in your lands. I will assist you in raiding south and will pay you each year for securing our lands from the east when I go a-Viking with your brother. Soon the talk will be of Blood Axe's deceit and your luck. Everyone wants to sail with luck. What is your second request?"

"If I am to stay at my stead, I would have the boy I have hurt today. I would teach him how to fight and sail. I would help him become whole again."

"Granted, but you will get more than you bargained for. The boy is my daughter, Gun."

CHAPTER ONE

Sausalito, California: November 16, 2000

The small parking lot in front of the Seahawk restaurant was, as usual, filled with cars, most of them luxury models, which left precious little room for walking to the entrance. It was peaceful, the sounds of piano and guitar floating from the bar inside. Ed Falcon moved across the pavement with a firm stride that belied his eighty years. The sour, salty smell of the outgoing tide below the pier comforted him.

Behind him a large black BMW entered the parking lot, cruising slowly as it sought a space. As it came to a stop, the old man stepped aside and up the first of two stairs to the small landing that fronted the restaurant.

"Good luck finding a spot. Thank God for the public parking lot half a block down," Falcon thought. He did not have to worry about such things, as he had walked the four blocks from the home he shared with his son, Mats, who now ran the restaurant.

The BMW hesitated behind a Lexus before moving slowly toward the exit, not having found a stall. Falcon couldn't see through the windows, so deeply tinted that even the sun's late afternoon rays did not penetrate the car's interior.

"BMW ... Basic Marin Wheels," the old man said under his breath as he turned toward the entrance.

A sudden tortured screech of tires spun Falcon's head around. The BMW was re-entering the parking lot at an uncontrollable speed. It slammed to a stop directly behind the Lexus. The rear doors of the Lexus flew open and three men jumped out, waving pistols. They were met with automatic gunfire from the back window of the BMW before they could fire. Riddled with bullets, they slammed back against the open doors before falling to the ground. The driver of the Lexus, seeing the fate of his companions, opened his door. Partly screened by the rear doors and the men on the ground, he leaped over the hood of the Mercedes parked next to him, escaping the hail of bullets that had left his companions writhing on the ground. As he jumped, he fired three shots, making small popping sounds as each round entered the side of the black sedan.

The old man watched as the rear door of the BMW opened and a dark-haired man rolled out onto the pavement, returning the fire in short bursts. With no immediate shelter around, Falcon dropped to one knee on the restaurant's entryway, eyes wide, alert, watching the scene in front of him.

Between the front of the parked cars and the water, the driver of the Lexus was picking his way toward the restaurant, firing as he moved. He jumped to the top step, but before he could find safety in the restaurant he was caught by a burst of automatic fire. The driver went down, twisting spasmodically, staggering against the old man and grasping him for support as he fell toward the ground, his weapon clattering to one side. A smile spread across the face of the assassin as he straightened and walked toward them.

The assassin slowly climbed the steps until he stood directly over the fallen gunman, who had pinned the old man under him as he fell. Raising the gun from his hip, he pointed it down at the man's chest.

The old man had pulled a fisherman's knife from his pocket. He shouted an oath in the language of his youth, trying desperately to push the fallen man off his chest. Age had diminished his strength but had not dulled his instincts, nor the look of ferocity in his eyes. Pinned as he was, however, he could not provide the needed power as he threw his knife at the gunman standing above him.

The assassin's head snapped upright as he heard Falcon's words, seeming to understand their meaning. Then, hesitating for a second as the knife hit the stock of his rifle and smiling, he stood over the dying gunman and the struggling old man beneath him and fired four quick bursts. "*La morte viene a tutti noi* – death comes to us all!" he said, as if answering the old man, and then moved quickly down the stairs to his car.

Mats Falcon, the old man's son, was in the small office behind the reception desk. The first shots had not fully registered with him. Then he heard the second burst of gunfire, and recognizing it for what it was, he bolted past the reception desk.

Mats Falcon heard his father's death scream as he tore through the front door of the restaurant. He watched as the killer ran down the steps, stopping briefly next to the Lexus to spray the three men on the ground with a final fatal burst before climbing into the BMW.

Kneeling, Mats grabbed the blood-soaked man still covering his father, casting him to the side. He saw his father's eyes staring up at him, wide and dead, his chest torn and bleeding, his blood mingling with that of the other man.

"No...No!" Mats clutched his father and buried his face in his limp shoulder. Then he heard the dying gunman groan.

"Leca...Leca..."

Mats tore his eyes away from his father. The man was reaching for Mats' arm, his eyes riveting him. He gasped his last breath as he moaned to Mats a last time.

"Leca..."

CHAPTER TWO

Mats skipped a rock across the abnormally placid waters of the Bay, bouncing it softly off the bronze statue of a harbor seal perched some fifteen yards offshore. Without showing interest in the task, he scanned the ground for another suitable stone. He had inherited his father's build and grace of movement; his dirty blond hair and blue eyes contrasted with his olive complexion, which was often mistaken for a tan but was with him all year.

"Mats, you're exhibiting the classic signs of traumatic loss. I've treated enough cases like yours to know the typical recovery patterns." Mike Ferrera flipped the rock he was playing with to Mats.

"Yeah, swell. Any of your other cases involve seeing your father shot down in front of your own eyes?"

"It's been six months now, Mats."

Five years ago, they had met playing racquetball. What had started as a weekly game had matured into a strong friendship. Since the murders, Mike had been coming around more often than usual, forcing Mats into playing several times a week and to have a beer or two afterward. It was an indication of how distracted Mats was that he had not realized Mike was gradually changing their relationship. He was functioning more like the therapist he was at the office than like the close friend he had been to Mats.

"Six months," Mats repeated. He heaved a sigh and skipped the stone, which flew just over the seal's head. "And I still expect to see him when I come home. Or hear him greeting the patrons as they wait in the bar."

"I've noticed," Mike said. "And I know you miss him, Mats. Six months is not very long, but clinically speaking, you should be starting to move forward ... getting on with the rest of your life, realizing it'll be a life without your father. You show few signs of coming to grips with this. If anything, you are slipping into a deeper melancholy."

"I can't get past it, Mike." Mats turned to face his friend, tears streaming down his cheeks. "Every time I turn around, I'm reminded of him ... passing the boat ... getting mail addressed to him. Eating pizza, for Christ's sake."

"It's okay to miss him, Mats. It's okay to be reminded of him. He was your dad, and you were as close a father and son as I've ever known. But you can't keep your dad alive and maintain your own sanity."

"I know I have to move on with my life, but how do I do that, Mike?" asked Mats, looking back at the Bay. "How do I 'move forward'? He was my only family. He was my life and I was his. He was my only parent since I was six years old. We were so close that we knew what the other was thinking. We'd be walking to the restaurant and I'd look at the dock and know that he wanted to go for a sail without him saying a word. The restaurant, my wealth, hell, I wouldn't have this life but for him."

They both sat down on the single bench, ignoring the crusted salt that filled the cracks in the wood grain.

"Don't get me wrong, Mats. You still have grieving to do, and that's all right, but you can't let it consume you. When was the last time you went out on a date?"

"Don't get on that, Mike. I'll date again when I'm ready. And it's not what I wish I had said to him or told him. He was the one who kept secrets. How many times have you been over to our house? You didn't even know his real name was Egel Falconi, not Ed Falcon. Did you ever hear him talk about himself? Sure, he would go on about the boat, or sailing, even about the buying of the pier, and building the restaurant, but did you ever hear him say a word about himself before he came here, or even what he did during the war?" *Even his will has added to the mystery,* Mats thought; it had left everything to him, including Egel's gold ring and the contents of a safe deposit box, which had had only one item in it—a heavy leather notebook with about twenty pages of loose computer paper filled on both sides with his father's precise hand folded around it. The bundle was wrapped in plastic and secured with clear packing tape. A note was attached with the same tape: *You will know when to open this. Do not open it until then.* What the hell did that mean?

"The restaurant has been good for me these past months. It's given me a focus, an outlet for my energy, and a few hours a day that I'm forced to think of something else."

"That's true, but for now it may be too much of an anchor to your everyday life with your dad. You have a good staff. The Seahawk could run itself for a couple months. What do you think about taking a vacation? There must be someplace you've always wanted to see. You've worked damned hard to get to a place where you can take a break. So, take it. Take a break now when you need it the most."

It was difficult for Mike Ferrera to advise Mats so directly. All of his training as a therapist told him to lead patients gradually into realizing what they needed, having them come to the conclusion themselves, but Mats was more than a patient. He was a friend.

"Dad and I always wanted to go to New Zealand, sail around the island." Mats tossed another rock, which skipped three times before striking the seal's head.

"Would that be bringing your problem with you?" Mike squeezed his friend's forearm.

"You're right. I'd feel guilty for going without him."

"Is there a place that you alone have wanted to see? Maybe a place you've never mentioned to anyone?"

"Dad came from Corsica. I've always wanted to see where he grew up. He didn't talk about it much, but when I was a child, he used to tell me bedtime stories about knights and pirates, with Corsica as the background. I once asked him if the stories were true, and I remember he just smiled and got real quiet."

"There you have it. You might learn about the life that formed your dad. I think it's a great idea. The restaurant will take care of itself. I'll watch it if you need someone to make an appearance." Ferrera stood up. It was a technique designed to close a session, which was exactly what he wanted to do: to have Mats' comment become a decision.

Mats didn't get up with him. Instead he stayed sitting on the bench, staring at the water. He was thinking of what he had truly known of his papa. He knew he had come to Sausalito in the thirties as a teen, working as a fisherman, then buying the dock on which the restaurant now stood. He had married late in life. He had anglicized his name; Falconi became Falcon, and he gave his first name as Ed to all but his family, who still used Egel or "Papa." Only when he spoke did he give himself away as a naturalized citizen. But he was a quiet man, and he spoke very little.

Mats closed his eyes. The lapping water against the shore brought back memories of his father's bedtime tales. It was the only time he spoke of his homeland. So many stories were filled with sea voyages, his father painting a picture of the shores of Corsica. The lapping of the waves on the rocks reminded Mats of those tales. *He let the smell of the receding tide fill his mind, remembering…*

Egel Falcon looked at his son and smiled. The five-year-old was half sitting, half lying against his bedstead. The boy's eyes were already drooping, but every few minutes they would flick wide open, as if startled, before slowly relaxing again to their almost closed position.

"In the fourteenth century, a young knight was returning home. In those days, it was common for young men from noble families to leave home to study with a scholar and learn the use of weapons at the castle of another nobleman. Now, after two years, the young knight was traveling from his training place to his island home. Traveling with him was his mother, the Baroness, and his manservant, Carlo. His tutor, Master Margaux, and the rest of the company traveled behind with two carts containing the Baroness's acquisitions from the trading fairs in Paris. The roads, rutted and uneven, caused their weapons to jangle and clank as the horses kicked up small puffs of dust behind them."

Young Mats interrupted. "Papa, did the boy have a sword?"

"Yes. But the preferred weapon of his father, and his father before him, was the battle axe. His manservant named Carlo carried his master's axe as well as his bow."

"Is the story true, Papa?"

"Yes. All the stories I tell you are true, and you must remember them."

The young boy exaggerated a nod up and down three times just to show he understood. "What was his name, Papa? The young knight?"

"Thomaso. His name was Thomaso.

South of France 1328

Thomaso's mother looked at him as they rode side by side. She was proud of him and how he had matured in the two years he had spent in Burgundy. When he had left Ajaccio at sixteen, he had not yet started to fill out the muscular shoulders and chest she now found so like her husband's. She had prevailed on her husband to let her travel to Paris. Returning with her son could be one of the last motherly acts she would be permitted before Thomaso moved completely into the world of men. Now she knew that it had been worth the effort. Thomaso had not only matured physically but had also assumed the quiet air of authority that his father possessed. Carlo, who had joked with him just two years before, now showed him deference, addressing him as 'milord' without a hint of familiarity.

"'Carlo!' Thomaso called over his shoulder, beckoning him to ride abreast. 'My mother has need to rest.'

"'Yes, milord. I will find a camp along the banks of the Rhône. Tomorrow we will surely be sailing to Corsica.' Carlo galloped off ahead of the small party, disappearing around a curve in the road, leading the four pack animals.

"Half an hour later, Carlo came back and led the travelers through a small stand of live oaks into a small meadow. He had already cleared an area and built a fire pit with freshly cut boughs at the ready. As soon as they dismounted, Carlo started to unpack their horses. Another half hour saw the Baroness's tent raised and the evening meal starting to cook on the fire. The baggage carts, and the servants and men-at-arms who guarded them, camped several hundred meters to the rear, providing privacy for the lead group.

"The river next to the camp ran freely, too deep to cross at this point and almost fifty meters across. Thomaso, seeing the camp set up, took his bow and rode downriver in search of game to liven up the evening's fare."

"Was he a good shot, Papa?"

"Yes, Mats, he was a good shot," his father said. "In those days people still depended on wild game such as deer to provide variety to their meals, but already wildlife was becoming too scarce to allow the common people to hunt it. Nobles were designating large tracts of land that only they could hunt."

"Then wasn't Thomaso worried about hunting?" asked the boy.

"He shouldn't have been. You see, there was not much traveling done in those days. Nobles would take soldiers to a distant war or go on a pilgrimage, but the common people usually spent their lives within sight of their lord's castle. Nobles in transit had certain privileges, but Thomaso was still cautious because the nobles of southern France were never on the best terms with those of Corsica, whose allegiances were often to the city-states of Italy."

"Oh," Mats said, as if comprehending.

"Thomaso had bagged two rabbits and was closing in on a third when he heard the sound of swords clashing coming from the camp. He ran to his horse, startling the rabbit he was stalking. It took only minutes to gallop the distance, but already the sound of combat had ceased. Drawing his sword, Thomaso rode into the camp and reined up in front of his mother's tent.

"There were six armed men in his camp, one dressed as a noble in an embroidered jerkin over a shirt of chain mail. Two of the others were holding Carlo, who had a gash down his left forearm, still bleeding through the pressure of his fingers. Thomaso saw a man's legs stretched out on the ground behind his mother's tent. Another had blood running down his leg. Carlo had done well before being captured.

"'What is the meaning of this?' Thomaso asked in his deepest voice as his mother emerged from her tent. 'I am Sir Thomaso Falconi and this is the Baroness Falconi, my mother. What right have you to seize my man-at-arms?'

"'I am Claude d'Avignon, son of Charles d'Avignon, lord of this region. Please put down your sword. You are to come as guests to my father's castle. Your man disobeyed my command and drew his sword, killing one of my men. You are fortunate that I had my father's orders to bring you to him alive, or I would have returned the favor.'

"Thomaso gauged the situation. Mounted, he could easily take two of the remaining guards, but the man with the weapon at Carlo's back would surely kill him at the first sign of hostility. His tutor and baggage guards were still some distance behind. When they arrived, they would still be outnumbered. Still...

"'Thomaso, put away your sword.' It was his mother, who had read his thoughts and stopped him a moment before he would have struck Claude down. 'D'Avignon wants us to be his guests while he holds us for ransom. A despicable practice, but one we have come to expect from the lesser nobility of this region. They would rather live on the wealth of others than manage their own affairs properly. Your father will pay the ransom price and after we are free, he will manage the insult.'

"'There is no need for unpleasantness here,' Claude d'Avignon said to the Baroness. 'I am sure that when your husband understands why my father requires the coin, he will want to help. Your presence as our guests is only intended to draw attention to our need.'

"'I can only hope that your need will one day bring you to Corsica, where we might return your hospitality,' replied Thomaso, placing his sword back in its scabbard. He dismounted and walked to his mother's side. 'And my men? You will offer them your hospitality as well?'

"'They will be taken care of if they cause no further trouble. My men will break your camp while you accompany me to our castle.'

"The trail to the castle of Avignon, which was much closer to Arles than to the Pope's residence at Avignon, wound south along the banks of the Rhône. Several times it broke away from the bank, traveling up small tributaries, past fields cultivated with grapes, wheat, and rye. 'Do not think so badly of my father and me,' said young d'Avignon, pulling up aside Thomaso as they rode the trail. 'It is not his desire to waylay nobles such as you. He would not do it now except his need for funds is extraordinary.'

"'Not nearly as extraordinary as the amount he will spend on his defense once we are free,' replied the Baroness Falconi under her breath, riding just ahead.

"'Please understand, my father has been excommunicated by the Pope. Only a payment of three hundred florins will lift the edict.'

"The Baroness kicked her horse in response, opening two lengths between herself and the young d'Avignon. They passed through a vineyard, the trail winding between its ancient vines before skirting the cliffs above the river a hundred meters below. The trail was narrow at this point, requiring the party to ride single file.

"Carlo was riding behind Thomaso, his hands tied, with one of d'Avignon's men riding between them, holding Carlo's reins. The Baroness had cleaned and stitched his wound, binding it with clean linen. The flow of blood had stopped but not before staining through the bandage. Another of d'Avignon's band rode behind Carlo;

this man was the brother of the man Carlo had killed. As soon as they mounted, he had whispered threats to Carlo, assuring him that he was a dead man. When they reached the castle, Carlo would not be watched and then he would have his throat cut. Carlo tried several times to turn, receiving a sharp poke with the point of the man's sword for his effort.

"As the column rounded a sharp bend in the trail, Carlo reared his horse, spinning it into the mount of the guard behind him and causing him to drop his sword. The sudden movement also jerked the reins from the man ahead.

"With his hands tied, Carlo relied on his knees and feet to urge his horse down the trail. He had acted out of anger and fear; now his only hope was to escape. The guard in front of Thomaso was slow to realize what had happened, but when he did, he acted quickly. Shouting a warning, he drew his sword, racing past the man who had been guarding Carlo from behind. With no one to stop him, Thomaso followed, bringing his mother and the rest of the party charging after them.

"Carlo made it to the cliff before his pursuer caught him. The first sword thrust caught him across his back, just below the shoulder blade. His cry of pain caused Thomaso to spur his mount even faster down the uneven trail. Twice he caught sight of Carlo, his hands still tied, the guard in pursuit. The swordsman was having trouble getting a good swipe at Carlo due to the narrowness of the trail, with a cliff falling to the river below on one side and dense brush on the other. But when the trail widened in the vine-yard, he would have no such trouble. Then, in clear view of Thomaso, Carlo's horse stumbled, pitching him over its head and sending him sprawling on the uneven ground. The swordsman was having difficulty reaching him without dismounting. Dazed and unaware of the danger, Carlo started to rise. Thomaso, seeing the threat to his manservant, urged his horse hard into the flank of the swordsman. The man acted instinctively, turning in his saddle, slashing back with his sword. Thomaso, unarmed, had no chance to defend himself. The blade sliced cleanly through his neck, severing the carotid artery, his life's blood spurting from his body as he fell to the ground.

"'No!' yelled Claude d'Avignon as he saw Thomaso receive the stroke.

"His man-at-arms had dismounted, ready to make sure of what was already a certainty, the death of Thomaso Falconi. At his lord's shouted command, he stopped his thrust, aimed at Thomaso's heart. Thomaso, growing weaker with the loss of blood, turned toward d'Avignon and hissed through injured vocal cords, blood bubbling from his wound, 'You will pay...'"

Egel Falconi looked at his sleeping son and smoothed the covers, arranging Mats' favorite blanket next to his cheek. "Sweet dreams, my son," he said as he bent and kissed Mats' forehead. He realized the absurdity of the wish: few Falconi dreams were sweet.

Sometimes Egel wondered if he was robbing his son of too much of his heritage. Egel had left Corsica as a teenager, partly to escape a fate that had seemed preordained. Corsican life depended on family ties and alliances. His family had never produced more than a few children each generation so that slowly, over the centuries, its power base had eroded until he was the last of the line. Vendeta had cost him his own father and had shown him how tenuous his legacy was. He had looked at Europe as he was growing up and even as a teenager had seen the inevitability of further warfare, and with it the threat to his own survival. So he had left his homeland. He had sold much of the Falconi land. Those properties he could not get a fair price for he had given to loyal friends. At 15, already with the body of a man, he had immigrated to the United States. He was smart and well educated. He had arrived during the latter part of the Great Depression with enough cash and the training to start a small fishing business that had thrived in Sausalito, the community it served.

Falcon glanced away from his son to the dirigibles depicted on his wallpaper, wondering if he had done the right thing in leaving Corsica, the home of his ancestors for almost a thousand years. He never spoke to either his wife or his son about his youth in Corsica. His only concession was to teach his son the Corsican dialect. Both Mats and his mother, Katarina, knew of his origin, of course, but they never asked about it. He was the kind of man whom one did not ask questions of a personal nature, not even his own family.

Now he wondered if he was denying his son important information he might one day need. At five years old, Mats already showed all the traits of the Falconi line. He had even taken to the languages so well that as the boy grew older, Egel could tell his stories in English, French, or Corsican.

The bedtime stories he had told Mats from the time of his birth were his way of passing on the Falconi legacy, the stories his father had told and his father before him. When he was old enough to understand, he let his son know that the bedtime tales were in truth the oral history of his family. He also told his son that he must keep the stories a secret. The boy would remember them and perhaps more on his own, if he had the Gift. Even though Mats was asleep, he would remember, as Egel himself had, and as his own father had. But Mats was young, and he was old. He made up his mind to write the stories down and add them to the notebook that had been passed down over the generations. Should he die before the stories had been repeated enough to stamp them indelibly on the child's memory, the heritage would survive.

He brushed the child's hair back from his forehead and continued the story, as if impelled to imprint it on his son.

Southern France – 1328

"The Baroness was slow to understand what had happened to her son. D'Avignon's back obscured Thomaso. Then she saw the stream of blood still flowing on the rocky surface of the trail, as if trying to reach and mingle with the flow of the Rhône River below. She felt faint, grabbing the rim of her saddle with both hands before slipping to the ground with barely enough strength to stand. Slowly, she recovered and moved to her son's side. D'Avignon relinquished his kneeling position, allowing her to cradle Thomaso's head in her lap. His eyes were closed, and the pulse of blood had slowed to a trickle. His body was already starting to lose color. She sobbed, at first so softly that even d'Avignon, standing behind her, did not hear her. But as her grief overcame her, she moaned, crying openly with the anguish of losing her only son.

"D'Avignon also grieved the young noble's death. The practice of detaining nobles for ransom was not uncommon. It had its strict rules of conduct and chivalry. They must not be harmed. They would, in most cases, live as well as their captors while staying in their household. Young Falconi's death would be a further smear on the reputation of the d'Avignon family, even though it had been an accident. It might even require that the mother be set free with a written apology and an honor guard of the House d'Avignon to assure her safe travel to Corsica.

He was not sure. His father would know what to do. His father would also punish him for failing in what had seemed a simple assignment.

"As the Baroness's sobs subsided, d'Avignon reached down, clasping her shoulders from behind, urging her to her feet. She rose slowly, turning to face him.

"'I am truly sorry,' he said. 'There was to be no fighting. You were to be treated as guests.'

"Without warning she lashed out at his eyes, scratching and tearing at his flesh. Her screams, naming him a murderer, echoed off the cliffs as a guard moved to restrain her.

"Carlo was lying on the trail facedown, unmoving. He had recovered full consciousness but had forced himself to lie still. Only when d'Avignon dismounted had he risked a glance back down the trail. He saw the body of his lord and the anxiety of his captors, but he decided there was nothing he could do. He lay quietly, watching for an opportunity through squinting eyes. By the time the Baroness arrived at her son's side, he had flexed all of his extremities, detecting no broken bones. The cut on his back was not deep. His arm hurt far worse. He had also become lucid but had so far been unsuccessful in his attempt to devise a plan of action that would improve his situation.

"When the Baroness Falconi dismounted and raised Thomaso's head to her lap, Carlo for the first time saw the extent of the wound. Thomaso surely was dying or already dead, the amount of blood covering his riding garment a testament that the wound had been a fatal one. Carlo knew that it was partly his fault, his responsibility that his lord lay dying. Had he not panicked under the threats of his guard, had he not attempted an escape, then in all probability his lord would not have been struck the mortal blow. Now, with Thomaso dead, Carlo knew there was no guarantee that the entire entourage would not be murdered once inside the d'Avignon castle.

"Carlo heard the outcry of grief from the Baroness. By then the two other guards had arrived, and even had he not been in a weakened state, Carlo would not have been able to intervene effectively. Their arrival made his decision for him.

"Slowly he inched his body toward the side of the trail. All attention was focused on his mistress. He crawled until the shoulder-high scrub brush hid him from their view, then moved through it, careful to make no noise that would alert his captors to his purpose. Hunched over, he continued through the underbrush until he broke through into a vineyard. The guards had not yet noticed his absence, but it would not be long before they would pursue him.

"The ground was rocky, and it took little effort to hide his tracks. Without a horse he could not hope to outdistance his captors, but there were tricks perfected in the hills of Corsica, tricks that the Falconi clan had devised over centuries of being island-bound, that would serve him well now. He moved into the vineyard with care, so as not to disturb the dirt where he stepped. When he was ten rows deep, he found what he had been seeking: a natural depression in the ground, surrounded by loose dirt and close vines. He quickly took off his riding cloak, reversing it to expose the brown inner lining. Then, making sure there were no tracks or blood droppings marking his position, he lay down in the depression and pulled the cloak over himself. His back ached where his pursuer's sword had cut through the skin and lightly into his muscles, but he worked to overcome the pain. Scattering the loose dirt over his cloak, Carlo gradually camouflaged his presence until all but his head and arm were covered with dirt. Ducking under the cowl, he finished the job, tucking the last exposed corner into the depression and thereby letting the last pile of soil fall into the furrow.

"Unlike the men's horses, the Baroness's mount had not been trained for combat. She had chosen the mare in Paris strictly for comfort and reliability, not for agility in combat. Now, with the scent of Thomaso's blood filling her nostrils, and the shouts of the guards ringing in her ears, the mare was on edge. The Baroness broke away from the hold of the guard and again assailed d'Avignon, screaming in rage at the death of her son. Just then, the guard to her left looked down the trail and sounded the alarm that Carlo had escaped. As he ran toward the spot where Carlo had lain, the hilt of the guard's sword struck the already excited mare just behind the cinch. The screaming, the blow, the smell of blood—it was all too much for the frightened animal, and it lashed out in protest with its rear hoofs. One of them struck the Baroness in the back of the head.

"The Baroness Falconi's scream stopped mid-breath as she pitched forward into the arms of her captor, the basal area of her skull crushed by the kick from her own mount.

"'Oh God in heaven!' wailed Claude d'Avignon. She was dead before he caught her.

"Meanwhile, on the trail, left behind with the pack animals loaded with the sum results of Thomaso's studies, as well as with his own reference manuals, P. Margaux, master scholar and Thomaso's tutor, was left alone. Not a brave man under less trying circumstances, Margaux was badly frightened by the sounds coming from down the trail. First at a walk, then at a trot, he continued down the trail, letting his mount choose the route at each fork. Without trying to escape, without really knowing how to escape, he moved slowly away towards the mountains, seeking only safety where he could again be alone with his books and his teaching."

CHAPTER THREE

The flight to Paris from San Francisco took nearly eleven hours. Mats spent most of the time reading. Now as the 747 touched down on the runway at Orly, just outside of Paris, he wished he had forced himself to sleep, as almost every other passenger had managed during the trip.

It took less time than Mats had expected to clear French Customs and retrieve the lone bag that comprised his luggage. Too many of the things he'd thought of bringing with him had memories of his father attached to them. A cashmere sweater, a pair of slacks that Papa thought suited him particularly well—one by one Mats had discarded these items until finally he'd decided to take only his father's ring, the small, tightly wrapped notebook, and a few changes of clothes, and to shop for whatever else he needed after he landed. Starting fresh, without the emotional baggage that Mike Ferrera had pointed out, allowed him to ward off some of his grief.

The next day Mats left his hotel to experience one of the glorious late summer days that Paris sometimes provides tourists. The air was fresh, and the smell of flowers and freshly baked bread helped clear Mats' mind, dulled with the effect of the nine-hour jet lag.

At the car rental agency, he chose a Fiat over the Peugeots and German makes, threw his bag into its small trunk, and drove toward the wine-growing regions to the south. As soon as he cleared the congestion of Paris, he took a deep breath and sighed. There was an almost audible click deep inside his mind. Suddenly he felt the tension release like the unbuckling of a fat man's belt. For the first time in months he smiled to himself, actually feeling his grief slide away into the green mosaic flashing by his car's window. He smiled once more and pushed the small engine of the Fiat toward its red line as he sped down the highway.

He had left Paris shortly after noon, avoiding both the traffic that snarled the roads and the personalities of the French motorists. He had purposely made no hotel reservations past his first night in Paris. This was how he wanted to travel, by necessity letting the trip unfold without a schedule and with no itinerary.

He allowed himself to think of his father now, as the restful scenery passed by: how they would bicker good-naturedly over rooms and toilet facilities. But his eyes soon welled with tears, blurring his view of the roadway ahead, and he flicked the button on the radio to break his reverie.

He glanced at the map spread on the passenger's side seat. The radio spouted French at him through the two small speakers. The sound quality was the negative reward for renting one of the least expensive cars. Finally, he stopped at the side of the road, wiped his eyes, and looked more carefully at the map.

The next day Mats arose early, driving two hours before stopping for breakfast in Toulouse at a small café across from the Basilica of Saint-Sernin. Even before he pulled into the small square, Mats had begun to feel at home with the language filling the car through the small, squeaky speakers. He had switched from music to a station that featured talk and interviews, listening, deciphering the words and phrases with alacrity as the hours passed, his two years of Latin and three years of French, taken at the University of California's program for gifted high schoolers rather than at Tamalpais High School, finally coming into use.

Another hour in the car brought him to a bluff with an unobstructed view of the Mediterranean Sea. The sight of it filled Mats with a sense of serenity he had not felt since the day his father was murdered. The azure of the water was different from the blue-gray hue of the San Francisco Bay waters that washed the shore of Sausalito.

The small engine of the Fiat was no match for the high-powered luxury cars continually passing on their way to destinations on the coast, but Mats didn't mind the lack of power, availing himself of every opportunity to pull to the side of the road and look at the sea. Closing his eyes, he could envision the details of the coves and inlets below him.

The highway swept north away from the sea, crossing the Rhône River at Avignon. On the way north, Mats passed through the wine district whose vineyards produced hardy, robust wines from vines planted by the Romans before the birth of Christ. Mats looked over the vine-covered hills cascading down toward the river and his mood darkened. There was no clear thought of his father associated with the emotion, just a deep sense of foreboding.

He wasn't able to shake the dour feeling until he drove into Avignon. The sight of the Citadel and the stonework of the old buildings helped his mood. Lunch completed the transformation. The warming sun and the wine made him feel at home in the surroundings. He was relaxed with a feeling that he was accomplishing something by the time he climbed back into the car.

As Mats drove south, following the course of the river, he passed several stone ruins of castles perched on small steep hills, and his mind wandered to the days when they had housed noble families: days of knights and chivalry, moats and maidens, the jocular sounds of rebecs and horns, the pageantry. He recalled days his father had described in great detail as he told and retold his bed-time tales...

Corsica – Summer 1329

A brisk wind washed waves over the bow of the small trading vessel, making the ten men-at-arms nervous but having no effect on their leader, the Baron. He, like his ancestors before him, felt at home on the sea. Although he had a large fiefdom stretching far inland, the fact that Corsica was an island demanded that he be a skilled seaman, equally at home on the Mediterranean waters as onshore in his island home. His ancestors had made their fortunes as sea raiders before coming to the island from Italy with titles and lands given to them by Roger the Great. His family had proven its loyalty many times, taking to the sea in the island's defense, battling to discourage those invading noblemen who thought the island would be better off aligned with France or with the king of Aragon than with Norman Italy.

Now, with the winds howling and waves threatening to capsize the boat, the Baron Falconi took command from the ship's captain. He moved swiftly among his men, giving them a sense of purpose with orders that were instantly obeyed. The ship slowly came into the wind and the waves were cleaved by the sharp bow, easing the equine confusion in the bowels of the open boat. The horses, now able to orient themselves and stand steady against the action of the waves, calmed down.

The squall had come upon them suddenly, hot and dry off the sands of Africa. The waves it produced were not large, but their choppiness and lack of rhythm were hard to predict. A wave of any size was a concern for a coastal vessel. A diminishing freeboard of scarcely three feet made it necessary to head for the shelter of a bay at the first sign of foul weather. In a storm such as this, the angle at which the waves hit posed as much danger as their size.

They were only three hours from their destination of San Remo. If the winds would abate even a little, they could turn and run with them directly to the port where men and supplies awaited.

Mats came out of his daydream with a start, the crunch of rocks on the shoulder of the road bringing him to the realization that he was still driving. He swerved back onto the pavement and brought the car under control. He silently blamed the wine at lunch for the daydream and his lack of concentration. Then, unable to shake the reverie, he slowed and pulled to the side of the road. Two hundred yards away on a bluff guarding a bend of the river stood the ruins of a castle with two massive stone keeps. Mats brought the Fiat to a stop partway down a dirt road, which diminished to a slim path before reaching the structure.

The sun beat through the windshield onto Mats' chest as he turned off the engine. As he rolled down the window, the balmy air and the earthy smell of lilac, combining with the residual effects of the wine and the remnants of jet lag, made it impossible to keep his eyes open. Then sleep...

South of France 1329
San Remo provided a beach on which to land the animals and men. Waiting, as was expected, were five additional

knights sent by an Italian lord who had more than once relied on Baron Falconi for help. They brought with them food and supplies for a week, enough to provide for the party of fifteen on their trek to Avignon. Falconi spent little time thanking his ally before sending the boats on to Arles at the mouth of the River Rhône. Mounting his horse, he led his small band west.

The sun was setting as they pitched camp at the end of their second day. Falconi had purposefully avoided staying over at castles or inns where a sympathetic noble or inn-keeper might guess his intentions and dispatch a runner to warn d'Avignon. They traveled light. They hid their armor and most of their weapons on the pack horses, along with several bundles that had come with the Italian knights.

It was virtually impossible to overrun a castle strong-hold once the gates were closed, and this was especially true of d'Avignon's because with its two massive towers, it was designed to guard the southern approaches to the city and control all traffic on the river below. There would be supplies of grain and wine, enough to withstand a siege of many months. Natural springs were almost as impor-tant as a defensible terrain, and the castle of d'Avignon had several fine sources of water, virtually immune to poisoning from without. D'Avignon would be safe inside his stronghold against ten times the number that rode with Falconi. Long before a siege would have any effect, a relief force would come from the city. Still, the men who sailed from Corsica with Falconi passed on their confi-dence and faith in their leader to their new comrades in arms. The cause was a righteous one; chivalry would be served with the strength of their sword arms. In any case, the knights of the city-states of Italy and Corsica had no great love for the nobles of southern France, who, unlike their northern French counterparts, talked loudly and ran fast.

At the end of the second night, Falconi gathered his men at the fire. He addressed them with a soft voice, his features fixed, his blue eyes deep-set above his chiseled cheekbones.

"You know of Charles d'Avignon and his sins against God and my family," began Falconi, hissing his words through lips that had hardly spoken in the preceding days. "I intend to make him pay for his crimes and see if he fights as well against men as he does against women and boys."

Several of the knights stirred, shifting their weight in readiness for his call to action.

"He will pay for his son's crimes! I swear this before God and my ancestors. But he will not fight us if we give him any other recourse," Falconi said, his features set hard and cold, without a hint of the father or husband, only the warrior remaining. "We must not give him the opportunity to do anything but fight and die."

Rising from the fire, he went to one of the pack animals and, loosening the leather ties that held the load, pulled a piece of fabric through the opening. Holding it before the group, its folds catching the light from the fire, he revealed a cloth bearing the insignia of the Cardinal of Rome on its red background.

A knight called Marco, with Falconi and two others in clerical garb, approached the castle alone. The other eleven, several hundred yards to the east, well hidden from the castle, awaited their signal.

Falconi had timed their arrival at d'Avignon's castle keep for just before dusk. It had taken two and a half days of hard riding from San Remo. On the last day, he, Marco, and two others donned the clerical garb. One of the outfits, the one he had shown his men, was predominantly white with a red cross. It was the attire of a knight pledged to serve the Holy Mother Church, and he had given it to the most skilled of his knights, Sir Marco. Falconi and the two others followed Marco toward the castle, wearing the brown cloaks of priests, hiding their mail armor, their broadswords and axes strapped to their backs. The others, while still out of sight of the walls and the guards that must be on them, swung wide, approaching a small wooded hill just to the north of the castle.

"Hail Charles d'Avignon! I bring a message from my master in Rome!" The knight raised his shield, displaying his own heraldry as well as the insignia of the Cardinal in the upper corner, to the guard standing on the tower to the right of the gate. The entrance gate was reached by a long ramp that passed under the two wings of the castle. High and imposing, they would render anyone attempting to storm the gate prey to the arrows of archers above. The sentry was joined by another, who after a brief conversation left the wall.

Only Marco, dressed in light armor, was equipped with lance and sword. The three dressed in priestly garb appeared unarmed, busy handling the pack animals, themselves riding mounts that looked better suited to pulling carts than to a warrior's pursuits. All were dusty, showing the effects of many days of travel. As they waited below the walls at the first of four gates, Falconi, who rode directly behind Marco, dismounted. He went to one of the pack animals, removing a leather packet. He presented it, along with an exaggerated bow, to the knight still mounted on his great war horse.

"If they don't admit us, wave this at them and say that we will answer their lack of courtesy by giving this to Clement in Avignon instead of to Charles."

Since 1309, when Pope Clement V had made his palace in Avignon the papal seat of the Roman Catholic Church, the Italian nobles had chafed under his authority. The force of arms of the Church was at times formidable, but the real power of the Church came from its ability to legitimize the ascension to titles for the nobles, and the constant threat of excommunication. Even the king of France depended on the Pope to affirm his legitimacy.

Falconi returned to the pack animal, leaning on one knee as if inspecting the beast's hoof, his sandals protruding beneath the rough fabric of his cloak.

"I have a message from Rome for Charles d'Avignon," said Marco from the back of his prancing horse.

The sentry on top of the wall was joined by the soldier who had disappeared along with another, whose gray hair and fine doublet proclaimed his noble heritage before his commanding voice did so.

"I am Charles. Who brings me a message from the Cardinal?" The man now standing between the ramparts was slender, the hollowness of his eyes making him appear older than his carriage would indicate.

"I am Marco of Carrera, bound to the duty of my lord, and I have been instructed to bear no discourtesies. I come with the authority of the Cardinal. I will not shout God's work for all to bear witness. This being the case, I will deliver this to the Pope in Avignon rather than to Charles." He waved the scroll over his head and roughly reined his horse in a turn that almost knocked Falconi to the ground.

"Hold, sir knight!" bellowed the figure from the wall. "You'll receive no discourtesies here. Open the gate."

Immediately, the sounds of great bolts being released could be heard from the other side of the huge doors, and then one half of the wooden gate swung open, revealing a courtyard behind a second set of already opened gates. Falconi mounted and followed Marco into the keep. What they would see in the next few minutes would determine if they would remain alive or soon be dead men. They had no way of knowing what force of men Charles would have inside.

At the far right side of the courtyard was a stable and next to it the kitchen. To the left were a small chapel and a well. From the number of horses that appeared in the stable, they had been lucky in their arrival. The empty stalls indicated that only a small number of defenders were present.

"See to the horses," Marco ordered the two trailing priests. "You, accompany me." He gestured to Falconi, who showed his deference by bowing his head.

A man-at-arms came forward and took the reins of Marco's horse, extending his hand toward the knight. Marco unbuckled his sword and scabbard and, as was the custom, handed them to the man before dismounting.

"Lord Charles will see you in the great hall," said the servant as he received the sword. Turning, he carried the weapon in front of him toward a stout doorway leading from the courtyard into the largest of the inner buildings.

Marco and Falconi followed. The passage past the door was long and narrow. Falconi noted with displeasure the slots in the walls on either side that would allow defenders to spear or stab anyone who might force his way past the outer walls. After twelve paces, the corridor took an abrupt ninety-degree turn that ended after three strides at another stout door. A man-at-arms opened it and the three of them entered the great hall.

At the far end, behind a large wooden table, stood Charles d'Avignon. At his side and in front of the table stood four nobles dressed in the French tradition, with bright colors and tight breeches. They eyed Marco with interest and suspicion.

"I am Charles d'Avignon. I do not recognize your colors, Marco of Carrera."

"Nor would I expect you to, sire. They were given to me along with lands in the East during the Crusade against the Turkish infidels who now occupy the City of our Lord."

"A cup of wine after your long journey?" Charles waved at a servant, who rushed toward Marco with a goblet and a pitcher.

"Perhaps later. I have forsworn personal comforts while under the orders of my Lord. After I have delivered his message, I will be free to avail myself of your generosity." Marco turned to Falconi, holding his hand palm up as if to receive the scroll.

Falconi looked at him, bewildered. "Your bag was left on your horse, sire."

"Retrieve it then, as Lord d'Avignon, a goblet of fine wine, and I are waiting."

Falconi bowed and shuffled quickly toward the door. Laughter rang out behind him as Charles and the other nobles enjoyed Marco's quick wit. Once outside, Falconi hurried to the stable, where one of the other priests was tending to the mounts.

"Four inside, besides Charles. How is it out here?" Falconi looked quickly around the inner walls of the castle.

"No more than ten men at arms and a like number of servants. It can be done. We have already placed the fire package in the kitchen."

Falconi glanced toward the kitchen and saw his other false priest nibbling on an end of bread, nodding to him as he stood poised in the pantry. "Good. Give me time to reach Marco and get in position; then set the fire and open the gates. I depend on you." Falconi loosened the large leather bag from the saddle of Marco's mount and started again toward the great hall. He held in check his excitement, his blood lust that was now so close to finding expression in his actions. All of his restraint went toward maintaining the appearance of the humble priest that his dress proclaimed him to be.

"Are you ready now, Father?" asked Marco as Falconi entered the hall with the leather case.

"Yes, sire," replied Falconi, giving Marco the case and moving off behind the nobles.

Marco reached into the pouch and removed a roll of paper, hefting it, ignoring the outstretched hand of d'Avignon. Inside the case he could feel the weight of the dagger that remained hidden below its flap. He started to unroll the document, taking time to look at it as it inched open. D'Avignon was starting to show annoyance at the delay. Falconi didn't know if d'Avignon could read the scroll or if he would have to rely on a cleric, as did most nobles.

He did not get the chance to find out. Cries of alarm from the inner courtyard interrupted their proceedings. D'Avignon reached for his sword while moving quickly toward the door to the courtyard. Halfway through his third step, Marco grabbed his arm and swung him around, the dagger at his throat. One of d'Avignon's knights saw what was happening and moved to his aid. Falconi, who had loosened his battle axe from beneath his robe, now swung it with great force at the hilt of the man's drawn sword. The attack, coming from an unexpected quarter and from a weapon that had seemingly materialized in thin air, took the man by surprise and his sword clattered to the floor. Falconi whirled and struck the back of the man's head with the flat of the axe, rendering him unconscious on the floor. The other three knights were not as alert. Faced with an axe in the hands of a wild-eyed priest, and with their lord being threatened with a knife at his throat, they surrendered their arms. Falconi herded them into a corner, making sure they had no hidden weapons, then pushed d'Avignon in with them.

"Kill anyone who moves from this corner," ordered Falconi, giving d'Avignon's sword to Marco.

Outside, Falconi found confusion as men hurried to fight the fire in the kitchen. On the ramparts above the gate he saw his man, still dressed in priest's clothing, in position above the gate. The hand of one of the guards lay draped over the edge of the rampart. They had been given instructions to first signal the group hiding in the trees, but not to open the gates until just before they arrived at the castle. The fire would only keep the attention of d'Avignon's men as long as there was nothing else amiss. The raising of the gate would attract attention, and Falconi wanted the rest of his band inside to prevent the gate from being recaptured. It seemed like an eternity before the gate finally swung open and the men of Corsica rode through the opening beneath the walls and into the inner courtyard.

Falconi turned, already knowing the outcome. Once inside the enclosure, his men would have little trouble with the defenders. It was d'Avignon who demanded his attention.

Marco had not moved. He had d'Avignon's sword held at high guard above his head, at the ready for any movement. He acknowledged Falconi's return with a slight twitch of his head, not taking his eyes from his three prisoners. Falconi, still in the robes of a priest, looked directly at d'Avignon, then hoisted the robe over his head.

"Killer of women and children. Do you know he who will take your life?"

"Falconi? I assume by your question that you are the Baron from Corsica."

"You may also assume that I come for revenge."

D'Avignon held up his hand. "You should first know that, while it is true that your wife and son were accompanied by my men, their deaths were an accident. Your son took a blow meant for his servant, and the Baroness was killed by a kick from her own mount. I grieve with you, Baron Falconi, as if I had lost my own."

Falconi was glad to know for certain that Carlo had related the truth in his telling of the incident, for d'Avignon's account differed only in perspective, not in substance, from Carlo's. In the two months he had waited before leaving Corsica, Falconi had decided that d'Avignon's sin was in putting his loved ones in the position where they could be harmed. His wife and son were dead because of d'Avignon's actions and his greed. He would pay in the same coin.

The warning, a soft drum of a bowstring, gave scant time for action. Still Marco moved just quickly enough for the arrow to pierce his left arm just below the shoulder, rather than entering his back and passing through his heart. Falconi looked up the flight of stairs and saw the tip of another arrow being readied through a slot in the stone just past the place where the stone stairs disappeared in the upper chambers. Almost simultaneously, the door to the courtyard flew open and several of his men surged in, proclaiming victory in their loud Corsican dialect.

"Watch out!" screamed Falconi, watching the arrow tip swing around in their direction. "Bowman! Top of the stairs."

Marco had regained his balance and was still holding his four prisoners, but he was now flush against the wall, creating an impossible angle for the archer.

The second arrow thudded as it sank into the oaken door just a few inches from the head of one of the men from the courtyard. Even as it was in the air, Falconi was racing toward the stairs, leaping up them three at a time. The door swung shut as Falconi came up the stone steps. He tried it and found it barred from the inside. It came under immediate attack by his battle axe. As the door splintered, he kicked it open and jumped aside, watching the arrow hit the stone at the top of the stairwell and clatter harmlessly down onto the floor below.

Charging into the room, he found a small chamber with a bed, in front of which was a young man drawing a sword from a scabbard of red leather. Its point never cleared as Falconi's battle axe sliced down in a vicious stroke halfway between the shoulder and neck of the youth. The blow was the standard one used in combat against a foe wearing armor of plate and chain mail; it was a fatal blow when a man was wearing armor. Against this lad, clad only in a woolen doublet, there could be no doubt of its effect. He was dead before he fell back on the bed, his spine crushed by the blow.

"My son!" screamed d'Avignon as Falconi stepped out onto the top stair. "My son!"

Falconi ordered his men to sack the castle but not to harm any of d'Avignon's men unless they resisted. It was Marco, after having his wound treated in the upstairs compartment, who discovered the treasure.

"That's the church's money. It is to buy my absolution from a decree of excommunication by the Pope," said d'Avignon.

"That it is still in your possession tells me it is not yet the Pope's," said Falconi. "I am sure the Holy Father would not want this tainted gold; better that your soul burn in hell. Put it on the horses from the stable," instructed Falconi to one of his men, "and ready the others to leave."

Falconi took d'Avignon up the stairs and put him alone in the upstairs compartment with the body of his son. D'Avignon's death would come, but only after he had had time to reflect on that of his son. Falconi left him no doubt that death was imminent. He wanted him to fully appreciate the depth of sorrow he had inflicted by killing Thomoso. Closing the splintered door and wedging a chair from the room against the stone of the landing, preventing it from being opened from inside, Falconi joined his men packing the spare horses in the courtyard.

"My lord!" the sentry on the rampart cried to Falconi as he was inspecting the last of the pack animals in the courtyard. "A column of twenty horses approaches from the north."

"How far?"

"Three miles or so. They ride slowly."

Falconi quickly crossed the yard into the main hall, yelling instructions to his men to ready themselves to leave immediately. Then he sprang up the stairs and pushed aside the chair that jammed the door to the compartment shut from the outside. He would fulfill his vengeance, then ride quickly to the coast.

He pushed on the door, but it would not yield. Splintered as it was, he could see the bed wedged against it from the other side. In blind fury he began hacking at the barrier. Suddenly, one of the bed posts, splintered to a sharp point, thrust at him through a small opening, nearly impaling him as he raised his axe for another blow.

"Milord! Two riders have left the band and are riding at a gallop in the direction whence they've come. The others have picked up their pace toward the castle," a voice from below bellowed.

Falconi struck again at the door and again the shaft thrust blindly out. The instincts of a warrior prevailed over his rage, making him realize that he risked being trapped in the castle if he took any more time getting to d'Avignon.

"Be it so, then, jackal!" he cried. "Live with the death of your son, as I will live with mine. May it give you great pleasure and comfort in your old age."

Falconi turned and leaped down the stairs to the courtyard, where his men waited on their mounts. The gate opened, and they rode out at a full gallop, toward the coast and safety.

CHAPTER FOUR

Mats peered at the waves breaking off the bow of the ferry. He had boarded in Marseille, arriving just minutes before the boat left for Ajaccio, Corsica. Whatever he had expected when he decided to take a ship rather than fly to Corsica, he was unprepared for the reality of the ferry he boarded. He was used to the ships that ran between Larkspur Landing and Sausalito to the Ferry Building in San Francisco. This vessel had staterooms six decks high, a cross between a car ferry and a cruise ship. The design was explained to him by a crewman after casting off. They would shut down for five hours during the night. The passengers would sleep, and the ferry would arrive in Ajaccio at 8 am the following morning. The fee he had hurriedly paid, thinking it high, included a private stateroom.

The motion of the waves and the sound of the water slicing off the hull calmed Mats and cleared his mind. He had awakened from his nap at the ruins of the castle with the realization that his vision was an extension of a remembered bedtime story. The need for sleep he could still blame on jet lag or the wine at lunch, but the emotion that lingered after his dream was derived from the reality of the ruin so closely matching his father's description. He had driven fast, dangerously fast, to Marseille. Arriving just before four, he used his improving French, along with animated gestures, to turn in the Fiat. Finding that the ferry was leaving within the hour, he bribed the agency to take him to the dock.

The dream at the roadside had left a strange feeling of urgency. Mats had come on this trip to leave behind his useless baggage of guilt and to alleviate the feeling of loss resulting from his father's death. The reality of the nightmare—the avenging of the murder of the Baroness and her son—brought back memories of his father telling him as a child that the stories were real. Mats remembered his father telling him the story of Baron Falconi's revenge. That his dream matched his father's tale, and the physical description of the ruins he had parked near, was unsettling.

"What would Dr. Ferrera think about this one?" he thought, noticing a change of speed in the ferry. *"Am I losing it?"*

Both his father's story and the dream were about revenge. So, thoughts of his own revenge for the murder of his father did not seem so strange to him. In the months following his father's murder, revenge had been foremost in his mind. Mike Ferrera had explained that it was the most normal of emotions but also one of the most destructive, since there was almost no chance of fulfillment.

The police and the FBI had taken his description of the gunman. They had the dying statement of the man killed on the steps of the restaurant, which had given them the name "Leca." The agents were stingy with information, sketchy at best. They did say that a big mover had been taking over the major distribution of heroin and cocaine in Northern California over the past year. This guy was clever, a shadowy figure, and the FBI hadn't even begun to infiltrate his network. He was called Leca, but the name had no substance attached to it. They thought he was Mexican, but he didn't employ the usual Central American drug channels. He dealt in large amounts, both in money and drugs, staying near the top of the distribution chain. He had reputedly killed several drug lords in Oakland and San Jose and now ran their network by phone and internet, without personal contact.

"Only a matter of time until he slips up," the FBI had told Mats. "In fact, you being alive and capable of identifying him is a big slip in itself. Thanks to you we now at least have a face to go with the name. Don't worry. It is only a matter of time till we get him."

But months had gone by and nothing had happened. No new leads surfaced, no new information, only the persistent rumor that a new source was now supplying the druggies of Marin. Mats' thoughts kept intruding on his efforts to go to sleep, but finally the rocking of the ship and the quiet, broken only by the muffled ringing of the ship's bell, overcame his racing mind.

An hour after Mats awoke, the island of Corsica rose off the starboard bow, at first just a haze over the horizon, the morning sunlight filtering over the mountain range to the east. Then splotches of color separated the emerging blue of the sky from the azure of the sea. Slowly, cliffs and breakers became visible as the ferry continued south toward Ajaccio. They swung around the promontory that protected the ancient port from the north and eased into the large bay.

Ajaccio had originally been a Roman settlement called Adjacium, surrounding a fort north of the present city. With raids from Saracens occurring with fearful frequency in the eleventh century, the inhabitants had fled to the mountains. The present town, existing to the south of the original settlement, had grown to a population of nearly seventy thousand.

Only the slightest of bumps, accompanied by the quieting of the throbbing sound of twin diesels, announced that the lines were fast and the car ramp secured and lowered. Mats grabbed his bag and was among the first to depart, hesitating only for a moment before he set his foot down for the first time on Corsica.

With his bag over his shoulder, he trudged north along the Boulevard du Roi Jérôme, drawn to the ancient center of the city. Everywhere there were reminders that this was the birthplace of Napoleon: a great statue, directions to the house of his birth, and finally the grand Avenue Cours Napoleon.

Mats had deliberately read only the introduction to a guidebook about the island after deciding to take Mike Ferrera's advice. He had learned general information, such as how best to get there, and positioned it on a map. He'd avoided the information about tourist attractions and "must see" towns and resorts. He wanted to discover things at his own pace and according to his own inclination. He knew that Corsica was an oval-shaped island approximately a hundred miles long by forty-five miles wide, with a population of 250,000, about the same as Marin County. It had been occupied by various cultures for ten thousand years, continually invaded by Romans, Normans, Etruscans, Carthaginians, the Italian Lombards, the Germanic Vandals, and eventually the English and French. Consequently, the island had a language of its own, having evolved long before the birth of Christ. A Roman in 111 B.C. was exiled to the island and described its inhabitants as "ferocious" and "speaking an incomprehensible language." Mats knew from his father that the Corsican language was a bastard of Italian, or a Tuscan dialect of it with many words and phrases from each of the invading cultures thrown in, but that French was now taught in schools as the official language.

The map in the guide book showed there were two mountain ranges running north-south which, before the advent of the automobile, separated the island into two discrete halves: the east side, colonized mostly by Italians, and the west side, studded with a rocky shoreline with many coves and towering cliffs, where a mixture of Italian, French, Greek, English, and German prevailed. Understandably, through centuries of invasion and territorial conflict, the island had seldom enjoyed any prolonged period of peace, which might provide a motive as to why his father had left and why he didn't talk about his past.

Corsica's finest hour had probably come during World War II, when its inhabitants mounted a fierce resistance first to fascist Italy and then to Germany; it was the first French land to be liberated by the Americans in September of 1943. Corsicans acquired a reputation as tough, almost sacrificial, warriors given to dedicated friendships, obsessive loyalties, and strong passions in every venture, from war to food to lovemaking.

Mats was glad that he had entered this land knowing only the basic history of the island. He could feel the rightness in his choice as he moved away from the water and the tourist establishments that ringed it. After walking uphill for half an hour, he found a hotel occupying a two-story stone building in the center of the block. A café fronted the street, its bar doubling as a front desk. Heads turned as he walked in. It was obvious that tourists did not often enter the establishment. Behind the bar stood a thick bald man wearing a green short-sleeved golf shirt that had been washed to almost a dirty gray. He had a pouting expression which made his lower lip look swollen, protruding, lacking all but the cigarette to balance on it. He was bent over a bowl of bouillabaisse sitting on the bar, his posture accentuating his double chin. As Mats approached, he muttered something to the two customers opposite him at the bar.

"Can I help you?" he asked in an accent almost indistinguishable as French.

"A room, please," answered Mats in English.

A smile crossed the face of the man as he noisily slurped another large spoonful loaded with chunks of fish. "You will want the English hotels. You will find them on Cours Grandval." A flip of his hand to the east served to dismiss Mats as well as provide amusement for his audience of two.

"If you have a room, this hotel will be fine," Mats retorted. "My father was born near here and it would have suited him. It will suit me."

The men shot sidelong glances at Mats while the proprietor put down his spoon and wiped his hands on his jeans. "How long will you be staying?"

"Two or three nights. Perhaps as long as a week. May I see what you have available?"

A sideways nod of the head and semblance of a smile showing chipped and missing teeth served as both an answer and an invitation to follow as the innkeeper moved from behind the bar and toward a flight of stairs in the back.

Mats chose a room that looked west. The Citadel was framed through a small window that opened above the red tile roof that covered the café. It was smaller than the first room he had been shown but the view suited Mats better. It was also further away from the bathroom and shower, so it promised to be less noisy. On the way back down the stairs, the proprietor took an advance of two days at what Mats figured was three times the rate for a local.

A man had entered the café, following Mats' heels, escaping from the heat of the street. Coming down the stairs Mats noticed that the man had not taken a seat but was standing in the shade, just inside the enclosure, sipping a glass of wine.

As the proprietor slipped back behind the bar, Mats ordered some stew as well as some bread, olives, and wine. Grabbing the bottle of wine and olives, he walked to a table near the front where he could look out on the street. The two men at the bar glanced back at him over their shoulders. Mats didn't much like their looks, or those of the proprietor for that matter, but it didn't diminish the feeling of contentment and accomplishment now that he was in Corsica.

The wine was surprisingly good, a full and rich red, but it was the olives that offered the most pleasant surprise. They were large and green, stuffed with anchovies, the saltiness of the stuffing perfectly complementing the tartness of the olives. He was already on his second glass of wine when the stew arrived at his table and with it the only other occupant of the café. Mats had noticed him enter the café before he had chosen his room. The man had a different bearing from the others. His head was held high, his shoulders square, and his face showed a stubble, but it was more likely the result of fast growth than a neglect of shaving. As he approached, he held eye contact, and Mats intuitively responded positively to it.

"Monsieur, would you mind company as you eat?" The man had a rough Corsican inflection to his French. It was not unpleasant, though, and it came from a face that was open and smiling, unlike the stubble-framed sneer of the proprietor.

Mats looked at the man. It was true that it was his first day on the island, and he was not familiar with the local customs, but the man's familiarity put him on edge. He now thought that the man had probably followed him into the café, and the thought added to his concern. The man stood, waiting for a reply to his request for several seconds before Mats' curiosity overcame his uneasiness.

"Please." Mats offered the chair to his right.

"Thank you, monsieur. You are an American, are you not?"

"Yes," said Mats, offering the neck of the bottle to the glass the stranger had brought with him to the table.

The man pushed the glass under the bottle's neck as an answer. "Merci. Your first time in Corsica?" He used French as if it were vinegar passing his lips, giving Mats the impression that he would prefer another tongue—most likely, from the looks of him, the mountain dialect of Corte, or perhaps Italian.

"Yes, this is my first time, but you probably overheard. My father was born here."

"My name is Guibega," said the man, extending his hand across the table. He said the name as though it should be familiar to Mats. His eyes were dark and intense under strong, straight brows. Mats felt the power in his handshake. With no recognition by Mats of his name, he nodded toward the bar. "These men …" He shrugged and fluttered his hand above the table. "They will overcharge you if they have not already," he said, switching to heavily accented English and softly hissing rather than whispering.

Mats smiled. "I thought as much, but I will not be staying here long. I'm a tourist and expect such things."

"I would be your guide and overcharge you only half as much as Arnot. Besides, you do not appear to be a tourist. You have the appearance of a Corsican. What was your father's name?"

"Falconi," answered Mats, copying Guibega's subdued tone. "Egel Falconi."

"Humph. I would not mention that around this place. You will see much more with a guide. If you are a Falconi, I will not even overcharge you. My grandfather knew your father. I will be here for you tomorrow." With that, Guibega downed the rest of his wine and abruptly stood and left the room.

"If that man bothers you, let me know," shouted the proprietor with bravado across the bar. It was not lost on Mats that he had waited until Guibega left.

That night Mats walked the streets, following curving roads with no plan other than to feel the essence of the town. When he returned to the room, he had made up his mind. He locked the door behind him and opened the small window, allowing a light breeze to circulate. Turning on the small bedside lamp, he removed the package from inside the large chest wallet that also held his passport, his father's ring, and several thousand euros. His father's instructions not to open the package until the time was right came back to him. Holding the package, he felt the urge to open it. It felt right. Carefully, he peeled off the outer layer of oil cloth. Under it was a sheet of thin lead that had the appearance of being removed and replaced several times, as creases in the metal did not line up perfectly. The last covering was a soft cloth with its seams sealed in wax. Even before it was removed, Mats could feel the familiar outline of a book. He removed one protective layer after another, until it lay unopened in his hands.

Opening the book to a random page, he found handwriting in a small, cramped, but legible hand. Mats stared at the writing. It was clear enough, but the words were unfamiliar, written in a language that was completely incomprehensible. Thumbing through the pages, he could identify some words that he was sure were Latin, but not the Latin of his schooling, and in the same sentences were words he was sure were not of that tongue. He felt sure it was a journal, as many of the passages were separated by what appeared to be dates. On examining the text, however, the book became a complete mystery. On some pages there were sketches in ink that took up half a page. The first drawing was of a stack of rectangles with X marks in two of them. There were other sketches as well, but none that were any less enigmatic. Disappointingly, there were no maps, but stuck in the rear of the journal were a dozen loose, neatly folded pages in his father's handwriting, in the same unusual Latin script. It had been thirteen years since Mats had studied the language. He found he could read his father's pages after a fashion, but not well enough to make a translation. He decided to leave his father's writing for last and try to read the journal in chronological order, somehow deciphering the unruly text. Still, he scanned his father's pages as he carefully refolded them.

On the second page, in the first sentence, he stopped at a familiar word, a word not in Latin: Guibega. The text seemed to be remarking favorably upon some deed by Guibega. It could not be about the man in the bar—the ages would not nearly match up—but the mention of his name gave truth to the man's words and relieved some of the doubt Mats had about the offer to act as his guide. A half hour trying to make sense of the pages left him exhausted, and he soon found further study impossible. Turning off the light, surprised that it was almost three o'clock, he fell into a deep, dreamless sleep.

Mats was awakened by sunlight streaming through the open window. He looked at his watch and was surprised to find it was already ten-thirty. He had slept longer than he had planned. Dressed, with a splash of water on his face and his teeth brushed, Mats came down the stairs, his pack slung over one shoulder. Looking around the café and not seeing anyone, he stepped outside onto the Boulevard du Roi Jérôme. The sunlight hit him full and warm on his back as he turned toward the Citadel. He had only walked a dozen paces when he saw Guibega, sitting on a motorcycle at the curb. His smile stretched unevenly, showing straight white teeth with a space between the two front teeth.

"That offer of a guide still stand?" Mats asked, pleased to see the stranger from the previous afternoon.

"I have a cousin who works little and knows much. He has a car. He will show you Corsica."

"And I have an appetite. Do you know of a good café?"

"Ha Ha! Spoken like a true Corsican. But do you want breakfast or lunch?" Guibega patted the rear seat of the bike and kicked the starting lever. His comment made Mats think that Guibega had been sitting there waiting for him for some time.

Mats hesitated, entertaining a sliver of doubt as to whether he should risk the seat or the man. Then he remembered his father's seemingly positive reference to Guibega in the journal and straddled the rear of the Ducati.

Five minutes later they had climbed above the harbor and pulled into a small courtyard. Walking through a gate in a windowless wall, they emerged into a café that opened through three shuttered doors onto a large sun-drenched balcony. Bougainvillea framed white stucco arches in brilliant splashes of red. Over the middle archway, between two shields carrying a pair of crossed battle axes, was a painted sign in the same shade of red as the bougainvillea: ALTA MIRA.

Mats followed Guibega to a small table near the edge of the balcony, away from the other customers, who almost filled the restaurant. Even with the balcony open to the inside, the aroma of the food on the plates they passed made Mats' mouth water. In the center of the balcony, already prepared with three place settings, rested a Reserved sign. They'd barely had a chance to sit before a waiter arrived and clapped his guide on the back, addressing him in the distinctive Corsican dialect. Guibega answered in the same tongue, accompanied by vigorous hand motions, several of which he directed at Mats. As quickly as he had appeared, the waiter spun on his heel and departed, still talking over his left shoulder to Guibega as he entered the kitchen.

"I have taken the liberty of ordering your meal," Guibega said. "And I have sent for my cousin." He looked expectantly at the entrance. "The one with the car – our grandfather knew Egel Falconi in the old days."

Mats was excited that he had stumbled upon people who might have known his father but still wary of the circumstances that had led Guibega to find him the day before. Now a cousin was being thrown at him.

"Remember, if I choose to use your cousin as a guide, I don't want to be a tourist."

"Signor Falconi ..."

"Falcon. My name is Mats Falcon. My father dropped the 'i' in America. And why is it I'm being pawned off on your cousin? I don't even know your last name," said Mats, smiling, but with a serious undertone that was not lost on Guibega.

"Signor Falcon, Guibega is my family name. The Guibega have been on this island longer than the French, the Genovese, even the Phoenicians, but that is not what is important to you. I work in Ajaccio. I manage a warehouse we own near the waterfront. My time is my own. I saw you enter Arnot's yesterday, something that is not often done by tourists. I was curious. That pig deals in drugs, but he has not yet been caught at it. I thought that was why you went upstairs. I knew I was wrong when you said you were the son of Egel Falconi. All things changed at that moment. The Guibega and the Falconi have known each other for centuries. I am a Guibega but please call me by my given name, Mario."

Mats noted that Guibega appeared uneasy, as if unused to speaking more than a few words at a time. Relief spread across his face when the waiter arrived with three plates of food, one with a large soup plate inverted over it.

In what Mats assumed was the entrance to the kitchen, he saw the figure of a woman staring at him from the shadows. She had striking blue eyes that seemed out of place in a face framed with dark hair pulled back in a bun. Her stature and coloring made Mats feel sure that she was related to Mario. Their eyes met, and she abruptly turned and disappeared into the rear of the building.

Mats was about to take his first bite of eggs when they were joined at the table by Mario's cousin Carlo, who could have been his brother, so much did the two men look alike. Both were dark, with eyes shadowed by prominent brows, and while not extremely tall, at just under six feet, they moved with the grace and power of athletes. Mats soon felt as comfortable with Carlo as he did with Mario, and within five minutes had agreed to hire him and his car, a twenty-year-old Renault, for a hundred euros a day. He would pay for gas and Carlo's food but not for his lodgings. Their business arrangements concluded, they ordered a liter of red wine, which the waiter brought with four glasses. Mats did not have time to wonder about the extra glass, as the waiter immediately pulled up a chair and poured for himself as well.

"I am Tony Campanelli. I have the good fortune, as I am sure Mario has told you, to be married to a Guibega. Welcome to Corsica, Falconi," he said. "It's good that Mario brings you here for food instead of letting you eat at that fleabag hotel of Arnot's." He made a spitting gesture over his left elbow in the direction of the harbor. "Now at least you will not have to throw up on your shoes."

"Falcon," Mats corrected.

"Falconi," the waiter corrected back.

Mats shrugged and continued enjoying the meal of eggs and spicy sausage. He joked that he would steal the recipe for the rich salsa spread over the eggs for his own restaurant in Sausalito – and the sausage, could it be exported? The men laughed. Mats observed with both pleasure and curiosity, but no longer suspicion, that these three men were now treating him with uncommon familiarity bordering on respect simply because of his Falconi heritage.

They had finished the meal before the three Corsicans could agree on what to show Mats on his first full day on the island. When half the bottle was gone, Carlo turned to Mats and finally asked if there was anything specific he wanted to see.

Mats looked down on the palm-lined streets of Ajaccio where his father had departed from Corsica more than seventy years before. He couldn't help remembering how silent his father had been about his past. Mats had always wondered if he was trying to hide something. Now, with men whose family had known his father, he felt he might have been wrong to associate guilt or shame with his father's departure. Mats thought these men, or perhaps their relatives, might solve that mystery for him.

"What I really want is to get a feeling for the island, get to know where my family came from. Maybe see where they lived, if that's possible. My dad didn't talk about his past on Corsica, but I got the feeling that the war had a lot to do with his leaving the island." Mats caught a sharp sidelong glance between the Guibega cousins, but they said nothing. "Please don't misunderstand," Mats continued, answering the question that lay in their silent shared glance. "I don't know why he left. I'm only guessing. He only told me of Corsica in stories. I want to know the land he described in his stories."

"And know it you will, if you are truly a Falconi," said Carlo, standing and slapping Mats on the shoulder. "It is still early enough in the day. We can have dinner in Evisa and still be back before dusk."

Mario Guibega followed Carlo and Mats outside, handing Mats change from the bill he had left on the table. "No sense in overpaying, even if he is a relative, eh? Tony offers you the use of his kitchen if you would like to swap recipes. I should advise you, though. Tony's okay, but it is his wife Jennette who prepares all the dishes and runs the café. She is the best cook of all the Guibega, which of course means she is the best cook on Corsica."

Mario started the motorcycle, belching a puff of blue smoke from the tail pipe, and was out of the courtyard before Mats could thank him. The roar of the engine reverberated against the stone walls of the houses that flanked the narrow street. Mats watched him go, then moved to the Renault. As he got in, he glanced toward the entrance to the Alta Mira. Standing half shadowed in the doorway was the woman, Jennette, watching him with a cell phone pressed to her ear.

Twenty minutes of driving brought the old Renault, with Carlo driving, into the mountains north of Ajaccio. Mats rested his head on his arm halfway out the passenger's side window and watched the scenery flash by. As they crested a final rise, he was treated to a beautiful panoramic view of the Gulf of Sagone.

"We call this the Cinarca region," explained Carlo as they crossed the bridge at San Bastiano. Mats looked out at groves of pine and chestnut, their distinctive odors mingling in the air rushing by the open window. Trees alternated with mountain meadows as the car continued to climb. "For centuries this land belonged to the Falconi," explained Carlo. "My grandfather believes that it was given to your family in the early eleventh century as a reward for some great service, but it may even have been before then."

Mats nodded. "When my father left before the war, did he still own much land?"

Carlo slowed the car, pulling to the side of the road. "He really did not tell you of your history?"

"Nothing," Mats said. "It was as if he was ashamed of something."

"Egel Falconi? Ashamed?" Carlo stifled a chuckle, confusing Mats even more. Then, with a slow shake of his head, Carlo killed the engine. "If you came here to find your father's shame, you came on a fool's errand. The Falconi were a noble family. Can you see the sea?" Carlo pointed to the west. "The Falconi controlled all the land between here and the coast, from Ajaccio in the south to Evisa in the north. When the first Baron Falconi came to Corsica, we Guibega were primarily a hill tribe. The Falconi were seafarers. Still, there was a bond between our two families. The Falconi have always held the well-being of the people of Corsica as their first concern. They were the only nobles to support the common people when the Pope handed over our land to the Spaniard Aragon. They also openly supported our greatest hero, Pasquale Paoli, who twice declared Corsica's independence.

"In 1794, when Corsica was declared an appendage of the British Crown, the Falconi and the Guibega fled to the hills, where we directed attack after attack on the British. Napoleon helped us. He put pressure on the English after his Italian campaign until they finally pulled out two years later. But instead of independence, the island came under the control of the French. The French stole much of the Falconi land, some through excessive taxation, some through plain thievery. When your father left, he still owned much. He was a rich man, but nothing like his family was before the French. When he left, he gave my father and his two brothers what he did not sell. He gave us the café we had lunch in today, a farm not far from here, another winery near Evisa where we will have dinner tonight, and warehouses in Ajaccio. In doing so, he gave us standing and security for which we will forever be in his debt."

Mats took a deep breath. So that was it, why Mario and Carlo treated him with respect. He had learned more in the last ten minutes about his father's Corsican past than he had in his entire life prior to this moment.

"What did your father do in America?" asked Carlo.

"He worked as a longshoreman in San Francisco until he mastered English," Mats said. "Just before the war he moved to Sausalito, started a fishing business, and bought some waterfront land with a dock and a boat. He never said where he obtained the money. When my mother died, Dad became both father and mother to me. He hired a captain for the fishing boat so that he could be with me full time. As I grew older, he bought a second boat and built a restaurant, so he could be with me when I was not in school. On weekends he taught me how to sail, and during the evenings, when I was older, I worked in the restaurant. He was like a kid with me, always telling stories, playing games. He even made some wooden swords and we would play pirates on the fishing boat."

"To us your father was a great man. A man whose deeds exceeded valor," said Carlo. "The Guibega owe much to him. Corsica owes much to him." He pulled the car back onto the road that led deep into the mountains.

"Deeds?" Mats thought. He decided to let it lie for the time being.

"We will take this road, the D101, to Vico, then the D70 to Evisa," Carlo said. "It's a little longer, but it goes through mountains that have always been a source of strength to our people. We'll take the coastal route back to Ajaccio, which will be best at sunset."

The variety of landscapes they traveled astounded Mats. Back in Marin County he'd had a mental image of Corsica as a rocky, treeless land, but the road they traveled now took them through vineyards, orchards, and valleys that wound up into the hills and forests. In other places, rocky outcroppings that lined the road forced them around exaggerated twists and turns. They often had to avoid pigs, and goats with slashes of paint on their sides proclaiming ownership.

They drove through the Lisicia Valley, past the scattered village of Sari-d'Orcino and on toward Vico. The road became tortuous a few kilometers out of the village, and the Renault labored with every change in elevation. Carlo several times had to ride the clutch and increase the gas to overcome a tendency of the car to misfire on the uphill sections. Finally, it sputtered to a stop. Carlo coasted the car to a level area along the side of the road.

"What's wrong, Carlo?" asked Mats.

"We will see." Carlo started the car with a great deal of sputtering, put it in reverse, and backed smoothly up the incline that had defeated the car seconds before in its forward gears.

"It's the fuel pump," he answered Mats' questioning look. "The fuel tank is in the back, the engine in front. As long as the gas is higher than the engine, there is a positive flow. We won't make it to Vico this way, though. I can't back up every hill. Reverse won't hold up and I'll have a car that will need a transmission as well as a fuel pump. I will have to go back to Ajaccio for the pump and some tools. I'll catch a ride from Sari-d'Orcino. You stay with the car till I return."

Mats looked around the landscape. To the west there was a small rift between two boulder-strewn hills. In the distance he could just catch a glimpse of the Gulf of Sagone.

"Why don't I go with you?" asked Mats, not relishing the idea of being left alone.

"Two reasons, signore. First, I will get my cousin to ride me back. His motorcycle will carry two but not three. Second and more important, it is not unusual to have a car completely dismantled if left alone on these mountain roads. There are vehicles in some of these villages with heritages as mixed as the French bastards that own them. No, better you stay here. I will be back long before dark."

Carlo hit Mats up for fifty euros, which he said he would deduct from his wages, and was off with the promise to return in two hours. Mats watched as Carlo moved quickly up the hill that had defeated the old Renault, a man used to the motion of walking.

An hour later, Mats had exhausted all the reading material in the glove compartment, memorized the two dog-eared maps, and drunk half a bottle of unlabeled red wine. The day was hot and getting hotter as the sun moved toward the western horizon. Several cars had passed and asked him if he required help. Mats detected more than one greedy look at the car's headlights and tires accompanying the offer of a ride. Tired of the inactivity, he got out of the car and stretched. He took another long swallow from the bottle and walked down the pavement in the direction of the village. He was still on the flat ground, not having started up the hill, when he saw a small path leading through the boulders in the direction of the gulf. It was not well defined, and Mats could not decide if it was a game trail or just the sandy wash laid down by runoff from the road. However, it clearly offered an opportunity to relieve himself out of sight of passing vehicles. Mats looked back at the car before stepping off the road onto the trail. He would hear a car easily in the dead quiet of the countryside.

The trail wound sharply around several large russet, lichen-covered boulders before straightening out, following roughly the fall line of a dry creek that guarded its left side. It was not a difficult path. Carlo's Ducati could have maneuvered along it if it were pushed. Rounding a curve, the trail ended in a small clearing.

To the west, Mats could see the red-tiled roofs of the village of Tiuccia and, beyond, the azure of the Gulf of Sagone. Carlo's words came back to him. This had all been Falconi land.

He remembered, with sudden clarity, one of his father's stories describing a path and a meadow such as this one with a hidden cave, but before he could look, he heard the motor of a car from the road pause briefly and then move on at a faster pace. He decided he should get back before Carlo returned with Mario and the fuel pump only to find a car with no tires.

CHAPTER FIVE

Walking back to the car had only taken minutes, far less time than Mats had expected. The clearing couldn't be more than fifty meters from the roadway, but from the road there was absolutely no indication that it existed.

The Renault appeared undisturbed. Evidently no one had stopped by since he had left, at least no one with a vandal mentality. Within minutes Mats heard the staccato exhaust of a motorcycle coming toward him. The heads of two riders were visible atop the Ducati as it sped over the crest and down the hill toward him.

The Guibegas, Mario and Carlo, hopped off the bike and immediately began jacking up the Renault. Mario pulled a package and some wrenches from the saddle-bag on the back of the bike and shimmied under the car. Seconds later, a curse echoed off the surrounding boulders as his wrench slipped off a nut, skinning his knuckles. Ten minutes passed before he emerged, sweat dripping from his forehead, a mud-encrusted fuel pump in his hand.

"Give it a start," he mumbled to Carlo.

Carlo climbed into the driver's seat, leaving the door open, and started cranking the engine while Mario looked under the car at his handiwork. Finally, after a minute of trying and a noticeable slowing of the starter motor, the engine caught. First in fits and starts, then humming as smoothly as four cylinders could, the engine evened out as it obtained a constant flow of fuel.

"Takes a while to pump the air out of the line and get the gas up to the carburetor," Mario said with confidence to the other two men. "Let's try it on the hill."

"I smell gas," said Carlo as he put the car into first gear and began accelerating toward the hill that had earlier defeated his efforts.

"It's just the petrol I spilled making the repair. There is no leak."

Something was different, something Mats thought he should be picking up on, but nothing came to mind, except the unusual clarity of his father's description of the meadow he had just experienced.

"Looks like it's fixed," said Carlo as he powered over the crest of the hill and made a U-turn.

The maneuver sent Mats sprawling across the back seat, but as he regained his balance, he knew what had been tugging at the edge of his consciousness: the two men in the front seat were speaking in the Corsican dialect he had found barely decipherable just the day before. Now he could understand what they were saying—not each specific word, but the general meaning – the teachings of a father to a five-year-old son bearing fruit.

At the bottom of the incline, Mario got out and Mats took his place in the front seat. Then Mario had a second thought.

"As long as I'm out here," he said to Carlo in their native dialect, "I might as well go with you to Evisa. It's been a while since I've seen Paulo and his family, and we could even stay with them this evening. It's getting late. We could tell Falconi that we can't make it all the way back before dark. It's not much stretching of the truth." Mario was leaning across the open window on Mats' side of the car, talking across him to Carlo.

"Who is Paulo?" asked Mats in the Corsican dialect, the sounds of the words coming haltingly to his lips.

"Our cousin who runs the vineyard your father gave to us." As he answered Mats in English, Mario's eyebrows rose. His glance at Carlo conveyed his surprise as well as his acceptance of the fact that Mats could speak and understand Corsican. "We didn't know you understood us," he said, a bit haughtily. "Why didn't you tell us?"

"I...I just picked up a few of your words. My father spoke it to me when I was very young, and I guess it is coming back. I haven't used it in twenty years."

Mario nodded impatiently. "The vineyard is just north of Evisa. Paulo would consider it a personal affront if you did not visit him."

"I'll bet," Mats replied, remembering the phone at Jennette's ear as they had left the Alta Mira.

An hour later, with Carlo and Mats in the Renault following Mario on his motorcycle, they came to the mountain village of Evisa. The view was breathtaking. Red-tiled roofs topped buildings outlined by the sharp peaks of the mountains rising behind them, peaks so near that they lost themselves in each other's shadows. The trio pulled into a small square dominated by a large stone wall with an open gate near its center made from stout timbers and iron braces. Carlo parked the car and got out to buy cheese and bread to take to the vineyard of Paulo Guibega.

"What's beyond that wall?" asked Mats of Mario as he parked his Ducati next to the Renault, his interest piqued by what appeared to be a rampart at its top.

"It's an old mountain fort that has been converted into a hotel. The food is terrible."

Mats got out and looked toward the top of the wall, another of his father's stories vying for his consciousness.

"I'd like to take a look," he said and started toward the gate, giving Mario little choice but to dismount and hurry after him.

Inside the gate was a courtyard which contained a memorial in its center. It was little more than a pile of rocks. At its base was a ring of smooth-faced stones bearing the names of villagers who had lost their lives in each of the world wars. Disturbing to Mats, there were a number of similar stones that were empty, waiting for the next group who would add their sacrifice and names in the next conflict. Beyond was a three-story building, obviously constructed to defend the keep in a previous era. The windows at the ground level were mere slits that pierced meter-thick stone. The upper stories overhung the courtyard, giving free access for archers of old to take full aim. The stone wall and the building at its center seemed familiar. There was something about them that nagged at Mats.

Mats, now followed closely by Mario, entered an arched doorway into the ground level of the old fort. It had been fitted with electric lights and converted into a museum of sorts. Even with the lights on, the area was full of shadows, grim and cold.

Mats walked quickly past the caretaker to a stairway cut into the rock leading to a second story, where the lighting was better, and the colors of the rugs and drapes overcame the dinginess of the stone. To the side, away from the staircase that Mats had ascended, was a desk with squares of dark wood mailboxes behind it. A woman in a colorful flowered blouse stood before the boxes.

Mats looked around the room, which appeared to comprise most of the second level. There were tables and chairs arranged along the side wall opposite the registration desk. Although there were no signs proclaiming such, Mats presumed this was the restaurant that was allegedly not very good. With Mario on his heels, Mats crossed the room and approached the receptionist.

"I would like to stay here this evening," he said in English.

The clerk made an obvious show of turning and looking at the keys in the boxes behind her. At the same time, Mario laid his hand on Mats' arm and shook his head sharply from side to side.

Mats was concerned about spending the night at the Guibegas' winery. Even if he had felt comfortable with the invitation, it was likely that someone would have to give up their bed. He thought it would be good to have an excuse to leave if he felt awkward. And despite Mario's displeasure, something about this building intrigued him. He wanted to spend the night in this parador.

"You are in luck. We do have a vacancy," the woman said, turning with a smile and speaking heavily French-accented English.

"We should stay with Paulo, Signor Falcon," Mario whispered. "Even if we do not, this is not a good place. There are better."

"This place appeals to me. It has a charm about it. How far away is Paulo's?" Mats asked politely.

"Only five minutes, but …"

"I'll stay here, Mario. You and Carlo can stay with your cousin."

Mats followed the woman to the stairwell, where he took the stairs two at a time. At the top landing was a small corridor with four doors off it. He found himself hesitating in front of a door with a brass "A" nailed to it.

"That room is taken," said the clerk, moving around Mario. "Room C is available."

"This is the room I want," Mats said evenly. "I am sure you can make some new arrangement with the current occupant." Mats reached into his wallet and withdrew several large bills, pressing them into the woman's hand. "I will go to dinner with my friends for a few hours. This will be my room when I return." Without waiting for a reply, he turned back down the hallway. "Let's go, Mario."

As they rode to the winery, Mats wondered at his assertiveness with the hotel clerk, as well as the level of authority he had begun to assume with the two Guibegas. He had been raised in Marin County, a mecca for political correctness and non-confrontation, except as practiced by their U.S. Senator. His father had been strict with others at times, but never with him. Now Mats recognized the decisiveness in his own actions and words that had been ingrained in his father's make-up and wondered when his personality had changed.

The perplexed Mario followed Mats. They left the clerk standing in the hallway, looking at the three folded hundred-euro bills in her hand.

The vineyard was less than five kilometers from Evisa. They arrived just before dark. Jennette had indeed telephoned ahead. Paulo was waiting for them in the winery courtyard as they drove in. He was obviously related to the Guibegas—same size, same muscular shoulders and arms. Only his nose, which had clearly been broken, perhaps more than once, separated them by looks.

Paulo welcomed Mats, introducing his wife, five daughters, and two sons. Their large stone house, separated from a substantial crushing and storage building of the same construction butting against the rock face of a cliff, guarded the entrance to the valley. A sharp tang of fermenting grapes struck Mats. Even with his eyes closed he would have known it was a winery. A well and a barn completed the small grouping of structures. On the way to Evisa, Carlo had explained that the Guibega family all shared equally in the profits of their various enterprises. The vineyard, extending over a hundred and fifty acres up the valley, produced the grapes that, when picked, produced a wine bottled and transported by the Guibegas to the family warehouse, where Carlo's brother brokered it. The same principle held true for the family's other concerns: a drayage company, numerous rental houses, a hotel, and the restaurant that Mats had already seen.

The table was already set for the family and three guests, the smell of roast chicken filling the house when they arrived. By the end of the meal, Mats had grown more comfortable with both the language and his treatment. He felt good about the developing relationship. He sensed he could trust these men and women and count on their honesty. The language Mats had learned from his father, and taken to be Corsican, he came to understand was probably better termed a private language of the Guibegas. It was heavily laced with slang, different pronunciations, and phrases from utterly forgotten cultures. Clearly they did not speak it outside of the family, as evidenced by the number of times conversation stopped so they could explain a word or phrase to Mats.

As they were finishing a dessert of baked apples laced with strong aromatic liquor distilled in small quantities from a special stock of grapes grown in the far end of the valley, the front door opened. A young man came in, supporting the arm of an impossibly grizzled old man.

"Grandpère! Nonno! Grandpapa!" A chorus of voices rang through the room while everyone stood in respectful greeting.

The old man looked crankily at his progeny and bellowed, "Am I too old to be told when the son of Egel Falconi eats with the family?" The old man cocked his head as he shuffled toward Mats. "Welcome, Falconi. In truth, I was told with plenty of time but had to pick something up that delayed me."

As he reached Mats, he held out both hands, and Mats extended his own in return. As they touched, the old man seemed to falter, going down on one knee in front of Mats. At first Mats thought had it not been for his grip, the old gentleman would have fallen. Then he realized that he had not slipped but merely knelt, holding Mats' hand firmly pressed to his lips. Mats looked around in embarrassment.

As quickly as he had knelt down, the old man rose and embraced Mats with both arms. "Welcome, Falconi. I am Nando Guibega, your father's oldest friend."

Mats was aware of all eleven members of the Guibega family watching the old man. They said nothing, as if waiting for something to happen, waiting for Mats to respond. Mats felt his father's ring in his pocket, pressed against his thigh by the tight fabric of his jeans. Without knowing why, he reached into his pocket and slipped the ring over the third finger of his right hand. He had the powerful feeling that it was the right thing to do as he removed his hand from his pocket, showing the ring to the ancient Nando Guibega.

The effect was immediate. Seeing the ring, the old man grasped Mats' hand tightly in his own gnarled and bony fingers, his grip surprisingly strong. He held the ring finger up for all to see. Tears flowed from the corners of his eyes, running obliquely down the deep crevices in his cheeks to the edges of his mouth.

The old man said nothing for a long while as everyone stared at Mats. Then he spoke. "Your father was a great man. You have his look." He pulled Mats with him as he sought a chair, three of his grandchildren scattering to assist him.

"Paulo!" he bellowed. "What kind of house is this where I must ask for a glass of wine?" The old man, still holding onto Mats' hand, sat down with his young companion standing behind his chair, nodding to Mats to take the chair next to him. "Your father, even as a youth, was a remarkable man. I was saddened when he decided to leave Corsica. We all were."

"He died six months ago," said Mats. "He was eighty and had had a good life. Still, it was too short. You look of an age."

"I worked as a boy for his father, your grandfather, then later for your father. He was four years older than I. And your mother?"

"He met my mother when he was already in his fifties. She was Swedish, twenty-five years younger than he was. She was killed on the Golden Gate Bridge when a drunk swerved over the divide. I was just seven years old. All I really have to remember her by is a few words of Swedish. She used to laugh that I would only be able to use it with seven million people. My father said that was seven million more than the twenty thousand who speak Corse." Mats looked straight at Nando. "Do you know why he left Corsica?"

"Then he did not tell you? He was true to his word. But of course, he would be." The old man grinned through teeth which, while not straight, were still mostly intact, only one in the rear missing.

"I explained to Mario and Carlo that my father never spoke of Corsica. I know nothing of his life before he came to the United States."

"Then how is it you have this?" The old man lifted Mats' hand, again showing the ring to the rest of the family.

"It was left to me at his death."

The old man's eyes narrowed, the wrinkles deepening at their corners. "It bears the dual-shield crest of the Falconi family. I first saw it on the hand of your grandfather."

Mats wanted to return to the earlier subject. "Signor Guibega, why did my father leave?"

The old man sat back and took a long pull on the water glass full of wine that one of his grandsons had given him.

"Your father vowed when he left here that he would spare his sons and daughters, if he was so lucky as to have them, the responsibility... the fate... of his Corsican ancestors. It was for him to tell you. I cannot go against his wishes. It must be yours to discover."

Mats could feel the strength of the old man's conviction, his loyalty to his father's wish. "Still, you could tell me something of my family, of my father. When did you last see him?"

"Your father left Corsica in 1935. He was just sixteen years old, but he was already a man of substance—intelligent, and faithful to the bond between our families. He was the last of the Falconi line. He left not for fear for his own life, but because he desired children who could grow up without the harshness of the conditions on this island."

"Then you last saw him when he was sixteen?"

"No. I only tell you this because it will serve to show you what type of man your father was. During World War II, the Nazis and the Italian fascists overran Corsica. As so many conquerors before them, they used our harbors to control the sea-lanes of the Mediterranean and, as so many times before, the Guibega fled to the hills. We fought, but technology had changed warfare. Their airplanes found our positions, and superior guns with greater range put us at a disadvantage that made us ineffective as a fighting force.

"In 1942, your father returned. He swam ashore from a passing boat, slipped through the German lines, and joined us in the mountains. From that day forward, we became the heart of the Corsican resistance. Over the next three years, we lost only one Guibega. Your father took the code name 'Maquis,' after our tough mountain shrub, a rock rose that is almost impossible to pull out from between the boulders, and the name and the man became a legend. No enemy troops were safe from attack. No consignment of food or weapons was beyond our reach.

"De Gaulle, that pig, later took credit for forming the resistance on Corsica, but in truth he only contacted 'Maquis' long after your father had severely crippled the Axis's ability to use our island as a comfortable base. After the war, when he became president of France, de Gaulle tried to find out the identity of 'Maquis' to bestow on him the Croix de Guerre, the highest of military honors, but only the Guibega knew his identity and we kept your father's secret."

Mats was incredulous. His father, a war hero? "No one in the States knew of it either," he said. "What an incredible secret! I knew that he was gone during the war, but I always assumed he was with the U.S. forces. He didn't talk about the war. I don't even think my mother knew what you have just told me."

"Signor Falconi, I do not tell you this to break your father's wishes. He often said, *Home is not where you live but where men understand you.* Envy of the Falconi is what made Corsica so dangerous for your father. Your father left Corsica because of the threat of reprisal to his unborn heirs. He returned in the most dangerous of times because my clan needed his leadership. Without him, the Germans would have killed us all. He wanted no medal, no fame, no recognition, but only to fulfill the responsibility that his family had recognized since the first Falconi on Corsica met his first Guibega. He taught us the way and our lot has prospered with the Falconi ever since. It is his legacy."

"His 'legacy'?" Mats asked.

"The Guibega family is part of it, the only part I can tell you about. These men and others of our family are yours to command as helpers or friends. Their allegiance to the Falconi is bound in blood over the centuries. Every Guibega is taught the history of the Falconi and their importance to our survival over the years." The old man drank and leaned back. "The rest of it I cannot speak about. There is much I do not know, and my guesses over the years have sometimes been very wrong. But now let us drink wine."

Mats raised his glass, now filled with a deep red wine, and was answered by the uplifted glasses of the Guibegas. Mario and Carlo both had smiles on their lips. It was plain that they had increased in status among their clansmen by bringing him to the house, and they both considered Mats their personal responsibility.

Mats' mouth opened, but before he could speak, Nando spoke again. "I said I would have arrived earlier, but I had to pick something up. Your father gave it to me before he left Corsica for the second time. It was then he told me that he would not burden his children, were he so lucky as to have them, with the vendettas held against his family. I was to keep this until his sons or daughters returned on their own seeking answers, then give it to them, but only if they had come seeking the truth. You have come and the Guibega who are here will rejoice. I am the only one in this room who has had the opportunity to know the Falconi. All the others were too young."

Nando pointed to a young boy of about ten. "Julius, bring me the sword." The young boy moved quickly to the back room, returning immediately with a short sword with a jeweled pommel.

Nando turned to Mats. "This is yours, given to me to safeguard until you came to claim your legacy." Nando handed the blade to Mats while the Guibegas watched in awe. Mats drew it from its scabbard. It was short, the blade no longer than the length of his arm from the elbow to the tip of his thumb. It showed a few specks where rust had tried to gain a hold on the blade but was glistening with a light sheen of oil. Its grip was well formed and seemed to be covered with some type of skin that adhered to his palm like Velcro.

As he examined the grip more closely, Nando said, "It is shark skin. It prevents slipping even when drenched in blood."

The drinking now began in earnest, with Guibega after Guibega offering toasts to Mats and Mats offering them back.

After several hours and many emptied bottles, one of Paulo's daughters drove Mats back to the hotel, being one of the few left sober enough to drive. They had tried to convince him to stay at the farmhouse, but Mats had only to say once that he wanted to sleep at the hotel. They had not tried to dissuade him after that, only arguing as to who was going to accompany the girl in the car.

The money had done its job. The receptionist was not happy at being roused from bed, but when she saw that Mats was with the young Guibega girl and the unsteady Mario, she tried to be polite as she handed him the key. Mats thanked the girl and lurched towards the stairs with the key in one hand and the other holding the sword against his leg, unseen through the fabric of his pants.

Once in the room, he removed his shoes and took the sword out. He had planned to study more of the journal before he went to bed, but the wine and the hour … after only two pages, he put it down. Even the best laid plans …

He fell asleep in his clothes, one arm wrapped around the hilt of the sword, the journal opened beside him, a series of rectangles covering the page.

CHAPTER SIX

Corsica 1329

The small column of men rode hard up the dusty, boulder-strewn trail southeast of Porto. Their leader, Baron Falconi, who rode the magnificent gray war horse previously ridden by Sir Marco, reined up at the top of a particularly steep grade and looked back down the trail. He could not see the pursuit, but he could hear the sound of their mounts and occasional shouted cries echoing up the mountain pass. He tried to gauge how long it had taken his men to ride the distance from the faint dust cloud rising in the air below them to their present position. At most they had twenty minutes. Short as it was, this cushion seemed like a luxury compared to the obstacles he had faced over the last two days. Despite the sinking boat that had forced him to land at Porto, his plans had gone well. There had been so many chances to fail that he did not take the relative success of his deeply felt quest for revenge for granted.

Falconi's plan to overrun Charles d'Avignon's castle had gone perfectly, better than he could have hoped. They had not lost a single man. He had killed Claude, the son responsible for the deaths of his wife and son, and had taken d'Avignon's treasure, gold destined for the Pope in payment for the reversal of the man's excommunication. But the relief column, outnumbering his own force, had made it necessary to flee the castle before he could fulfill his vow to kill Charles d'Avignon as well. The castle damaged, the money taken, and the death of d'Avignon's son would have to suffice to soothe his own loss, at least temporarily.

Falconi turned his mount back up the trail, spurring it past the animals that carried the two chests containing the treasure, past the men who had sailed with him from the mainland.

Leaving the castle, they had had no trouble eluding the relief column riding to d'Avignon's aid. The rescue force had pushed their horses to get to the castle and could not keep up the pursuit of Falconi's men at the same pace. Each of his party had helped himself to a fresh mount from d'Avignon's stable, leading a spare animal each and scattering the few remaining horses over the fields as they rode away. Still, they were in a hurry to board their vessels and be gone from the coast before the serious reprisal force arrived.

Even with a head start over their enemies, their attempt to leave the port city of Arles was almost thwarted. Of the two ships they had sent from San Remo, where they embarked on their quest for revenge, only one had made it to Arles seaworthy. One had hit a submerged rock at the entrance to the harbor and was afloat but listing, water visible just below the thwarts. Worse, there was no suitable replacement for it in the port. Although the pursuit was still hours away, word of the raid had spread through the waterfront, and though d'Avignon was not a popular figure among the coastal people, none wanted to risk his displeasure by helping the dangerous-looking armed knights and their men.

Falconi had his men drag the damaged vessel onto the beach and turn her over so he could examine the damage. Three strakes had been split by the collision. The rest of the bow was intact and solid. There was no time to replace the planks, but a double thickness of canvas tacked in place and covered with tar should allow the boat to sail to Corsica.

Falconi loaded most of his men and horses into his original vessel, taking only four men, their mounts, and the booty with him in the recently repaired ship. Even then, both boats were dangerously overloaded. They were clear of the harbor and below the horizon when d'Avignon rode into the village. His rage at their escape was evident to seafarers and longshoremen alike, who scurried around in feigned activity whenever he rode by, laughing at him silently beneath their serious countenances. To people who made their living on the water, a man who knew the sea as Baron Falconi did was to be respected, unlike d'Avignon, who was known as a poor seaman, liable to get lost on the river.

It would be days before a ship would leave port in pursuit, and even then, it would be well if they did not meet Falconi at sea. Generations of accounts of the Falconis' prowess as sea fighters had gained them a healthy respect from the men who made their living on the Mediterranean.

The repaired ship started taking on a small amount of water almost before they had left the safety of the stone breakwater. It was enough that Falconi could not risk raising a full sail as the added speed would loosen the patch at the bow. Each hour they dropped farther behind their other boat. Falconi signaled it to proceed without them. There was no room to transfer any more people, even if it became necessary. With luck, the first vessel would arrive in Ajaccio, unload, and then hurry back to escort them into port.

As the northwest tip of Corsica came into view, one of the horses, its fetters loosened by the water in the hold, broke free. Frightened by the slapping of a rough wave, the animal kicked, striking the boards just behind the patch. Immediately water started squirting past the repair and into the hull. Falconi had the men stuff their cloaks and blankets against the breach but only accomplished a slowing of the leak. That done, he set his men to bailing. Marco's injured arm prevented him from being of much use. Of the other four, three were experienced sailors and the last was an archer Falconi had sent to Scotland the previous year, ostensibly to trade wine and olive oil but really to learn the secret of the English longbow. He had smuggled out eleven of the six-foot yew-honed weapons. Now he seemed more interested in keeping his bow in a long water-proofed sleeve and the bow strings beneath his cap dry than in bailing.

As they sailed down the coast of Corsica, it became apparent that the boat was shipping too much water to make the run down the entire west coast. The men had been bailing constantly and they were tiring, the result of almost fifteen hours in the saddle and the delay in Arles repairing the boat.

Falconi had one of his men take the tiller while he lent a hand with the bailing. The seas were just high enough to start taking advantage of the reduced freeboard. The water had risen to a critical level. He urged his men to give a last heroic effort as they made for Porto. With pride he watched these men who were so loyal to him, loyal beyond the expected bonds of allegiance, bend to their task. As they struck the floating dock at Porto, the men bent over the lines that secured them. Breathing deeply, muscles quivering with fatigue, they gasped in great gulps of air.

Despite the early hour, three men had gathered at their approach, helping to secure the lines. Falconi now ordered them to assist with the unloading of the horses and the chests once destined for the Pope. One by one, his men followed the animals onto the pier, up the steeply inclined wooden gangway that gave access to the stone jetty. As the cargo of horses and men climbed out, the boat lightened, but the leak had opened to a point where the rails remained low in the water. Falconi was the last to leave the sinking vessel, but only after walking its length, waist deep in water, exploring the hold with his feet to make sure all items had been removed.

Porto was situated north of his own lands and was ruled by the Duke Colletti. Teodoro, the present duke, held all of northern Corsica from Porto in the south to Bastia in the northeast, and he was Falconi's bitter foe. Only a balance of power in the numbers of knights prevented bloodshed. The ill will between the families stemmed from the Falconi having been awarded the southern lands which the previous dukes of Colletti had once administered for the Romans and which they still considered rightfully theirs, despite documents proving the contrary. The Colletti forces had always been superior in number but had not fared well against the Falconi, nor against the men the Baron had recruited and trained. Hostile was the term that best described their relationship.

Any intrusion into the other's territory was invariably met with violence; thus, Falconi's forced landing at Porto put him and his men at risk. Seeing his men sitting on the quay, their shoulders hunched in exhaustion from rowing and bailing the last six hours, underlined the seriousness of his position. The treasure would have been enough of a temptation even if it had not been defended by only five weary knights. The horses now unloaded onto the jetty in contrast seemed fresh, having been idle in the hold; their soft snickering and blows gave evidence that they were happy to have firm, unmoving land beneath their hoofs.

"What do we do now, sire?" asked Marco. The blood from his wound was now dried black against his over-garment.

"Yes, what to do?" Falconi repeated. There were only three options: steal another craft, wait for his own boats to sail north to find him, or take the horses south over the coastal mountains to the safety of his own land. Falconi suddenly felt the weariness that was so apparent in his men.

Despite the early morning, the sun, still hidden by the mountains to the east, was casting its reflected light off the high clouds to the harbor below. The three men who had helped them stood idly on the jetty, curious as they saw the ship sink to the height of half the mast. One looked at the Falconi crest still visible on shields attached to the horse's saddles, then at Marco, obviously wounded, and noted the arms carried by the other knights.

"Lord Falconi," the man said, "it appears you have exacted your revenge on the lords of Avignon." The shrewdness of the man was undisguised in his sidelong glances at the treasure chest. The deaths of the Baroness Falconi and the Baron's son were common knowledge on Corsica. The timing and method of the anticipated payment of the vendetta had been the subject of many a conversation.

"Tend to your own affairs," Falconi said with a force of voice born of authority.

"Aye, sire," said the man, bowing and backing away down the quay.

Watching him go, Falconi understood the consequences. Halfway to the corner the man broke into a run, pausing to shoot a glance back over his shoulder before he was out of sight. He would surely bring Colletti's men. The number of men Falconi had with him could not defend the quay, there was no other vessel on the dock, and his own miserable craft had settled to the bottom.

"Mount up, men. We'll find an inn that has soft beds." Falconi picked up one of the chests and secured it to the wooden frame on a pack horse. His men, seeing his actions, followed suit and in minutes they were mounted and moving off the pier.

Porto was a small settlement compared to Calvi and Galéria to the north, where the bulk of Colletti's forces were to be found. Falconi knew the land. They would have to ride into the mountains before turning south. The coast was cut with steep, rocky inlets that sliced their way to the sea, making it impossible to take a more direct coastal route. With luck they would be in their own territory within two days. He would lead his men to Evisa following the river road that had been built by the Romans. It was still Colletti's land, but just an outpost, most likely poorly defended. From there he could travel south to Vico and the safety of his own men.

Once off the waterfront, Falconi spurred his mount to a trot. His men responded without question. "We must make it to the mountains," shouted Falconi as they quit the town, the road stretching toward the south-east. Six mounted men and two pack animals would be impossible to hide even in the hard, rocky territory of Corsica.

Falconi looked at Marco, their eyes meeting despite the rapid gait of the horses. Marco nodded. Understanding his Baron's wishes without spoken command, he nudged his mount to a faster pace.

The Baron smiled. Marco was a Guibega. He could sense his wound caused him pain, but it would not interfere with his performance. He would be at a disadvantage if they had to fight, but just riding, even at this pace, he would block out the pain, using his good arm and resting the injured one on his thigh. Hearing Marco's horse's hoofbeats quicken, the other four turned in the saddle and looked at the Baron before spurring their horses after Marco.

Falconi watched them pass through a series of boulders and out of sight. He turned his great horse around and dismounted. From his vantage point he could look down the five kilometers of road to the outskirts of Porto. After five minutes, with no pursuit yet visible, he began to wonder if his concern over Colletti had been necessary. Possibly he had given the rogue at the dock too much credit. Perhaps there were insufficient men, perhaps no leader, to take the initiative in the city.

He was about to leave his concealment and remount when he saw the commotion. Riders shot forth from not one street but three, converging on the road that Falconi's men had taken. He stood, keeping out of sight, as he counted over thirty mounted men stretching their horses in full pursuit. With a small oath, Falconi realized it was much too large of a group to be permanently stationed in Porto, that it must be a visiting patrol. His luck had not held. Unhurriedly, Falconi moved to his horse. The animal had been trained for combat, but still it made no sense to risk startling him by running. This race would not be won or lost by the seconds he would gain by reckless haste.

It was soon apparent that the horses, despite the comfort of being on land, were too worn out from their sprint to the French coast and the harrowing experience in the boat to sustain the pace they had kept at the onset of their escape from Porto. Falconi had hoped to be at Evisa by now. After observing the amount of ground their pursuers had closed, he now just hoped to be able to get to that mountain village. He had scouted the fortress town two years before. It had a small well-built fort that was likely to be poorly manned, but they were at least ten kilometers away and still had to climb the red rock side of the gorge.

No one had spoken in almost two hours. The faces of the men were etched with fatigue as they crossed the last ancient Roman bridge and began the ascent to Evisa. Falconi turned to watch for their pursuit. He did not have to wait long. Around the bend, less than a kilometer behind, came the first of the horsemen, close enough for Falconi to make out the crest of Colletti on his shield. Less than three minutes separated them from their foes.

Falconi looked at Marco. With a quick jerk of his head toward the small fort nestled against the side of the mountain less than two kilometers away, he gave his instructions.

"Leave me the archer. Take the others and secure the fort."

"Yes, milord."

Marco called three of the men to him and rode hard toward the sanctuary.

The man left at the top of the trail with Falconi was the best bow shot in the company. A stonemason by trade, he, as most of Falconi's men, belonged to the Guibega clan.

"Now we will see if you have learned well your lessons from the English," Falconi said to him.

The longbow could not be used from horseback, as could the Saracen bow preferred by most of the Guibega, but it had the advantage of extended range and the power to pierce armor.

"We must give Marco enough time to secure the fort," said the Baron, dismounting from his horse with his bow already in hand.

"Sire, let me take the right side of the trail. It will expose me but will offer a wider field for my bow. If you can climb that rock on the other side, they will have no place to take cover. They will have to retreat."

Falconi smiled. The positions he had chosen were the best to stop the advance of Colletti's men up the final hundred meters of the trail. The trail narrowed as it rounded a large boulder, becoming so constricted that two horsemen could not pass at a time.

They could hear the horses laboring before the first rider came into view. Falconi held his arrow until four men occupied the narrow section, and then he let fly. The twangs of the two bows followed each other so closely that they might have been mistaken for one. Falconi had aimed at the first man in the column, striking him full in the chest but not knocking him from his saddle. The mason had not been so chivalrous. He had aimed directly at the unexposed chest of the horse, and his arrow had flown true and with great force. The animal tumbled, throwing his mortally wounded rider off and blocking the trail to those already pressing from behind.

The archer unleashed his second shot as Falconi was drawing his aim. This arrow found the second rider just above the heart, piercing his chain metal tunic. The shot spun the man around in his saddle so that he was facing back down the trail as he fell, his blood mingling with that of the dying horse. His horse, panicked by the loss of its rider and the smell of blood, was unable to turn on the narrow trail. It leaped over the dead mount obstructing the trail in front of him and toward the archer.

Falconi held his next shot, watching the man fall before readjusting his aim for the third of the pursuers. He caught the man as he was trying to turn his mount back into the pressure already surging from behind, his arrow buried deeply in the man's hip. The last two men visible to Falconi showed signs of panic as they backed their mounts around the turn and out of sight.

Falconi waved at his archer, gesturing at him to mount and follow the column that had already made it to the fort's keep. Without hesitation the man mounted, carrying out the order and starting toward the small fort.

Well-trained and intelligent, thought the Baron, as he watched the man break into a gallop in the distance. It will take Colletti a while to devise a strategy, and I'll wager that it will be to send someone around on both flanks.

He moved from his vantage point seconds after sending a third arrow whistling past the corner of the trail. On foot, he moved thirty meters down the side of the rim, being careful to stay close to his mount, which was grazing on the top of the plateau. He had chosen the high side of the trail, reasoning that it would take longer for a man to circle from the downhill side.

Falconi just had time to take another arrow from his quiver when he saw them: two men moving through the rocky hillside, keeping low and heading toward the crest of the trail, the spot he had just vacated. They had come faster than he had anticipated. Colletti was not to be underestimated. His tactics were good.

Falconi fleetingly wished he had kept the archer with him. He had not anticipated two men. Still, it had been the right decision. It was imperative that they control the keep and a good archer's presence might make the difference. If they did not control it, then nothing done here at the head of the trail would influence the outcome.

He took two extra arrows and laid them on the rocks in front of him. He would be able to get his first shot off, and possibly his second, before compromising his position. He hoped he would have no use for the third shaft. He waited until both men had exposed themselves before sending his first arrow through the back of the trailing man. Without looking to discover the result of the shot, he strung his second arrow and let fly at the lead man, who had turned toward his fallen companion. The shot took him in the groin, eliciting an immediate scream. Falconi looked back toward his first target and caught sight of the man crawling toward cover, bright feathers still protruding from just below his shoulder blade. Turning, Falconi jogged to his horse, mounted, and took off toward the safety of the keep.

As Falconi had anticipated, Marco and the men had encountered no resistance at the fort, one inebriated man-at-arms and three servants being the total occupants. Having made the fort secure, they stood on the abutments, within Falconi's view. They had found water and food stored, enough not only for them but also for their horses, and had locked the man-at-arms in a storage room. As Falconi spurred his horse forward, he could see servants passing through the gate and the horses being led out and into the hills by the archer.

Falconi saw Marco standing at the gate and watching the horses disappear between the large rocks that fell toward the keep from the mountains to the west.

The Baron rode through the gate with apparent lack of concern. As he dismounted, Marco apprised him of their situation, mentioning the horses placed in the mountains above the keep.

Falconi turned to the man who had just closed the gate. "Peter, take my mount. Take it to the other horses. Take them farther up the mountain and hide them. Then ride to Vico. There should be at least ten of our men there. Bring them to our aid. Bring them no later than morning two days hence."

Peter nodded and slipped out of the gate, which Falconi himself re-bolted.

Fifteen minutes later, Colletti had surrounded the fort with the twenty-one men remaining to him. He was careful to keep them out of bowshot. When they were in position, he approached the keep under a white flag hung from the tip of his sword. Falconi stood on the abutment and called down to him.

"Far enough!"

"Why did you attack my men, Falconi?"

"Why did they pursue me in battle gear?"

"I offered escort."

"I want none," Falconi answered.

"It will be your casket we escort, unless we come to terms," yelled Colletti. "Give up the chests you took from the waterfront, and you are free to ride south."

"We are free now, Colletti, with men on the way to provide for our safety."

"If you desire death, then I will be glad to oblige. But think on it. The chests will allow you to return to your own lands." He turned his horse and trotted back to where his men had already started to set up camp.

After a few minutes Falconi saw five riders leave Colletti's camp, galloping to cover the road to the south. He has a fine mind, thought Falconi of his foe, hoping that Peter had seen the men leave from his vantage point in the hills. It was imperative that Peter get through, as Colletti had undoubtedly sent for more men already. Colletti did not have enough men to completely surround the keep, especially in the dark, but the noose would only tighten with time. For all his bravado, Falconi understood the danger of the position he and his men were in.

"He knows about d'Avignon's chests," said Falconi to Marco, who stood at his side. "Perhaps his greed is more important to him than his desire to capture me. He will send for more men but will first try our defenses tonight after dark."

Falconi turned and walked the perimeter of the wall surrounding the keep. Then he went down to the courtyard and into the building, a plan already formulating in his mind. Colletti would know his strength in numbers, or nearly so. He would not want to lose any more men to the bows used so effectively on the trail. He would wait for more men to completely surround the small keep, letting the fatigue from watching and responding to constant small probes take its toll.

"Marco!" he called, summoning him down from the wall. "Did you find wine among the supplies here?"

"Yes, but the guard in the lock-up has undoubtedly put a dent in the amount."

"Tonight I want a large bonfire here in the courtyard. Make sure the men don't look at it, and stay down to avoid being silhouetted. Also, can you chain the guard to the wall, so his door can be opened?"

"There are chains in there. It is not the first time it has been used as a gaol."

"Do it and send the archer to me."

Falconi went to the rear gate. It was small, only wide enough to allow a single horse to pass, and was studded heavily with iron. There were four more hours of daylight. The two pack animals stood quietly eating hay, already comfortable in their new surroundings. The chests that had put them in this predicament were still strapped to their backs.

The archer arrived, holding his bow, a quiver of arrows on his back. He was, like most of the Guibega men, powerfully built with dark hair and eyes, and shoulders that would serve him well both as a bowman and as the mason that he was.

"Tonight I will need you as a mason. But first help me carry these chests upstairs. I would ask you something."

In the bedroom, Falconi pointed at two large stones in the wall that held the window. "Would it be possible to remove these stones and open a space behind them to place these two trunks without it appearing that they had been tampered with?"

"If the trunks were smaller, yes," said the archer, looking out the window and measuring the distance from the inside and outside with his hands.

"I saw several trunks in the stable. Bring them here and see if they would fit."

The archer returned carrying two saddle boxes. Putting them down, he removed chisels and mallets from one of them. "These will fit." Falconi and the archer-turned-mason transferred the coins and jewels from d'Avignon's chests into the smaller containers.

As night fell, Falconi went to the prisoner with a liter of wine. "We do not want to harm you, only to get to our own lands," he said as he gave the man the bottle.

Up in the bedroom, the mason had begun the process of removing the stones. "The first one will be hard, the second much easier," said the mason as Falconi entered. "Help me with the wedges."

It took almost two hours to remove the first stone, setting it on the floor of the bedroom. The facing was unmarked, but the sides showed small chips caused by the wedges. "Those will be hidden when the stone is replaced," said the mason, watching the Baron run his fingers over the scores in the stone. "When I am finished, no one will be able to tell they have been removed."

Falconi left the man to the second stone, went to the courtyard, and lit the fire. Walking to the ramparts, he reminded each of his men not to look at the flames and to keep hidden. "When the fire is high, sing as if you are slightly drunk. Throw an empty bottle over the wall as the night goes on. Colletti might attack if he thinks we are drunk, but I believe he will wait until more men arrive."

Back at the courtyard, he got another bottle of wine and went again to his captive, who was pleasantly drunk on the Baron's first offering. "My men often sing when they are drinking. It would be good to hear a better voice tonight."

Back in the bedroom, Falconi found the second stone removed. The mason had chiseled a score line around each of the removed stones. "The line must be deepened. Then with luck and wedges, the stones will fracture, leaving the face unbroken to be replaced when the chests are inside. It will be loud."

"With luck, Colletti will hear other things," said Falconi and set to work gouging the line deeper while the mason applied himself to the second stone. The singing started and after it the first hard chisel strikes. Half an hour later, the first stone was done.

The next day broke clear and bright. Falconi had stood watch, relieving his men at midnight. No attack had come that night. He let Marco sleep, taking sentry duty by himself, but ordered the archer to take his sleep on the parapets close at hand. Marco would heal better with the extra sleep.

Twice during the next day, Colletti sent men to test the keep's defenses; once he tried the front gate, and later, around mid-afternoon, he sent five men with a ladder to try to storm the rear wall. Both times they were easily repulsed. The walls were too high, the gate too stout to be breached without exposing the men to attack from above. Colletti lost an additional two men in the effort. These attempts seemed more designed to gauge the reflexes and fire power of Falconi's guard than to gain the fort.

That morning, Falconi had helped place the boxes holding the treasure into the recess in the wall, then watched as the mason carefully replaced the stones, which had been shortened by two thirds in depth, back in place. The mason's final act before putting the stone chips in d'Avignon's treasure boxes was to pound dirt into the cracks between the stones, leaving no trace to show that they had been removed. There was no hint of the treasure now hidden inside the bedroom wall. If they were captured by Colletti, the hidden treasure would be their best bargaining chip to saving their lives. Falconi and the mason carried d'Avignon's chests back down to the courtyard, and after spreading the stone flakes behind the animal enclosure, secured them again on the pack animals.

Falconi woke at dusk. He washed and then went to the storeroom, where he again gave the prisoner a bottle of the rough red wine.

"Marco, come down here," Falconi whispered harshly to his man on the parapet.

"Yes, sire." Marco came down the stairs two-by-two after alerting the other sentry to his intention.

"We will leave an hour after dark for Vico, just before the moon rises. Ready the men. Put the dummies on the wall and give the prisoner another bottle of wine. Tell him his singing was bad." After giving the order, Falconi climbed to the parapet over the back gate, looking hard into the encroaching gloom, trying to visualize the placement of Colletti's men who partially ringed them. Colletti's reinforcements would be arriving soon. They must not spend another day in the keep or it would become their death trap.

An hour later, Falconi opened the back gate and motioned his men and the pack horses, their hoofs wrapped in layers of wool, silently through. Closing the gate, he bolted it from the inside. In the courtyard, he lit the bonfire, as he had the first night. The Baron had used clothes belonging to the man-at-arms now chained and into his second bottle, filling them with straw and placing them on the ramparts. The fire outlined their shapes but at the same time made it impossible to open the gate again without alerting Colletti's men. Falconi watched the sparks rise into the night sky as he barked orders to the stuffed figures and started singing. He was immediately drowned out by the prisoner, who provided truth to the saying, "If you can't sing good, sing loud."

At the top of the wall, hugging the southwest tower wall, the Baron had secured a rope around a stout stone drain. He dropped the end over the wall and quickly followed its descent with his own. With luck, it would be hours before Colletti realized that the sentries had not moved. Once on the ground, Falconi made off toward the spot where he had directed his men to wait.

There was no way to be sure that his plan would work. The moon would not rise for another hour, and a light cloud cover made the dark even less penetrable. He had reasoned that in the darkness, anyone riding fast or directly away from the keep would be challenged. Falconi led his men away from the fort, halfway to the pickets. Then he moved in an oblique route, so it would appear that he was approaching from the side. Slowly, making little noise, weapons muffled with cloth, his men moved away from the keep toward where the archer had left their mounts.

The plan worked better than Falconi had hoped. The horses had not been found. They mounted and started to move south, picking their way through the rough ground until they found a narrow trail. As he came close to where he sensed the picket would be, he signaled Marco to stop, proceeding only with the archer.

"Guido, is that you?" Falconi whispered. They had moved only a scant twenty yards from Marco and the rest of his men.

"No, Guido's still at the main camp," a voice responded.

"We just arrived from Galéria." Falconi kept walking his horse unhurriedly toward the voice. He was not certain if the man would be alone, but he felt that Colletti would more likely have two men at each post if his numbers permitted it.

"Have you attacked yet? Are we in time?" Falconi dismounted and continued walking toward the man, leading his horse by the reins.

"No. Can't you hear their singing? Everyone seems to think we will storm them tomorrow. With you here to help, we should have little trouble. How many came—" The thought was never finished, as Falconi's knife sliced through the sentry's throat before he could identify his enemy.

"Seven." The Baron continued the conversation. "Now be quiet and my men will spread out." If there was a second man, he was either asleep or hiding, a better soldier than the one lying dead beneath Falconi's legs. The archer went back, bringing Marco and the animals with him as he returned. Now they had only to find the road south. With fresh horses, an hour's head start would be enough to get them safely into territory loyal to Falconi.

As quietly as they could, they rode straight toward a small notch in the rocks that marked the southern trail to Vico. Falconi tried to remember the extent of the trail, but only the ten kilometers north of Vico would come to him with any clarity. The dark that had aided them so well in leaving the keep now worked to their disadvantage. He could only guess at their exact position and that of the cart trail south.

From the keep Falconi had observed a detachment of men leaving to guard the trail. His plan was to get by them by any means and as quickly as possible. Hopefully they would be as negligent as the picket had been.

The Baron smelled the camp before he saw the tents, the odor of human sweat mixing with the open sewage pit.

"Stop. Who goes there?"

The voice was alert and immediately accompanied by the sound of weapons being unsheathed just to his right. Falconi had almost ridden directly into their camp before being hailed.

"It's Guido, you fool. I've come from the main camp," whispered Falconi, harshly disguising his voice. He hoped the same ruse would work with these sentinels.

"Why do you ride here at night? You know the orders."

"Why, indeed—" Falconi did not finish the sentence. A man jumped out from behind the rocks.

"It's Falconi! Falconi!" The alarm spread and a horn blew, surely heard in Colletti's main camp as a signal that they had escaped.

Falconi spurred his horse forward. As he did, the sentry swung his sword at his waist, but Falconi was able to deflect the blade with the head of his axe. The parried blow bit deep into the leather of the saddle and for an instant the man had trouble freeing it. An instant was too long, as Falconi's axe struck down from the height of his horse, bisecting the space between the man's neck and shoulder.

Marco and the archer whipped their mounts forward past their lord, quickly passing the body of the man who had hailed them to stop. Others, unseen in the dark, continued the cry of alarm.

Falconi rode his animal quickly down the wide trail, trusting the horse to find footing that he could not see, the sword still stuck in the saddle just in front of his thigh. "Follow me!" he shouted. Arrows whizzed by their heads as they galloped through the camp. A grunt signaled that one of his men had been hit.

Riding south, Falconi could hear Colletti's men pursuing them, getting closer at every turn, their knowledge of the road giving them confidence and speed that Falconi could not risk. Another hail of arrows helped to make up his mind. Their pursuers were now close enough to shower them every time they came to a straight stretch of road. If they kept riding, they would all be dead long before reaching Vico.

The moon had risen over the backdrop of the mountains, and with its light Falconi detected an outcropping of rocks with a space behind them for the horses as well as for his men. It was their last chance. They arrived just in time to thwart another shower of arrows, which clattered harmlessly off the boulders. Here they might hold off Colletti until daybreak; then he would have to rely on Colletti's sense of chivalry.

"Milord." Falconi turned toward Marco as he dismounted. A man had his arm around the waist of the archer, supporting him in his saddle. An arrow's feathers protruded from his back, and the point and most of the shaft, glistening black with blood, extruded from his chest.

Falconi rushed toward the stricken man, gently lifting him to the ground. For a moment their eyes met, a confirmation of service and appreciation explicit in the contact. Then the man closed his eyes, his wound mortal.

The Baron softly laid the man's head on the dirt and again took his position against the boulder, guarding the trail. The loss of the archer, of all of his men, had the most impact. Their position could only be held by keeping Colletti's men at a distance. In a hand-to-hand fight, there was no natural formation to protect them. Their only hope was to keep the main force away from them with arrows. Now, not only were they just four in number, but the best of them with a bow was on the ground, dead.

Falconi was positioning his men when he heard the sound of horses behind him on the trail. Colletti knew this land well and had somehow used a bypass to surround them. They could now expect an attack from both sides at once—an attack that could have only one conclusion.

"Duke Colletti!" shouted Falconi into the night, his voice gravelly with the emotion of defeat. "I desire a conference."

The sound of the attack from the rear did not slacken. Falconi turned to his men.

"Swords."

His remaining men turned to meet the onslaught—not with fear but with resignation in their eyes.

The first rider hesitated only momentarily as he passed the Baron's position, the battle cry of the Falconi screaming from his lips as he charged north toward Colletti's men, his shield proudly painted with the crossed axes of Falconi. The Baron counted over twenty men following the lead horse. There was a brief clash of weapons before Colletti's cry of retreat was heard. Peter had gotten through.

Within half an hour, his men, led by Peter, returned with a dozen horses laden with shields, weapons, helmets, and armor. It would be days before Colletti could recover his losses and come after them.

After making sure Marco's wound had not opened, Falconi decided to bury the archer where he had fallen. The boulder would forever mark the site of his bravery and sacrifice. Falconi swore silently that one day he would take this land from Colletti. On the boulder set as a headstone, he instructed that a message be chiseled: "Lorenzo Guibega, a man of Falconi."

When the burial was complete, Falconi stood and addressed the men who had come with him and those who had saved them from Colletti's soldiers. "The Guibega have once more served the Falconi with their lives," said the Baron. "Marco, the archer's family is to be sent to me when we arrive at Ajaccio."

Falconi's ancestors had given the Guibega clan special privilege. For the most part, nobles fought and their serfs died; that was their lot and their duty. Between the Falconi and the Guibega, however, there was more: the Falconi gave leadership, protection, and respect to the Guibega, who provided their loyalty and strength of numbers. The archer's wife and sons would be provided for by the Baron. It had always been so between the families, and his son Thomaso, had he lived, would have continued the tradition.

CHAPTER SEVEN

Evisa, Corsica

Mats turned over in bed and was jabbed by a hard metal object. He reached behind him and felt the blade of the sword at his hip, the hilt pressing uncomfortably into the small of his back. Swinging his feet to the floor, he grasped the hilt in his right hand and swung the sword in front of him as he sat on the edge of the bed. His heart was still beating furiously from the adrenaline aroused by his dream.

The floor was cold, and its reality helped Mats get a grip on his own. He had gone to bed heady with wine. Still, the inevitability of a major hangover could not account for the total disorientation he felt. The surroundings were familiar, but his orientation in time did not seem so. The dream had been too real, its effect on him powerful and lasting. Standing, he placed the tip of the sword on the floor, using it as a pointed cane to ensure his balance as he stood. Memories of last night at the farmhouse came back to him and he was warmed by them. There was no doubt in his mind that the room and the journal had triggered the dream. Flashes of his father, sitting by his bed in the dark telling him the story of Baron Falconi, kept intruding. He remembered that he had been looking at the journal. It was lying on the bed, half hidden by the pillow where it had dropped from his hand the evening before, opened to the drawing of the rectangles, two with

Xs marking them. Morning light was just filtering in the small window. Below the window he looked at the pattern of the stones, then back at the open page of the journal. There was no mistaking it; the pattern was the same. All that was missing were the two Xs on the real stones.

A hot shower restored Mats almost to normalcy, averting the hangover that he had expected and probably well deserved. As he felt better, he realized that his disorientation was due more to his dream than to his debauchery.

In the small dining area on the second floor, Mats found his two guides. The previous evening had not been as kind to them, as was visible in their haggard, hollow-eyed looks. They were sitting at a table, bent over large cups of steaming coffee, heads bowed. There was no reason to expect them to be present so early in the morning, but somehow Mats had known they would be there, waiting for him.

"The Guibega should be kinder to their own," Mats said, smiling at their condition.

A grunt, closer to a groan, was the only reply he received as the two men brought the cups of near-scalding coffee to their lips.

"I have changed my plans slightly. I will hire both of you at twice the agreed upon wage."

Mario glanced up over his cup and without looking at his cousin said, "After last night, we would gladly work for less than we agreed on."

"I understand, but that is not how it will be." Mats looked at them closely, drawing their attention to his lowered voice. "You will justify the pay if I correctly understand our relationship and that of our families."

"What would you have us do, signore?"

There was no questioning, no definition of limits placed on his request. The relationship described by Nando the evening before would be unconditional.

"First, I want to take the car a little way back toward Ajaccio. Then we will return here for breakfast. Perhaps by that time your stomachs will accept the thought of food."

Three kilometers south of the hotel, Mats pulled to the side of the road. The sun had just crested the mountains to the east, casting long shadows across the road. The day would be hot without the usual breeze to help moderate the afternoon temperatures.

Mats got out of the car, followed quickly by Carlo and Mario. He looked up and then down the road, trying to get his bearings. The stretch of road was barren of houses and farms, nothing but boulders framing the side of the macadam. Mats walked slowly down the road for twenty paces, then turned, his actions now filled with purpose. He scrambled over boulders pushed to the side of the road during its construction, stopping in front of one three meters from the paved surface, which was twice as large as a man. Kneeling at its base, he rubbed his hand over the inscription chiseled there centuries before. Now rounded and indistinct from the passage of time, a cross made by battle axes was still identifiable. Underneath it was inscribed the name Guibega, followed by smaller, less legible letters that disappeared below the sand.

Falcon stood looking down at the inscription while Mario and Carlo exchanged short exclamations of surprise behind him. The dream had seemed real, like many dreams. However, for the first time he was not surprised to discover that this one had actually been true. He remembered asking his father decades ago if his stories were true and wondering why his father had smiled. Mats could not separate his father's stories from the dreams. He only knew that both had basis in truth.

Moving away from the rock, he allowed the two Guibegas to move forward and touch the stone. Mario started to scoop out the sand at its base, exposing more of the inscription. Mats did not watch. He knew what it would say.

The dream had been real, most certainly an unconscious retelling of his father's bedtime stories. The journal was the catalyst that had brought it to his unconscious mind even through the haze of drink.

"Carlo! We should get back to the hotel." Mats had the car started, driving back to the city of Evisa somewhat faster than he had come.

As the town came into view, Mats said, "Mario, you and Carlo go and order breakfast for the three of us. I have to get something."

Mats climbed the stairs and unlocked the door to his room. He looked around, noticing his bag open and emptied on the floor next to the bed. The small notebook was still on the bedside table, but his sword was gone. He ran down the short hallway and leaped down the stairs three at a time, ignoring the danger presented by their age-rounded stone risers. On the ground floor on the back wall he found a heavy door unlatched and open.

As Mats ran toward the back door, Mario followed him down a narrow flight of stairs into the courtyard between the hotel and the inner aspect of the outer wall. Outside, after the gloom of the interior, the bright sun blinded them, and they almost collided with Carlo, who was holding a man by the scruff of his neck. The man, sallow-faced and powerfully built, was holding Mats' sword.

The man looked pleadingly at Mats and held out the sword, hilt upward with the tip pointing at the ground.

"Monsieur, I am Marc Dupree. My sister is the front office clerk. I was just borrowing your sword to show a friend who has an interest in such things. I was going to bring it right back. Your man here misunderstands my intentions."

Mats took the sword by the hilt, holding it in front of the man in Carlo's grasp. He handed it to Mario, who had come up behind him. "This man is a thief and a liar," said Mats. "I am new to this island and unfamiliar with how the authorities would handle this matter. I leave it to you and Carlo to decide what should be done."

Looking at the thief, Mario replied, "Part of what he said is true; he is related to the housekeeper. What is also true is that he is a thief and has always been one. However, he is French, as are the police and the judge, and he will get off lightly enough with his lies and their tolerance." Without warning, Mario brought the pommel up sharply under the point of the man's jaw. An audible crack echoed off the walls as the man's head snapped backward. At contact with the chin, Mario reversed the direction of the sword, jamming the tip of the blade into the man's sandal, piercing it and severing the small toe. The man screamed in agony, blood oozing between the straps of his sandal.

"You will not steal from the Guibega again," said Mario in a low whisper. "And you will not say anything against me or my friends or you will lose more than a toe. Do you understand?"

The man had been on the verge of unconsciousness when the sharp pain in his foot forced him to regain his focus. Now he nodded quickly and emphatically.

"Good. I'll take you to a doctor," said Mario. "You had an accident." Turning to Mats he added, "It should only take a few minutes. Will you still be here?"

Mats nodded, turned, and, followed by Carlo, walked into the hotel through the back entrance. They passed the reception desk and were halfway to the stairs when Mats noticed the wizened face of Nando smiling at him from the relative darkness of the eating area. He was sitting at the farthest table, fast against the stone wall, his hands cupped around a mug of coffee. Mats smiled in return, and he and Carlo approached the table.

"Please take this, put it in my room, and lock the door," Mats said to Carlo. He sat down with Nando as Carlo left with the sword for the upper floor. "You knew?" he asked Nando.

"This morning I came to see you, but age has made me soft and I slept too late. You had already left with the boys. I was drinking coffee when Dupree, a thief from a family of thieves, came in, slipped behind the desk, and got a key. He did not see me in the corner, which is just as well. I followed him upstairs and watched him slip into your room. When you came back with Carlo, Dupree had just left. Carlo saved me the need to detain him myself." The old man looked up and smiled again, the creases around his eyes crinkling like a spider's web.

Mats gazed at the old man. It was as if he had shed years since the evening before. It was not evident whether the effect was temporary or if he had truly regained his vigor upon the return of a Falconi to Corsica, but clearly, he was different today. Mats was still lost in these thoughts when Carlo came down the stairs and returned to the table, giving Mats the key to his room.

"Carlo, we will have a gathering here tonight. This time the party is on me." Mats peeled off six bills of large denomination from his wallet. "Invite all the Guibegas on the island. I would like to meet all of your clan. Get Jennette Campanelli to come up from Ajaccio and bring some of those recipes that you were bragging about. While you're doing that, I will talk privately with Nando here."

"Jennette is known by Guibega, Jennette Guibega," offered Carlo as he stood up. "She would not change her name to Campanelli. It is the way with many of our women." Carlo moved to the reception desk to find the clerk while Mats and Nando climbed the stairs to the top floor.

Once they were behind the closed door, Mats turned and asked Nando the question that had been on his mind. "Nando? Since I arrived in France, I have been having dreams about my father's stories. How is it they tell me things that I have no right to know, that my father had no right to know?"

Nando smiled the smile of the old when they know something that the young do not. Taking his time, he looked straight at Mats and said softly, "I do not know all of what you ask, but what I do know I will tell. Like your father, your grandfather never told all that he knew of anything. It is sad that your father did not pass on his history or the legacy of the Falconis' Gift to you, but it seems you are finding it anyway."

"What is this gift you speak of?" asked Mats.

"Falconi's Gift!" The old man shrugged his shoulders. "We Guibega can only guess. It is said that when the first Falconi came here, they could read each other's thoughts. The first children also seemed to have the ability, but it has been lost over the centuries. You seem to have inherited another part of the Gift – the ability to know what will happen before it does."

"I don't think I have that ability," said Mats.

"Carlo said you drove back here very fast after finding the stone. That you didn't even let them uncover all of the writing. Why was that if you did not anticipate the theft?"

Mats recalled the feeling of urgency he'd had in returning to the hotel, but he could not find any reason for it. "Is there anything more to the Gift?" he asked.

"Your ability to lead men and inspire loyalty," said Nando with a smile. "Surely you have recognized that part?"

"Nothing more?"

"The Guibega have always thought that the Falconi symbol, the one on your father's ring and on the door of the Alta Mira—the battle axe, which is a favorite weapon of seafaring people—was a clue to the Falconi origin."

"But what about the dreams?"

The old man looked up at Mats, intelligence shining in eyes yet unclouded with age. "As for your dreams, I know nothing. Would you like to tell me about them? Perhaps I can help you to interpret them."

Mats detected a curiosity in Nando's offer. The Guibega did not know of the dreams. It would not be he who revealed them, then. "No, no need. They interpret themselves, and events prove or disprove their truth."

A soft knock on the door interrupted their conversation. "Come in."

The door opened immediately. Mario entered, nodding first toward Mats and then toward Nando. "The thief will not trouble us. It seems he slipped with the sword coming down the stairs. He is being cared for by the doctor."

Mats looked up at him. "I just told Carlo we are having a party for all the family here tonight. Help him with the arrangements and phone calls? I want loud, lively music. Have Paulo provide the wine. It will be paid for."

Again Mats reflected, looking at Nando, and again it was as if the old man had shed years. When he had first entered the house the evening before, he had seemed frail, supported by a young boy. Now Mats wondered if this had been an act. He could believe that the Guibega patriarch was the eighty-four years he confessed to, but his handshake, Mats remembered, was strong. He now moved without assistance. He no longer bent over as he stood or walked.

"I have a task for you as well," Mats said to Nando after Carlo had left, "one that must not arouse any curiosity. I want you to bring chisels and crowbars here to this room, tools that could help us move two of these stones out of the wall." Mats gestured with the back of his hand toward the wall. "Do this by yourself. Do not tell even Carlo or Mario."

Nando nodded, and as he closed the door, Mats went to it, latching it behind the old man. Then he picked up the notebook and carefully began studying the pages he had tried to read the previous night. He was no more successful, but he now recognized the rectangles from one page: there they were, in exactly the same configuration as the stones in the wall. The only difference was that there were no Xs painted on them.

Later, with the morning not yet half over, Mats left the hotel, climbed onto the motorcycle, and rode toward Porto. He wanted to let the Guibegas arrange the party as if it had been their idea, not his. He drove for an hour, taking side roads that were little more than wagon tracks, stopping often to look at the view of the sky and the land. Shortly after noon he found a small café, really just a single table outside a farmhouse next to a wide spot in the road, and stopped for lunch.

It was after three when he pulled back into the courtyard at Evisa. A bustle of activity was discernible even from the back of the Ducati. Carlo and Mario had apparently been successful in their efforts to organize an instant party. Equal numbers of men and women were scurrying around with food and decorations. A platform had been erected in the courtyard with the trappings of a band already on it. A fifty-five-gallon barrel of wine was set on a stand, its bung hole already filled with a brass spigot. Mats shook his head and walked inside, nodding to several Guibegas he had met the evening before.

GARY DOC NELSON

Carlo was sitting at a table with Mario and Nando. Mario was involved in an animated conversation with a good-looking woman who appeared to be more than holding her own. They stood as they saw Mats approach.

"This is Jennette Campanelli Guibega," Carlo said. "She has somehow managed to alienate the hotel chef. Now he will not even let her in the kitchen."

The woman curtsied and was about to launch into a staccato list of complaints, but she was stopped short by Mats' upraised hand.

"Please, ask the chef to come out here," he said to Carlo.

Mats could see the open hostility in the chef's face as he came around the corner and noticed the woman standing next to the table. Mats raised his hand again as the chef began to sputter a protest, his finger pointed at Jennette. The chef had heard of the early morning confrontation in the courtyard. Word had spread quickly about how Dupree had been caught as well as about his broken jaw and severed toe.

"This woman has come a good distance to provide you with help for the party," Mats told the chef. "Her family expects some of her special dishes. I would consider it a personal favor if you would extend to her the use of your kitchen. I would also like you to evaluate the dishes she prepares and see if you can provide their equal."

Turning to Jennette, Mats added, "I expect you to respect his wishes. It is my party and your food, but his kitchen. Also, share one of your recipes with him. That will be part of your gift to me."

Without waiting for assent from either party, Mats stood up and went quickly upstairs to his room. He walked directly to the small window cut in the stone and looked down on the preparations for the band in the courtyard below. Nando entered a minute later, latching the door behind him as he entered.

100

"There will be no trouble from those two. I think the food will be beyond expectations. The tools you requested are under the bed. I brought them separately. No one saw them," said Nando.

"We will use them tonight," answered Mats in a voice just louder than a whisper. "See that Carlo and Mario do not drink this evening. I will need them after dinner when the festivities start." Mats walked to the inner wall of the room near the corner and kicked two large stones that made up three feet of the wall just above the floor. "What do you think of these, Nando? Do you have any thoughts on how to move them?"

The old man walked to the wall and stooped, running his fingers over the joint between the stones.

"I worked as a mason for forty years, but we might need Mario for his strength."

"This evening, then."

The evening brought with it a warm southerly wind that added to the pleasantness of the festivities. Mats moved among the Guibega, shaking hands and greeting the numerous cousins and uncles. He watched the children dance as their parents filled their plates. The eating soon gave way to music and singing. Mats moved with Mario into the hotel and up to the room where Nando had already started on the stones. Mats stationed Mario at the door to make sure no one would interrupt their work. The band covered the rhythmic beat of the old man's chisel as he gently wedged the stones from their resting place. With Mats helping, it took less than half an hour to remove the first stone and only half that time to move the second to the center of the room. Both had been cut so that their depth was only a third of that of the surrounding stones, leaving a space behind them.

Mats waited until the second stone had been moved aside before reaching in. Slowly he dragged out two simple wooden chests, sliding them across the floor. As he was moving the second chest, the band outside came to a sudden stop, and the screech of the box across the stone floor filled the room. Mats and Nando both froze in place. Mario tensed at his position at the door. But soon the band started again, the people in the courtyard again taking up their singing.

"We have been gone long enough." Mats nodded at Mario and started toward the door. "Nando, please stay here. Let no one in. We will be back in within a half hour."

To Mats' relief, none of the partygoers seemed to have noticed the sounds that had been so loud in the confines of the upstairs room. After a number of toasts, and after proving to those around him that although his voice was pleasant, he could not carry a tune, he and Mario made their way back to the room. Inside, Nando and Mario gaped as Mats opened the first chest. Mats knew what he would find, but the two others gasped when the open lid revealed a store of gold coins and a fair number of jewels. The second chest had the same contents but in reverse proportions.

A quick nod set Nando to replacing the stones, and Mats turned to help.

"The wall must look as if it had never been touched. We will also need a way to get the treasure out of here. These boxes will not stand to be lifted."

"I know just the thing," said Mario. He went to the door, listened before opening it a crack, and peered out carefully before slipping outside. He was back within minutes, giving the door a knock with his foot, a ten-gallon cask of wine under each arm.

"These have already been emptied," he said, removing the end boards and beginning to transfer the content of the two boxes into the cask.

CHAPTER EIGHT

The ferry trip back to the mainland of France was uneventful. The anxiety that had accompanied Mats' arrival just nine days before was gone, and a feeling of purpose filled him in its stead. Marin County and the San Francisco Bay had been his home. He had known no other, but now he felt that in discovering his father's heritage, he had found another home in Corsica. He knew that the friendship of the Guibegas had a lot to do with the feeling of comfort he was experiencing. He had boarded the ferry with Carlo and Mario, leaving them with the Renault in the vehicle hold.

Now, with a small portion of the treasure hidden in the panels of the old car, guarded by the two loyal Guibegas, Mats felt at ease. The rest of the treasure was hidden in Paulo's storage cave, inside an empty oak barrel with a bung that spurted the deep red wine of his vineyard from a five gallon skin attached to its inner boards. It seemed that the Guibegas were adept at hiding things, that they'd had that talent long before Mats had arrived in Corsica.

In the days that followed the discovery, Mats had cemented his relationship with the Guibegas. With the help of Nando, he had used the sale of a necklace, two jewels, and ten of the gold coins to buy fifty acres of land just north of the winery, giving it to the Guibegas. The land was peppered with rocks that would need removing, but it was suitable for grapes, as it faced south and received sun nearly all day. Mats purchased another fifteen acres just off the D6, five kilometers north of the Alta Mira. The land was already planted with lemons, oranges, and a particular lime that ripened to a lemon-like yellow exterior while retaining an overwhelmingly fragrant green interior. According to Jennette Guibega, the fruit was the best to be had in Corsica. Behind the orchards was a steep hill topped with the ruins of a small stone watchtower. As he walked the exterior of the ruins, Mats envisioned using them as a basis for a permanent modern residence. It was only a fifteen-minute drive to Ajaccio, and the view was superb.

While Mats had come to accept that his dreams were reenactments of his father's bedtime stories, understanding the journal became his obsession. His father's stories and his own dreams were helping to guide his actions, and at their root were historical truths. Both had the same cadence, and he heard both the stories and the dreams in the same voice. Mats had come to believe that the stories his father had told him had in some instances been dreams of his own, real and precise and much like the ones Mats had been having since his arrival in France.

It had been more than three weeks since Mats' last dream. Still, there were times during the day when he felt directed to perform certain tasks. He often had an awareness of what he was about to see around a bend in the road, a feeling of familiarity in a country he had never visited before. That was how he had come to buy the hilltop acreage. He had driven by it with Carlo on one of their excursions from Paulo's winery after hearing about it from Jennette.

"What do you know of the structure on that hill?" asked Mats.

"It is known as Falcon's Roost. The French think it is called that because peregrine nest there, but Nando once told me that it was built by the Falconi in the old days. The Guibega named it for them, not for the birds."

Together they climbed through the orchards to the summit of the hill, the smell of the ripening fruit so strong it was like an aphrodisiac. At the top they discovered the low ruin of a building attached to the northeast side of the watchtower, hidden from the road below by the crest of the hill. The structure had an unquestionable effect on him, but one he struggled to define.

"Carlo, will you find out who owns this property?" Mats asked.

"That I already know," answered Carlo. "Jennette told me before we left. It is owned by a foppish Frenchman who is indeed trying to sell. A coffee importer named Collette from the north, near Porto, has made the only offer, an insulting one according to the owner. The Frenchman had too much to drink a week ago at the Alta Mira," he added, answering Mats' inquiring glance. "Jennette inquired about buying it, but even the amount that the Frenchman had already been offered would have been too much for her to handle easily." Mats' interest was piqued. Even if the property had not spoken to him, the name Collette—so close to Colletti, remembered all too vividly from his dream— would have been enough to prompt him to pursue the matter.

The French owner was more than happy to find that there was another potential buyer for his property. He had once intended the land to be a mountain retreat before his own lack of funds, and the Corsican bureaucracy's demands for permit after permit, had forced him to reconsider his plans. However, Collette's offer was only a third of his original purchase price. The one thing you could not do to a Frenchman was insult him, and Collette's offer was an insult. Mats had Jennette Guibega present an offer to the agent at double Collette's price. The offer was accepted the next day.

Mats sat with Nando at the Alta Mira, as Jennette brought them lunch and then sat down with them.

"Did you give the chef in Evisa a recipe, as I asked?" Mats smiled as he lifted a forkful of linguini into his mouth.

"Of course, although I might have forgotten one ingredient," she said, smiling back.

Mats shook his head but couldn't suppress a laugh. "Are you happy with both the land and the sale price of the two parcels?"

Nando and Jennette looked at each other. Jennette took the lead. "Both land and price are better than good. Better yet, they fit perfectly with our other businesses."

"Good. That was my thought as well. We have two weeks to raise the money. I could cover it with funds from the States, but I would rather obtain it by selling some of the treasure. That might be hard, as it is obviously old and will be sure to raise questions of origin and ownership. Do either of you have any suggestions as to how that might be done?"

"The Guibegas have been evading French taxes and laws for over two hundred years," said Nando, taking a sip of wine. "Of course it can be done. Maybe not here in Corsica. Such a transaction would surely be noticed, but I have a niece in Monte Carlo, a shop owner who knows a man who discreetly deals in all sorts of interesting items. He is always looking to turn money that he might not be able to account for into hard items. It should be no problem."

The sale was concluded a week afterward, as soon as Mats had received the necessary cash from the sale of the items from the chests. Jennette had flown to the mainland

and taken a train to Monte Carlo. She was back in five days with shopping bags filled with wrapped presents. One in particular was for Mats. The broker who bought the jewels understood that they were museum-quality pieces and made sure Mats knew of his interest in any other pieces that might come into his possession.

While the people and the land of Corsica had become less of a mystery, the small notebook became more of one. Every time Mats looked at it, he felt an increasing desire to translate the volume. He remembered reading somewhere that the French, so proud of their heritage, had scholars, even whole divisions, at the Bibliothèque Nationale that dealt with the languages of the Middle Ages. Mats hoped he would find someone to help him with the translation of his journal.

He had also decided to use what was left of the cash from the sale of the jewels to set up a business on the French mainland, a wine-exporting company that would specialize in the wines of Provence and Corsica. His restaurant background made it a natural extension of his business, and his contacts on the retail end in California would ensure an air of legitimacy. The business would also provide him a reason to travel between France, Corsica, and the United States. Instinct told him he would need such a cover, if only to provide a conduit for the treasure.

Paris, France

The Bibliothèque Nationale was impressive from the outside. A great grim building of gray stone, it had occupied the former palace of the Cardinal Mazarin since 1721 and had since been expanded from area to area, floor to floor, building to building until it occupied an entire city block.

The main reading room was magnificent, 360 seats surrounded by more than 40,000 volumes. Most of the new works and all of the digital content had been placed in new structures away from the Bibliothèque, which despite its size was cramped for space. The historical manuscript section and the heart and spirit of the famous depository remained inside its walls.

Mats presented his coveted pass to the guardian librarian before entering the fabled reserve of knowledge. Only the sound of pens against paper, balanced by the sound of strokes upon computer keyboards, broke the quiet as he passed through the main reading room with a feeling of awe. But once inside the labyrinth of scholars, Mats had a different feeling. The hallways were narrow and poorly lit. By the time he wended his way to the third floor and found the section for old manuscripts, he was even less impressed. Rare books might be displayed on the main floor rooms of the library like royalty, but the men and women who studied and restored them were not afforded such spotlights.

Checking the address on the note he had scribbled, he opened the door and entered a small reception area flooded with light that was almost blinding in comparison to the dimly lit hallway. He greeted the middle-aged man who appeared around the partition that separated the entry from the room behind.

"Hello."

"Bonjour!" The man was balding and slightly plump. He didn't try to hide his contempt for Mats' use of English.

"My name is Mats Falcon. I have an appointment with Professor Gilbert." He made a great show of saying the man's name in proper French, *Jheel-bare.*

"I am Professor Jean Gilbert," the man said in French. "You are an American. I thought from my phone conversation with Commissioner Bluschel that you were French."

"Monsieur Bluschel is too kind." Having taken an immediate dislike to the man, Mats responded to the professor's French in English, enjoying the chance for one-upmanship. "I have the book with me that I believe Monsieur Bluschel mentioned."

"Ah, yes. An ancestor's diary, he said." The professor looked over the rim of his glasses at the small package in Mats' hand. "I will take a look at it." He extended his hand as if about to touch something unclean.

Mats' inclination was to turn and leave. Gilbert was not a man with whom he would work by choice. But he held himself back.

"I could not decipher it with just my high school Latin," he said as the professor opened the book and studied the script.

"With an old book, you can, in fact, tell a lot by its cover. The more important the book, the more accomplished the scribe assigned to copy it, and the more ornate and substantial the cover. This," he said, gesturing with the back of his hand at the book, "This is a poor example both of binding and penmanship."

"But can you translate it?" Mats' tone clearly showed his displeasure with the man's observation as well as with his general attitude.

"Parts of it. Although it would probably not be worth my time. It is only partially written in Latin. Some words are an idiom of the early French used in Normandy, and some are in a language whose origin I cannot even guess without further study. I can give you the Latin, but the early Norman French will require you to leave the thing. Perhaps in a month?"

"Is there someone else who can help me now?" asked Mats, losing patience with the man and showing it by leaning menacingly across the counter and grabbing the journal back.

Gilbert stepped back, protecting himself from Mats with the counter and increased distance. "Suzanne! Suzanne! Would you come out here, please?"

A young dark-haired girl wearing large glasses with maroon rims pushed up over her forehead came around the corner from a back room, taking more time to do so than the flustered Professor Gilbert would have liked. The rims of the girl's glasses matched the auburn highlights in her hair when the light struck it from behind.

"This ... individual has a diary of some sort, written in a jumble of Latin and Norman French and God knows what else. He was referred by Minister Bluschel, so I guess we must help him despite his American manners. Would you please tend to it? I have important work at my desk."

With that, Gilbert, obviously relieved, bowed ever so slightly. "May you have a good day, sir."

"I'll try to salvage it," Mats said snippily, and turned to the woman, Suzanne. "What's he like when he's not turning on the charm?"

"Monsieur?"

"Never mind."

Suzanne reached under the counter, taking out a pair of latex gloves which she snapped over her slender fingers. That done, she held out her hand for the book, a slight smile curling at the corner of her mouth.

Mats handed it to her. She looked to be in her mid-twenties and was stylishly if conservatively dressed. Her figure was camouflaged by the cut of her jacket and shoulder pads, although neither could conceal that she was a very poised young lady. Her hair was drawn back in a bun, and her lips and eyebrows carried only sparse makeup. Her eyes were dark and happy.

Mats decided that Suzanne's smile was occasioned by her superior's obvious discomfort. He smiled back and felt warmth passing between them. She slowly lowered her eyes to the book, which Mats had not released. Mats followed her gaze and let out a soft laugh. "I'm sorry. I think I got a little protective of this with Professor Gilbert. It's a family keepsake, very old, and despite what Monsieur Gilbert said about its worth, it is very important to me."

Suzanne gently took the book and opened it. She looked at Mats, wondering what it was that had upset her boss. "I overheard a little of what the professor said. He was correct, of course, when it comes to copied manuscripts, but this appears to be an original work. The vellum and ink quality are good. The binding is also good. I suspect from the look of the cracks that it has not been opened often until recently. The year on the first page, 1326, could be accurate. It can certainly be confirmed, if that is what you wish."

After Gilbert, this young woman seemed not only helpful but kind. "I don't think that will be necessary," said Mats. "I am virtually certain that this book was written by my ancestor in that year. Can you translate it?"

Suzanne carefully turned the pages, reading speedily, trying to take in the context of the narrative. On the second page she discovered one of the sources of Professor Gilbert's testiness. There were passages in ancient Norman, a language Gilbert was familiar with but by no means an expert in, and she guessed that he had relied on pomposity to hide his ignorance.

Whenever she read a new document or book, Suzanne preferred to get a feel for the subject by going over whole chapters before sitting down and laboriously translating each word into correct modern usage. It was a trick that enabled her to decipher complex documents while retaining the feel of the original, an ability that, over the last few years, had gained her a reputation as a linguistic genius, at least within her department.

"This is very interesting," she finally said in a softly lyrical voice. "Do you know what it says?"

"No. I know some of the words, but the overall meaning is not clear to me. By the way, Professor Gilbert left without introducing us. I'm Mats Falcon."

"Nice to meet you, Monsieur Falcon. I am Suzanne De Lacy." She took the hand Mats offered, accepting a slight squeeze instead of the typical American shake. "I think this might have been written deliberately in a way that is difficult to read." She turned the book ninety degrees so that they could both read the script from opposite sides of the counter.

"See here." Suzanne pointed with a manicured fingernail visible beneath the thin transparent latex gloves she had put on before accepting the book. "He starts in Latin, giving the date and place, as if in a diary, but by the fourth sentence he lapses in mid-sentence into Norman." She flipped the page over. "Later, on this page, he uses a series of words from what I think must be a Teutonic language, perhaps early Norwegian or Danish, and then he turns back to Latin for the name of a place described in the other language. At first this switching of languages looked haphazard to me, but at least in the first twenty pages or so, it comes to seem quite consistent: dates and places in Latin, hard facts in Norman, and names of people and their actions in Norse. It might be intentional, as with a code of some sort. Who wrote this?"

"I don't know for sure, but I suspect a man called Thomaso," said Mats, looking at the pages she had pointed to. "A distant ancestor, I think." Suzanne was right. Looking at it now, he could begin to understand parts of the text. It was as if a shade had been raised and he was inspecting the book for the first time.

"Are you in a hurry for this?" Suzanne asked in English. "It seems to be a typical American trait." The smile that flashed across her face and the twinkle in her eyes made it clear that she intended no insult but was probably poking fun at her boss.

"That makes me typical," laughed Mats, "but that wasn't why I got upset with the professor. I feel it's important, yes. There is some urgency." He liked this girl. No deception, no posturing as with the pompous Gilbert, just a professional expertise that was apparent in her actions as well as her words.

"I have never personally seen any manuscript of this age that was purposely encrypted. Could I make some photocopies to study overnight?"

Mats tried not to offend her. He wanted to sound casual. He drew a deep breath and exhaled, as if making a momentous decision. "I'd prefer no copies were made right now," he said. "It's not a question of money, it's just that until I know what the book says … I hope you understand."

"Of course, but as soon as you are comfortable, you should have it photographed. It is in as remarkable a shape as I have ever seen for a manuscript that is so old, if indeed this is the original. That could easily be checked by testing the ink and paper. But regardless, it is very fragile and really should be protected." She softened her words with a smile.

Mats watched as she straightened herself from the countertop. In doing, so the fullness of her figure became apparent despite the severity of her suit. He felt a curiosity, a flickering of desire he had not experienced since the death of his father. He returned her smile, forcing himself to concentrate on their discussion.

"What I would really like is for you to teach me how to read it. I sort of have a way with old languages. I'm sure I'll be a quick study. I have studied Latin, and my French is good."

"Your French is excellent."

"Thank you," said Mats with sincerity. "As is your English."

"Would you like a cup of coffee?" she asked. "I have an office just down the hall that would be more comfortable for us than leaning across this counter. I have several reference books on old Norse languages there as well."

"Coffee sounds great," said Mats, retrieving the book.

Suzanne knocked on Gilbert's office door and informed him that she would be checking some reference books in her office.

The coffee was strong and flavorful. It filled Suzanne's small office with a mingled aroma of paper, leather bindings, and ink—a rich European aroma. The room was set up in an efficient fashion, with a large desk as its focal point. Two walls were totally covered with reference books. A third wall featured a small window that opened on a view of another wing of the building only meters away. Mats took it all in, particularly the desk where only a photo of an older couple was displayed, then chided himself for having done so.

They worked for three hours on the manuscript, only stopping to refill their cups. Finally, Suzanne got up and stretched.

"You do pick up things quickly," she said with some admiration. "Do you mind if we continue this tomorrow? I would like to go on, but I still have to finish up a critique for Professor Gilbert this evening."

"Not at all," said Mats, also rising. "I appreciate your taking the trouble."

Suzanne reached down and tore a piece of paper from a notepad to mark the place where they had stopped after thirty pages. She casually turned the remaining pages as she spoke. "We covered enough to understand the particular use of languages and unusual wording. These two reference books fit the writer's use of language perfectly. The rest should not take as long as…. Maybe tomorrow, we can…" She trailed off as she looked at the remaining pages. "Ooh lala! Had you noticed this before? The penmanship in the last pages of the book isn't the same as that in the beginning. It's not the same handwriting."

Mats looked down as she flipped quickly but carefully from the first page of the book to the last. He had looked at the back pages and noted the differences in the script, observing that these pages were written mostly in Latin, though not a form of Latin he could understand; but he had made up his mind to read the journal from front to back. Now he saw that there was a decided difference in the handwriting as well as the language. The stroke was thicker and bolder in the final pages, less loopy and apparently hurried.

"Curious," Suzanne said. "It couldn't be simply the maturation of the author, even though the dates seem to follow, with a hiatus of about four years."

Mats knew she was right. They had already determined, in the pages they had translated, that the book was essentially a narrative of the life and travels of a man named Thomaso Falconi and that it included accounts of his schooling. It had seemed like a fairly common narrative of a young nobleman's education until Thomaso mentioned his dreams. Suzanne had not picked up on the mention of them as anything unusual, but Mats immediately realized why the writing had been encrypted. He remembered the name Thomaso from his father's stories. Thomaso had struggled to understand his dreams seven hundred years before, just as Mats was doing now.

Suzanne's suggestion of recessing until tomorrow was welcome to Mats. Once she had explained the key to deciphering the text, he had found that reading it was still difficult but not impossible with the help of the reference texts. During the last hour, they had referred to an old Norse dictionary and one of Norman-French. He was anxious to try to continue on his own. Besides, he wanted to see her again.

"Suzanne, I can't tell you how much I appreciate your help. What time would you like to meet tomorrow?"

"I will arrange for free time after three. That way, if we work late it will not interfere with my other projects. Why don't you come to this office directly, just after three? No use in raising the professor's blood pressure any more than necessary."

"Is he always that … er … officious?" asked Mats.

"Always, when it comes to people or things that are not French. Americans are a particular problem." She smiled again, making Mats wonder how she would look in a fitted dress instead of the suit she was wearing. "If you happen to see him, mention how difficult the translation is, and that I was only to sketch out the first five pages."

"Will do," said Mats, seeing her smile at his understanding of her position. "Could I borrow these for the evening?" he asked, hoisting the Norse and Norman-French dictionaries and placing them next to Thomaso's journal. "I'll be careful."

"Of course." She picked up her briefcase. "Oh, Mr. Falcon. Don't fall into the translator's trap and stay up all night with your book. We all do it when we get excited over a new manuscript, but it's like cramming for an exam. It's rarely effective." She placed her hand over his that held the book, maintaining contact just long enough to let him know that she was looking forward to their next session. He understood that he was an enigma, an American who was the owner of a French journal written in 1326. She must know that he was well off financially, since he had gotten Monsieur Bluschel's blessing. He watched her, hoping for a further sign, and was rewarded with a mischievous smile that remained on her lips as she lifted her head, looking directly into his eyes, telling him without words that she too was looking forward to their next meeting.

Mats phoned Carlo and had him pick him up outside the Bibliothèque. The two Guibegas had spent their time productively. Following Mats' instructions, they had leased a warehouse that had a back-loading dock on the Seine six kilometers southeast of the Louvre. They had also acquired furnishings, including two beds, a sofa, two chairs, and a desk for the small apartment upstairs, with two large plate glass windows looking out on the Seine. Mats looked out at the river flowing slowly past, the hard afternoon sun of summer filling the room from the west.

"This is too open. The room is too exposed to the river and anyone on the opposite bank. We should get some drapes," Mats observed. "But the warehouse is a good find. It is the perfect size and location. Place the money from the sale of two more pieces of jewelry into the account I've set up at the BPCE bank. Keep enough for yourselves. You deserve a good time. You can stay here for now. I'll see you here the day after tomorrow." Mats clapped them both on the back as a signal that they were dismissed, gave them each a thousand euros to hold them over until they sold the jewels, and then left to return to his hotel.

At the hotel Mats undressed to his skivvies, stretched out in a large overstuffed chair, and sipped a glass of wine. He picked up the journal and began thumbing through its pages. He had been correct in his guess that the discussion of dreams would take up most of the unread portion of the journal. It became obvious that these dreams had obsessed young Thomaso Falconi.

Mats read the first section for almost an hour, often stopping and rereading whole pages, not because he didn't understand the words the first time but because he wanted the full import of what he was reading to sink into his own consciousness. Thomaso had dreamed of the past, much as Mats was doing now, but he had not dreamed of knights and swordsmanship. Rather, he'd dreamed of his ancestors coming to Corsica, of sea raiders and pitched battles against men with matted black hair and foul-smelling fur clothing. Thomaso's writing showed that he was unsure of the meaning of his dreams and greatly troubled by them. He wrote of wanting to talk to his father about them when he arrived home.

As it turned out, the posturing Professor Gilbert had been correct. The volume was more of a journal than a book—thoughts and experiences jotted down hastily, to be expanded on at a later time. Several times Thomaso mentioned essays he had written as part of his education with his tutor, Master P. Margaux, and how he intended later to elaborate on a thought or a dream in more detail.

After an hour, curiosity made Mats turn to the second half of the journal. He had decided on Corsica that when he finally had the journal translated, he would read it in order from front to back. Now, knowing that the first part was a record of Thomaso's schooling and undoubtedly ended at his death, which Mats had seen in his first dream, Mats was drawn to the latter pages. As Suzanne had pointed out, it was written in a heavier hand and in Latin. But the Latin didn't sound right. It was stilted and uneven, and some sentences didn't make sense, the wording awkward. After an hour, with the two reference books proving of absolutely no help, Mats came to a series of words that puzzled him. The words seemed added to the narrative rather than an inherent part of it. Finally, he took to translating it word by word and realized that it was a poor translation of an expression that Nando had used that first night at the winery: *Home is not where you live but where men understand you.* The writer of this second half had translated the Latin from the spoken dialect of the Guibegas.

Finally, just before midnight, Mats' brain could not absorb any more. The concentration required to read a text that only that morning had been indecipherable had taken its toll, resulting in eye strain and a headache. He collapsed into bed, the journal's account of Baron Falconi's arrival in France to meet Thomaso's tutor vying with his exhaustion. What he could not decide, and it kept him from sleep, was whether he should let the enticing Mademoiselle Suzanne De Lacy see the rest of the book.

CHAPTER NINE

As had become his habit, Mats slept with the sword on one side of the bed—within arm's reach—and the book on the nightstand on the other side. Going to sleep thinking about what he had read led to dreams, and dream he did, the trail winding up in front of him into the Alps of France, east of Avignon ...

⚜   ⚜   ⚜

1329 Southern France

They could feel the air becoming thin, their breathing and that of their mounts labored with the climb. Baron Falconi had come to the mainland in response to a message from P. Margaux, his dead son's tutor. He had left all his crew but Carlo on the coast, preferring to make a quick two-man trip into the interior mountains rather than risk the probable discovery of a larger party.

It had been almost four years since the deaths of Falconi's wife and son and two since he had taken a measure of revenge on d'Avignon by taking the life of his son. There had been reason to be wary of the message that had been delivered to him in Corsica – suspicious of both the messenger and the information he carried.

Now, only miles from the monastery that was his destination, he went over the message, seeking any hint of deceit. It had been delivered by an Italian monk. The man, more a scholar than a priest, was much like the writer of the letter,

Monsignor P. Margaux—a man who had left the church and now worked for illiterate nobles, serving as a clerk and instructor to their children. Margaux was now the head of a library associated with a small monastery near Allos, at the foot of the Alps separating Italy and France. The monk's story had the ring of truth and was accompanied by a letter that contained a page written in Thomaso's hand.

The Baron could not be certain that the letter wasn't part of a trap set by d'Avignon to lure him to the mainland, but he suspected from the time of first reading it that it was genuine. First, the facts concerning Thomaso's education were accurate. Few would know these details. The messenger also seemed genuine, but just to be sure, he was left in the care of the mason's widow and commissioned to teach her son figures. He was watched carefully by the family and would find it impossible to get word to the mainland. Now, in France, the farther they traveled from the coast, the more certain was Falconi that there was no duplicity.

A cold wind off the mountains chilled them as they rounded a bend and came upon the monastery. It sat in a widening of the canyon. A crystal blue lake lay at its center, surrounded by several small buildings that housed the craftsmen who served the order. Their path took them past a small stone church built into the cliff at the side of the trail. Falconi dismounted and was greeted by an elderly man dressed in bright colors and a flamboyant hat, which hung down over his right ear.

"Monsignor P. Margaux, I am Baron Falconi."

"Milord. Thank you for coming." Margaux swept his hand toward the open door of the building nearest them.

"You have hidden well," said Falconi once inside the small room. "It has been four years since Thomaso's death. Why have you waited until now to contact me?"

Margaux turned at Falconi's question. "When I arrived here, the Abbey had just lost its founder. Without direction, the monks were lost and about to leave. I saw potential, as well as a place to hide, and prevailed on them to stay. I did not know of your wife and son's death at that time. I used my books and those of Thomaso to bolster the small library here. Without permission, I used some of Thomaso's gold to buy more books from the Vatican scribes in Rome. Over the first year, I taught the monks penmanship and set them to copying the volumes that were most in demand.

"As the reputation of the library spread, I began to attract students. I sent word to Normandy to send my things here. With them came my first outside student, a woman I had instructed previously. She brought me word of your successful raid to avenge the death of the Baroness and Thomaso. It confirmed my worst fears, for now I knew for certain that I would be hunted as part of the Falconi group as long as the elder d'Avignon lived."

Falconi could sense the man's nervousness. "So, this woman came with the news and you sent for me. How long did you wait?" asked Falconi, clearly unhappy with the scholar.

The small room protected them from the cold wind that whipped down through the valley, but not from its chill. Margaux shivered and motioned him to the door in the interior wall.

"Sire, I am not a courageous man. It took almost a full year after Lady Adelaine's arrival," said Margaux, opening the door on the interior wall.

Inside there was a fire that warmed the occupants, who were sitting at half a dozen writing desks. One was occupied by a beautiful young woman dressed in a fine manner, like the tutor. The softness of her blue satin dress contrasted with her stiff posture at the desk. Margaux sat down, after arranging a chair for the Baron. Falconi looked at the work spread on the desk in front of the woman. An ornate letter *F* done in a brilliant red color stood boldly at the top of the pages, colorful symbols and designs woven into it. The woman was working on an illustration at the bottom of the sheet of fine vellum, depicting vines and small blue birds sitting among berries in the same red used in the opening *F*.

"Milord, I must first apologize for the tardiness of my message, but as I explained, I did not know the outcome of that fateful day at the time. When I was told, I felt in mortal danger that d'Avignon might still follow me. I fear that I am rather easily identified. It took some months to build up my courage to finally send you the message."

"I hold you in no malice," Falconi said. "That I reserve for d'Avignon. You said you had items for me that belonged to my son?"

"Yes, sire. I had them packed for you when we received word of your arrival."

"Then you knew that I was coming? How?" Falconi was immediately alert for a trap.

"This village is isolated, which affords some protection, but only if we know what occupies the approaches. There are trails through the mountains, other than the road you have taken, and men who can travel faster than you on those trails. I knew of your coming early this morning."

"For a scholar, you have chosen your place of hiding well. Now what is it you have for me and why could it not have been sent with your monk?"

"First, let me stop myself from compounding my thoughtlessness. May I present the Lady Le Vere, daughter of Baron Le Vere? It was Lady Adelaine who brought my belongings from Normandy. I was the guest of her father while I instructed her and Thomaso. It was she who convinced me to send word to you."

"Thank you for that, Lady Adelaine," said Falconi, bowing to the stiff woman at the other desk and kissing her offered hand. "So, you knew my son, Thomaso?"

"I was a girl of twelve when he first resided with my father's sister, Baron De Lacy's wife. He had just begun his studies with Monsignor Margaux. We were taught together. That was almost six years ago. I knew Thomaso well, but I feel I have only really come to know him this past year through the study of his writings."

Falconi shot a questioning glance at Margaux.

"The abbey supports itself by copying books, sire. The valley produces sheep that provide not only meat but also excellent vellum and leather for the bindings. The lake provides fish. We sell our copies mainly in Florence, where we buy ink and brushes. The red tincture that we distill from local mountain berries is the only one we produce on our own. It is unique, for its color does not fade. There is a market for it as well as the copies, but we rarely produce more than we use, perhaps because we use too much.

"This is the room where we work on copying manuscripts." The scholar gestured at shelves that held several books, quills, and bottles of ink. "Some of the monks can't read as yet, but they copy faithfully, more artists than scribes. The Lady Le Vere was sent here to receive the rest of her education in letters and figures. She was allowed to read your son's works after she had completed all my other texts. No one else has had that privilege and no copies have been made."

Margaux got up. Falconi remained wary. "Come, sire," the tutor said. "I will take you to your son's belongings."

He led Falconi past an elderly woman sitting on a stool with needlework spread on her lap. She stared brazenly at Falconi as Margaux led him out the door down a narrow path leading toward the mountains behind the village. In less than a quarter of a mile, the path split. Margaux took the right fork into a narrow canyon. Within thirty yards, the path appeared to end at a wall of rock, but just before terminating, it turned to the left into a crevice scarcely wide enough to admit a man. After only three paces it roofed over, leaving the path first in deep shadow and then in the total darkness of a cave. Margaux reached out into the void and lit a small oil lamp. With practiced steps, he passed around the large vaulted area, lighting additional lamps and torches until the lower aspect of the cave was bathed in light. Arranged around the almost vertical walls were shelves filled with dozens of books of different sizes and colored bindings with the brilliant red predominating in their spines. Although Falconi was unusual for a noble in that he could read and write after a fashion, the number and variety of the books in this room held him in awe. His personal library consisted of five books. He had never thought to see so many books in one place.

"This cave, because of its position and the upward slope of its entrance, keeps dry and consistent in different temperatures all year long. The light is not adequate for copying the texts, but one can read, and it is ideal for safeguarding the books we copy." The tutor walked to the far wall, past a small wooden table and chair. "These," he said, indicating a line of books on the shelves, "are the originals. Each day we return them to this place." Moving further along, he hoisted three books and a chest from one of the shelves. "These are your son's."

"Could these not have been sent with your monk?" Falconi nudged the chest with the knuckles of his hand.

"I'm afraid that I am partly to blame for not sending them to you, milord." Lady Adelaine had silently followed the men into the cave, followed by the elderly woman still clutching her embroidery. "I suggested to Monsignor that you would not want to trust the information contained in your son's writing to the possibility of interception. I think he meant the texts for your eyes only."

"I had not read them as a total work, sire," explained Margaux. "I had corrected parts of them as he finished an assignment, not realizing that he was combining them at a later date as a full volume. It was only when I discussed the work with Lady Le Vere as part of her education that I realized what a prize Thomaso had created."

"I will read these books and then pass judgment on the appropriateness of your actions," said Falconi. "Now I need to be left alone."

The other three left without saying anything more. Falconi found the chair and desk comfortable, and in what remained of the day, he read the volumes written in his son's hand. There were three in total. Two were manuscripts similar in size to the other volumes in Margaux's impressive collection. One of those was unfinished, having to do with the final months of his formal education and the arrival of his mother. The other was in the form of a series of essays on growing up as a Falconi in Corsica, his relationship with his father and mother and the talents that made his line so special. He speculated on the significance of his dreams, as well as the steadfast loyalty of the Guibega.

The third book was little more than a small journal. It touched on many of the topics covered in the two larger works but only in outline form. It was written in the code that the Falconi used to hide their messages when being sent off Corsica. The last twenty written pages contained accounts of Thomaso's dreams. More than half the book had been left blank. From the handwriting, it looked as though the Baron's son had penned the dream accounts immediately upon awakening. The journal had been kept current, up to and including the first portion of the trip that had taken his life.

Falconi started with the unfinished volume. It was the series of assignments that Margaux had referred to before leaving. As Falconi read through them, Thomaso's writing became more refined, the content more descriptive. There were observations on the baking of bread and three full pages of detail describing an ancient oak tree. The last twenty pages diverged from the obvious lessons of Margaux to descriptions of Thomaso's dreams and his interpretations of them. The last page spoke of discussing the dreams with his father when he returned home.

Falconi leafed through the small journal and put it aside. It would be hard to read in the light provided by the oil lamps and seemed to be mainly first renditions of the essays he had just read in the first volume. He took up the last book and started to read.

Falconi had to stop reading several times as tears came to his eyes. Reading the words that his son had used to express his devotion to his mother and father broke through his warrior's demeanor. The loss of his wife and son had left a dark void, even four years after their murder. He saw in these words how his son had matured in the four years he had been exposed to P. Margaux's teaching and Edmond De Lacy and Baron Le Vere's instruction in the arts of war. Falconi's loss seemed even greater with his new knowledge of the man Thomaso had become, the promise never to be fulfilled.

Then the Baron came to a page with a heading that read in bold black ink, *On My Father.* After a moment of indecision, feeling he might be intruding on his son's most secret thoughts, the Baron read on.

I first knew my father when I turned ten. Oh, I knew him before. He wrestled with me, and when I was five years of age, he gave me a wooden sword and a small bow that I began learning to use with Luca Guibega, his weapons master. My father was kind and loving with my mother but stern-faced and strict with me. Then, the day I turned ten, he came to me while I was tending to the horses and said, "Come." Father took me outside and into the woods. He stopped some twenty paces from a gnarled apple tree. Without saying a word, he took out an axe from his belt and threw it with great force at the trunk of the tree. I watched the axe turn over and over until it bit deeply into the trunk. Without a word, he reached beneath his tunic and handed me a small axe, a duplicate of his except that it was two-thirds the size. He motioned for me to throw it as he had done. I did, but my axe hit the tree with its handle rather than the blade, bouncing off the hard wood to the ground. My father looked at me, but I could not tell if it was with surprise or disappointment. We walked together to the tree, retrieved our weapons, and walked back to the spot where he had thrown his axe. He placed me at his side and explained his grip and throwing motion. Then he threw the axe again, spinning and striking the tree only an inch from his first mark. He guided me slowly three times, until the grip and motion seemed natural. Then he stood back and I threw the axe. This time the blade struck the tree, sticking in the bark, but as we walked to retrieve our axes, mine fell slowly to the ground.

For the next four hours, long past the mid-day meal, he worked with me. He explained that you could kill a man with the edge or knock him out with the blunt heavy side. He showed that the speed of rotation was critical on which end struck. He told me that many could only stick the axe by standing at certain distances, but the real skill was in controlling the rotation. That afternoon I stuck the blade in the tree ten times from different distances. On the tenth time, before I could retrieve the axe, my father grabbed me by the shoulder, turning me to him in a hug. I looked up at him and saw pride in his face, a sense of warmth that I had never before felt from him, and I knew he loved me.

Six years later, when I arrived at Baron Le Vere's castle, one of the first things he did was test my skills with the sword and bow. Then he placed five axes on a barrel some distance from the inside of the castle gate. All were different, with handles and heads of varying length and size. He asked me to choose one and throw it at the gate. Without really thinking, I took the nearest and stuck it deeply in the planks. I followed it with the next and the next, until all five were sticking in the gate side by side. Baron Le Vere let out the loudest laugh I had ever heard and said to me, "You are your father's son." I had never felt so proud as at that moment.

Staring at the wall, the Baron's eyes filled with tears, the book open in front of him. He did not hear Lady Le Vere enter.

"Sire, I too was affected by your son's writing. I hope you agree that these works should not have been trusted to any courier."

Her words were slow to penetrate Falconi's consciousness. He wiped his eyes with the back of his hand and turned toward the beautiful young woman. The light from the flickering lamps combined with the tears he was still shedding to outline her in a shimmering halo.

"You were right to have sent for me. I hold only gratitude toward you and Monsignor Margaux. Now please leave me. I have much to remember."

At dinner time, Falconi emerged from the cave carrying only the small journal of his son. Carlo met him at the trail head, walking back to the village. Falconi moved swiftly to the dwelling, the place where Monsignor Margaux stayed when he was not at his precious books.

"We will be leaving tomorrow." Falconi's announcement was no less than a command. "You are certain that there are no copies of my son's manuscripts?"

"I am certain, sire. You can confirm it with Lady Le Vere, if you wish."

"Ah yes, the Lady. How is it that a woman has been given an education? What can she possibly use it for?"

"She is the second daughter and youngest child of her father, the Baron of Le Vere. When you sent Thomaso to him, giving him the task of educating your son in subjects suitable for a young knight, she was just a child. Le Vere dotes on her as his favorite. As the second daughter, she will receive little for her dowry, and she has less chance than her sister of marrying into land. Her father recognized her sharp mind and decided it would not hurt to have her educated, because the probability of matching her with an affluent noble is small, but with a knight, perhaps. As for her ability as a student, she is second only to your son in my memory. She has been ready to return to her father for months but has put off the journey because she cherishes her independence and doesn't want to exchange it for the constrictions of a lady-in-waiting or be fobbed off by her father in a marriage of his choosing."

"Remarkable! Her father would seem to have his hands full with that one." Falconi waved his hand at the tutor. "You may keep all of the texts, and the remainder of Thomaso's purse as payment for your last months of tutorship and for your loyalty to the Falconi. You have done well in both positions." The Baron turned quickly, a rush of grief for his son overcoming him, and walked back to his own hut.

Later that night, deep in the recesses of the valley, Falconi slept heavily in a small cottage with Carlo on a cot blocking the doorway. The Baron had given orders to have his horses packed in the morning. He wanted to be on the trail south before mid-morning. He was content, sleeping soundly with the memory of his son warm inside his dreams. Not in two years had he found such peace in slumber. The images of his son came again and again throughout the night, each time more vivid and real. In the last sequence, Falconi saw him bent over his manuscript, having a difficult time with a passage describing a dream. Then the form of Lady Le Vere entered the dream. Reading over his son's shoulder as he struggled with his task, she looked up and stared straight at Falconi with eyes full of wisdom beyond her years.

"Baron Falconi! Baron Falconi!" The urgent summons came from a man who had just made his way through the door, shouting, even as Carlo grabbed him and forced him against the inside of the jamb, thrusting a knife at his throat.

"Baron Falconi!" The man ignored the knife, looking past Carlo toward the dark corner where the Baron's cot stood against the wall. "Sire, men at arms on the trail! Monsignor Margaux sent me to warn you, sire."

"How many men? How much time before they arrive?" Falconi was already on his feet, buckling on his sword.

"At least a score riding as fast as they dare in the dark, sire. Our runner thinks they'll arrive two hours after sunrise, three hours from now."

Carlo had released the man but still kept between him and his lord, even as Falconi went through the door and out into the pre-dawn darkness.

Margaux was hurrying along the corridor between the few buildings to the cottage where Falconi had been sleeping, his way lit by a lantern held in front of him by Lady Le Vere.

"Milord!" Margaux looked disheveled. "You have been warned?"

"I have. Will we have further warnings?"

"Yes, milord. I have sent additional runners to report their progress."

"What are your plans for your community?"

"We will disperse into the mountains until the threat is gone," Margaux explained, his face barely discernible in the lantern light. "It is the usual way."

"And the library?"

"In the past we have packed the volumes and brought them with us, but we had more time and a smaller number of riders than now, milord. They are usually content with the sheep and with ransacking the dwellings. We will have to hope they don't find the cave."

"They are not after your books, Master Margaux. Carlo will see to it that your books are not discovered." Falconi nodded his head in the direction of the cave and looked at his man for a split second, an unspoken message passing between them, before Carlo moved quickly off onto the footpath that led to the library.

"Thank you, milord. I have a man, Pierre, who will guide you. He knows the trails to get you back to the coast undetected. The ground is hard. It will be impossible to follow you, but you must be careful in the coastal towns. If d'Avignon has spies to tell of your arrival, he might have set a trap to intercept you as you leave the mountains."

The scholar turned to go, but Lady Le Vere held the light steady and did not follow him. She looked Falconi straight in the eye. "I will be going with you to Corsica," she stated in a flat, unemotional voice.

Falconi looked at the young woman holding the lamp in front of her like a sentinel. "You will not!" He turned to walk back to his room, but she grabbed his arm, turning him around.

"I can and I must! D'Avignon knows that my father took your son into his keeping. He knows I am here. He will not treat me well. If he cannot capture you, Baron Falconi, he will consider me an alternative. Would you leave me to the fate of your wife and son? If you do not protect me, you will have betrayed my father's friendship."

Falconi met her steady gaze, feeling the strength of her conviction. Margaux turned away, sensing the silent struggle between Falconi and the girl.

"Pack your things and be ready to go when Carlo returns. One horse, only one." He turned and re-entered his sleeping quarters.

Carlo took a lantern and climbed up above the narrow cleft that led to the cave. Thirty feet above the entrance, he found that a crack in the cleft had spread around a large segment of the rock on one side of the divide. It was prevented from slipping down into the narrow gap only by a narrow horizontal step at its base.

Carlo secured the lantern in a niche above his left shoulder and placed his sword into the crack, slowly wedging the slab of rock out toward the edge of the crevice. Fifteen minutes of hard work allowed him to place his feet into the widened crack, providing more strength and leverage to the task. Finally, the slab moved over the ledge that was holding it and down the crevice. As it skidded and bounded against the sides in its downward fall, it loosened other smaller rocks, sending them cascading into the narrow gap as well. Carlo, hanging on to the rocks above, had to close his eyes against the dust that billowed upward.

Carlo waited several minutes, letting the sound of crashing rocks slowly subside, and then he climbed down, careful of the loose debris when selecting his handholds. The light he held in front of him barely pierced the dust that still hung in a gray cloud in the narrow entranceway. The opening, in fact most of the length of the crevice off of the main trail, had been filled not only with the large chunk of rock that he had levered free but also with thousands of pounds of smaller ones, effectively sealing the opening of the cave without a trace.

Still sweating from his labors with the rock and the run down the trail, Carlo entered the small sleeping room and found the Baron packing the last of his things into his riding case. Carlo's own things had already been packed by the Baron. They were ready to leave.

Extending his hand toward Carlo, the Baron said, "Give me my son's manuscripts. They will go in this pack with the small journal."

Carlo froze, alarmed. "Sire, I—I did not retrieve them," he stammered apprehensively. "You said nothing about them."

"Have you sealed the cave yet?"

"Yes, sire, as you ordered. It would take many days to reopen it even if one suspected its presence. I am sorry, sire. I should have known you would want them."

"It cannot be helped. If we cannot get them, then d'Avignon will not either." Falconi was already moving toward the door with his pack. "We will retrieve them in the future."

Outside, a man was standing beside their horses. "I am Pierre, your guide. We should go."

Pierre held the horses while Carlo packed them. As he was finishing, a silent figure on horseback approached. In the dim light Falconi could not make out the rider until the horse was reined to a halt next to him. He had taken the figure to be a man, but it was Lady Le Vere, dressed in leather pants and a long-sleeved jerkin. Falconi could not help but smile in admiration at the speed with which she had made ready and her practical selection of garments. He wondered if her pack held clothes that would be more suited to a woman of her youth and status.

"Take the lead, Pierre, and I will give you the name of the town to which we will head when we are well away from the village."

CHAPTER TEN

Paris, France, August, 2000

When Mats awoke, the mid-morning sun was splashing across the floor below the window. The sword by his side was warm. His other hand clutched the small journal of Thomaso's. He let the message of the dream replay in his mind, going over the important points, letting them fill in around the areas he knew from reading the journal. Before he was fully dressed, he knew that he must uncover the manuscripts if they still existed in the sealed cave.

After a long shower and an even longer breakfast, and after giving instructions to Carlo and Mario, Mats made a phone call to the office of Monsieur Bluschel, Minister of Antiquities. When he had first arrived on the French mainland, it had taken several days and fifteen thousand euros in contributions to gain the minister's ear. This call was more complicated. Mats wanted permission to search for the library he had seen in his dream, but also to involve Suzanne De Lacy in the effort. The afternoon they'd spent together had affected him deeply. Her participation was as important to him as finding the library.

He need not have worried about Bluschel. With the promise of financing the search to the tune of a hundred thousand euros, and an additional donation to Bluschel's department for the preservation of the books if they were still there, the Minister quickly agreed to endorse his efforts, to call Professor Gilbert and inform him, and to place Mademoiselle De Lacy in charge of the operation.

Just before noon, Mats stood on the Rue de Richelieu in front of the seventeenth-century palace that served as a centerpiece for the Bibliothèque Nationale. The sun still beat down on the streets of Paris, the proximity of the Seine lowering the temperature only a few degrees. He worried that Gilbert might still be difficult and want to lead the effort, preventing Suzanne from doing so.

Mats was still trying to sort things out when he opened the door into the small room off the third-floor hallway, the bell attached to the inside of the door announcing his presence.

Professor Gilbert came around the counter and shook his hand. "Suzanne tells me she was able to help you with your translation, and Minister Bluschel phoned, saying that you might have found a lead to a deposit of manuscripts. I want you to know how pleased I am that my department was of assistance."

"Thank you, Professor." Mats was relieved to see that Bluschel's phone call had had its desired effect.

Gilbert turned, seeing his assistant coming from the back of the room. "Suzanne, Monsieur Falcon seems very happy with the translation you did for him. I think he has some good news for us."

"Suzanne may in fact have uncovered some clues to the location of a cache of books left by my family in the fourteenth century. Minister Bluschel was quite pleased with the prospect that they might be uncovered."

"Yes, yes," said Gilbert. "He phoned me earlier this morning to thank me. I explained, of course, that the work was mostly Suzanne's. But thank you, monsieur, for the kind words."

"Minister Bluschel had a couple of suggestions concerning the possibility of unearthing the books," said Mats. "That is, of course, if they are still where the journal says they are."

"This is the first I have heard of this. What did he suggest?" asked Suzanne, her tone firm, her face an unsmiling mask.

"When I mentioned that I might finance the dig for the library myself, he was insistent that I would need the assistance of an expert. Evidently, France has many regulations concerning digging for artifacts, and it will be necessary to notify his bureau immediately if and when any manuscripts are found at the dig."

"What dig are you talking about?" Suzanne was not happy at losing the trend of the conversation.

"I'm sorry, Miss De Lacy," said Mats in English. "With what you taught me, I was able to read a few pages in the journal past where we stopped yesterday afternoon. It described a library that was concealed in the south of France by one of my ancestors. Minister Bluschel suggested that you offer technical assistance for the next week or so while we look to see if the books are still in their hiding place."

"But I have projects that I am working on here," Suzanne protested. "I can't just drop them to look for something mentioned in your diary." It was obvious that Suzanne De Lacy did not like being manipulated even if it was to her benefit.

"Suzanne," said Gilbert, "Minister Bluschel mentioned you by name. Our American friend here was evidently quite effusive in his praise of us and particularly our help with the translation. I can transfer the rest of your work. It will do you good to get out in the field." Gilbert had taken her hand and was holding it like an indulgent uncle.

Suzanne had begun to protest again when Mats looked directly at her. "Please. I know this seems like a whim, but it could be important," said Mats, the first part for Gilbert and the last for Suzanne.

"You can't just go digging up the countryside," said Suzanne. "This will have to be researched, permits obtained, crews brought together." Suzanne was already reviewing in her mind a list of items that would be needed before anyone set foot out of Paris. It was sinking in that this American with a seven-hundred-year-old journal, and enough pull to get Bluschel's patronage, could be giving her the opportunity of a lifetime.

"I brought the journal." Mats displayed it at chest height. "Perhaps we could go over the translation in your office to correct any errors or misunderstandings on my part."

Gilbert nodded. "Go," he said, and officiously ushered them down the hallway toward Suzanne's office.

As they entered her space, Suzanne turned on Mats and said, "This isn't really a whim, is it? You know where some manuscripts have been hidden."

"I know I should have talked to you before I had Bluschel commit you to the search. I'm sorry for being so inconsiderate. But the journal…" He opened the book carefully, past the point where they had stopped the previous afternoon, at the place where the handwriting changed. "I was able to read part of the journal last night and some of the passages are private affairs that I would like to keep to myself for now. The description of the manuscripts and their location is here." Mats marked the end of the pages dealing with the concealment of the cave with a torn piece of paper. "Your promise to stop at this point?"

"You have it, Monsieur Falcon."

Suzanne read the passages swiftly and when she had finished, she turned toward Mats and whistled softly through pursed lips.

"This morning I sent my men to arrange accommodations at Allos in the Maritime Alps. There will be a crew of stonemasons there in two days with all the necessary equipment. I need to know from you what items we might need for the preservation of the manuscripts once they are uncovered. I'll try to buy those while you secure the legal papers."

"You were quite sure of my participation, weren't you?" asked Suzanne, trying to be upset with this man who had surged into her life.

"No, but I certainly hoped that you would be pleased with the prospect." Mats got up and faced her. "But I was going to proceed in any event, so I arranged for the parts I could already anticipate. I was very much hoping you'd lead the effort, but it was your decision to make."

"It seems I can't lose, Monsieur Falcon," said Suzanne, a smile spreading across her face as she looked at the journal again. "The least that will come of it is that I get a two-week paid vacation in the Maritimes." She pulled a map of France from her desk and let her finger trace a line from the Mediterranean to the small village of Allos. "And what do you get out of this, Mr. Falcon?"

"Oh, I get a two-week vacation in the Maritimes, watching you work," he said with a smile as he took the journal back from her. "And of course, the thrill of uncovering a literary treasure."

From the smile that reached Suzanne's eyes, causing small wrinkles in the bridge of her nose, Mats sensed that she might feel the same.

Five days after their first meeting in Gilbert's office, Mats and Suzanne boarded a high-speed train from Paris to Nice. Mats carried his canvas bag, the same one he had arrived in France with. Suzanne had a huge suitcase and an official-looking briefcase.

Mats had watched Suzanne obtain the final permits and marveled as her firm but professional attitude cut through the red tape of the French bureaucracy. He had tagged along while she purchased the items she required that he had not been able to find himself, and they slowly filled five cases which they shipped ahead of them.

As the train slipped by the French landscape at a hundred and sixty kilometers per hour, Suzanne remained silent, preferring to watch the passing countryside rather than talk to Mats. Ever since the meeting with Gilbert where she was told that she had been assigned to the effort to uncover buried manuscripts, she had treated Mats courteously but without the warmth he had felt at their first meeting. Mats could tell she was excited about the prospect of unearthing the library, not only for the literary value of such a discovery but for what it would mean to her own career, by the way she acted as each item was checked off her list. He suspected that her coolness toward him was a direct consequence of his arrangement with Minister Bluschel to have her supervise the dig without asking her permission first.

"Did you grow up in Paris?" he asked, trying to break the impasse.

"No. I grew up in the country on my father's estate northwest of Paris. It is on a small tributary of the L'Oise, just before it joins the Seine."

"And where did you learn your language skills?" Mats asked as she lapsed back into silence.

"I got my love of languages from my father. He is a professor of art and an overseer of the Impressionist collection at the D'Orsay. He is quite remarkable," she added with pride. "He speaks seven languages fluently and gets by in three others. I inherited my love of languages and the written word from him."

"And your mother?" asked Mats, completely taken by this intriguing young woman he had spirited away from Paris.

"Mama was an opera singer studying in Austria, but when she met Father, she gave up singing professionally. One of my most cherished childhood memories is the sound of her voice as she sang her favorite arias while preparing meals." As Suzanne spoke about her parents, she abandoned the flat tone that she had used with Mats for the last few days.

"Suzanne, the evening after our first meeting when you translated the journal and lent me the books, I read further and learned about the library that was buried. I knew it would be an important discovery, and I very much wanted you to be part of it. I was afraid that if your boss, Mr. Gilbert, found out about it, he would want to take over, perhaps even to the point of leaving you out. That is why I bypassed him and went to the Minister to have it set up for you before Gilbert had a chance to minimize your role. I apologize for not asking you first. It was my mistake."

"I also am remiss in not thanking you for including me in this opportunity. It is just that it is hard being a woman in a male-dominated profession … one is always being told what to do instead of being able to use one's own initiative."

"Good," said Mats, offering his hand. "Then we can be friends again?"

Suzanne took his hand and smiled. It was better than words.

At the Nice station, Mats rented a car, and after loading their gear, they took off to the north. With Mats driving, they covered the eighty-five miles in a little under two hours.

"I know you mentioned that you had already obtained workers," said Suzanne as they drove away from the coast. "Where did you find them? Uncovering artifacts requires special handling."

"I have used them before. They are Corsican. You will find no fault with either them or their work, I assure you."

As the road bent around the last of the curves leading to the village of Allos, the closeness of the terrain to that in his dream amazed Mats. The two-lane road was paved but still followed the path of the old wagon track that he had visualized in his sleep.

"Allos is just around the next turn," Mats said with excitement. The sun was still high above the mountains as he negotiated the car around the curve and came into the small mountain valley in which the village nestled. The mountains provided the exact backdrop that Mats remembered, but he was not prepared for the changes in the village. Instead of the cluster of stone and timber dwellings that he had seen in his mind, there was now a small town with a market square nestled next to the pure blue lake. To the north of the town and its single dwellings were apartment buildings obviously built for winter skiers. Ski lifts rose from the valley floor to the top of the mountains that ringed the small valley, now idle in the mid-summer heat.

Carlo had arrived before them, renting a three-bedroom house from an absentee owner on the proviso that he keep it for a full month. He was waiting for them as they arrived at the house and took charge of their belongings, storing their supplies in a small garage.

"The men are staying at a hostel back down the road," Carlo told Mats as he passed him on the way to the house. "Nando insisted on coming with the men from Corsica and has taken charge of the group. We found the main trail and the offshoot you described, but we haven't found any trace of a cave."

Mats watched Suzanne's reaction in silence as the dark muscular man lifted all their bags with ease, climbing the stairs and depositing her things in a room on the second floor before placing Mats' belongings in the room next door. Carlo had spoken in a harsh dialect that, even as a linguist, Suzanne had had trouble understanding. When he finished his task, Carlo came back down the stairway without making a sound, despite his bulk. He moved quickly to Mats' side, where he stood looking at Suzanne.

"Suzanne De Lacy, this is Carlo Guibega. He is my personal friend and helper. Carlo, his cousin Mario, and their grandfather Nando will be supervising the excavation crew. You can trust them implicitly. They will do anything you ask." Mats looked at Carlo. "She is to be trusted and followed as if the words came from me. Speak French or English from now on and tell the Guibega of her status."

Carlo smiled, his white teeth contrasting with his dark features as he extended his hand to Suzanne. "Glad to meet you, boss."

Carlo drove Suzanne into town to call on the mayor and present their permits and authorizations. Ten minutes after they left, a van arrived with Nando as its only passenger. As the old man climbed down from the passenger's seat, Mats could see the difference in the man since they had first met on Corsica. He still had a way of carefully placing his hands and feet that so often accompanies old age, but now he had a look of confidence and his movements were more elastic. Mats recognized the change and attributed it to having a purpose. The Falconi had returned and the old man had been restored.

Mats and Nando left the house and started walking toward the mountains. It took them twenty minutes to reach what was now the start of the trail, partly because of Nando's age and partly because the house they occupied was located away from where the mountains rose steeply from the valley floor.

Mats moved down the trail, exchanging information with Nando. He stopped abruptly at the cleft. The centuries had filled in the narrow opening until it was flush with the wall of the narrow canyon from which it had once diverged. Mats explained to Nando how it had been sealed off and that the opening to the cave was eight feet from where they stood. The old man picked at a fist-sized rock, loosening it with his gnarled fingers.

"We will have to shore up the loose fill at this level as we proceed. If not, it could collapse and bury the workers. We have what we need in camp." Nando looked up with difficulty against the bow in his back, looking toward the top of the depression. "As long as there is only this type of fill, it should not take more than two days to go eight feet."

"As soon as we start the excavation, we will have to keep a guard posted." Mats tried to dislodge a rock similar to Nando's but found he did not have the strength in his fingers to lever it free as the old man had done. "I want you to make sure I am the first one to enter."

"There will be no need for a guard. We will work through the night and I will not leave this spot." The old man slowly lowered his head and looked at Mats. "You will be the first to enter. Unless you allow the woman go before you." Nando smiled. It was one of the benefits of being old; you could often be truthful without giving offense, and he had heard of the way Mats looked at the woman. "A beautiful Frenchwoman! Perhaps you will find more than one treasure at this place in the mountains, eh?" The old man winked.

❧   ❧   ❧

The next morning at sunrise, Mats dressed and went to the kitchen. He found Carlo already frying eggs and ham at the stove, a pot of coffee on the table.

"Would you knock on Mademoiselle De Lacy's door? We should be starting soon, before we pick up any sight-seers from the town."

"I don't think that will be necessary," answered Carlo. "I heard movement up there a while ago, and if all else fails, the smell of this ham should bring her out."

As if answering their summons, Suzanne De Lacy came down the stairs and walked straight toward the coffee.

Mats led Suzanne and Carlo up the trail in the soft light of dawn. He had chosen the time in order to arrive at the site undetected by the villagers, whose curiosity had been piqued by Suzanne's contacts with the politi-cos the day before. Then she had worn blue slacks and a white silk blouse. Today she was dressed in jeans and a long-sleeved shirt, work gloves hanging from her belt. As they rounded the corner and started down the nar-row canyon that led to the cleft, they heard the muted sounds of digging. As they neared the end of the trail, they found Nando supervising eight heavily perspiring men. They had progressed two feet into the crevice at a height of six feet.

"Buongiorno, Signor Falconi," said the old man softly as he came forward to greet them.

"Good morning, Nando. You're starting a little early, no?"

"I thought it would be good to get the crew in place before we had too many visitors," said Nando, glancing back at the cleft where a large rock had just been rolled free out onto the floor of the trail. As quickly as it came to rest, two men hefted it and carried it further back into the canyon.

"Wise thought, but it will only be a matter of time before the locals find us."

"Perhaps not, signore. I left two men with some impressive equipment and maps at a place not a hundred meters from the old stone church." Nando smiled, showing the loss of a posterior tooth. "They have some yellow plastic ribbon and are marking off an area with some signs that tell people to stay away. That should hold most of the attention. It would help if the lady would slip back there and give some orders before noon. The men will complain and call her names when she is out of earshot, but they are expecting her."

"You old fox!" Mats smiled at the man, his respect and affection showing as he gripped his shoulder.

"It is the Corsican way. Only let them see what you want them to see. It is why our houses open their windows onto our courtyards and not onto the street." Nando broke off the conversation to move back to the cleft, where another rock had been dislodged.

Every six inches a device that looked like an automobile jack, except that it had a foot on either end instead of on just one, was placed against the rugged rock-studded walls of the cleft, roofing over the excavation that had already deepened almost a meter. Mats saw that the purpose was to prevent further slippage of material into the tunnel below. Four had already been placed securely against the sides of solid rock.

Mats tried to envision how much deeper they had to dig, but his memory of the dream had now faded by four days and was not as clear as it had been.

"I will call you when we are about to enter," said Nando. "You should be seen in the village."

It was a wise suggestion. Nando's crew, not residing in the village, might not be missed. But Mats' and Suzanne's absence would be noticed.

Mats turned to Suzanne, but she was already walking back on the narrow trail. He followed her to where the canyon met the trail running from the village into the mountains.

"Your man Nando seems quite competent. He is right. It is best if they come get us when we are needed," she said as they left the valley. "I suspect we are just in the way in those close quarters. It looks like you chose the crew wisely."

"Nando chose them. I just chose Nando, or rather, he seems to have chosen me."

The day went by slowly. Suzanne did as Nando had suggested and several times during the day harangued the men who were digging near the church. The ruse worked to perfection. There were dozens of people watching the two men dig. Some were young boys, flexing their muscles and inflating their hairless chests, hoping to be asked to use the shovel. But most were adults, curious about the woman with the permits and the authorization to dig in their village. Suzanne got into her part, giving the men money to hire villagers to help them when they took their breaks at mid-day. She also confided in a female onlooker that they would have to dig many feet further before they would be close to finding anything. The information given in confidence had already spread through the onlookers as Mats led Suzanne back toward the village square for lunch.

Mid-day, Carlo found Mats at the house. Suzanne had gone to make another appearance at the church, leaving him alone to pack the equipment they might need from the crates into a backpack. Nando had run into a setback at the tunnel and Mats was needed for advice on how to proceed.

A large slab of rock had been uncovered, filling most of the crevice. Nando had already considered several ways to handle the problem but needed information from Mats as to the size of the items that would be removed from the cave once they had it opened. One look down the excavation was all Mats needed to see why he had been called. The huge rock had slid down the narrow cleft, wedging just above the trail. Supported on the rubble that had preceded it from above, it was too large to be removed. Nando already had it supported vertically with two of the jacks.

Nando pushed the boulder with the gnarled knuckles of his fist, his disdain for the obstruction apparent. "We could split it with dynamite, but it would be noisy and possibly bring down more rock, filling what we have already cleared. We can chisel it out but that would take many days. The other possibility is to tunnel underneath it. With luck we can clear a crawl space that will allow us to get to the cave. But you have not told me what we will find inside. Will an opening wide enough to crawl through be sufficient?"

Mats closed his eyes, rehearsing the dream in his mind. He tried to bring a recollection of the cave into clear focus. There had been tables and chairs, but those were not important to him; they could be removed later, either in pieces or through a larger opening. The books could be removed through any opening that would pass a man.

"Go under it. The entrance is not more than a meter past the rock, if it has not been filled with rubble as well."

Mats turned and walked back to the house. He was on edge and couldn't put his finger on the reason. When they had uncovered d'Avignon's treasure on Corsica, he had felt only elation. This was different. He was nervous and didn't want to be part of the process of digging the passage clear. His apprehension increased with the return of Suzanne.

"How is it going?" she asked as she entered the front door.

"The workmen encountered a large rock and it slowed them down somewhat. They're going to dig under it."

"This probably isn't the time to ask, but are you positive there is a cave behind all that rock?" She knelt beside him and began placing additional items from her bags into the knapsack. "I know what the journal said, but it didn't give very specific directions."

"It's there. The journal tells of the existence of the cave and the general area. The rest comes from family history that I believe is true. At least, it has been up to this point." Mats smiled at her. "I'm sorry if I seem distracted. I'm missing something important, something I know isn't registering as it should. It will come, but right now it's making me nervous."

"Did Nando give you any indication of when they would gain entrance?"

"It depends on how much of the cave was filled by the slide, but judging by the rate they've been progressing so far, I would guess they will break through early this evening."

Suzanne looked up from her packing in surprise. "That soon? It looked like such an extensive job."

"I don't think they've taken a break since last night. The old man took the large boulder as a personal insult."

"I've never seen workmen like them," said Suzanne. "Most digs have a crew chief and workers who are more worried about wages than about the amount of work they accomplish. Are they being paid by the job rather than by the hour?"

"They're Corsican. They've known my family for generations. Their pay is of little importance to them. In some cases, it was taken care of generations ago. What they ask for I will pay." Mats stood up. "We should get some rest."

"You mean that we will explore the site at night? Wouldn't it be better to wait until daylight?"

Mats smiled broadly at the young scholar. "It's a cave. What difference does it make if we look at it in daylight or darkness?"

Mats saw the mirth her oversight had brought to her previously troubled countenance. She hesitated, then laughed. It was the first time Mats had heard her laugh, and it was delightful. He thought it sounded like a musical shower of small bells. As he listened to the sound echo off the walls, he thought again that he was missing something. He just hoped that it would not put this interesting woman in danger.

"Good thinking, De Lacy," he heard her admonish herself as she moved toward her room. "Wait for daylight to explore a cave!"

The shadow of Mats' body partially obscured the tunnel below the boulder from the light cast by the lamp Nando was holding. It was almost midnight. There was the smell of dirt in the air, but not nearly as bad as it had been that morning. Dust still swirled in the lamplight.

"Carlo cleared the last of the rocks away from the opening. No one has entered," hissed Nando. "Once past the boulder you should be able to stand up before you enter the cave itself. That is what took the extra time. With more time, we can enlarge the entrance. The ground under the rock is packed dirt and sand. The bottom of the rock had a jagged point that stuck down into the crawl space. It took some time to chisel it off."

"You've done well." Mats turned and held the old man by the shoulders. "Please have your men guard this place well. Let no one but Suzanne and me inside."

Suzanne had already taken two miner's lights out of her backpack, adjusting one to her own head. Mats took the other. As soon as Mats had his in place, Suzanne asked, "May I?"

Receiving a nod, she lay down and started headfirst down the warren-like tunnel under the boulder. As her feet disappeared, Nando gave a chuckle and winked at his men. Suzanne's backpack seemingly moved by its own will as she pulled it behind her down the passageway. Mats followed the bag quickly into the darkness and bumped his nose against it for his trouble.

Blocked in the tunnel, Mats experienced a shiver. He had never had a fear of enclosure before, but he was starting to panic. His breath came faster, as if he could not get enough oxygen. The knapsack still blocked his progress. He was about to crawl backward when the bag was jerked forward. After a body length, the tunnel came to an abrupt end, going up but not at the gradual incline of the entrance.

Suzanne was waiting for him on the narrow ledge just past the step that restored the passage to the level of the cave entrance. Two meters behind her, Mats could see the cave expanding in width from the narrow cleft that the excavation had been following.

"Suzanne, wait a minute. I have something to say before you go in." He hoped that she had not noticed the sigh of relief that accompanied his exiting the tunnel below the boulder. On the train from Paris to Nice, he had learned that her only previous field exercises had been painstakingly slow excavations of broken pottery and one small

mosaic floor. Not only was this process much more accelerated, but they also expected to find in the cave items
that were her particular specialty, rare books.

Suzanne turned, flipping her light up so as not to
blind him with a direct beam. He knew it could not be
put off any longer. "Yes?"

"Before we go further, I want you to know what to
expect. If we've been lucky, and it appears we have, we will
find the complete library of a medieval scholar named P.
Margaux. No saint's relics, no finger bones, nothing to
bring pilgrims to this place—just books. These will rightfully belong to the people of France. However, away from
the main collection, we will find two volumes written by
the same man who wrote my journal. These were written
by my ancestor, and I tell you now that those two books
belong to me and not to France. I don't want there to be
any misunderstanding about this."

"And you wait until now to tell me this!" said Suzanne,
her anger barely contained.

"I could have done this on my own, but after our first
session translating the journal, I trusted and respected
you and wanted you to be a part of the discovery. All that
is in here is yours and France's except for Thomaso's volumes. They are personal."

Suzanne looked hard at Mats. "What you say goes
against every tenet I have learned from my father and
my training. History is full of scholars who were little
more than grave robbers. Why do you ask this of me?
Why now?"

"If I had given you my conditions earlier, you might
have refused. Then I wouldn't have led you to the correct
location. It would have ruined our friendship. If we had
found the cave pilfered since my ancestor wrote of its sealing in the journal, then our friendship would have been
ruined for no reason."

Mats could see the conflict on Suzanne's face. It was obvious that she thought her integrity was being challenged. She started to turn toward the cave without answering. Mats reached out and gently held her forearm.

"Suzanne, you have the opportunity to preserve the life's work of a little-known fourteenth-century French scholar, and you will raise both his and your own status in doing so. The entire contents are yours to announce as your discovery, all except Thomaso's books. They deal with my family's history and I do not want them to be public knowledge. So before you take any photos that might cause people to ask questions, please let me remove them. Do we have an understanding?"

Mats could see her features softening in the reflected light.

"You say you only want two books, written by the same individual who wrote your journal. No coins or paintings or anything else valuable?"

"No, only Thomaso's volumes. I have not lied to you or misled you before, nor would I do so now."

"If I say yes to your request, do I have your promise that I can examine them before you hold me to my word?" she asked. "I'd like to be certain that they are what you say they are before allowing their removal."

"Of course," he answered.

"Okay then. I trust you, Mats Falcon." Suzanne reached out and held both of Mats' hands, the pressure of her touch informing him of her decision as much as her words.

She turned, still holding Mats' hand in hers, and entered the cave.

CHAPTER ELEVEN

"My God!" Suzanne stopped two paces into the cave, Mats at her shoulder. She had led him into the confines of the cave, her headlamp illuminating first one section of the high vaulted room and then another. Mats, still holding her hand, turned off his own lamp. He wanted to experience Suzanne's wonder as she took in their discovery.

The cave was as he remembered it from his dream. The walls had been smoothed by humans, and the ceiling, over four meters high for most of its depth, tapered in a sharp V twelve paces toward the back. A bench and writing desk stood against the far wall facing the master's desk, and books lined the rough shelves behind. The walls contained a dozen niches holding copper oil lamps, green with the disuse of centuries.

Suzanne swept her beam from one section of the cave to another. Twice she completed the circuit before moving to the center of the cave.

"This is wonderful!" she exclaimed finally. "Unbelievably wonderful!" She dropped Mats' hand, turned, and threw her arms around him. He returned her hug and they stood motionless, the light from Suzanne's headlamp illuminating the books on the wall. Suzanne broke the embrace, suddenly becoming the academic. She opened her backpack and took out gloves.

"Mats, put on gloves, but don't touch anything, not even the desks, until we have recorded everything. We have no idea as to the books' condition. They could fall apart at a touch."

She left his side, moving to the books behind the master's desk, looking carefully at the writing on the spines. "My God, it's true. It's true. Look, this is the *Otia Imperialia*. We have a copy at the Bibliothèque, but it is nothing like this." Her hand rose toward the book, stopping an inch away. Even from the center of the cave, Mats could see her fingers tremble as they wavered in front of the book. His heart went out to her. He realized her excitement, the passion she was showing, was the reason he had wanted her to be part of the discovery, and with that realization he fully understood his own infatuation with this woman he had met just ten days before.

"It would appear that you have found your library," said Mats, trying to keep his voice measured, countering the excitement shown by Suzanne. "We may never find out what happened to Margaux and why he did not return to uncover his books, but it is good for us that he didn't."

Switching on his own lamp, he moved to the smaller desk. The wall behind it had held a small shelf, but one of the wooden supports had loosened over the centuries, collapsing one end to the ground. Among the pieces of shelving lay two books. One of them had fallen, binding up, in an open position on the dirt of the cave floor. Mats bent over it, reading the inscription on the front cover. Ignoring Suzanne's warning not to touch anything, Mats carefully lifted it. The pages were dry and cracked, but the leather binding and print were both in good shape. The pages revealed the same strong, cramped hand he had become acquainted with in the first half of the journal.

"Suzanne, look at this handwriting." Mats brought both the books to where Suzanne stood in front of the collection and held the open volume in front of her. "It's the same hand as the journal I brought you."

Mats sensed that Suzanne was about to admonish him for moving anything prior to taking pictures, but she could not help but look at what he held before her. The handwriting should have been enough for Suzanne, but he could see that the inscription on the bottom corner of both volumes dispelled all doubt. It read "THOMASO FALCONI, 1328."

"No doubt about it. They're yours. I'll say nothing about them. The vellum looks in good shape, which bodes well for the rest of the collection. But Mats." She placed a gloved hand softly on his cheek, her eyes looking deeply into his. "Please don't touch anything else."

"Of course not. Do you want me to help with anything?"

"Not right now. You could look around the cave for animal droppings, spider webs, or water seepage. Humans are not the only problem we could face here."

"I'll see to it," he answered as she returned to the racks of books.

From inside his backpack, he removed a folded leather satchel lined with soft wool, into which he placed the closed volume. He hesitated with the second book, unable to make up his mind whether to close it and risk cracking the binding or place it into the pack opened and risk damaging the pages. Slowly he closed it, watching with care as the leather came together, slightly cracking the spine. Then he slipped it into the bag with the other book and placed the bag gently near the entrance.

Mats took only ten minutes to examine the cave floor, then took another five shining his light into the upper reaches of the cave vault. When he was finished, he stood back, watching as Suzanne took an hour to walk the length of the library, carefully writing a description of each volume without removing it from its resting place. She would note the title and position of each book on the shelves, occasionally saying a title out loud. After recording ten volumes, she would step back and take a photograph of the section just completed.

"Would you like me to take the photographs for you?" asked Mats.

"Not yet, thank you. Mats, look at this. I can't believe the vibrancy of the red color on the spines. Inks, particularly the red hues, always fade with age. Whatever ink they used must have been unique. It alone would make this library distinctive."

Mats watched her, completely absorbed in her task. "Suzanne, I'm going to tell Nando and the men what we found. I will let them come in just to the entrance one at a time to see what they uncovered. I'll be back in a few minutes."

He crawled out of the cave, holding the sack with Thomaso's books carefully in front of him, pushing with his legs to get forward momentum. As he came out of the excavation, he met Carlo and Nando standing side by side in the narrow canyon, the rest of the men crowded in anticipation in the dark behind them. Mats showed Carlo the satchel with the books. He opened the bag so that several of the men could see its contents.

"Books, old books of an ancient scholar. A treasure for the scholars, but we'll find no gold or jewels. Still, it must be guarded. Keep three men at the entrance. We must protect the find until other historians arrive to authenticate the contents of the cave and relieve us of the responsibility. Also, Suzanne is concerned about rats or bugs getting in as well as men. Could you fit a screen tight for when we are inside, and a secure door for when no one is inside?"

Mats took Carlo aside. "We need your lantern inside. Let all the men see what they have uncovered. Send them in one at a time after I go back inside, so they may see what their labor has achieved."

Taking the lantern, Mats handed Carlo the backpack, Carlo testing its weight as he received it. "The books in the knapsack belong to me. Take them away from here and hide them. No one is to see them, not even Suzanne." Mats was aware that entrusting the books to Carlo meant his complete faith in the Guibega. He was anxious to read the books, as they were sure, like the journal, to have Thomaso's thoughts on his ability to dream of events long past.

After all the men had rotated through the cave and Nando had set up the watch schedule, Mats began helping Suzanne with her cataloging. She had been working without a break for over eight hours, without sleep for over twenty-nine. In the darkness of the cave, she was not even aware that dawn had broken in the village. Mats took the camera from her, insisting it was necessary to have multiple pictures of her working with her notebook, the books in the background. They would prove that the find was hers and hers alone.

"How much more do you need to do today?" Mats asked softly, so as not to startle her.

She straightened up, stretching, then rubbed her eyes. "What time is it?"

"After seven. You've been working all night. Maybe we should get some rest and lay plans for preserving your discovery."

Suddenly the strain of working through the night in the poor light of the cave came over Suzanne. Rest and time to contemplate the significance of their find were a good idea.

As they exited the cave, the crowd of workers stood and applauded. Mats and Suzanne were surprised by the reception and squinted against the glare of the morning light. It took several minutes to become accustomed to the harshness of the sunlight after the dimness of the cave. The air was also different, fresher and easier to breathe. For the entire trip back to the rented house, Suzanne told Mats enthusiastically about the books she'd examined in the cave.

By the time they got back to the house, they were both hungry. Mats went to the kitchen and broke five eggs into a mixing bowl. Within minutes the room was filled with the aroma of frying bacon, scrambled eggs with onions, and browned squares of potatoes left over from the previous day's meal. It was the first time Mats had cooked for Suzanne, and he wanted to impress her, but he was not hopeful as she sat at the table and began working herself into a near frenzy of excitement as she continued telling him of the library.

"Several of the works might be originals, ranking alongside the most treasured volumes of the Bibliothèque Nationale," said Suzanne. "Others appear to be copies of rare books that I have never before had the opportunity to study. One, the *Liber Facetiarum*, has only been mentioned in the literature. I don't believe that there is a surviving copy. The red ink alone makes this collection unique. I can't wait to use mass spectrometry on it. "

"I don't know about the ink, but I need to use a shower on my body after crawling in and out of the cave," said Mats, putting the dishes in the sink.

Mats had finished his shower and was already downstairs as Suzanne came down the stairs in a bathrobe with a towel around her head as a result of forgetting her hair dryer in Paris. There was a flush in her cheeks, but she seemed to have her elation under control. In Paris when he first met her, he was taken by her self-assurance, her ability to decipher the riddle of the journal, and her skill in translating the languages. More than that, she had been willing to teach him what she was doing, knowing that her boss would have been pleased to give him nothing in the way of help. He knew he was becoming attracted to her in other ways as well over the past week, but other than the smile she had given him when he thwarted Professor Gilbert and the hug she had given him in the cave, she was showing no signs of interest, other than in his connection to the books.

"Now that you have discovered the library and have an idea of what it contains, have you thought of what you will do?" asked Mats.

"I will phone Professor Gilbert and perhaps Minister Bluschel this evening, as it was he who recommended me, thanks to you."

"May I suggest something?" asked Mats, sitting down beside her. "Wait a few days before phoning them. Do everything you can, not only documenting each book, but researching them so that you are not only the discoverer of the library, but also the foremost expert on what you have found. And most of all, make sure it is you who announces the discovery to the world—not Gilbert or Bluschel."

Suzanne settled back into the sofa, the towel around her head touching the blue terrycloth bathrobe she now wore. Her face wore a thoughtful expression, taking in what Mats had said.

"And let's be realistic," Mats continued. "Don't you want to remain in charge of the categorizing and preservation of the library?"

Suzanne looked at him, her intelligence showing through the excitement that had earlier dominated her mood. "Do you think there could be a problem with that?"

"You saw Gilbert take partial credit for translating the journal," said Mats. "He would do the same with your discovery, given half a chance."

"I have taken pictures from before the cleft was dug out, and every step of the way," said Suzanne with a frown. "That should be enough to prove whose find it is beyond a doubt."

"It should be, but they're still debating whether Salk or Sabin developed the polio vaccine. Damn—just look at the battle religious bigshots are having over control of the Dead Sea Scrolls. This ranks as one of the most important literary finds in recent history, and you deserve all the credit."

"Why is this important to you?" Suzanne asked. "You have what you came for—Thomaso's writings."

"It matters to me. I was at a dead end until you translated the journal. Gilbert is an overbearing ass. Other than putting together the crew, you have done all the work. Besides, I like you."

Suzanne looked at him, tilting her head and giving him a slow smile. "So how would you handle it?"

"First, please make sure that the Guibegas and I do not appear in any of the photos you have taken. Other than that, I don't know if I can advise you, but I guess my first question would be, do you leave the books in the cave for study, or do you move them to another place?"

"The books should be left in place until several experts are able to see them to verify the find." Suzanne's mind was now working like an academic. "But they shouldn't analyze the books at that time. That has to be done in the laboratory with moisturizing agents, photocopying, and constant humidity for their protection. That is why I didn't want you to touch them. But experts must see the books *in situ* to authenticate the place of discovery."

"Okay, so we get some experts to come down and look at the cave and the books. Then what? A press conference?"

"Yes, a press announcement. Then the books are packed in constant humidity cases to a secure lab where they can be studied. We're lucky most of the books are written on vellum and not papyrus. In this case, the older the books are, the more likely it is that we can preserve them. Since the mid-1800s, most paper has been acid-treated and pulp-based. As the paper ages, the acid used in its manufacture actually eats away at it, hardening it and making it brittle. We have to use chemicals, or more recently Zilberstein's proteomic film, for the newer acquisitions at the Bibliothèque. That won't be necessary with anything in this find."

"Well, then," said Mats, "I think you should do everything you can before you invite the experts. Arrange for the lab. Procure the carrying cases and have them ready, arrange transportation, and most important, you make the announcement to the academic community by calling the press conference. Don't let anyone else put his name on any part of your discovery. One other thing. You know what I think of Gilbert, and Bluschel can be bought. Any man who can be bought is untrustworthy. I would arrange a meeting away from this place and get full assurance as to the handling of the find before they are brought here."

Mats was rewarded with a smile. He could see that Suzanne still did not fully trust him, this American who had led her to the greatest achievement in her life yet wanted no credit. It was as if she sensed the sadness in him as well as a mystery concerning his motives.

"We should go to bed," he said, rising.

She looked at him in mock alarm. "Who is being French now?"

"No, no," he added quickly, smiling at her. "Even an American can be more subtle than that, or at least I used to be. I mean, we need to get some rest. I'll see you at dinner."

But Mats could not keep himself from remembering Suzanne's excitement upon entering the cave: the hug, feeling her body pressed against his. He kept picturing her in her robe, smiling, and these thoughts made sleep difficult…

Mats knocked on Suzanne's door at two in the afternoon, waking her from a sound sleep. She had asked to be awakened, as she told Mats it would be best for them not to sleep too long but rather to get into a regular cycle after working through the previous night. After lunch and a quick round of haranguing the workers at the church site, they went to the cave.

"What!" said Suzanne, coming to a stop in front of the cleft. There were three Guibegas standing in front of the cave entrance and Nando grinning like a gnome. A white metal door had been placed over the opening, hinged and locked. Mats laughed, recognizing it as the rear door of the van the crew had rented. The opening had been finished with rocks and cement, a rubber gasket visible around the frame of the door.

"You said you wanted it closed off to rats and insects," said Nando, handing Suzanne a key. "I've run a power cord into the cave, and I sent someone to buy a gas generator that we can run out here." Nando kicked his boot toward a black wire that was sealed by cement at the bottom right of the door.

Suzanne bent over and kissed Nando on the cheek. "You are a treasure."

Mats had to check himself from becoming jealous.

The generator came in less than an hour along with three electric lights and a multiple-outlet plug. While Nando had men readying the generator and installing the lights in the cave, Suzanne walked back toward the village, stopping at the house to use her computer to research the effect of halogen light on ancient texts. Satisfied as to the safety, she crawled back inside the cave and had the men turn on the power. The cave was filled with a rather harsh bluish light. Nando had positioned the three flood lamps so that there were no shadows as Suzanne stood in front of the shelves of books and began her work.

"I can't believe we can hardly hear the generator," said Mats as he grabbed the camera, intending to retake all the shots he had taken previously under flash. After two hours he crawled back out and solved the mystery of the quiet generator. Nando had removed the muffler from their car and attached it to the already efficient generator exhaust with silver duct tape.

"Suzanne better hurry or we'll have nothing to drive back in," he laughed, slapping Nando on the back before squirming back into the cave.

Mats took multiple pictures of Suzanne and the books, indulging himself with several closeups of her face, mostly in deep concentration, but more than one with her smiling as she removed a book from the shelf, revealing a front cover of intricate design that she wanted him to photograph. For the most part Mats felt he was just in the way, but he enjoyed watching her work, listening to her exclaim at each new discovery.

"I am going back to the house," he said after five hours. "I have some arrangements to make. Don't be too long. You want to get a full night's sleep this evening."

At ten, after seven hours of work, Nando stuck his head into the cave and told Suzanne that dinner was being prepared back at the house. She looked at her phone, surprised at the time, except that the mention of food made her realize she had not eaten in hours and was hungry. She took her notebook and the camera and followed Nando out, locking the van door behind her.

Mats was in the kitchen when Suzanne came in. He had made a meat sauce and had water pre-heated to just below boiling to receive spaghetti that was already sitting by the stove top.

"Dinner will be ready in twenty minutes if you would like to take a shower and clean up," he said over his shoulder as she came in.

"It smells wonderful. I'll be back in fifteen."

True to her word, she was back down soon wearing the previous day's work clothes, which had been washed and pressed to the point of knife-edge creases on both shirt and pants. Nando's crew had been busy.

"What are you making?" she asked, looking over Mats' shoulder, the smell of garlic almost irresistible.

"Spaghetti Bolognese and artichokes, along with a reasonable bottle of Pinot noir that Carlo found in the village."

They sat down at the table. Mats had topped the artichokes and scooped out the center leaves, filling the depression with mayonnaise. The spaghetti was perfect, the wine an excellent complement. All that was needed were a few candles, which Mats had thought of but rejected as being too blatant.

"This is wonderful. Where did you get the mayonnaise?"

"It's easy enough to make. The eggs that we had for breakfast are local. I've told you that I have a restaurant in California, haven't I?"

"Yes, but that doesn't necessarily mean you know how to cook."

"Well, I may not be able to put a truck door on a cave entrance for you, but I can cook, and I can make reservations for us in Monaco in three days," said Mats, taking a rather large sip of wine. "You can have Gilbert and Bluschel meet you there before bringing them here."

"You did? Why Monaco?"

"Two reasons. It would be best to work out the details of your role in the preservation of the library before those two know precisely where it is, and second, after watching how hard you worked over the last few days, I think you should get some rest before you announce your discovery and all hell breaks loose. Besides, I have never been there, and it would be delightful to see it with you."

He was rewarded with another smile spreading over the rim of her glass. "I haven't been there either. That's a very nice gesture." Mats noticed that her right eyebrow lifted more than her left following the smile; it was enchanting.

Over the next two days, Suzanne spent the morning researching the volumes in the cave on her computer. She noted where other examples were held, and how many copies were known to exist. Since all copies were done by scribes, it was not unusual to find variations, sometimes large variations between works that were copied centuries apart. It was another aspect of the discovery. It could be known with virtual certainty that these were copied before 1328. Even more startling was the fact that there were two volumes that appeared to be written in Old English.

Suzanne spent some of the afternoon hours in the cave, but more time at her desk at the house, writing the press release, arranging for transport for the following week, and deciding on the three authorities she would invite to authenticate the find.

"I would like one of the experts to be from the National Geographic Society," said Mats as they discussed the selection. "Gilbert will have to be one, of course. Who do you want for the third?"

"There is an Englishman who would be perfect, but I will have to find out if he is available," said Suzanne. "Professor Gilbert will not be happy with an American and a Brit, but he would probably be unhappy even if I invited him three times."

The announcements would contain attachments of the pictures with only Suzanne and the backs of the Guibega workers in the frame. There would be no mistake as to whose discovery it was.

Nando kept half of their men working at the church site, where they leaned on shovels and told stories in the typical manner of French laborers. The other half guarded the canyon or went with Carlo to buy packing crates, bringing them by van from Nice to the village. When even Suzanne was satisfied that all that could be done in the cave without removing the books had been carried out, Mats sat down with her again and discussed the strategy and timing of the announcement.

On the morning of the third day, they drove down with Carlo to the principality, leaving Nando to guard the cave with his men until they returned. Carlo had replaced the muffler on the van. If Suzanne was nervous about leaving the find in Nando's hands, she did not show it. The drive to the coast seemed shorter than the trip north just seven days before.

"Carlo has a cousin who owns a shop in Monaco," said Mats as Allos disappeared behind them. "She will take you shopping for clothes when we arrive."

"Why would I need to go shopping?"

"When you put your terms in front of Gilbert and Bluschel, it will be important to look like a serious businesswoman. A dark blue business suit and white blouse will call attention to your academic accomplishments rather than the dig."

Monte Carlo, September, 2000

Mats made reservations for the scholars at the Princess Hotel in Monte Carlo in two days' time, just one block away from their hotel, the Monte Carlo, where he had booked three rooms, for Suzanne, Carlo, and himself.

Mats sent Carlo to gather up his cousin and sat next to Suzanne in her hotel room as she phoned Gilbert and Minister Bluschel on a conference call.

"This is a truly great discovery," Suzanne said, the excitement evident in her voice. "Just wait until you see the list of volumes, all of them in very good condition. The cave is absolutely dry and cool. It was perfect for their preservation."

"Why must we wait two days, and why meet you in Monte Carlo rather than just go to the site?" Minister Bluschel asked impatiently.

Prompted by Mats with hand signals, Suzanne said, "I am still arranging security. The site is rural. So far, we have been able to hide the find from the locals. Having two well-known experts such as you show up would make it more difficult."

"That I can understand," said Professor Gilbert. "But I think it would be better if you and I worked on the press release together. It hasn't gone out already, has it?"

"No, the formal release has not gone out, but based on the titles in the library, I have selected two other experts, one from the National Geographic Society, Paul Georgus, and Professor David Davenport from Great Britain. I have just now sent you and them an email explaining the enormity of the discovery and attached a number of photos."

"You did what?" exclaimed Gilbert. "This is a French discovery, on French soil."

"I will make the release public after you look it over and we meet in Monte Carlo," said Suzanne, watching Mats barely able to hold his laughter. "The others will not arrive at the site until a day after you."

"You will be lucky if one of them doesn't announce it with his own press release, trying to take some credit," said Gilbert. This sent Mats to the floor, holding his stomach. It was exactly what he had warned Suzanne that Gilbert himself would do.

"You have rooms reserved at the Princess Hotel. I'll meet you there the day after tomorrow at three. We can discuss the find and how best to preserve it then."

Mats had suggested it would be more dramatic to bring the men to the cave together rather than let them straggle in on their own. Two days in Monte Carlo would also give Suzanne a little time to unwind and relax. She had been working fifteen hours a day since first entering the cave.

After the phone call, Mats said, "From what you have said, the library will belong to the Ministry and probably be administered by Gilbert. Credit for the discovery is another thing. It would be good if you got assurance from Gilbert and Bluschel that you will have control over the site and be involved in the translation and preservation of the collection. I think you might even suggest to Bluschel that the site be preserved as it is, as a sort of national monument – a literary tourist attraction."

"That is a lot to ask for," said Suzanne. "I'm not sure they will agree."

"It might be too much. But you can let them have something in the negotiations. Try to keep as much control as you can, but keep all the credit for the discovery. We'll get the papers written up before they arrive." Mats caught himself dictating the terms Suzanne would present to the experts. He recognized the change that had come over him in the last month. In Sausalito, with Mike

Ferrera, he had been unable to make up his mind what to do the next day; he could never have plotted out the plans of another. Now he was becoming decisive, his relationship with the Guibega clan radiating into the rest of his personality. He wondered about the change and the nagging feeling that he was still missing something.

Mats had reserved the first evening for their own private celebration. A knock on the door announced Carlo, who entered Suzanne's room followed by a woman in her early thirties who was obviously a member of the Guibega gene pool. "This is Leda," he said as an introduction to both Mats and Suzanne.

The woman had flashing dark eyes and the same sharpness to her features that both Carlo and Mario exhibited. In the men it tended to make them appear intense and brooding, but on Leda it accentuated the intelligence in her eyes and added to her beauty. Small, scarcely over five feet tall, she had the square shoulders and erect posture of the Guibega, giving her a look of both grace and strength.

"I am proud to meet you, Signor Falcon," she said, thrusting her hand into his. "Aie-e-e-e," she then exclaimed, turning to look Suzanne up and down. "Carlo said you needed my help, but this will be easy. What a beauty! I am Leda. You must be Madame De Lacy."

"Mademoiselle," Suzanne was quick to correct.

Leda's smile and openness were infectious. It was impossible not to like this forward, exuberant woman.

"It would be impossible to spend too much on a figure like this. The problem will not be finding the right clothes, but not buying everything that looks good on her."

"Price will be a factor," said Suzanne, shaking Leda's hand.

Carlo interrupted the two women's assessment of each other with a torrent of Corsican. Mats joined in with his cursory Corsican.

Leda nodded and smiled at Mats. "Give us five hours. I will bring her back to the hotel."

"Carlo just told her what is needed in the way of outfits and instructed her that all the bills should be brought to me," said Mats in French, in answer to Suzanne's questioning glance. "I told them that price is indeed not a factor. Don't say anything. It is my way of saying thank you for your help in retrieving my family's legacy. Have fun."

Carlo slipped Leda a credit card as they left the room.

Leda Guibega was as good at estimating the time needed to make the rounds of Monte Carlo's best shops as she had been at assessing Suzanne's figure. Precisely five hours after Leda and Suzanne had left, Mats answered a knock on his door. In the hall, accompanied by a bellhop and a cart laden with boxes, stood the two women.

"Looks like you were busier this afternoon than you were at the site," laughed Mats, tilting his head toward the pile of boxes.

"This woman knows absolutely everyone in Monte Carlo. I can't possibly keep all these things, but I can return what you don't like or what I don't wear."

"That would be a crime, Signor Falcon," chirped Leda. "Those clothes belong on her like Michelangelo's fresco belongs on the ceiling of the Sistine Chapel. What a figure! Carlo has already taken care of everything," she added in response to Mats running a finger across his palm in the universal signal for a check.

The bellhop had opened the door to Suzanne's suite and was arranging the packages on a desk and on the bed. Both Suzanne and Leda followed him into the bedroom, Leda giving him directions and tipping him on his way out.

"What a wonderful room!" exclaimed Suzanne, crossing to the window that had just been opened. The view looked west over the harbor, literally filled with gleaming white yachts both at dock and at anchor.

"Would you mind if Carlo stayed with my family?" asked Leda. "We don't get to see the rascal very often since we moved to the mainland."

"I'm sorry, but I want him to be near Suzanne during the negotiations that she will be conducting … talks that I will not be able to attend myself. We also have some items of value that would be safer with Carlo next door."

Even as Mats spoke, he was surprised at his tone of command. He had taken charge before, in dealing with Professor Gilbert, in explaining to Suzanne about Thomaso's special volumes, and now with Leda. His manner and tone of voice left no doubt that he was to be obeyed. The smile left Leda's face as he spoke. The seriousness of his remarks dispelled the euphoria produced by the shopping.

"But," continued Mats, a smile radiating over his face, "I would like you to join us for dinner this evening. From the number of boxes alone, it appears you have done a fine job this afternoon. It is only fair that you help us enjoy the fruit of your labor. We have reservations in the Crown Room at nine, but I would like to introduce Suzanne to the gaming rooms about eight. Does that give you enough time?"

"Barely. Suzanne, you know the shop with the blue dress that we liked?" she asked. "I could not go to the Crown Room without a new dress."

Suzanne grabbed a fistful of euros from Carlo and thrust them into Leda's jacket pocket. "Of course not," she said. "We'll see you here at seven thirty."

Mats and Carlo had been fitted for tuxedos and suits in Mats' suite while the women were shopping. Mats could see that Carlo would rather have gone with the women. His shoulders looked constricted, the collar too high and uncomfortable for a man used to hard work and loose clothing. Mats, on the other hand, with his tall, spare frame, looked as if he were made for the garment.

Mats saw Carlo look down at his hands, sticking through his jacket sleeves, showing exactly three-quarters-of-an-inch of white cuff and half of a pair of eighteen-karat-gold links. Carlo looked at his fingernails, clean but notched and broken from the labor that had produced the hardness in the rest of his body. Carlo was ill at ease, but this was how Mats wanted him dressed. The suit he would wear in front of Bluschel and Gilbert would give exactly the same impression.

Mats' reasons for wanting Carlo by Suzanne's side and in attendance at the next day's negotiations were clear-cut. Carlo would help ensure that the bulk of the credit would go to Suzanne while acting as her site foreman. His presence would allow Mats to monitor the meeting through a small microphone without having to be physically present. In the tux and the suit, Carlo looked even more rugged and hardened than he did in his open shirt and loose trousers. He looked exactly as Mats had hoped he would—like a bodyguard—a very dangerous man.

❧ ❧ ❧

At seven-thirty, Leda phoned Suzanne from the front desk to announce that she would be up to help her with final touches in less than a minute.

Suzanne was shocked at the transformation that high heels and the blue dress had produced in her guide. During the day she had been a very efficient fashion expert, guiding Suzanne from shop to shop and advising her on outfits and accessories while negotiating proper prices from her fellow shop owners. Her dress was that of a very chic professional, effortlessly and stylishly practical, much like what Suzanne herself wore in Paris. Now, dressed for the evening, she looked beautifully extravagant, and somehow, she had found time to have her hair set.

"I brought these over for you," said Leda as she moved quickly into the room. "The gown would not be complete without them. They are on loan, so don't get too attached, though," she laughed.

Suzanne took the black velvet case Leda offered and opened it, finding an eighteen-inch strand of nine-millimeter pink pearls and a matching bracelet. She took them out and let them fall from her hand to the neckline of the gown. Their light pink radiance complemented the off-white satin of the fabric.

"They are perfect, Leda."

"So are you, but you still must hurry. We only have ten minutes."

It took no time for Suzanne to put on what little makeup she used. Her hair was another story. A week of tangles had accumulated. Now, bringing it under control was giving her problems. Luckily, Leda again proved more than equal to the task. A few strokes with a brush and light spray, and she had deftly curled Suzanne's hair into lush, soft waves.

Suzanne was putting on her shoes when the phone rang. It was exactly eight.

"How are things going over there? Do you need more time?"

"We're ready. Leda is with me. We'll wait for you here." She hung up the phone and yelled to Leda, who was checking herself in the bathroom mirror one last time, "They're coming."

Suzanne's dress was made of cream-colored silk with a neckline that plunged just low enough to show her figure to best advantage. Its hem reached almost to the floor.

"You look beautiful," said Mats, taking her hand.

"You don't think it is too formal?"

"It's perfect for the Crown Room," said Leda, "and you are perfect for the dress."

The casino floor looked nothing like the cavernous main floors Mats was used to in Lake Tahoe and Las Vegas. There were fewer gaming tables, and it felt as if the gambling was occurring in private areas of a ballroom under chandeliers rather than in a casino. According to Mats' quick conversion, the stakes were much higher than in the games for the working-class clientele of the Nevada desert.

"We have sufficient time before our reservation for a little entertainment," said Mats, stepping to a roulette table and exchanging a handful of bills for a stack of violet and rose chips. "You play, Suzanne. What you win is yours to keep. What you lose will be my responsibility."

"But I do not know how to gamble. I have never played roulette."

"There's not a lot to learn. I'll help you. It's actually a better game here in Europe." Mats looked at the table, drawn toward the red section on the betting surface. Even before recent events, he had been more successful than most people who relied on their intuition when gambling. He felt good about red now. "Place a chip on the red diamond, here," he instructed, pointing at the proper place.

Suzanne did as Mats instructed as the ball was released, following its high track around the wheel.

"You can bet on either red or black. If you are right, you double your money, but if the other color or the green space captures the ball, you lose. In America there are two green slots; here there is only one, and thus much better odds." The ball continued its circular course without seeming to lose any of its momentum. "You can also bet odd or even or on any of the individual numbers. There are combination plays, but let's keep it simple."

As if on cue, the ball suddenly fell with a clatter into the numbered track of the wheel, bouncing wildly. Mats watched as Suzanne seemed mesmerized, her head rotating slightly with the movement of the ball.

"Vingt-deux, rouge!" said the croupier. "Twenty-two, red!"

"Red!" Suzanne repeated, watching in fascination as the croupier placed a matching violet and rose chip next to hers.

Mats looked again at the board and then at the hand of the croupier. He still felt good about red. "Let them stay on red and let's see what happens," he whispered into Suzanne's ear.

Again they heard the sound of the smoothly rolling ball followed by the sharp ratcheting of its fall into the center of the wheel. The smooth velvet voice of the croupier called, "Sept, rouge!"

"How much are these things worth?" asked Suzanne as Mats added two more to the growing stack still perched on the red rectangle.

"A hundred euros," Mats answered in an even tone. He was looking at the board, but he could get no feeling one way or another as to which bet he preferred. "Why don't you leave just one on the red?"

Suzanne removed three chips and a minute later experienced the gut-wrenching feeling of losing one hundred euros with the spin of the wheel.

"Black with three chips," whispered Mats to Suzanne. He felt a reinforcement of his intuition and saw Carlo and Leda both looking at the wheel.

"No more bets," announced the croupier as the ball started to lose momentum. Then, seconds later, "Noir, dix-huit! Black, eighteen!"

What had started as one thousand euros in chips grew in less than half an hour to over seven thousand. Mats enjoyed watching Suzanne play, even with an occasional loss that surprised Mats and anguished Suzanne.

"Put them all on odd," whispered Mats. "It's time we went to dinner."

The croupier raised his eyebrow as Suzanne fumbled with the stack of chips, at the last minute taking away the ten she had started with. The ball was paused to roll high on the wheel. "I want these on the odd," she said, smiling sweetly. "Is this correct?"

"Oui, Madame," came the reply, accompanied by a slight straightening of the chips.

Suzanne stared wide-eyed as the ball bounced wildly into the depression on seventeen and the croupier added stack after stack to the table, finally pushing them to her. She counted as he did so.

"Mats, I can't keep this. There is a small fortune here."

"We'll talk about it."

"Why are you doing this to me?" she whispered into Mats' ear. "I agreed to your terms before we entered the cave. Is it part of that?"

"Please, let's talk about it later." Turning to the others, Mats said, "All this excitement has made me hungry.

Leda, will you lead us to the Crown Room? I don't see how Suzanne could expect to have much more luck this evening." Mats took her by the elbow and turned her from the table. "Carlo, would you see that the winnings are credited to Mademoiselle De Lacy's room and then join us?"

The Crown Room more than lived up to its reputation. Mats' restaurant in Sausalito served a mixture of Italian and Nuevo California cuisine, with just enough turnover in the menu to keep the regulars interested. It consistently received excellent reviews and had never failed to make a healthy profit since the year Mats' father had opened it in 1955. But the Crown Room was on a different level. Eight courses, each done to perfection, the presentation exquisite, and the sauces for each dish, unique but complementary, were superb.

From the time they were seated, Mats began to experience a headache. By the time they reached the last dish of Zabaione—more a custard than a drink, but served in massive, wide-brimmed wine glasses—he was having trouble following the conversation, and the smell of cognac only seemed to add to the pain. Leda had suggested they follow dinner with a show a friend of hers was in not two blocks from the casino. Suzanne, still excited from the roulette, was eager to go. Mats, his headache reaching terminal levels, excused himself, using a business call to the States as an excuse, while making sure that Carlo would accompany the women. On his way back to his room, he realized it was the first time he had been alone since they had entered the cave and found the library – the first real opportunity for him to examine Thomaso's writings.

CHAPTER TWELVE

Mats sat in his room, directly across the hall from Suzanne's suite. The room was large by European standards, with a bed, a sofa, and an ornately carved desk. Mats had discarded his jacket and tie, loosening his shirt while quickly thumbing through Thomaso's first book. It was more an exercise in writing than a manuscript. Mats could see the improvement in sentence structure and phrasing as he read through it. It was crafted as a polished version of his journal and was in several different languages. Often in the earlier pages, the same paragraph had been repeated in both Latin and French. The first writings were mostly descriptive in nature, illustrating the appearance of the castle and the meadow that flanked it. In the second volume, Thomaso was more introspective, exploring his own experiences, thoughts, and dreams.

Mats sat back and rubbed his temples. His headache confirmed what he had suspected: using his intuition as he had done in Corsica when he had first met Nando, and in finding the treasure in the wall, had physical consequences. When he had first noticed this with Nando, he had thought the headache part of his hangover. Now he thought otherwise. He had only had two glasses of wine during dinner, not enough to cause a headache, which had started before they were seated anyway. They had played roulette for over half an hour and he had been concentrating, guiding Suzanne while she played. He had noticed both Carlo and Leda concentrating on the wheel as well. He would question them to see if they were suffering ill effects too.

Perhaps Thomaso had discussed what Mats was experiencing in his writings. With that thought, he pushed on, despite the searing pain centered deep behind his eyes, making translation difficult. He put the first book down and picked up the second. Immediately Mats could see the difference. In the second volume, Thomaso was beginning to explore the same questions and feelings Mats had now, seven hundred years later. Thomaso seemed to have a similar problem understanding why he had knowledge of events that had happened to his ancestors generations earlier. He called it Regalo – the Gift— the same word Nando had used. Perhaps because he had lived with the Gift for years, Thomaso had drawn certain conclusions based on repeated experience, and he had used these conclusions as subjects for his essays. The first thing Mats learned was that Thomaso first experienced the Gift in his late teens; before then he had noticed his father looking at him, expectant in his expression. Like Mats' own father, Thomaso's father had said nothing about the ability. Thomaso was uncertain if his father even had the Gift.

The discomfort in Mats' head was finally too much for further reading. He pushed away from the desk. Carrying the book to the couch in the sitting area, he sank deep into the embroidered fabric. He let his head lean back against the roundness of the top cushion, closing his eyes against the light in the room, sleep enveloping him immediately. With sleep came the dream ...

❧ ❧ ❧

1329 – Cannes, France

Baron Falconi followed Pierre out of the last canyon and onto a gentle slope that spilled from the hills into the Mediterranean twenty kilometers in the distance. The horses were tired.

"The village to your right is Cannes," said the guide. It was only the third time he had spoken in more than fifteen hours of hard travel. Once he had grunted when Falconi gave him their destination, and once he had said "halfway" to Carlo, who rode in the rear, making sure they were not pursued.

Cannes was where Falconi's men and boats awaited his return, with escape to Corsica no more than two hours away. The horses were at the end of their endurance. Falconi had come to respect Lady Le Vere during the trek. She had not once asked them either to stop or to slacken the pace. She often had ridden ahead of Falconi, following Pierre with a quiet determination, her shirt clinging to her skin with the sweat of exertion.

"In Cannes I will arrange for Carlo to bring you back to your father with an armed escort," said Falconi, looking at the red-tiled roofs and the long white beach fronting the blue of the Mediterranean.

"That will not be necessary. I will accompany you to Corsica," said Lady Le Vere, focusing on the trail in front of them.

Falconi saw the same determination in her that he'd seen when she defied him at the village. "But you are safe now, and I will see to it that you remain so until you are under your father's protection."

"I understand your meaning and your concern, but I am still going with you to Corsica."

"And if I don't let you?"

"I will follow you."

"You are very strong-willed, my Lady. Why won't you do as I say?"

She answered by kicking her horse into an easy trot toward the coast. Falconi had no option but to spur his mount into motion as well. Only Pierre remained stationary. Having done his job, he was already planning an exchange of mounts and a return to the village. As Carlo rode past, he reached out and gave the guide a small purse and a nod.

"Will you not tell me why?" asked Falconi again when he had pulled up alongside the beautiful young woman.

"I will tell you, but it will make no difference whether you accept my reasons or not. I will still go with you to Corsica." She kept her eyes focused straight ahead as she spoke. "I was just a girl, not yet thirteen, when Thomaso came to study with Monsieur Margaux. Margaux was retained by my father as a cleric. Thomaso and I became friends, and I knew that when I grew up, I would marry him. As I grew, he did not notice that I was becoming a woman. Instead he treated me as a sister. We both liked reading and were good at it. We also liked to hunt and ride together. It was something else, though, that gave us our closest tie. While he was under my father's roof, he pledged me to secrecy about what he called the 'Gift.' It concerned his dreams. I had experienced the same kinds of dreams since my twelfth year, when I became a woman."

"You have the Gift?" Baron Falconi's voice reflected the same surprise that registered on his face. "It cannot be!"

"I assure you that it is so. It is also the reason that you must protect me." The young woman was smiling as she rode light in her saddle next to him. "Soon after Thomaso and his mother left, I convinced my father to let me travel to Corsica to visit with your family. Then word of Thomaso's murder reached us. Shock and grief overcame me. I spent the next year alternately taking care of my father and letting him take care of me. I was considering entering a convent when word came of your revenge. Then Monsieur Margaux sent for his books, letting us know of his whereabouts and the circumstances of his escape. I convinced my father to let me travel with Margaux's belongings and finish my studies with him."

"You still have not told me why you wish to come to Corsica."

"At the village, I studied with Margaux. He told you that I read Thomaso's works. He suspected that I had been in love with Thomaso. Thomaso's writings are now buried. So I will tell you about them. The first is merely an exercise book. Margaux had me make one also. The second was pure Thomaso. Twice Margaux caught me crying as I read it, so much of himself had Thomaso put into the work. It dealt with the Gift, its discovery soon after he came to us, and other subjects that were unique to your family. I met you through your son's eyes, a respect that turned to love the more I read. When you came to the village, I saw the strength that Thomaso would have possessed if he had grown to full manhood. I saw the intelligence that begot him. I will go with you to Corsica because you are alone, and I would be alone without you. I hope that you will feel love for me, and that my journey will not have been in vain. I will not lessen the chance by returning to my father's home. I expect to marry you and bear you sons."

Falconi stopped his horse and looked in astonishment at this bold young woman. She returned his gaze with an even, intense one of her own and a mere hint of a smile, her eyebrow upturned as though daring him to reject her. There was no embarrassment in her eyes, only pride. She sat straight in her saddle. Her beauty suddenly took on a meaning that had been outlandish to him a few minutes before. The realization of a great truth fought through his fatigue as he looked at her.

"I am an old man, older than your father."

"Yes, but you have the strength and spirit of a much younger man. I am young, and I will easily and happily bear you children."

Baron Falconi looked at her and then at the blue waters that separated them from his island home. His eyes began to fill with tears as he thought of his beloved son and of the sheer goodness of the woman before him. "Lady Le Vere," he said softly and as if for the first time. "Come with me then. Come with me to Corsica, and we shall let the future take care of itself."

Monte Carlo, August, 2000

The knock came, jarring Mats from his sleep. His neck was stiff and would not move from its position on the couch. The knock came again, forcing him into full awareness. "Yes," he called, looking at his watch. He had been asleep for almost two hours. His headache, while still present, had diminished.

"It's Suzanne. May I speak with you, please?"

Mats walked to the door, his stiffness decreasing with each step. Suzanne, still in her evening dress, stepped into the room and he closed the door behind her.

"I'm sorry to intrude so late, but I had to talk with you before people start arriving tomorrow. Several things are troubling me, and I won't be able to sleep unless my mind is clear."

"I think I know some of your concerns already," said Mats as he led her to the couch.

"First of all," she said, "I cannot accept the gift of the clothes Leda and I purchased this morning. Neither my family nor I am poor. I have savings and I want to reimburse you. I also cannot accept the money I won this evening at roulette. It was your money that I gambled and your suggestions that guided me. It's your money, not mine."

"The money and the clothes are just symbols, aren't they?" said Mats with a smile. "It is the books I took from the cave that trouble you. You guess that they must be very valuable for me to want nothing else. Your ethical code tells you that the find should not be tampered with, and the clothes and the winnings seem like a payoff for your silence. That's what's bothering you, isn't it?"

"How do you know my feelings so well? This isn't the first time I've felt you knew my mind."

"It's part of the answer. First let me show you the books. This is the first one, which mimics the journal. Many of the outlines you have already read in the journal. These are expounded upon in his essays, but there is nothing really new. You can see that the handwriting is the same." Mats passed the book to Suzanne. "I have gone through the entire volume. There is nothing in it that I would object to you reading. Evidently it is an exercise that Margaux had his students complete before he let them go on to anything original."

Mats watched as Suzanne flipped through the pages, recognizing the tight, upright script of the journal. She took time to read a passage dealing with the flight of a hawk. The manuscript was as Mats had described it in the cave. It was written by his ancestor. It was the first time since the discovery in the cave that she had seen either of the books. As she thumbed carefully through the pages, Mats could see the tension on her face dissipate.

"You're right. I had started to doubt you. I had even concocted a scenario in which these were the two most valuable books in the collection and held directions to more tangible monetary treasures. I was willing to stand by what I had promised in the cave until the gift of the clothes and the money won at roulette. It made me wonder if it was all a bribe for my silence. And there's something else…It's about why you don't want any credit for these discoveries, why you don't even want to be present tomorrow. What are you hiding?"

"I'm hiding nothing. Credit would not benefit me, but it will you. I want the discovery to be yours alone. Here, read this. It is the second volume. It starts to deal with matters that are private to the Falconi family. I have not read all of it, but it attempts to answer some questions that I myself have—like how it was that I knew the exact location of the library we have just discovered. I must make sure that I understand Thomaso Falconi's conclusions. I would prefer that you don't read it, but if you must know the truth of my words, then do so." He handed her the open book and received in return the first volume.

"It's the same hand," Suzanne said. She read far enough in the second volume to know what he had said was true. "I don't need to know your family's secrets," she said, gently closing the book and returning it to Mats. "The books are as you said. They are yours, and I will say nothing of their existence."

"Thank you," Mats said with sincerity. "Part of Thomaso's story does concern you. Thomaso had dreams of past ancestors, like I have. Only his family was supposed to have the ability, although occasionally one of the Guibega would have it too, to a lesser degree. He found one exception in the daughter of his host, Baron Le Vere, who was born in the district where you were raised. It might mean we have a shared heritage. Whatever the reason, you seem familiar to me, and have since our first meeting." He paused. "Do you believe me?" he asked, leaning toward Suzanne and reaching for her hand.

"Yes," came her surprised answer. "It's as if I have known you for years." Her hand rose to touch his cheek.

Mats froze, her touch warming the skin beneath. Slowly he stood, and Suzanne rose to meet him. His arms encircled her in a hesitant embrace.

"Suzanne," he said softly. "Suzanne ..."

"Yes, I know," she whispered.

Suzanne cupped Mats' neck and drew his head toward her, no longer denying the shared feeling that had been building in them since Mats had first walked into the Bibliothèque. Neither Mats nor Suzanne was prepared for the surge of raw emotion that coursed through them. They tried to step back, to pull away from the embrace, but they could not. Mats took her hands tenderly and kissed her, first gently, then with passion.

When they finally broke apart, he slid his hand underneath the thin silk strap of her dress to the point of her shoulder, then slowly lowered the strap down her arm, bringing the dress with it. The fullness of her breasts was accentuated by the gathering of the silk below and the pearls rising and falling with each breath. She pressed against him. He felt her warmth against his chest. He kissed her again, his tongue finding acceptance in the welcome that hers gave.

"There's so much I want to tell you, so much that I suspect about the past and our future."

"Later," she whispered. "We'll have plenty of time later."

Something had been bothering him and now, with Suzanne in his arms, he saw why he had been unable to pinpoint it until this moment. He had thought it was something about the books, but the books had not been the source of his worry. They had given him the answer. He had been searching his reality, his own mind and recent events, to find the source of his discomfort, but last night in his dream about Baron Falconi and Lady Le Vere, he'd realized that he should be looking in the past, not the present, for the answer.

Last night he'd realized what hadn't made sense. In his dreams, Thomaso, the author of the journal and the family histories, had been killed, murdered along with his mother, the Baroness Falconi, before he could marry or have children. It was clear in the dreams that Thomaso had no brothers or sisters, so how could the Falconis be Mats' ancestors? This question had been answered while Mats was dozing on the couch. Baron Falconi had taken Lady Le Vere to Corsica at her request. Despite his grief and lust for revenge, she must have found a spot in his heart receptive to a woman's love. Now, in Mats' own grief, Suzanne had come to him.

Mats bent and lifted her in his arms. Her lips thrust upward, seeking his mouth, inviting, as he carried her to the bed.

CHAPTER THIRTEEN

Suzanne awoke in Mats' arms, sharing a pillow, the sheets rumpled around them. The scent of sweet sweat mixed with that of sex conjured up the memory of every moment of the previous evening. They had discovered each other, not only in the passion and patience of their lovemaking, but also as they rested, spent, describing their personal histories to each other in soft words of release.

Suzanne basked in contentment, keeping her eyes on Mats, his breathing slow and even. She had wept openly when Mats told her about the murder of his father. She had suspected, even back in Paris, that there was some underlying grief submerged in Mats' being. The thought had again come to her after the excavation at the cave. Mats was happy at the find but not as ecstatic as she was, and his mindset had been difficult for her to grasp. He seemed preoccupied with some inner struggle, but she had been too engrossed in the cataloging of the books to pursue the reasons for his melancholy. Now she understood, at least partly, the enigma that was this man she loved.

Love. How strangely and suddenly it had come over her, yet looking back, she could see it building from the first encounter. His good looks, the way he had handled Gilbert so easily, his courtesy and respect for her intelligence and her ability to translate his journal—each day had brought her closer to his side without her conscious awareness that she was falling in love. Last night he had disarmed her with his candor when she had voiced her doubts about the books he had taken. How easily he had recognized her concerns, convincing her they were groundless. She knew men found her attractive, but her studies had taken most of the energy of her teenage years. Her work to earn honors as a student and then her fight for recognition in the academic world of France, where French attitudes still tended to keep women in subservient roles, had taken precedence over romance.

Mats had also told her of his life. He spoke of his father and their loving relationship, and of how he had come to Corsica and then France to release his soul from its grief. The telling for both of them had been interrupted frequently, a provocative touch or caress prompting them into new passion. Finally, exhausted, they had fallen asleep, still joined in love's embrace.

Now Mats stirred and blinked awake. He looked at Suzanne, still next to him with her eyes on him. He realized now that his relationship with his father had always been at the heart of his attitude toward women. He enjoyed their company, but he hadn't wanted to chance a relationship that could possibly change the living arrangements he had with his father. As his father aged, Mats' resolve to stay uninvolved had grown more steadfast.

His attitude toward women, polite but distant, had remained firm until last evening. Only now did he recognize that the change had been weeks in coming. Ever since he had met Suzanne in Professor Gilbert's office, he had liked and admired her, and with the translation of the journal, he had known she was different.

It was as if a deep shadow had passed across Mats' own heart and in its passing allowed light into his life. Like the Baron some seven hundred years before, he knew he had found love. His father had been unlucky. He had found his love very late in life, when he was almost sixty. He had almost been destroyed when his wife had died. Needing to take care of five-year-old Mats had been his father's salvation. It was part of their bond.

"Good morning," he said as he turned toward Suzanne, then hesitated. Last night they had made love, discovering each other in bits and pieces. Now it was as if he were seeing her for the first time. She was magnificent, perfection, more than the sum of all the parts that had occupied his attention the night before. Now she rose on her elbow, proudly, not embarrassed, and moved over him, kissing his forehead, then his cheeks, then his lips. Then, feeling his reaction, she straddled him, moving slowly until they were both sated with the pleasure of each other's newfound desire.

Mats looked down the hall, assuring himself it was empty, and allowed Suzanne to cross the hallway unobserved in her evening dress and heels. When the door to her suite closed, he went to the house phone and ordered a full breakfast for two to be served in her room. He showered and shaved, dressing casually in shirt and slacks. Crossing the hall, he knocked on Suzanne's open door as room service was setting up the breakfast in front of the window overlooking the harbor.

Suzanne looked out from the bedroom as he entered. "I will be out in a minute, Mats. Make yourself comfortable."

The minute stretched to five as the waiter stood by the table, making a show of fussing with the silverware. Their early morning activities had deprived them of several hours they had needed for discussion before the arrival of the invited scholars. The waiter started pouring the coffee as Suzanne entered the room. She was wearing the skirt that went with the blue business suit Mats had suggested for the meeting with the Bluschel and Gilbert. A light yellow blouse awaited the jacket. Mats thought she looked radiant as they took their chairs. The waiter opened napkins with the polished flourish of a torero, placing them on their laps, taking covers off the meal of crêpes, strawberry preserves, and thick bacon, a generous fruit bowl to the side.

"You look beautiful," Mats said in a soft voice as the waiter closed the door behind him, the tip Mats had slipped him hidden in his palm. "It is the perfect outfit. Gilbert and Bluschel do not have a chance. Also, the money you won last night at the tables is important. Money is often power, especially in dealing with administrators. A show of it here in Monte Carlo, if nothing else, implies that you could continue to work the find without their financial backing. It gives you a bargaining piece and might be important in your discussions. Did I mention that you look beautiful?"

Suzanne picked at the crêpes in front of her, blushing slightly. Mats could see her trying to find a flaw in his reasoning.

"I agree, as long as you take back the thousand euros that you gave me to start last night," she said with the impish smile to which Mats was becoming accustomed.

Mats reached across the table and took her hand. "You will be busy with the library. I have to return to Corsica. So far, I've been following my dreams, or more likely, they have been leading me through the events of the last month. Perhaps answers will be provided in Thomaso's last volume. What I have read in it deals with dreams and premonitions—dangers to be anticipated. My dreams lead me back to Corsica, but I'd like you to follow as soon as you have the library under control. Gilbert will not want to give you the necessary management, but in the end, if he keeps overall control, he will give up enough control for you to receive the credit. Get separate agreements with England and America. The National Geographic representative will be cooperative, but the other two might strike a deal between themselves."

"What is the danger you just spoke of, Mats?" Suzanne asked. She had sat quietly, absorbing Mats' directions. She was disappointed by his pronouncement that they would separate so soon after finding each other, but only the threat of harm had gone unexplained.

"I'm not sure. There has been so much violence in my family history and in my dreams, and it's always centered around loved ones. I have a feeling that it's not finished yet."

Mats watched Suzanne's emotions flash in her eyes: first defiance, then resignation, then something much softer.

"I love you," she said, touching his cheek.

Carlo picked up the two French officials and brought them to Suzanne's suite at two in the afternoon. His jacket strained across his shoulders and there was a poorly disguised lump between his shoulder and his hip, just above his elbow. Suzanne introduced him as one of the foremen of the dig crew in charge of security. He sat and watched the deliberations in a chair apart from the other three, every now and then grunting at a description of the find or a point made by Suzanne. Every few minutes he would shift in his chair, as inactivity was difficult for him.

It took only an hour for Suzanne to describe the contents of the find and outline her plans for the library's future, going over the points that she and Mats had discussed that morning.

"You seem to have thought of everything," said Bluschel after ten minutes of hushed discussion with Gilbert following her presentation. "I see no problem with the plan you propose, especially since it falls within the budget I negotiated with Mr. Falconi earlier this month."

"It would still have been better if the announcement had come from the Bibliothèque," added Gilbert. "It would have underscored the connection between our division and the discovery."

"Well," said Suzanne, "I know I got carried away with my excitement. It can't be helped now. Professor Davenport and Paul Georgus will be arriving tomorrow, but we still have time to get to the site this afternoon."

Carlo loaded their luggage into the van. As it pulled away with Suzanne at the wheel, he took out his cell phone.

"Nando, Suzanne is driving the two Frenchmen up there now. They should be there in two hours. Mats says to have Mario take over the role of crew chief. I will be going with Mats to Corsica."

Carlo bounded back up the marble stairs, knocking on Mats' door before entering. "We will miss her, I think," he said to Mats, smiling. "She did well. It went just as you said. She was so prepared, they had little option but to agree to her plans. Even Gilbert's objection was just as you thought it would be. I think they were surprised that she had security already in place. And as you suspected, my presence made them nervous." He reached up under his shirt and removed the thick guidebook that had been taped to his side, grimacing as a swath of hair came with the tape.

"We have six hours before the ferry sails from Nice. Shall I ask Leda to join us for lunch?" asked Carlo.

"Yes. How long will it take us to drive there?"

"It's only fifteen kilometers or so. About a half an hour, but best give us an hour. Leda can drive us. The ferry terminal is downtown. There is usually traffic. "

Leda took them to a café just around the corner from her shop. The food was good, the wine excellent. The waitress was friendly and familiar with Leda and placed them at a corner table. Mats' meal was filling, and he supplemented with two glasses of wine.

Leda let Carlo drive her small white Audi while Mats took the back seat. Traffic was light, and they arrived at the ferry dock in just over half an hour.

Chapter Fourteen

The departure of the ferry from Nice was delayed for almost an hour while maintenance was done on the port diesel. From the sluggish way the ferry left the slip, Mats suspected that the repairs were not as complete as they had been told as they boarded. His suspicion was fortified when he saw another ferry approaching the slip they had just vacated. "More likely they needed the dock, rather than finished the work," he thought.

"Damned French." Mats, taken by surprise, turned to see Carlo smiling at his side. "French mechanics are the best because they get so much practice fixing their own machines." Mats couldn't help but laugh, glad that the remark was made while they were standing at the railing and not in the crowded galley.

The incoming ferry was almost abreast; fewer than thirty yards separated the two vessels. The inbound ferry had its deck lights on. Mats heard the deep exhaust noise of the ship's engine kick into astern, slowing its speed as it neared the slip. Passengers bent over the railing, watching their boat's bow edge toward the dock. A movement at the incoming ship's rail caught Mats' eye: a head, turning toward the shore, a man's profile in the deck lighting—something familiar. As if the man sensed being watched, he turned slowly toward Mats.

It was Leca, the man who had murdered his father. Even at this distance, Mats knew he was not mistaken.

"Leca!" he screamed over the sounds of engine and prop wash. "Leca!"

The man heard his name and grinned, the same grin he had worn when he'd slid back into the BMW in Sausalito. Mats ran aft, down the deck, followed by Carlo, losing the race to the widening distance between the two ships.

"Watch that man!" Mats yelled at Carlo as he gave up the futile attempt to keep contact with the passing vessel. Wheeling, he raced up the ladders to the bridge deck. The door to the bridge was locked, a precaution taken since the hijacking of the Achille Lauro. "Captain! I must see the captain!" Mats yelled, pounding on the door with his fist.

A face appeared through a port in the door—a face too young to be captain of anything, looking confused. Mats repeated that he must see the captain, this time in French.

"My name is Falcon, Mats Falcon. I must speak to the captain. We must go back."

The face disappeared, replaced seconds later by another that assessed Mats with hard, weathered eyes. "I am the captain. What is the emergency?" he asked through the port in the door.

"My name is Falcon, Captain. My father was murdered six months ago. I just saw the killer on the incoming ferry, the one about to dock. You must turn around."

"Surely you could be mistaken, sir."

"There is no mistake. You must return to shore."

"That I cannot do. I could not dock with the other vessel in the slip. But, I will use the radio to phone the harbor master for you."

Mats was about to protest when Carlo came quickly up the ladder. "He has already left the ship. There was a car on the dock waiting, a black sedan."

It took a moment for Carlo's information to sink in and another to methodically click off the possibilities. Mats could see that it was useless to try to change the captain's mind, especially now with the man in question gone. Even if he could get ashore, the chances of finding the car would be small in the streets of Nice.

"Captain, please," he said in a calm and, he hoped, persuasive tone. "Your suggestion to use the ship-to-shore is greatly appreciated. Could you do it immediately?"

The captain squinted at Falcon, assessing the risk of letting him on the bridge. He spoke to the seaman who had first come to the door. He and another crew member stood to the side, weapons at their side.

"Come in."

As Mats entered, the captain was already working the buttons on the ship-to-shore phone, then handed the handset to Mats.

"A murderer has just left the ferry," shouted Mats into the phone. "There is a reward. The man in question is six feet tall and he has dark eyes and jet-black hair. He is tan or naturally swarthy and is wearing a dark blue double-breasted suit. He was standing on the port railing when the ferry docked. He was one of the first off. He did not have a car on the ferry but was picked up immediately in a black sedan. His might use the name Leca."

"Do the police want this man?" came the reply.

"The American FBI and the international agencies do. I don't know about the French."

The man on the other end took Mats' name and phone number and told him he would look into the ship's records before disconnecting.

"Captain, you have been most helpful. Thank you for your courtesy. One last question: where was the other ferry coming from? Where did he board?"

The captain looked at him strangely, as if the answer should be obvious. "From Calvi after stopping in Ajaccio. The ship is on the same run as we are, monsieur."

Mats left the captain, rejoining Carlo outside on the flying bridge.

"Carlo, please phone Leda. See if she can return immediately to the ferry terminal and collect any information and leads that Leca might have left."

While Carlo was placing the call to Leda's cell, Mats came to grips with the fact that he would be on the ship for the next eight-and-a-half hours. The ETA at Ajaccio was set. As much as he might want it to, it would not change. He felt as if he were in prison. He could do little more until they arrived in the morning.

Mats' room, which had been described as a state room when he booked it, was small and narrow, allowing only a thin bed, a miniscule desk, and a door to a private shower. He had drunk two more glasses of wine at a dockside café while waiting for the delayed boarding. Now he was beyond tired. He knew he needed sleep if he was to function the next day. He climbed into the narrow bed, the gentle motion of the ship and the low, dull sound of the diesels deep in the vessel's bowels providing sedation, slowly counteracting the adrenaline that was coursing through him. He knew he would sleep; he only wondered if he would dream.

CHAPTER FIFTEEN

Off Corsica, Autumn 1329

Baron Falconi loved the sea. Many of the stories his father had passed on to him had dealt with great battles and daring raids from the sea. Lost in all but his own memory was the origin of his title and claim on the lands he now occupied. Some of his holdings had been given to his family for service by Robert Guiscard in 1084. This he knew from documents held safe. His family's ties in Corsica went further back than that, though—some of them much further, but those were indistinct, being consistent only in that they dealt with the sea.

They had sailed through the night, escaping from the mainland far ahead of the pursuit of d'Avignon and his men. This was Lady Le Vere's first time on the water, and the Baron had expected seasickness to diminish the proud self-assurance she had shown in demanding to accompany him to Corsica. It did not. She had shown no signs of illness other than to curl beneath the stern-most thwart and go to sleep. As often this time of year, the seas were calm and regular, providing an easy rhythm to the movement of the boat. The skies were clear of clouds, allowing the helmsman to steer by the stars.

As dawn broke, Falconi squinted into the mist off the port bow where the northern coast of Corsica was just now becoming visible above the haze. "Ease to larboard," he shouted. "Fifteen degrees." A small patch of red was barely visible on the horizon, interspersed in the waves between

Falconi's ship and the outline of the island. The helms-man carried out his order immediately and the vessel swung sharply to the left, heading straight for the flotsam.

Gradually the red outline cleared, revealing the shape of a sail and mast. Falconi had been in enough sea battles to recognize that the wreck coming into view was the result of violence. The way the sail hung ripped and sev-ered from its natural position on the mast, the absence of men exerting frantic effort to keep their ship afloat, told him the nature of the disaster. Over the generations, the Falconi had inflicted upon many vessels the condition of the one the Baron now viewed.

A single shark circled the wreckage. Only the bow of the ship now remained above water, its mast sticking above the waves at a rakish angle.

"Ho there!" bellowed Falconi.

There was no response. The helmsman brought Falconi's ship slowly around the sinking ship.

"Hello..."

The Baron was first to see the movement. Lying at the base of the mast was a man, his beard wet with the sea and his own blood. He raised his arm inches and waved at Falconi, who was twenty yards away, far enough to avoid the risk of hitting the submerged wreck. The motion caused the man to shift, slipping slowly down the slope of the deck into the sea, seemingly unable to muster the strength to hold on to life a moment longer.

The shark that had been circling the ship closed on the man, attracted by the red stain that floated on the water. Falconi reacted with a speed that surprised even his men, who were used to his acts of bravery. Diving into the water that separated the two vessels, he made half the distance before he came up for air, the remaining few yards taking only three powerful strokes. He grabbed the man around his chest and with his free hand hoisted him back up onto what remained of his ship. The man's eyes opened, fixing Falconi with a glazed look of recognition, and then closed as he lost consciousness.

Falconi's ship was alongside the other in seconds, two men securing lines to the wreck and another two coming to his aid with the unconscious seaman. Quickly, they hoisted the man into waiting hands, which laid him in the shade of their own sail as Falconi and the others leaped back to safety.

"Cast off," commanded Falconi, looking down at the man he had saved from certain death. "See to this fellow."

The man had been exposed to the sun and sea. His face was sunburned and beginning to blister, while his feet were bluish and puckered from long immersion in saltwater. But exposure was not the main threat to his survival. Starting at his left armpit and extending almost to his navel was a gaping wound. His ribs were exposed and whitened from the constant lavage of the seawater, which had probably saved his life. The wound was not deep, the blade having bounced off bone before reaching vital organs. The salt in the water had helped to cauterize the wound, and while it was still bleeding, the flow was manageable. His pulse, Falconi could feel, was weak but regular.

"Give him water, slowly at first, but keep him drinking. Then bind him with cloth to keep the wound closed."

He had given the orders to his men, but it was the Lady Le Vere who responded. Kneeling down on the thwarts, she raised the man's head and poured a small amount of water into his open mouth. One of the men placed a torn length of cloth into her hands, which she saturated with fresh water and laid on the man's head, pouring even more water over it. She placed a second bandage over the wounded man's side, wrapping it around his chest and securing it against movement.

"Now what do you suppose this is about?" the Baron muttered as he set the tiller to their original course. "A boat with a single man, attacked, by the looks of it. Too small to be on a raid. Very strange. Let me know if he comes to."

Almost six hours later, as they rounded the Gulf of Sagone and drew into sight of Ajaccio, the man stirred. The injured sailor was still lying amidships with his head in the lap of Lady Le Vere. She tended him as he gradually regained his faculties.

"Where am I?" The words came as a barely audible rasp of a whisper.

"You have been saved by Baron Falconi. You are on his ship," said the Lady Le Vere, as the man weakly surveyed his surroundings. She related to him the story of his rescue and Baron Falconi's bravery, as well as the extent of his wound, while feeding him water in measured amounts.

"Baron Falconi. Baron Falconi." The man breathed the words with obvious pain.

Falconi guided the boat softly against the jetty, then moved from the stern to Lady Le Vere's side. "I am Falconi. Who are you and how do you come to be injured on a wrecked boat?"

"My name is Edmund Auvray. The boat was mine, but under the hire of the Duke Colletti. I thank you for my life, sire."

"Well, Auvray, how is it that you were left for dead, alone in a sinking vessel?"

"I will tell you, milord, but I must ask that you forgive me the past and give me protection should I live to see the future."

Falconi looked at this man who would barter on what could be his deathbed. *His tale must be worth the telling, for him to be so brazen,* he thought. Falconi turned to the woman who had taken over the man's care since he had been dragged off his sinking boat. "Will he live?"

"If his wound is kept clean and does not corrupt, he will live," she answered, wiping the man's brow.

"The protection is yours until you are finished healing. The forgiveness I withhold until I hear what it is in your story that requires it."

"Fair enough," whispered Auvray. "I have reported your movements for the last year, to Duke Colletti. I was to tell him immediately if you left Ajaccio for France. This I did. I then was sent to France to give the information to a French noble called d'Avignon."

"D'Avignon," hissed Falconi through clenched teeth.

"Yes. Duke Colletti's daughter was to marry d'Avignon's son. Both hate you, milord."

That was how d'Avignon had been able to find him at the village so quickly. Things were starting to fall into place. This Edmund Auvray must be a fine sailor not to have been detected, thought Falconi.

"I was to wait at Nice, ready to sail. If you were killed or captured, I was to sail directly to Colletti. I believe he meant to attack your holdings before your men returned with word of your death. If you somehow escaped capture, then Colletti was to put forth a fleet of warships to intercept you on your homeward voyage. I was on my way to deliver the message when my ship was sunk."

"And your injury?"

"A man-at-arms, who had been with d'Avignon, had ridden quickly to the coast and told me of your escape. He was to sail with me to Calvi to ensure that Duke Colletti followed through and made up for d'Avignon's failure. He was a foul fellow in an even fouler temper when he boarded. We had not even cleared the harbor breakwater before he emptied a wineskin, then filled my bilge with his excess. He would not clean the mess he had made and my orders to do so infuriated him. By the time we had sailed halfway to our destination, he had drunk a second skin. In his drunken arrogance, he insulted my mother, my boat, and me. He was a bully, not used to men standing up to his insults. He drew his sword and killed my two crew members, and then he came after me at the tiller. His sword missed me but stove the bottom of my boat. His second swing bounced off my ribs and broke the mast. It was his last act before my knife found his throat. I tried to bail and re-rig the sail, but I must have lost consciousness. My next recollection is of seeing your ship closing on me."

"You have done much that needs forgiving, Edmund Auvray," said Falconi in a hushed voice. "Your deceit could have cost me many good men."

"You have saved my life, Lord. I tell you this that it may make forgiveness for my deeds easier in your eyes. Twice I ferried men between d'Avignon and Colletti. One of these trips was a single passenger who I first thought was a priest. He dressed in clerical robes, but his demeanor was that of a warrior. During the voyage, I saw weapons concealed beneath his robes. I think he was French, closer to d'Avignon than to Colletti. This man was sent to kill you."

"Does he have a name?"

"None that was given to me or that I overheard, milord. He spoke not one word while in my care. It was Colletti's man who told me he was to kill you."

"His appearance? What does he look like?"

"He has dark eyes and a beard that looks like it was colored with black ink, and I tell you, there is no chivalry or honor in this man."

"You have made your bargain well. As for protection, you will be a guest until you are well. My forgiveness will be withheld until we have further discussions of this stranger." Falconi's face hardened as he climbed to the lichen-coated stones that held fast against the rail of the boat.

"Are you all right?" Lady Le Vere asked, unable to read the emotion behind his cold eyes.

"The man's tale rings true. I must hunt this assassin rather than let him hunt me."

CHAPTER SIXTEEN

Corsica, August, 2000

The first time Mats sailed to Corsica had been magical. He had come to discover the birthplace of his father. He had taken in the mountains rising from the sea and the ancient stone jetty that protected the harbor from the unpredictable storms that thrashed across the desert and into the Mediterranean. Now it was different. Spurred by the urgent feeling that came from seeing Leca, the sights and sounds of Ajaccio were lost on him. As soon as the gangway was lowered onto the bow of the ferry, Mats and Carlo rushed to the front of the line and were the first passengers off the ship. Carlo's cell phone rang just as they reached the pavement. He listened intently before turning to Mats.

"The man's name is Leca all right. Leda found that he is an importer of coffee and art. He is French, a Corsican. He travels the ferry at least once a month, boarding at Calvi. He is picked up as soon as he arrives. If he is Corsican, the Guibegas can find him."

"Do we have Guibegas living in Calvi?"

"Not many, but a few. Calvi has never been a good place for the Guibega, or the Falconi either, for that matter. I have a cousin who married an artist. She will know about this Leca."

"Leca, a Corsican!" Mats mused. "The U. S. police thought he was Colombian. My father's murder was drug related. Colombians aren't the only ones with their fingers in that dirt. Make sure when you call your cousin to tell her this man is dangerous and to be careful, very careful."

"Yes, Signor Falconi."

Mats considered the events of the last few hours. His entire perspective had changed. Seeing Leca had wrenched him back to the reality of the events that had sent him to Corsica. Where relief from grief had originally been his objective, the appearance of Leca now filled him with the desire for revenge.

He had been foolish to shout Leca's name. The man had turned, had seen him. Sooner or later he would make the connection. The police in Sausalito had told Mats that he was the only one who could identify the man. Now, warned, Leca could cover his tracks and again drop out of sight—or attempt to repair his mistake in leaving Mats alive. Mats realized that he probably wouldn't have to do much looking; it was likely this Leca would do the looking for him.

"We must get to Calvi," Mats said to Carlo. "Is it faster to fly or drive?"

Calvi hugged the northwestern coast of Corsica a hundred miles north of Ajaccio. It was guarded by a high rocky ridge that ringed the harbor and city to the east. It had only one tenth the population of Ajaccio, and while it couldn't claim to be the birthplace of Napoleon, it was reputed to be that of Columbus and was the place where Admiral Horatio Nelson lost his eye during the siege of Calvi. It no longer relied on the defensible position of its port for its existence, but on tourism. As Carlo drove through the curved streets, they saw only cafes, artists' displays, and rental cars.

"Angela grew up in Ajaccio," said Carlo waving his hand at the streets passing by. "She married a French artist, Marc Forget, a painter of considerable skill but poor character. It was a marriage that the Guibega did not condone. He is a liar and a drug addict. He borrowed several hundred dollars early in his courtship of Angela and used it to purchase drugs, something that is not allowed in the Guibega family. Angela ran away with Forget, marrying him and settling in Calvi…it is only a hundred miles from Ajaccio, but few Guibegas live there."

Carlo drove Mats up a street leading past the harbor, climbing the hill on which the Citadel was perched. If he was hampered in his search for Angela Guibega by the absence of street signs, Carlo didn't show it. Halfway up the street, he pulled his old Renault to a stop.

"There it is," he said, pointing to a building with a red-tiled roof, distinguishable from its neighbors by the pale blue paint of its stucco exterior and brick-red door.

Carlo got out of the car and knocked. Mats was already standing behind him as a woman of almost square proportions answered. Dark hair streaked with grey cascaded past her shoulders to her waist, but it was her eyes that caught Mats' attention. They shone from below brows that had to be linked to the Guibega clan. In Jennette and Leda, the combination was quite pleasing, pretty if not beautiful, but in Angela, slight differences made her look plain and somewhat coarse.

Mats could tell she was troubled. She waved them inside, looking down the street in either direction before she closed the door. Mats sensed that she had separated herself from her family in more ways than just physically.

"It has been many years, Carlo," she said in the dialect that Mats had come to understand as the Guibegas' version of Corsican.

"Nearly fifteen, Angela. This is Egel Falconi's son, Mats."

Angela's head snapped around as Mats smiled and put out his hand. Every Guibega he had previously met had been happy to meet him. Angela was not. Mats watched Angela's reaction and hoped it had not been a mistake to come to Calvi to ask for her help.

"What is it you want to know?" she asked briskly, switching to heavily accented English.

This woman has much to hide, much to feel guilty about, much shame to conceal, thought Mats as he withdrew his hand. *Is she defensive of her choice to separate herself from her family?*

"There is a man who uses the ferry from Calvi to Nice," Carlo said evenly. "He is an importer of coffee and art. His name is Leca. Do you know of him?"

At the mention of the name Leca, Angela gasped, staring at her cousin with wide eyes and a slack mouth. "Leca?"

"You know the name?"

"I know of him. He is a businessman."

She is startled by Carlo's question, thought Mats. *She is afraid of Leca.*

"What kind of business does he do here?"

"He sells coffee beans to all the coffee houses and restaurants from here to Bastia. He buys paintings here in Calvi and sells them in Paris and America." Angela looked from Carlo to Mats and back to Carlo.

"What else does he sell?" Mats asked, speaking for the first time.

"What do you mean, Signor Falconi?" she replied, her halting words leaving no doubt that she was hiding something.

Mats fixed her with his eyes, making her squirm like a child in the headmaster's office. He let her discomfort build and then repeated his question.

Before Angela could answer, the front door opened and a tall, gaunt man stepped into the room. His arms were bare to the shoulders and, in contrast with the rest of his frame, strong and sinewy. His eyes were set deep under unkempt brows and accented by the dark circles below them. His hair was tossed and had not recently seen either comb or soap.

"What is this?" he asked in unpleasant, demanding French. "You entertain men in my home when I am gone?"

Carlo stepped into the center of the room, away from the wall where he had been partly obscured by a hanging mobile. "Marc, we are discussing some family matters with Angela. You weren't here when we phoned and asked if we could come."

The man whirled to face Carlo, rage contorting his face. "Carlo!" he spat with surprise and disdain. "You are not welcome in my house, you or any other of your pig-sucking family."

Carlo stepped forward, stopping only when Mats put out a restraining arm.

"She is my family now," Forget said. "You ask her nothing."

Mats studied the man as he insulted Carlo. There was something unnatural in his actions, a wildness in his eyes that had been present even before he had recognized Carlo. His pupils were constricted to pinpoints, even in the darkness of the room. He stood a foot taller than Carlo, outweighing him by perhaps thirty pounds, but as Mats looked at a barely restrained Carlo, he thought it would be an even match.

"They asked about Leca," said Angela hurriedly, hoping to divert her husband's attention from Carlo and delay the inevitable blows about to be thrown.

"Leca?" The husband turned slowly back to his wife. "What about Leca?"

"They asked about his business," she answered, stepping away from her husband, now frightened to be the center of his attention.

Mats was watching the man closely, but the swiftness of the attack still took him by surprise. The man seemed to deflate, then sprang forward toward Carlo with a knife that suddenly appeared from his boot. Mats was not prepared for the move. Carlo was, but nevertheless the knife flashed past him in an upward arc, tearing his shirt and penetrating the skin of his chest. As the knife went by, Carlo hit the man, missing his face by inches while landing the blow solidly on his neck below the angle of his jaw.

Forget gasped for air but regained his balance, keeping the point of his knife directed at Carlo's chest as he feinted a thrust with it.

Mats felt a surge of adrenaline flow through him. Since he had been given the short sword of his ancestor, he was comforted by its presence and certain that some of his dreams and premonitions were instigated by its close proximity. At times he carried it in a sheath strapped to the small of his back, feeling comfort and a certainty in its usefulness.

Reaching behind his back, Mats now drew the ancient blade from its sheath between his shoulders. The blade felt light in his hand, warm to his touch. One step and a thrust embedded an inch of the blade into the biceps of Angela's husband. Forget's fingers opened involuntarily and his knife clattered to the floor.

As the blade was pulled from his arm, Forget turned and faced Mats, pausing only momentarily to gauge the distance before leaping. Mats stepped deftly to his right and allowed the man's momentum to carry him against the couch. In one fluid movement, he brought the sword around in a wide arc, smashing the flat of the blade against the back of Forget's head. There was a sound at contact like that of fingers being caught in a car door. The man slumped forward onto the couch, then to the floor.

"Are you all right?" Mats asked Carlo and received a nod in reply. Mats turned to Angela, who was still standing with both hands over her mouth in a noiseless scream.

"We don't care about your husband or the life you live here away from the family," he said. "We're interested in Leca. Don't lie to me! Tell me what you know."

"Is he dead?" she asked, looking at the unmoving figure on the floor.

"Not yet. The information. Quickly!"

Angela sobbed. "What is it you want to know?"

"Does this Leca deal in drugs?"

"Yes." The fear in her eyes had been replaced by resignation.

"Why did our question make your husband attack Carlo?"

"My husband needs no reason to attack Carlo. It was Nando and Carlo who forced him out of Ajaccio, and tore me from my family, by not offering Marc the protection of the Guibegas."

"We would not let him sell drugs through the family's operations," said Carlo, pressing the rolled-up portion of the bottom of his shirt to the three-inch gash below his chest.

"That wasn't the reason he attacked Carlo," Mats said urgently. "Don't try to hide anything!"

"My husband works for Leca. Leca supplies and Marc distributes."

"And uses."

"And uses," admitted Angela, her head drooping to her chest. "Will he be all right?"

Mats ignored her question. "How does Leca get the drugs into the country?"

"At first he hid them in the coffee imports. The coffee stops detection by dogs, but for the past few years the authorities have been checking coffee shipments very carefully. Marc still uses the small bags of coffee to hide the drugs that he supplies locally, though."

"You said 'at first.' How does he import the drugs now?" As she gave her information, Mats had purposely changed the tone of his voice, his harshness diminished. "Give us the information and we will treat you fairly."

"It is more than your husband has offered you these last years," added Carlo.

"Leca killed a man for his dog—one trained to detect drugs. He brought the animal here and tested all types of masking methods on it. The dog was always able to detect the drugs, always, except when placed in coffee beans. Then one day the dog couldn't detect any drugs at all. It turned out that Marc had just brought two canvases from his studio and the smell of the oils was still strong. Leca was the first to figure out what was obscuring the dog's sense of smell. He made us promise under threat of death that we would not divulge his discovery that fresh oil paint masked the drugs." She stopped for a breath, but Mats' glare urged her on.

"Leca became an art dealer, buying my husband's canvases. The crates he ships them to the mainland in have false bottoms, allowing many kilos to be smuggled in each container. If the canvases aren't new enough, he puts some broken tubes of oil in with them. The ironic thing is that in order to do it, he has to sell the paintings, and in doing so he has made my husband wealthy. Patrons and collectors now commission Marc's landscapes, and he no longer has to forge the Impressionists."

"Tell me about this Leca. How often does he come to Calvi?"

The more openly Angela talked, the more her Guibega heritage became apparent. She stood taller, her straight back and shoulders showing the proud attitude Mats had noticed in the other Guibegas. "He first came to Calvi about eight years ago. He claimed to be Corsican, from Bastia, but I have my doubts that that is true. He recruited my husband with the promise of free drugs to run his distribution. Within the year, he was supplying most of the west coast. Now he comes only once a month or so."

"When is he expected again?" Mats asked. He was sure she was withholding nothing from him now.

"He was just here two days ago, and he left with a shipment of three crates with at least five of Marc's works. He does not tell us when he will return."

Mats had watched the steady pulse of blood from the man's arm as his wife had given him the information. It had been steady but slow. The man would have a concussion but was in no danger.

"Will he live?" Angela asked as Carlo bent over her husband.

"Bandage his arm. The drugs will kill him before the Guibega have to," answered Carlo with a hiss.

"Angela." Mats took the woman by the shoulders and looked deep into her eyes. "Do not fear the Guibega or the Falconi. No matter what has happened, or the guilt you feel, you will be accepted back into the family. You never really left. You are still a Guibega. If you free yourself of this filth, go back to Ajaccio. They will accept you as before. You have my word."

Carlo stood, lifting Marc Forget onto the couch. The painter moaned softly in response to the movement.

"One last thing," said Mats. "Do not tell anyone what you have told us about Leca." He added, "I will know if you do." Mats looked directly at Angela. "Tell your husband that we ran out of the house thinking we killed him." He did not have to ask if she understood. Angela kept nodding as she sat on the couch, resting her husband's head in her lap.

Carlo followed Mats from the room, stopping to pick up Forget's knife, a two-edged blade with a blood groove down its length.

They stopped to buy antiseptic, gauze, and adhesive tape at a Pharmacia at the edge of Calvi. Carlo had taken off his shirt, revealing a network of scars that covered his left shoulder and back. Mats was astounded by what he saw— evidence of a life of violence he had only suspected before he'd seen his companion sidestep Forget's knife attack.

As Mats drove, Carlo taped adhesive butterfly bandages every half-inch along the cut on his chest, closing it neatly. The knife had penetrated only a fourth of an inch, not deep enough to cut muscles or major vessels, allowing for easy closure of the wound, but still Carlo added several two-inch strips of tape extending from his shoulder over the cut to his hip. They would remind him not to stretch and accidentally reopen the wound.

"Please stop," Carlo said when they had been on the road for a little less than an hour.

Mats pulled to the side of the road, and Carlo pushed open the door and threw up. His face was pale, while the wound under the tape was red and swollen with the edges of the cut already turning grey. A hand to Carlo's head told Mats that he was spiking a fever.

Mats lowered the passenger seat so that Carlo might rest more comfortably, then drove the old car hard while he phoned Jennette at the Alta Mira on his cell.

"Carlo has been cut, and his wound is acting much worse than it should. Get a doctor. We will be there in forty-five minutes."

"We have a doctor. I will have him phone you."

Seven miles farther along the rock-strewn countryside, Mats' cell phone rang.

"Hello. This is Doctor Theo Debove. Is this Mr. Falconi?"

"Yes."

"Could you describe Carlo's wound and his condition?"

Mats described the cut and Carlo's treatment. "Forty-five minutes after he was cut, he started throwing up."

"And what is his condition now?"

Mats glanced at Carlo where he lay next to him before putting his attention back on the road. "He is pale and breathing rapidly. When I felt him a few minutes ago he was feverish, and the wound was red and angry-looking with the edges looking almost blue."

"Carlo has been wounded before," said the doctor. "I doubt that he is in shock, especially if he had the ability to tape his own wound. I suspect the blade was poisoned. How far are you from the Alta Mira now?"

"I'm guessing half an hour," said Mats, the tires on the car squealing as he took a turn one-handed, the other on the phone.

"Good. I will meet you there. It will save ten minutes in getting him to the hospital."

Mats remembered parts of the narrow two-lane road. Driving up to Calvi, the pigs and goats one frequently saw—splotches of paint on their sides declaring ownership—made the scene picturesque. Now it was just a narrow road as he pushed the old Renault to its limits. He pulled into the parking lot of the Alta Mira, sending gravel across the driveway and coming to a stop just outside the archway to the restaurant. Waiting for him stood Jennette, her husband, and a small man who rushed to the side of the car as it stopped. He opened the flimsy door and felt Carlo's neck, held back his eyelid, and stuck a needle in his arm.

"Carry him inside. Don't let him try to walk."

Inside they lay Carlo on a cot in a small day room behind the kitchen. The doctor placed a cuff on his arm and examined the wound, removing the tape that Carlo had applied. The wound immediately spread open, angry and engorged.

"There are three likely poisons that could have been used. It would help if we had the blade," said Doctor Debove as he took a swab of the now bleeding gash.

"I think it is in the back seat of the car. Carlo picked it up."

"Bring it here, but be careful."

Mats brought the knife back inside the restaurant and gave it to the doctor.

"That's a nasty piece of work," said Debove as he took the six-inch double-sided blade by the handle and sniffed the cutting edge. He licked his index finger and passed it along the edge of the steel, bringing it up to touch the tip of his tongue lightly. Without saying a word, he went to a black leather case that was sitting on the table and took out a vial. Taking a measured amount of the liquid out with a disposable syringe and tapping out a bubble, he came back and injected Carlo for a second time. Returning to his bag, he took out a plastic bottle that Mats recognized as contact lens saline and squirted it into the open wound until it was empty.

"It was fortunate that I was at the hospital when Jennette got hold of me. We are one of the two depositories for antidotes on Corsica. The other is in Bastia and would not have done. I brought the three most likely antidotes with me. This is a neural toxin derived from pit viper venom." The doctor held up the knife by its handle. "It was the most probable culprit of the three, having been used on a cutting instrument and with the signs you gave me over the phone. It is good that you arrived as soon as you did, though."

"What can we do for him now?" asked Mats, looking at the unconscious Carlo.

"Just let him rest. When he awakes, give him plenty of water – a little wine is all right— and soup. I gave him something to take care of any breathing difficulties as well as put him to sleep. The antidote will work quickly, but the periphery nerves have already been affected. It will take several days for the pain and fever to subside and for feeling to return. He should be kept quiet until then. It was good that it was a cut rather than a puncture. If it had passed through a major artery or vein, the poison would have acted much more quickly, and he would not have been so lucky."

Mats watched as Debove pressed the edges of the cut together and quickly started stitching them with short, quick movements. In seconds the entire length was held together with twenty tight, neat sutures.

"The tissue is swollen. When it heals, it will be puckered. It will not look as good as the Legion physician's work on his shoulder. I will be back tomorrow to check on him. Call me if he does not do what I have told you. Now I have to get back to the hospital."

Without waiting for a reply, the small man picked up his bag. At the door, he turned and said, "It is an honor to meet you, Mr. Falconi."

When the doctor had left, Mats noted, "I didn't ask him about payment."

"Theo Debove is a Guibega, Signor Falconi. It is a measure of the discrimination the Guibega receive from the French that Theo, despite his brilliance as a student, found it necessary to obtain entrance to medical school by using his mother's name, rather than Guibega," laughed Jennette. "He would have been affronted had you asked about payment. Carlo's wound and poisoning will not be reported."

"I will stay with Carlo while he recovers. Can you recommend a place to stay?"

"It would be an honor if you stay with us. We have a room and you will be near Carlo. Besides, you will not have to worry about eating. There is also something that you must know. Since you are going to be spending time in Corsica."

The tension of the drive back from Calvi was beginning to leave Mats. It was the first time he'd had a chance to talk with Jennette since she had taken over the kitchen at the keep where he had found the treasure. Since then he had learned much about the woman. Not only did she run the restaurant, but she also directed the brokering of the wine produced by the Guibegas and managed the family properties.

" And what is that?"

Mats saw a slight smile curl the side of her mouth and an uplift of the corners of her eyes. "It is because you are a Falconi. The Frenchman that you bought the land from on the hill. It seems that the permit system on Corsica had defeated him, and he spent lots of money on an architect's drawings, and on bringing water and power up to the ruin, but he was not allowed to restore or add to the structure."

"And the permits that are so much of a problem?"

"A problem for a Frenchman—not for a Guibega, and certainly not for a Falconi."

"And why is that?"

"We have people in the correct agencies."

"I take it you have looked at the property?"

"I don't have to."

"Jennette, could you please be a little more unclear?" Mats laughed and watched her smile like the cat that had eaten the canary.

"I said that I had not looked at it, not that I didn't know it. It is well known to every Guibega."

"And you think I will be able to sell it at a profit?"

"I don't think you would sell this land, Signor Falconi."

"Jennette, I understand that you are a fine business-woman, as well as the best cook on Corsica. Tell me the real reason you are telling me this."

Jennette laughed and reached behind her for a bottle of wine and two glasses. "Because it was your ancestral home, and we have started to restore it for you."

Paris, France, September, 2000

Suzanne was thrilled to hear that Mats was arriving in Paris by plane that evening. There were no direct flights to anywhere from Corsica, not even Paris. Everything connected through Marseille. It had been seven days since she'd last seen him in Monte Carlo. As busy as her days had been, she couldn't help but think back to the night in Monte Carlo when they had become lovers. She was certain it had not just been an infatuation, a one-night fling, but there was a doubt, not about her own feelings but about Mats'. It was small, but it was nagging, a shadow at the back of her mind. Part of it was that she had given herself to him so completely, but it had only been one evening. They had talked almost every day, but it was not the same as being together. One thing was for certain: she missed him with every fiber in her body.

The burden of working with the experts to move and preserve the library had fallen heavily on her. Professor Gilbert, whom she had expected to be a thorn in her side, had instead aided and supported her in every instance. Every now and then he would catch himself being pedantic and laugh, but he could not conceal the pride he took in the glory the discovery of the library had given his department.

Suzanne had suggested the cave be maintained as an in-situ museum for the residents of Allos and for the people of France. It was impossible to leave the original volumes in the cave, of course, now that it had been opened, but she had promised the Mayor of Allos that faithful reproductions of all the books would be placed in exactly the same positions as the originals. The scant furniture, consisting of only the desks and shelving, would also be copied and left in the cave, as would Nando's van door sealing the opening in the cleft.

She had originally envisioned being in charge, translating each of the works at her leisure. But it was soon apparent to her that this would be impossible at the speed the academic world, fueled by the National Geographic story, was demanding. As she realized the truth of the situation, she suspected Gilbert had seen it even before she had. By the time the sealed containers arrived in Paris, she had already started to delegate.

Gilbert had surprised her not only with his support but also with his knowledge of the ancient texts and his ability to translate the ancient Greek and Arabic. For the first time, she saw the ability that had brought him to his present position in the academic community. Up till now, she had not seen him carry his full load of work, but the prospect of his name being linked with a major discovery had rekindled in him a scholastic zeal that Suzanne had not seen in him before.

Over the three weeks, eighteen hours a day, with only the two days with Mats in Monte Carlo taking her away from her labors, Suzanne had worked on the library constantly. But her energy had begun to falter. The books had been characterized as to their value and rarity. There were five that were completely unique, four sets of duplicates, and some early examples of works that had become popular in later generations and thus were well known. She had divided up the work of translation among the scholars in the Institute and had started photocopying the originals, contracting for authentic replicas to be fabricated for study and for those to be replaced in the cave. All was in progress, but now Mats was coming, and she found it hard to focus on the tasks at hand.

Mats had told Suzanne of Leca over the phone, and he had described Carlo's brush with death. He always called late at night, but he still had the impression that he was interrupting her at work. He had not expected to be away from her this long. He knew that returning to Corsica was something that he had to do, but he'd expected that two or three days would be enough to fulfill whatever his dream had tried to foretell. Carlo's poisoning and recovery had taken six days – six days that Mats had spent at Carlo's side. Being away from Suzanne was hard on him. As the week wore on, his insecurity worked to persuade him that the night they'd spent together had just been her gift to him for the discovery of the library, not the genuine love they had both professed. On the phone their words were of love, but she sounded tired, as if she would rather end the call and get back to work or sleep. There was just enough doubt for Mats to worry about what their next meeting would be like.

Locating Leca was proving more difficult than he had imagined. He had so far been unable to find a trace of the man, either in Corsica's art circles or in the drug world of France. The police he had contacted had provided little help. Mario had joined Mats and the recuperating Carlo after his help at the find was no longer needed. It was good to have his two bookends together again.

Mats had read the third volume written by Thomaso. It dealt exclusively with the stories told to him by his father and grandfather and his own dreams. There had been dreams like Mats' own, but of different times, different generations, different feats of valor. Yet, as with Mats, the dreams spoke of truths and experiences known by the ancestor who had lived them. Thomaso had suspected he might be able to call on these memories rather than let them enter his sleep at random, but his writings revealed that he was not yet able to accomplish this.

The sword was another enigma Mats was trying to figure out. Ever since he had used it in the fracas with Angela's husband, stabbing Marc Forget in the arm, he had spent some time every day practicing with it. The skill had come easily to him in disabling Forget and now, with practice, his movements and techniques connected with fluidity; it was the type of skill that should be gained only by hours, even years, of practice and instruction. Yet it had come to Mats just as the dreams had come—seemingly effortlessly.

Both in the second volume and in the journal, Thomaso had mentioned his skill with the battle axe and his seamanship, talents which were his birthright. The first time Mats had read of this, he had thought Thomaso was simply describing a family trait, like being good at math. But since he had started practicing with the sword, he'd realized that Thomaso was describing instinctive behavior, learned and refined over previous generations. Like birds returning to their nesting place, his unexpected skill was instinctive. Mats' suspicion of what Thomaso was describing was confirmed when he purchased a wooden axe with a forty-centimeter handle at a hardware shop. Back at the Alta Mira, he confidently threw the weapon at the door jamb with a two-handed overhand motion and noted without surprise that it stuck with a thunk in the wood only inches from where he had aimed.

Mats had Carlo and Mario drop him off at the Bibliothèque Nationale, sending them on to finalize the paperwork on the export licenses for the wholesaling of French wine. With care, he should not have to dip any further into the treasure recovered in the wall of the keep.

Mats had a different treasure on his mind as he flashed his pass, running up the stairs to the same dark hallway he had crossed on the day he first met Suzanne. He was not prepared for the changes that confronted him.

The old frame door had been replaced with a heavy metal one with locks and alarms. It looked out of place in the dimly lit corridor. Inside, the counter had been removed, as well as the partition wall at the back of the room. Before him was a series of three tables. On one was a Nikon camera on a tripod secured to the table edge by a C-clamp arrangement and next to it another high-end Nikon digital, showing that nothing was being left to chance. The other two tables were laden with copies of the books they had found. Behind the third table, bending over one of the original texts, were Suzanne and Professor Gilbert.

"Hello." Mats stepped into the room and advanced toward Professor Gilbert with his hand outstretched in typical American fashion. "I heard my little journal helped you make a discovery. Congratulations."

Professor Gilbert shook Mats' hand. Mats knew from what Suzanne had told him over the phone that Gilbert had worked the situation to the department's best advantage and that she was happy with his help. Mats was glad to hear that Gilbert had assisted Suzanne with the extraordinary amount of work necessary to process, preserve, and delegate the translations of the original texts. The academic community had begun to consider him if not its discoverer, at least its gatekeeper. There was much credit to be shared, and she seemed happy to share it, although Mats could tell she jealously guarded the credit for the actual mechanism of the discovery.

"Mademoiselle De Lacy, how nice to see you again." Mats took her hand and squeezed it lightly. The look she gave him told him that the difficult nights he had spent trying to get to sleep, worrying about her feelings for him, had been unnecessary. She positively glowed with his touch.

"Monsieur Falcon." Suzanne nodded. "The library is even more spectacular than your journal indicated. It's the finest intact collection of manuscripts discovered in this century. What's even more exciting is that its existence wasn't even suspected. You have a good deal of credit due you for its discovery, and perhaps a reward. Without your journal, we wouldn't even have been aware of the library, let alone its location."

Mats saw the beginning of a blush starting to rise from her neck, conveying the message that she had missed him.

"I want no credit and certainly no reward," said Mats, catching an audible sigh of relief from Gilbert. "You translated the journal and must have done quite a piece of detective work. My little book only spoke in broad terms as to the location. Certainly, you and the professor deserve all the credit. After all, I am not even a Frenchman."

Out of the corner of his eye, Mats watched Professor Gilbert nod rapidly several times, apparently glad that an American could so quickly see the reality of his shortcomings. Mats' mouth twitched, suppressing a smile.

"Still, you do deserve some credit," Suzanne pressed.

"No," Mats said firmly. "You can say the journal belonged to an anonymous collector who wishes to keep his identity unknown. I'd be upset if my name were connected in any way with a cultural treasure of France."

"As you wish, Monsieur Falcon," said Gilbert with a quieting hand extended toward Suzanne. As Mats had suspected, the professor would not be averse to claiming the discovery, rather than sharing it with some American who had lucked into his office looking for someone to translate a notebook.

"Thank you, Professor," said Mats. "I knew I could depend on you."

Mats looked at Suzanne and saw the effort she exerted to keep from laughing.

"I don't want to interfere with the work you are doing, but I would like to hear about what you have done and your plans for the books. Would it be possible for me to offer you both dinner after you finish work? You could fill me in on what has happened since I left Paris."

Nodding her head as she glanced at her watch, Suzanne replied, "I'm sure Professor Gilbert and I would be happy to do so, Mr. Falcon. It is the least we can do to show appreciation for your contribution. Is that not right, Professor?"

"Absolutely. But I can't do it tonight, as I have a meeting scheduled. I would appreciate if you would entertain Mr. Falcon, my dear. I'll finish up here. In fact, you can leave now if you wish."

"That is impossible," stammered Suzanne. "It will take me at least an hour and a half to finish here and get cleaned up and ready." Suzanne bent over and wrote something on a piece of paper. "Here is a restaurant. It is quiet, has a fine chef, and is not too expensive. I'll let you make a reservation, and I'll meet you there at eight."

Mats looked at the note. It read: *What is the name of your hotel? I'll meet you there.*

"Fine," Mats said. "I will look forward to hearing about how you found the cave and the work you have done with the books. I am staying at the Crillon while I conclude my business in France." Mats turned away from Gilbert, winked at Suzanne, and mouthed "Crillon," leaving no doubt that the hotel would be their meeting place, not the restaurant.

"I'll see you at eight."

Mats shook Gilbert's hand once again and smiled at Suzanne before turning and leaving the office.

"Can you believe it?" asked Gilbert, rhetorically. "He doesn't even understand the importance of the discovery. I guess if you can afford the rates of the Hotel de Crillon, you do not value treasures of the mind for their true worth."

Suzanne entered the lobby of the Crillon, hesitating only a moment before deciding against checking at the desk for a message. Mats had made a point in Monte Carlo of keeping their relationship private, and his performance with Professor Gilbert left no doubt that he wanted it to remain so, while she wanted to proclaim it to the world. She would look first in the lounge. If he was not there, she would use one of the private house lines to connect to his room, a line that would ensure her own anonymity.

The lounge was small but divided with seating arrangements and large plants to create areas where conversations could be held in private. She felt conspicuous with her overnight case slung over her shoulder, hopefully disguised as a large purse. Her worries about propriety were quickly replaced by worries of another sort as she saw Mats in a secluded corner. He was leaning forward in deep conversation with a woman with flaming red hair. She was intently listening to him, dressed expensively in a manner that accentuated her figure. As Suzanne moved toward them, she became less sure of herself, trying her best to deny the jealousy that she instantly felt. Her uncertainty, coupled with her resentment of the other woman, caused her to fumble her purse as she neared the couch on which the woman was seated. Mats saw her and stood.

"Here's the friend I was telling you about. Audrey, this is Suzanne De Lacy. Suzanne, this is my good friend, Audrey Kent. She eats at my restaurant at least once a week when she's in California."

"So nice to meet you, Suzanne," said the woman, offering her hand without rising, but moving to one side, making room for Suzanne on the couch. "Mats has just been telling me you've discovered a fantastic treasure of medieval manuscripts. My Lord, the way he described your accomplishments, I thought you would be my age." She turned toward Mats. "You didn't tell me she was beautiful as well as young."

Suzanne took the woman's hand, recognizing the delicate scent of Joy, pleasingly noticeable from her extended arm.

"Like one of your paintings, Audrey," said Mats, smiling. "Why describe something that only takes one look to understand?" He turned to Suzanne. "Audrey lives half the year in California and the other half in Texas. She owns so many French Impressionist paintings that the Houston Art Museum constructed a new wing just to house her collection. I've been asking her about a Corsican artist, Mark Forget. Audrey's not only familiar with the man; she knows a dealer who sells his works."

"The artist, Forget, is a forger," explained Audrey, "as is often the case with Corsican painters. But he is one of the best, or at least he used to be. In his early years he would reproduce a painting by any of the Impressionists on demand. He has even painted canvases that passed as originals and that have been credited for years by museums. Only recently his own work has become sought after, as the penalties for forgery have become more severe. I am only interested because the new building needs more exhibits than my little ol' collection can provide. I thought an exhibit of the more famous forgeries would be unique and if successful could even be swapped with other museums. But tell me about your discovery, dear," she added, changing the subject.

Suzanne looked at the woman, then at Mats, but remained silent. Now that her eyes had adjusted to the light, she could see that despite the red hair, Audrey Kent was older than she had first thought, very well kept and still beautiful but with the small wrinkles of a well-maintained age. Suzanne's self-confidence surged back and with it her unease that she was carrying a large overnight purse.

"Oh, I'm sorry," Audrey said. "Mats told me it's still something of a secret outside your group. But don't worry. I won't mention it, scout's honor." Then, smiling like the Texas poker player she was, Audrey added, "Of course, it would be nice if we could arrange for the library to be exhibited exclusively in my little ol' museum in Dallas." Suzanne realized that Audrey had mistaken her silence for reluctance to discuss the find.

"Audrey is used to the intrigues of the art world," said Mats, "and is not only a friend but has my complete trust. I owe her a favor. Please tell her about the find."

This woman carries herself in a manner that suggests she's been rich long enough to be comfortable with it, thought Suzanne. "How did you acquire your paintings, Mrs. Kent?" she asked. Despite Mats' approval, she still wanted to know more about this woman before she told her any details about the manuscripts.

A twinkle came into Audrey's eye. "I spent some time in Paris before the war. In fact, I was in school in London when it broke out. In late forties, my husband and I came back to Paris. We just liked the Impressionists and started collecting them. You could still do that in those days."

Suzanne looked more closely at Audrey as she spoke. This woman must have been ravishing in her youth ... and this youth must have occurred far earlier than either her first impression or even her second guess at her age if she had been married just after World War II.

"We just kind of hung on to them," Audrey continued. "It wasn't until the seventies that things went absolutely wild with the Japanese buying up Impressionist art. But enough about ancient times. Tell me about yourself. Are you married?"

Suzanne felt taken aback by the question. She had just decided to tell Audrey about the library and now she was being asked about her personal life. "No, I'm not married, except to the manuscripts that Mats told you about. They take up fourteen hours of each day. Did he tell you how they were found?"

"Didn't you bring her a notebook to translate?" Audrey asked Mats.

"Yes, one my father had given me. It only mentioned that the books had been buried in a cave, however. Suzanne somehow pieced together the exact location."

"Egel was a great man, Mats," sighed Audrey in a tone that made Suzanne think she would have liked more from Mats' father than simply being a guest at his restaurant.

"I had a great deal of help and a lot of luck," said Suzanne after a silence that had become uncomfortable. "One manuscript might interest you particularly. It is a description of paintings transferred to the Papal Palace in Avignon in 1307, when Avignon became the seat of the Roman Catholic Church. We have not investigated it thoroughly yet. What makes the work so interesting to me is that the author used a pen-and-ink sketch of the basic outline of the paintings, along with his description of the work and a biography of the artist. As I said, we have only given this particular work a first rough translation for classification purposes. We have not advertised it to the academic community or to National Geographic. I think that it will eventually be worthy of its own issue. It still has to be studied in detail. I don't even know if it was to be an inventory or a brochure for viewers not well versed in art. But it is unique."

"My Lord! That one book alone would be worth a fortune!" Audrey's eyes reflected the interest that was obvious in her voice. "I could help you with the identification of the works and their present owners or locations. I suspect a lot of people and museums are going to be very upset, maybe even mine. I simply must see it before I leave. Would that be possible?"

"I'm sure it can be worked out, Audrey," said Mats, standing. "But right now, I'm afraid I have to go. Suzanne has agreed to be my principal in the purchase of wines from Provence, and I know she has an engagement later this evening, so our time is limited."

Suzanne took the heavy hint and stood up as well. "It's very nice to meet you, Audrey. I'm sure I can arrange for you to see the art manuscript, but please don't mention it to anyone else. It's hard enough to give it the attention it deserves without a horde of outside authorities demanding that you give their demands top priority." She took Audrey's hand as the lady rose. *This is the only thing that Mats has asked of me other than keeping Thomoso's volumes. It is a small part in exchange for his part in the discovery of the library,* she thought. *Mats has a talent for judging people. She already liked Audrey Kent.*

Mats took Audrey's other hand. "Thank you for the information on Forget and his agent. Keep my interest in them to yourself. It's extremely important. And be careful. There is danger involved with Forget."

"I will." Audrey pulled Mats' hand gently toward her and gave him a kiss on the cheek, whispering in his ear as she did, "She's a beauty, Mats. I like her."

After Audrey left, as they walked slowly toward the elevator, Suzanne asked, "What was that all about?"

"I didn't know it before, but Audrey is staying here at the Crillon while in Paris. We bumped into each other in the lobby. She's here looking at prospective purchases for her collection and knows Forget and a man who might be the one I'm searching for. It is a fortunate surprise that we met."

"Leca?" Suzanne asked as the door to the lift opened.

"Not now. I'll explain later."

"I have a surprise for you as well."

"What's that?" asked Mats, happy for the change in subject.

"I found a packet of maps and charts in the back of one of the books."

"One of Thomaso's books? How did we miss it at the cave?"

"It was in one of the duplicates, a rather sloppy Norman French translation of the *Al-Kitab Al-Rujari*, Roger's Book. I only discovered that the packet had Thomaso's name written on it when I got back to Paris. I was able to place the book aside as my responsibility. The packet was thin and contained only five charts, but I have the impression it was hidden in the book on purpose."

"What is Roger's Book?" asked Mats.

"To know that, you must know more about the Normans in Italy. Early in the eleventh century, Norman knights with weapons, mounts, and precious little else other than their fighting ability started drifting down toward the Italian peninsula from France. Sicily was at the time under Muslim rule for well over two hundred years."

"Sicily was an Arab land?"

"Yes, but they were Moors rather than Arabs. A family of brothers by the name of de Hauteville was among the Normans."

"Suzanne, the book? You were going to tell me about the book." Mats could not help teasing her. She was like a professor giving her favorite lecture. Her eyes shone, and her words almost made the men she was telling him about gain real form and substance.

"Oh yes, I was coming to that. Well, one of the youngest of the brothers de Hauteville was Robert. Later he was known as Robert Guiscard, the cunning one. By 1059 he controlled most of southern Italy in the name of the Pope. As a reward for his loyalty, the Pope made him the Duke of Sicily. It was a cunning entitlement on the Pope's part. The new duke and his fighting men were now in Sicily and less a threat to the Pope."

"Roger, remember? Roger's Book?"

"I was just getting to that. Two years before he was made Duke of Sicily, Robert was joined by his twenty-six-year-old brother, Roger. They formed a brothers' partnership like the world had never seen. Until Robert died at sixty-eight, they worked together to become the dominant fighting force in the Mediterranean.

"Roger became known as the 'Great Count.' In Sicily, he established four official languages—Arabic, Latin, Greek, and Norman French. He had a passion for science and poetry, but his most famous deed was commissioning a great book of geographical knowledge, one that stated that the earth was round three hundred years before Columbus. It is still known in the Arab world as *Al-Kitab Al-Rujari* — Roger's Book."

"And Thomaso's maps? Do they look important?"

"I don't know. Two of them look like lessons in chart-making. They are definitely in Thomaso's hand. One is of Corsica, one is of the countryside around a castle in Normandy, and one is of the route from Normandy to Marseille. The other two don't look finished—they have no names for any of the features—but they are drawn in great detail. One is of a town on a large river, and one is of a city on a large body of water, but neither is labeled as to the name of the river or the town. And of course, there are no latitude or longitude markings, just great detail about the waters and the various buildings in the towns. A computer search to match them up might prove successful, possibly assigning names to the water features and towns."

"Don't press," Mats said. "There's something much more important to occupy us right now, something so urgent we have to take care of it first." As the elevator door closed, Mats put his hand around her waist and pulled her toward him. She dropped her bag. Her hand cupping the back of his neck, drawing him to her for a kiss.

Yes, something much more pressing to take care of first, he thought. *Then take care of again, and perhaps even again.*

It was their third evening together. Mats was exhausted, and he could only guess that Suzanne was more so. Every evening they had dinner after she had finished an eleven-hour day at the Bibliothèque, which usually entailed at least one interview. She was existing on seven hours of sleep, if what they were doing several times a night could be termed sleep. He propped himself on one elbow and gazed at her as she slumbered, the soft light of dawn fil-tering through the curtains.

As if sensing she was being observed, Suzanne smiled, letting a feeling of contentment wash over her before turning toward Mats and opening her eyes.

"Good morning," he said.

"Good morning. Was I snoring?" she asked, her smile widening.

"You don't snore. A snoozle is as close as you get."

"What time is it?"

Mats raised himself, looking at the morning light just now filtering through the sheer curtains and trying to estimate the hour by the soft rose glow. Then he looked over Suzanne at the clock on her bedside table. "Three minutes before six."

Suzanne rolled over and shut off the alarm that was about to go off, then resumed looking at Mats. "I want to get into the office by seven this morning. We are copying the last volume today."

"You have certainly accomplished a lot in five days."

"The techniques are well established, and we have access to all we need in the building at the Bibliothèque. It was listing all the things to be done and assigning the personnel and the timetable that took the time. But except for the demand for interviews and requests to see the works from around the world, everything is running smoothly now. Today is different because a National Geographic crew is coming to take pictures of the restoration process and I'm to be interviewed."

"And Gilbert is behaving?"

"He has actually been wonderful. I've never seen this side of him. I have been allowed to do all that I asked for in Monte Carlo. Actually, now that everything is organized, I realize that I asked for too much. With everything set up, I find that I'm mainly doing public relations and administrative work. The translating I used to do in my old position is being done by others."

"Would it be possible for you to take some time off from the office during the day?" asked Mats. "It would be like a date. We would have time to enjoy each other, not just in the evenings, as wonderful as they are."

Suzanne smiled, thinking how much she would enjoy walking hand in hand with Mats, showing him all her special places. Perhaps she would even introduce him to her father at the D'Orsay. It was indeed possible for her to take a day or two off for herself. The more she thought about it, the more Mats became a priority over the work she had left to do at the Bibliothèque.

Suzanne moved toward him, kissing him fully on the lips, then tossing the covers aside and getting up. "There might be an opportunity after today, but not if I don't get to the office, and I still have to stop by my apartment, shower, and put on some fresh clothes. Stop looking at me like that. If everything goes well, I should be able to get away earlier this afternoon. There is no time for what you have in mind this morning."

After the National Geographic shoot and interview, Suzanne found that she was slowly resigning herself to leaving the manuscripts in Gilbert's care and spending more time with Mats. The excitement of finding the library and setting up the preservation and translation of the texts, and especially the announcement of it all to the world, had been exhilarating. Her training and personality had been perfect for the tasks. Even Professor Gilbert had admitted that she was a much better face for the project than he would have been, although he had made certain that he was in any number of the photographs. Now she could see that most of the work that remained would be administrative. She admitted to herself that she liked the action of discovery more than the task of maintenance, and that she would find the remaining tasks busy work after the excitement of uncovering the cave and the preservation of the works.

At first, she had thought it unrealistic when Mats suggested she drop her work and spend time with him. She had thought she would never be able to leave the books until they were finished being translated and were on display. But as the days passed, and the evenings with Mats loving her and being loved in return, she felt her priorities start to change. Mats added details to his plans that included her each night. He was sensitive to her needs, always maintaining that the library should be her first priority, but perhaps since the groundwork had been accomplished, she could be more of an overseer of the project. Suzanne thought that Mats had divined the truth: that her own personality would eventually make her work on the library feel stale, and that she would end up feeling trapped by the project rather than the master of it.

She took two days off after the final interview and pictures from National Geographic. It had taken an extra day, as she was photographed in each of the preservation steps and allowed them access to the many photographs they had taken during the uncovering of the cave and the discovery of the library. She had made sure that Gilbert and the individuals she now considered her assistants were also included in the photography. The process was exhausting, and there was no protest at all from Gilbert when she announced that she was taking a couple days off. Gilbert had even smiled and said he thought it would be an excellent idea. To Suzanne, it seemed an indication that he knew or guessed that Mats was the reason.

Chapter Seventeen

The days Mats and Suzanne spent together were magical, and they enjoyed learning more about one another's upbringing and the values each held dear. Paris cooperated with cooler temperatures and brilliant sunshine. The only disappointment was that they were unable to visit Suzanne's father at the D'Orsay. He had gone to Luxembourg for the museum and would not be back for a week.

"I will have to return to the States soon," said Mats as they walked along the west bank of the Seine on their way to the cathedral of Notre Dame.

Suzanne had known that at some point Mats would have to return home. Yet it still upset her as he spoke the words. "How long will you be gone?" she asked, fearing the worst.

"That depends. I thought I would be gone for a month, so I left the Seahawk with a friend looking over it while I was gone. I've got a good staff and crew, so I don't think it has been too much of a burden, but it's not a permanent solution. If I am to spend more time here, I would have to make a more stable arrangement. It also depends on how well the restaurant has been doing."

Suzanne's heart quickened at his words. She had worried about their work becoming an obstacle in their remaining together. Now Mats seemed to be offering a solution, and she felt joy in the prospect.

"Since I saw the Guibegas' winery on Corsica," explained Mats, "I have been planning an export business here, exporting their wine as well as lesser French offerings back to California. It would give me a reason to write off the travel expenses, as well as a tax break for the restaurant. I was hoping that you would become manager of the operation here in Paris, which would give you free travel as well. Carlo and Mario can do most of the work. They have already secured the license and a warehouse a couple miles upstream from here, and they've contracted with several wineries in Provence."

"How much time would that take?" asked Suzanne, thinking of how her work with the library had taken all of her waking moments for the last three weeks.

"At the present very little, but if it is successful, and as your work on the library diminishes, it might take as many as six or seven hours a week."

And it would keep us in touch, thought Suzanne, knowing that was the reason it had been suggested.

"I would keep an office in Ajaccio, because of the Guibegas, but it would look much better on the labels if the export license were from Paris." They had stopped midspan on the Pont Notre-Dame on the Rue de la Cité, facing each other, holding hands. Suzanne could see the conflict on Mats' face and suspected hers showed the same concern.

"Suzanne, dearest, we have just found each other. I suspect we both know it is not just a passing infatuation, that we have something rare and precious. Yet we both have major commitments. You have the library that has made your name academically. I came here to learn about my father, and now I find myself with the opportunity to find his murderer. I am greedy. I want it all, but if I had to choose, I would choose you."

Suzanne dropped his hands, raising hers to his neck, drawing his head down to hers and giving him a kiss that answered him more clearly than any words could. She held the kiss, her eyes closed, not an uncommon sight in Paris; but this moment was so filled with meaning and emotion that no kiss, no embrace in that city had ever mattered more.

On the eighth day after he had arrived in Paris, Mats brought Audrey Kent to the Bibliothèque, introducing her to Professor Gilbert. The book on the papal art collection had already been copied, and an unbound replica lay out next to the original for her inspection, along with a translation from the Latin.

Suzanne had told Mats that Gilbert had first been opposed to showing the manuscript to any outsider, especially an American woman, but since it was the only accommodation that Mats had sought, he agreed. However, Gilbert had still insisted that both Mats and Audrey sign a non-disclosure agreement.

The four of them pored over the copy for two hours. There were forty-two paintings described, all but two with a corresponding sketch. Audrey read the titles and descriptions and looked at each sketch before revealing the work's present location. Some she referred to her iPhone, pulling up information from one of several sites she had open before offering an opinion on where it could most likely be found. A large number of paintings, but fewer than Mats had expected, were still to be found in the Vatican. With each announcement, Gilbert wrote down Audrey's information. Five of the paintings were completely unknown.

"These five are not known to exist at present," said Audrey. "They might have changed titles, or more likely they are in private hands. An expert on medieval art might know more. As Mats told you, my major focus is the Impressionists."

"You are truly a wonderful resource," said Gilbert with the tone of a real compliment. He was as much impressed by Audrey's perfect French as by her expertise in art. With her professed lack of knowledge, she still knew more than many of the contacts he had been offered by his friends and fellow scholars.

"I'd like you to see these as well," said Suzanne, taking a manila file from a file cabinet behind her.

Gilbert put up a hand as if to stop her, then brought it back down.

Suzanne spread a series of single-page color copies out on the desk in front of them. Each had an intricate design around a large letter that started a paragraph. Some had birds, vines, or flowers intertwined, but all were highlighted with a brilliant red hue, vibrant, defining the illustration.

"These are copies of some of the title pages and chapter headings of the other books," explained Suzanne. "Some of the scribes were truly artists. I thought you might like to see them. The red pigment used here is unique. We have not seen its like and we are trying to find its origin. It appears to be local to the area of the cave, as it is seen only in the copies and not what we consider the original volumes from which the copies were made."

"They're magnificent," said Audrey. "Professor Gilbert, Mats may have told you already, but I am one of the directors of the Houston Art Museum. Professor, after all this hubbub is over, would you consider letting me show this volume in my museum?" She motioned to the work with the descriptions of the paintings. "I would pair it with the copies that Suzanne has shown us. It would be under glass and under the highest security, and I would hope you would be my honored guest at the opening of the display. It could be part of a traveling show that would make your find famous in the art world as well as the literary world."

Again Gilbert looked as if he would refuse. His eyebrows pinched together, and two frown lines showed on his forehead.

"Professor," said Suzanne, putting the copies back in the file, "it would be your decision, of course, but I think that what Mrs. Kent suggests is an excellent idea. The book itself transcends literature and art. Not only would it increase the exposure of the library, but it would bring in substantial fees."

"I agree with you that the book is unique, and while it is part of the library, it might well be considered by itself. How much time would it require to put together such an exhibit?" asked Gilbert.

"I think that you and Mrs. Kent could compose the contents. We already have the copies made and digitized. But this brings up something I was going to discuss with you later. All of the work on the preservation and copying of the library is completed. All that is left to do is the translations. The reproductions are being compiled, and Allos has formed a committee to place them in the cave and preserve the site for future generations. My work now is purely administrative, and you are by far the better person for that. I would like to take a sabbatical."

Mats observed the look on Gilbert's face; it read like the book in front of them. This was going to be his coup, his triumph—one to be shared with Suzanne, perhaps, but definitely his.

"What would you do?"

"Even though the National Geographic article is months away from publication, word of the find is now common knowledge. I have been asked by several organizations to give a presentation on the discovery and preservation of the library. An agent has even offered to represent me in securing dates, although I would not consider any before the article came out."

"Would you continue to work with the people from Allos?" asked Gilbert, his features softening and a trace of a smile curling the corners of his mouth.

"Certainly, if that is your wish."

Gilbert moved to his right and gave Suzanne a hug, kissing her on both cheeks.

"It sounds like you've given this much thought. I'll approve the sabbatical, and I wish you well."

CHAPTER EIGHTEEN

Mats was in the oversized tub of their suite. He was sudsing Suzanne's back, the hand-sized loofah sponge provided by the Crillon giving roughness to the soap that oozed out under the gentle pressure of his strokes.

The ornate telephone rang harshly in their suite, ruining the intimacy of the moment. Only Carlo and Mario knew how to reach them at the Crillon, all calls to Mats being on his cell phone, which was turned off or routed through them. Mats kissed Suzanne on the nape of her neck and raised himself out of the tub.

"Carlo wouldn't call unless it was important. I'll be right back."

He stepped gingerly out of the water, ignoring the trail of wet footprints he left on the tile floor.

"Monsieur Falconi?" The voice on the phone was stressed, hesitant with tension. It was not Carlo. "It is Jennette. Carlo thought you would want to hear this immediately."

"Yes, Jennette. What is it?"

"Marc Forget has been murdered."

"When?"

"Last night, just before sunset."

"And Angela? Is she all right?"

"Yes, signore, it was she who brought us the word. It took me a while to calm her down and piece together the story, but she is now safe with us in Ajaccio."

"You were right to phone. Tell me the details. Don't leave anything out."

"Just a second. I'll give the phone to Angela. She can tell you herself."

"Monsieur Falconi, it is Angela."

"Are you all right?"

"Yes, I am now. Jennette has been wonderful."

"What happened? Who murdered your husband?"

"It was Leca."

"Do you know for sure that it was Leca?"

"Yes, I was in the house."

Mats stopped short, taking a deep breath. If she was there, it was a miracle she had not died as well. He should have anticipated Leca's action. "Tell me it all. Don't leave anything out," he said softly into the phone.

"Ever since you and Carlo visited, Marc has been in a state of panic. He was sure Carlo would die, but he didn't tell me about the blade being poisoned. He was badly frightened by you, and the wound in his arm served as a constant reminder of his fear. It was like he was in a vise with Leca on one side and the Falconi and the Guibega on the other. It was hard to say whom he feared most, but Leca provided his livelihood.

"His terror increased his dependence on drugs, and he spent most of his time in our bedroom either taking them or sleeping them off. When he was awake, he would take out his anxiety on me. In the week after you left, I made up my mind to leave him, ignore my pride, and rejoin my family, as you offered.

"I was in the front room, gathering a few items to take with me, when I saw Leca parking across the street from our house. The shutters prevented him from seeing me, but there was no way to slip out of the house without being detected."

"How was it you escaped?" asked Mats, remembering his father lying on the steps of their restaurant as Leca shot him.

"Marc was in the bedroom. He had used drugs and was asleep. We have no back door. I was afraid. I did not want Leca to find me. Without thinking, I threw myself over the back of our front room couch. I slid down the wall into the small space between its back and the wall. I tried to find a comfortable position, but there wasn't one. I had just settled when I heard the door open and Leca entered without the courtesy of a knock. I was terrified. I was certain that my breathing was going to give me away. Leca went past me and into the bedroom.

"I could hear him as he tried to wake Marc. He spoke softly but insistently as he coaxed him back to reality. Even with the couch and the wall between us, I could hear them as Marc came awake. I heard Marc tell him that I was here when he fell asleep and that I must have gone to the market.

"They came into the front room, Marc's bare feet slapping the floor. Leca asked about the bandage on his arm. I could hear the fear in Marc's voice as he answered Leca's questions, which came with increasing force. He asked, 'How did you receive that wound? Where did the man come from? What is his relationship to Angela? Did he say he would return? What did he want to know about me?'" Angela's voice deepened as she mimicked Leca's tone.

"Marc's voice faltered. He tried to lie, but Leca cut him off sharply and in a voice as cold as steel said his only hope was to tell the truth. In almost a whimper, Marc told Leca that Mats had asked about drugs and had talked to me before he came home. Then, when Leca was sure there was no more to learn about you, he asked again about me. Marc repeated that I had been there an hour before and had probably gone to the market.

"Leca said, 'Then we will wait for her, to find out what she can add to our knowledge of this mysterious American,' and told Marc to take seat."

"Leca kept walking, passing back and forth. Marc tried to tell him that things were all right, but Leca cut him off. I had now been wedged against the wall for half an hour. My right arm was numb, but I dared not move.

"Then I heard Marc cry out, 'No...eeeeghh!' I heard his cry, so terrible, then the scrape of the chair legs, followed by the chair tipping over and a thrashing sound—the two men struggling only meters away from my hiding place. Slowly, the sound of movement ceased, and after a minute I heard the sound of a body dropping limply on the tile floor.

"I heard Leca say, 'You cowardly fool. Did you think you could inform on me and live?' His voice was soft, almost apologetic in tone. 'Now only one of us has to wait for your wife, or should I say, your widow.' I was so frightened.

"I heard Leca drag Marc's body back into the bedroom before coming back to the front room and sitting down on the couch. A burst of stale air from the cushions hit my face as he lowered himself to sit. It was stale and dusty, and I thought I was going to sneeze, but fear helped me hold my breath and keep still. I began to lose track of time. He might have been sitting above me for three hours, but in truth it could have been only minutes. I became fearful of dozing off, afraid I would snore or move and make a noise. My body ached, and my arm was now numb beyond pain. Then, just when I felt I could endure no more, Leca stood and said, 'Angela, Angela. Have you somehow discovered my presence? Well, I am sorry that I cannot wait for you any longer. You will know who killed your husband, but you will have no proof, and if you tell people my name, I will come back and finish what I cannot wait to accomplish now.'

"I was sure that Leca was talking to me, teasing me, torturing me in his sadistic way. I thought he would pull the couch away and find me. Instead, I heard his steps cross to the door, which opened and then closed.

"For minutes that seemed like hours, I remained there, listening for any hint of movement or life in the room. Finally, I could no longer endure the pain. I pushed against the wall, giving myself enough room to stand. I rose, bracing myself to find Leca standing there in the room smiling at me, but the room was empty. The feeling in my arm slowly burned its way back. Looking through the bedroom door, I saw Marc lying on his back across the bed. His neck was nearly severed, the garrote that had sliced it still looped around, its wooden handles dangling like earrings toward the floor. He was a bad man, but I still loved him.

"I was afraid that Leca might still be watching the building from the outside, but his car was gone. As dark fell, I phoned Jennette, then slipped out the door and into a passageway between the houses. Less than an hour later, Encio, a cousin I barely remember who lives on the outskirts of Vico, picked me up in his car and drove me to Jennette in Ajaccio."

"Well, you are safe now," said Mats. "Don't contact anyone in Porto. You must remain hidden until Leca is dealt with. Please, let me speak with Jennette again."

"This is Jennette."

"Keep her safe and hidden," said Mats. "I should have realized Leca wouldn't compromise his security by leaving a loose end like Marc Forget around to testify against him." Mats thought for a minute and then added, "Jennette, you did well to call me. He surely knows who I am now. Should anyone see Angela, tell them she has been visiting you since Tuesday. Make sure she is firm with that alibi. Let Encio know as well. That will protect her from being accused of her husband's murder."

Suzanne had followed Mats out of the bath, and after seeing that he would be on the telephone for an extended conversation, she draped the white Crillon bathrobe over his shoulders. She picked up enough of the conversation to know that the call came from Corsica and that some-one had died. She recognized the name, Jennette, as one of Carlo's relatives. She was already dressed when Mats finally hung up the receiver.

"I must hunt him, as he now hunts me," Mats said.

"Who?"

"Leca... Before I left Corsica, Carlo and I fought with an artist who was married to one of Carlo's cousins. He was the one who slashed Carlo. He dealt in drugs, beat his wife."

"This is the man you were talking to Audrey Kent about?"

"Yes. He was working for a drug lord named Leca, the same Leca who murdered my father. I'm telling you this because you might be in danger. An assassin in Falconi's time threatened the Baron and all that he held dear. The same may hold true for us."

Mats turned to Suzanne. He could feel his love for this woman swell inside him. He took her by the hands, and they sat down on the couch facing each other.

"That night in Monte Carlo, I told you that I first started dreaming of the past when I arrived in France. I don't know how much of what I know is the verbal history my father gave me as bedtime stories, or stories from the notebook or Thomaso's volumes. I do know for certain that they have relevance to our present situation. I love you, and I fear for your safety."

"But you are no longer on Corsica. Few know where you are and fewer still know that we are lovers," said Suzanne, squeezing Mats' hands.

"My dreams have changed. They no longer simply familiarize me with an area or tell me of the presence of a hidden treasure. Now it's as if they are warning me of future events. It is as if specific events that happened cen-turies before are being selected and presented to me, to aid me in my present danger. It's no coincidence that this man Leca behaves like the assassin in my dreams. I must accept the threat as truth. And if that is so, then everyone I love is in danger."

Suzanne reached up and touched her fingertips to his cheek. "If that is true, then tell me of your dreams and fears. Not only will it keep me safe, but it will help me to protect you."

"I must find Leca before he finds me, because there is no defense against an assassin."

"But if the police can't find this Leca, how can you expect to do it?"

"I can do it because I now know more than the police do about this man, and because I have my dreams to guide me."

Mats stopped, looking at a wall hanging, an original but uninspired painting of the Seine. He opened his cell phone and hit a phone number.

"Leda."

"This is Mats. I have a question for you. When you went to the ferry to check on Leca, was anything said about his picking up artwork?"

"No, nothing was mentioned about art, and I think they would have mentioned it to me. I was quite insistent about wanting any information about the man, and they seemed quite open. But while I was there, some cases of paintings were picked up. It was a dealer from Paris, not Leca."

"Are you sure?"

"Yes. I was in the office when the man came in to get the bill of lading, three crates full of oil paintings. I thought it unusual for a ferry to be carrying cargo."

"And no mention of Leca? Do you remember the name of the dealer?"

"I remember a gallery name. I saw it on the side of the van." There was a pause in the conversation as Leda scanned her memory. "There was something interesting about the name. I remember looking at it twice. Oh, I remember now. It was called 'Gallery of Flowers.' No, no, 'Gallery of the Lilies.' Yes, that was it. I remember wondering if they were referring to the Fleur-de-Lys of France, but a small water lily was painted beside the name instead. 'Of Paris' was written below the name, I'm quite sure. Do you want me to check on it?"

"No. You've given me all I need. Thanks for the information." Mats hung up the receiver. "Only one more call," he said to Suzanne, ignoring the questions in her eyes.

He touched one of his favorite numbers. "Hello, Audrey. This is Mats. I have a couple questions for you and some inside information for you as payment."

"You rascal," came her response. "What do you want to know?"

"When Forget shows his work in Paris, does he use a particular gallery?"

"Of course he does. One doesn't usually lug his paintings around like some street artist, not unless you ask for a special showing. His more recent ones are all the same size. Large. It's one of Forget's peculiarities. His early works, and of course his forgeries, had varied dimensions."

"What is the name of the gallery?"

"There are two that I know of, the Ambrage and the Gallery D'Ile. Why?"

"Because if you can lay your hands on any of Forget's paintings today, you might be pleasantly surprised at their value next week."

"Why is that, Mats?"

"Because Marc Forget was murdered on Corsica last night."

"Murdered!"

"Audrey, the people in the Gallery D'Ile might be involved or at least know the killer. Don't take chances.

251

And whatever you do, don't let on that you know Forget is dead or that you know me. Make up whatever story you want to about suddenly buying his work, but whatever you do, don't mention my name."

"I understand, Mats. I just happen to know where three of his paintings are hanging right now. And I can get a private showing at my hotel for any that the Gallery D'Ile might have. Honey, when you get back to Marin County, I owe you a dinner. Thanks for the scoop." Audrey hung up with the finality of a woman who was in a hurry.

Mats crossed the room and embraced Suzanne. He held her close for a long time.

"I think I've found a way to locate Leca. He doesn't personally pick up the crates that hold the paintings as they come into the country. He has a gallery do it. But I would bet my bottom dollar that he watches them as they do the pickup, watches to make sure there's no uncommon interest in the packing crates. Still, there is a time when he must lay claim to them, and that is most likely at the gallery. That's where we'll find him. We've lost the opportunity at the ferry, but we know the gallery here."

"Wouldn't it be best to let the police take care of this?" Before Suzanne had finished her sentence, she knew she would lose the argument. God, she loved this man. She realized that she would go after Leca herself if he asked it of her.

"I've spoken to the police, but they did not seem eager to help. 'Nothing but supposition' was their comment. I have the name of an inspector, their supervisor, and have made an appointment. Hopefully I can convince him."

CHAPTER NINETEEN

Carlo and Mario had rented a small warehouse outside of Paris. Built in an era when the River Seine provided much of the transportation to and from the city, it was still too far out to be converted into high-rent office space, yet the trappings of the inevitable transformation were beginning to be seen. A small, well insulated office had been added facing the river, with a large sliding-glass door looking out on the Seine above the loading dock opening to the warehouse. The office was comfortable by French standards. It was raised one story above street level, with a small walkway that looked down on the warehouse floor. There was a bathroom and shower and a small convenience kitchen. The two Guibegas had already brought in two single beds, a sofa, and a table with chairs.

"Carlo and I can stay here rather than at the hotel," said Mario as he showed Mats around the space. "Wine is beginning to fill the warehouse, and we don't have the security alarms installed yet."

Mats thought that a good enough reason, but he also gleaned that the two bookends would probably prefer living in this space than in the hotel with its maid service and fresh daily towels. With parking in the warehouse below and the view of the Seine flowing past, it really was a good location. He walked to the glass expanse looking out on the Seine; an impossibly long, narrow cruise ship was going by, headed downstream before docking in Paris proper. Several smaller boats were headed in the opposite direction only forty meters from where Mats stood, close enough for Mats to see the features of the men at the wheels.

"That's fine. It looks like you will be comfortable. I have an appointment with an inspector at police headquarters in an hour. Would you drop me off there?"

"No problem, boss. Will you need a ride after?"

"No. I'll take a cab back to the hotel."

Mario drove Mats to the Paris police headquarters, which was known by its address, 36 Quai des Orfèvres, or more simply as "the 36." Mats walked past the security barriers, both concrete and steel, and through two sets of metal detectors before arriving at an information desk, where he asked for Inspector Medau. A uniformed officer escorted him to the second-floor office with a desk staffed by another uniformed policeman, who took his name. Less than a minute later, a man in a business suit walked down the hall and offered Mats his hand.

"Mr. Falcon, I am Inspector Maurice Medau. Please come with me."

Medau led Mats down a long corridor. At a door marked 2-18 F, he stopped and stepped inside a small private office occupied by a desk and four chairs, one of which held another man, dressed like Medau in a suit and a tie.

"Mr. Falcon, this is Inspector Adrien Fuchs of the Brigade des stupéfiants. You told the interviewing officers that there were drugs involved as well as murder. Inspector Fuchs' division deals with drugs, so I thought we might as well all talk together." Medau motioned for Mats to take a seat as he himself sat behind the desk. "Why don't you tell your story from the beginning?"

Mats took a breath and told the story of his father's murder at the hands of Leca, seeing Leca on the ferry arriving at Nice, and going to Calvi in search of clues as to how to find the man. He related the argument with the artist Forget and how Forget had nearly killed Carlo with a poisoned knife. He explained how Leca smuggled drugs by masking them with fresh oil paint. He stuck to the truth, except for telling Medau that he had stabbed Forget with a kitchen knife, rather than his sword, and knocked him out with a fist. He deliberately withheld his knowledge of Forget's death. If the police did not know, there was a good possibility that his body had not yet been found. The discovery would put Angela and probably himself under suspicion.

Medau turned to his desk and picked up a sheaf of papers that had been clipped together, quickly thumbing through them. "This is the report of your interviewing officers. I have checked on several aspects."

"Thank you," said Mats, relaxing a little. "I didn't think they believed me or took much stock in my identification of Leca."

"Yes. Well, it seems that the California police—that would be the Sausalito police—are almost positive that this Leca is Colombian, not French. Also, there has been no report of any stabbing, either of your friend or of an artist named Forget. What is the name of the doctor who tended to the poisoned man?"

Mats could see where this was going. "Dr. Theo Debove. It was fortunate that he was at the restaurant, gave Carlo a shot or two and the anti-toxin, took his fee, and left." Mats made a mental note to have Jennette phone Debove and ask him to file an incident report on patching Carlo.

"I see," said Medau, jotting down the name in a small notebook. "Mr. Falcon, I am sure that you think you saw the killer. But it was from—" Medau checked the papers he held—"at least thirty meters away, in the dark, and with the ships heading away from each other. There is no report of anyone being stabbed in Calvi. Unless there is further evidence, I'm afraid there is not enough evidence to form an investigation."

"There is one thing we can check on," said Fuchs, speaking for the first time in heavily accented English. "We can check on the effect of oil paints on our dogs."

Mats looked at Medau. There was intelligence in the pale blue eyes. He sat quietly, as if he knew there was more to Mats' story and that if he waited, Mats would disclose it. After a minute of silence, Medau said, "Could I please have your cell phone number and where you are staying while in Paris? I should also let you know that this man you seek, Julian Leca, has no record and is not suspected in any crime. It may well be that he resembles the man wanted in California, but it is likely you are mistaken. There is no record of him being in America at the time of your father's death."

"I will be at the Crillon," said Mats, giving the inspector a card, newly printed for his wine export firm, with his cell phone number jotted on the back. Unable to hide his disappointment, he stood up and moved to the door, stopping before he reached for the knob. "Inspector, might I have your direct line as well?"

"Yes, certainly," said Medau, scribbling numbers on his own card and handing it to Mats.

Before Mats could turn the knob, Medau stopped him. "Mr. Falcon."

Mats turned around.

"I am inclined to believe your story, you know, but without any evidence, there is little my department can do to help. I would caution you that if there are drugs involved, you must be careful. Drugs are a major problem in France, and the trade is known for its violence."

"Same in Sausalito," said Mats sarcastically, as he left the room.

"What do you think, Adrien?" asked Medau of his colleague, after Mats' steps had disappeared down the hall.

"I think we have not heard the last of Mr. Falcon, especially if the oil paint does mask the drugs, as he says. If it does, it's most likely he'll end up on a slab. You should check on this Forget, though."

CHAPTER TWENTY

"Mats, you are a dear. I bought the three Forgets from the Ambrage, all at this year's prices." Mats was alone in the hotel room, Suzanne having already left for work. Just before he was about to leave, his cell phone had chirped with the particular ring he'd had assigned to Audrey Kent. "One is excellent and another quite good. The third I will either sell or trade when the value goes up. I wanted to let you know that I have also arranged for a private showing from the Gallery D'Ile in five days."

"You've done what? Audrey, I told you to stay away from the Gallery D'Ile. It could be dangerous."

"The gallery owner, Mr. d'Avignon, is not a dangerous man. He is—how shall I say it? Quite sweet. He arranged it all directly with Forget's agent with the understanding that he would still receive his commission. I will not be near the gallery. The canvases will be shown to me at my hotel. He's done it before for me. He thinks me a rich, eccentric ol' lady. But Mats, I didn't mention Forget's murder and neither did he, though he did say that the price, even for a favorite customer, had increased threefold."

"Then d'Avignon obviously knows."

"Yes. But I'm sure that he hasn't taken possession of the works as yet. He didn't know exactly how many he could show; he thought there might be five. Nor could he describe them to me, and he warned me that he might have to change the day."

"Have you met the agent?"

"No, but I saw him last year in the back of the gallery."

"What is his name? What does he look like?"

"I was never introduced, but he is a big man, thick, with dark features."

"Audrey, the police don't even know that Forget is dead! It says a lot that the owner knows already. Call me as soon as you have a firm date to see the paintings."

Mats hung up, sensing he now had the opportunity to set a trap for his father's killer. Suzanne's safety and that of Audrey Kent would be the first consideration, but it could be done. Audrey had already set the conditions by arranging the private showing in her hotel room—if Leca was indeed the agent. The trap would have to be sprung after he had left Audrey's room. He tried to picture the layout of the service entrance on the street backing the Crillon, but he could not recall specifics. He had much to work out before the final plan was in place.

Mats left his room and rode the elevator to the lobby. The front desk was as helpful as he would have expected. He was told that a package of large paintings being brought to one of the rooms for viewing might use either the front entry or the service portal in the rear, leaving Mats with the need to watch both.

"Would you please show me the service area?" asked Mats.

"Certainly," said the manager and called a bellhop over, issuing a few curt orders.

Mats followed the man to the rear of the lobby, where a door gave access to a moderately sized room with a rollup door at one end and the sliding door of a freight elevator on the other. A door to the outside was between the rollup and a glassed-in office occupied by a small bald man dressed in a drab brown uniform, which sharply contrasted with the red and gold costume of the front desk staff. The door opened onto a narrow back alley with an area provided for truck parking, allowing for one-way traffic to pass. Mats walked the alley in both directions, marking in his mind the entrance and the exit from the narrow street. Walking around the block, he had the Crillon bellhop whistle him a cab for the nine-block trip to the gallery.

The Gallery D'Ile was situated on a fashionable street inside the Latin Quarter on Rue Saint-Andre des Arts. Mats took a seat in a café on the other side of the street and ordered a coffee. He could see inside the gallery through a large window that fronted the street. The building was three stories high, the highest level appearing to be an apartment with an entrance to the right side of the gallery. After half an hour and one refill of coffee, Mats had not seen a single person enter, although several had stopped outside and looked at the three works displayed in the front window. Leaving a tip, he walked across the street and gazed into the interior himself. The gallery was divided into two areas separated by a half-wall extending from the left. To the right of the entry was a small modern reception desk. In the back area, Mats could see a door but could not tell if it led to a storage area, a restroom, or a back exit. He caught a glimpse of a slight, elegantly dressed man adjusting a frame on the wall of the rear area. There were at least twelve works displayed that Mats could see. Having learned as much as he could without entering, he joined the flow of walkers moving south along the sidewalk.

CHAPTER TWENTY-ONE

Early in the afternoon the day after their first meeting, Inspector Medau called. Mats agreed to meet him at his office at four. Undoubtedly someone had found Forget. Two days in the Corsican sun would have made discovery by nose as likely as anyone finding him by entering the house. Mario again dropped Mats off at the 36, and he again followed the officers in reception to room 2-18 F. His escort opened the door, announced Mats, and left. Both Medau and Fuchs were sitting in the same places as before, as if they had not moved.

"Please be seated," said Medau, motioning to the chair in front of his desk. "We found Marc Forget. It was as you said; he had a knife wound in the back of his arm and a contusion on the back of his head that was still swollen." Medau looked at Mats, trying to discern his reaction.

"Did he want to press charges?"

"That would have been difficult. He was dead."

"He was alive when I left him. Carlo and his wife are my witnesses."

"His wife is missing."

"Do you think she killed him?"

"Who said he was murdered?"

"Come on, Inspector. You would have told me if he had died of infection from my stab wound or of natural causes. He was a drug dealer. What do you expect?" Mats was annoyed and he let it show.

"Here in France we have the Napoleonic code as the basis for our justice system. It differs from America somewhat in that you are guilty until proven innocent."

"Both Carlo and I have been in Paris for the last four days. Unless Forget died four days ago, we have alibis. I tried to help you with this, and you blew me off. I told you Forget dealt for Leca."

"Calm down, Mr. Falcon. You are not a suspect. Both the knife wound and the contusion on Forget's head were on their way to healing. What you told us about the oil paint also proved true."

"Well then—find Leca."

"We are looking for him now, but there is no evidence that he knew Forget other than what his wife told you, and she is missing."

"I've met her. She isn't the type who could kill. How did he die?"

"That is still being investigated," said Medau. "Is there anything else you can tell me?"

Mats scanned his memory for details that he had not given in the first visit. "His wife said that Forget was delivering drugs around Corsica in coffee containers, but it didn't work anymore for shipments coming in and out of Corsica. She believed Leca had killed a man for his dog, and by accident, when Forget brought in a fresh canvas, he discovered that the oil paint baffled the animal. After that, Leca shipped the drugs to the mainland in crates containing paintings."

"You did not mention the dog or that his owner had been killed before or to the interviewing officers," said Medau, his voice taking on an edge that was meant to put Mats on the defensive.

"Quite frankly, Inspector, the first policemen I talked to were not as interested as you. They seemed skeptical of both me and my—more concerned about turning in their form than getting the entire account," said Mats in a voice that told Medau he was not intimidated. "And we were discussing Forget's paintings and Leca, not Forget's local distribution methods. I thought Carlo's poisoning and Leca's drug smuggling the major issues."

Medau rose, inclining his head toward Fuchs, who shook his head, indicating he had no questions. "Stay in Paris. If you must leave, call me." He stood and offered his hand again across the desk.

Mats hesitated. He thought about telling Medau that Angela had been present at the murder of her husband, but Leca was not in custody, and as the sole witness, Angela would be in danger. He was sure that the Guibega clan could protect her better than the police could. The same held true of Audrey's showing at the Crillon. If Leca did indeed show, and saw the police, Audrey would be in danger, and despite her West Texan bravado, he could not allow that.

Mats took the offered hand, looking deep into Medau's pale blue eyes, then turned and left the room.

"What do you think?" asked Medau of Adrien Fuchs, who had remained silent.

"I think what he says is true. He is smart and would not be caught in a lie. But he is hiding something—perhaps more than one something."

"Exactly how I feel. I think we should look more closely into this American."

"And Julian Leca?" asked Fuchs.

"Yes, and certainly Julian Leca. I would like to know where he was yesterday, in case what Falcon thinks is true."

"Hmm," said Fuchs. "Monsieur Falcon looks stressed, more tired than he was at our last meeting. I don't think he is sleeping well."

⚜ ⚜ ⚜

Mats left the 36 and decided to walk to the warehouse. The Paris afternoon traffic deadlock was in full effect, but it was the fact that he needed exercise that made him want to walk. If he had heard Inspector Fuchs' remark, he would have thought it perceptive. It was not that he wasn't sleeping well; Suzanne made sure of that. It was simply that he wasn't getting enough sleep. She had the ability to curl up and go to sleep immediately after making love, while he found that difficult.

He arrived at the warehouse and looked approvingly at the street-side display that had recently placed in the window with the name of his export company, a box of opened wine bottles surrounded by sawdust and the end of an oak barrel with a brass spigot attached as if protruding from the back wall. Mats used the wall-mounted keyboard to open the large rollup door and noticed that the rental car used by Mario was parked inside. Closing the door behind him, he walked among the ever-increasing stacks of cased wines and up the staircase to the office. Halfway up, the door opened and Mario came out.

"Hi Boss. Just in time for dinner. You hungry?"

"Perfect. Suzanne is having dinner with the big-wigs and won't be through until eleven. Gives me time to go over the books I've been neglecting." Mats went to the window overlooking the Seine, wondering when the bookends would put up drapes or blinds to stop the setting sun from filling the room each evening.

There was a folder of paperwork on the desk from the purchase of the wines now stacked on the warehouse floor. Carlo and Mario had found vintages that were both semi-neglected and suited to their tastes. Some of the papers showed the amounts for as few as five cases, others for as many as twenty. The prices were favorable, but Mats knew that the import tax that protected the California wine industry would add perhaps double to the eventual selling price. Still, the sales calls he had made to the Italian restaurants in Marin County had assured him that the business, rather than just serving as a front, could turn a profit and probably a significant one.

Carlo was in the small kitchen. "It's Jennette's recipe," he said over his shoulder.

"But not Jeannette's result," muttered Mario in a low voice to Mats.

"Be ready in about twelve minutes. Just have to put on some more pasta."

Mario set the small table and pulled the chair around from the desk to complete the seating. "Even with her own family, when she gives a recipe, she leaves out one ingredient," he said under his breath to Mats.

Carlo slung, rather than served, the dish onto the table in front of Mario. "I heard that. Jennette wouldn't do that to me."

The dish was risotto with onions, mushrooms, and sliced sausage, along with a side of asparagus. "Her secret is to warm the broth before adding it to the browned rice. It's faster and lets the rice release more starch without getting mushy."

Mats relished the risotto but ignored the asparagus, which Carlo noted for future reference. The wine was excellent, and Mats suspected that more than one case on the floor below would be light a bottle or two.

After dinner he started to check the books, but the tension he had been under since spotting Leca on the ferry had caught up with him. Unable to concentrate on the columns of figures, he moved to the couch and lay down. He took out Falconi's journal and read about Edmund Auvray, but even the journal could not hold his interest.

He put his head back, slowly succumbing to sleep, his dream coming unbidden and in much more detail than what he had learned from reading the journal. Carlo and Mario watched as his body slumped down on the couch, his face set as if in deep concentration, his breath ragged and uneven.

CHAPTER TWENTY-TWO

Ajaccio, Corsica, Late August 1329,

Baron Falconi had questioned Edmund Auvray repeatedly as he healed. After the third day, there was no smell of corruption from the wound, although much of the skin on either side of the gash had died and been trimmed away by Lady Le Vere. It would leave a deep scar, and the muscles of his right side would be weak should he survive.

"This assassin with no name. Where did you pick him up?"

"If you have a map, I will show you. It is a small beach, hardly even a village. Just a few huts, a barn, a chapel, and a shelter that serves as an inn. There is no dock. I had to beach my boat. He was well known at the shelter."

"Did they call him by name?"

"No, they called him Priest, but laughed as they did so. From their actions, I think that this is a normal landing for him."

The next day Falconi brought a map of the southern coast of France, and Auvray pointed out the stretch where the beach would be. It was not noted on the map, but the captain, who was now able to stand and walk, was positive of its position just to the east of Bandol.

Two weeks later, Falconi picked a crew of twenty-five men, four horses, and an ass, and sailed one of his ships to the small town of Bandol on the French mainland. Disguised as traders devoid of his coat of arms, his men inquired among the townsfolk about a priest in black robes. They found several people who recognized the priest by his description, but none who knew his name or habits. The Baron sent two men to the east, one disguised as a shepherd and one as a tinker, to spy at the beach shown to them by Auvray from the hills above. After the five men selected by Falconi and the animals had gone ashore, his vessel was to cruise outside the small inlet and come to them when a signal fire was lit. A mirror flashed from the hill overlooking the small inlet would tell the Baron and his men that the priest had been spotted at the settlement.

The Baron camped, hidden in a copse of trees twenty kilometers southeast of Bandol and several miles from the trail that led down to the beach. From the edge of the woods, he had a clear view of the shepherd he had stationed in the grassy hill above the small settlement and the beach.

"Milord, look at the hill."

At first he could not be sure, as the sun was so bright, glaring on the expanse of wind-flattened grass. Then he saw a flash of reflected sunlight, repeated again, then a third time. It was the signal. His men, weary of the inactivity, leapt to their saddles. Their horses caught the excitement as they were urged to a pace that endangered both mount and rider.

Falconi reined up next to a man who was just now removing his shepherd's garb, replacing it with the chain mail of a man-at-arms.

"A tall dark man dressed in priest's robes but riding an exquisite animal, and with a companion whose scarred face spoke of battles, not prayers, passed by here less than an hour ago. He scattered my flock but paid no attention to me," said the lookout.

"Have any boats entered the harbor since then?"

"No boats have arrived since he passed me, but before he arrived, a boat with a gray hull pulled up on the beach with four fishermen. They also went into the inn."

Falconi counted his men: the three who had ridden with him, the shepherd, and Paolo in his tinker guise leading his donkey, who now caught up with the rest of the band, made five. Falconi looked out to sea. He could see the sails of his ship on the horizon. The wind was offshore, hindering its approach. He had the option of waiting for it and the extra men it would carry, but if he chose caution, he stood the chance of once again losing the assassin, leaving with the favorable wind.

"Paolo, take your donkey and tinker's wares down to the inn. We will follow after you near the bottom. We will hide at the side of the inn. After you see what is inside, come out and walk back toward your wares. By then we should be at the side of the inn. Do not look at us, but tell us what to expect as you pass."

"Yes, sire." The man took a knife and a battle axe off a pack on the ass, fitting them under his shirt and into the small of his back. He started down the trail on foot, leading the pack animal, its load clinking and clanking as it made its way down the trail. The others waited, allowing him to reach the small valley cut into the side of the cliff before they started their own descent.

Only the initial portions of the trail could be seen from the inn. It was a concern, but it was the only way down to the small collection of buildings at its foot. Baron Falconi did not like being exposed and kept his eyes glued on the entrance of the inn. At the foot of the trail, they moved quickly to the side of the inn.

"We must get to the priest first," Falconi whispered. "You two dive through the door, low on either side. Depending on what Paolo tells us, the rest will follow." The door was wide enough to allow two of them at a time to pass through it together. Falconi took his position behind the man on the left. With his men positioned, waiting for Paolo to come out, he heard the warning.

"Beware, it is a trap!"

Falconi held out his arm silently as a barrier to the other men. "What awaits?" he shouted. Inside the inn, Paolo screamed.

Falconi had one bowman. If there were bowmen inside, they would be positioned directly in line with the open door. Realizing that it might be the last order he would ever give, he positioned his archer directly in front of the door. He left his men on either side of it, one with a mace and the other with a battle axe, with himself and his fifth man directly behind them. The Baron slowly pulled the latch on the door to the inn. As soon as it started to open, he kicked hard, slamming the door into the room. No sooner had the door swung open then the archer let fly an arrow at the dark shape that stood out against the white wall at the back of the inn. A cry of anguish proclaimed his success. The second arrow was already set in the string when the two men catapulted through the open doorway, one left and one right, diving to the ground as they entered the room. The assassin's remaining archer aimed at the right man with the axe but missed high. It was the last shaft he would ever notch. The second arrow whistled into the room over their hurtling bodies, and all three—arrow, mace, and axe—found their mark at the same moment. Falconi's men had both started wide roundhouse swings of their weapons as they entered the room. The arcs were low, aimed at the lower legs or ankles of the men guarding the entrance.

Falconi and his remaining man leaped deeper into the room, adjusting to the dark after the bright sunlight. A shape took form to Falconi's right. His sword came up instinctively and stopped the blow only inches from his shoulder. He slipped under his own sword and to the man's right, offering no target. At the same time, he slid his own sword off his attacker's and down across the man's midriff, leaving a thin line of red diagonally across his stomach, a line that slowly widened, separating, letting the man's bowels spill out over his belt to the floor as the man screamed.

The innkeeper was still in his apron, his sword held in a ready position signaling his loyalty to the assassin.

"Put it down!" shouted Falconi, glancing only for a second at the innkeeper, searching the darkened room for the priest. Seeing the carnage that Falconi had already wrought, the man put down his weapon on the bar and raised his hands in surrender.

Falconi looked around quickly. Both men behind the door were on the ground, with his own men standing above them ready to dispatch them if it proved necessary. Both of the assassin's archers were slumped against the back wall of the inn. One would recover in time, while the other would need a real priest.

"Aa-a-a-aghhh." Falconi heard Paolo's death cry and turned toward the kitchen. Only Paolo's feet, sprawled out on the floor, were visible from where he stood. Then, into the doorway, straddling the dead man, stepped the assassin.

"Baron Falconi, I claim the right of chivalry to fight you knight to knight." The man's sword dripped red with Paolo's still flowing blood.

"You have no right to demand this, assassin."

"I am Edmund De Brace, Knight Templar, bound in duty to the Temple of Solomon and Lord Charles d'Avignon." With his left hand, the man loosened the tie at his neck and let the clerical robes fall from his shoulders. Beneath the loose garment were a shirt and leggings of chain mail covered by a white tunic with a crusader's cross.

"A Templar!"

The knight-priest stepped into the room. Falconi heard the sound of an arrow being drawn taut in a bow just behind him and saw the look of uncertainty on the assassin's face.

"I demand that the laws of chivalry be observed."

"Templars are a blot on the very name of chivalry. Your order was disbanded and its members hanged. You are nothing but a hired killer. You have killed and tortured my men. I will kill you for the vermin you are."

"Then you will die like your men, squealing like women," said the assassin, as he swung the sword in an opening attack.

Falconi had watched the assassin carefully as he dropped his robe, never taking his eyes off the man's sword hand. Thus, he wasn't surprised by the first stroke, parrying it easily. The men moved back against the walls of the inn, the four loyal to the Baron pulling their fallen adversaries along the dirt floor with them. Among the group of ambushers, only the innkeeper was still standing.

The Knight Templar was a skilled swordsman and at least ten years younger than Falconi. It was apparent as the two combatants moved into the center of the room that the Baron had an opponent who was his equal in skill with the sword. The sound of steel against steel reverberated inside the wood walls. Back and forth the two men fought, each looking for an advantage or a weakness in the other's defense, neither gaining an advantage but learning the other's style.

Without warning, the Templar moved back two steps, dropping the point of his sword toward the floor. "You fool," he hissed. "You have been followed since you came ashore. We could have had you at any time, but we wanted to know how you knew of this beach. Your arrogance in searching for me could be relied upon, and it has helped me to kill you."

"Given the condition of your men, my arrogance seems not unfounded."

"We will see how well founded it is when Lord d'Avignon seals off this village. He will want to take your life, but he will forgive me your death at my hands."

The Templar was stalling for time that Falconi knew he couldn't afford. The Baron stepped forward, renewing his attack. He pressed the Templar back, striking the man's sword with such power that the impact forced it to the floor. Pulling his own weapon back, he swung it over his head in a great arc at the unprotected head and shoulders of the priest-knight. The sword reached midway in its path over his head and struck a wooden beam in the ceiling. The sudden stopping of his weapon startled the Baron. His grip was strong as he pulled the blade from the wood, but the effort wrenched the sword from his hand. It fell against the rough floor and skittered toward the feet of the assassin.

The laws of chivalry, the same code the Templar had called upon to fight the Baron in single combat, dictated that Falconi be allowed to retrieve his weapon. But now the assassin only smiled, with no sign of belief in fair play. With measured movements, he stepped over the Baron's sword, kicking it behind him. Raising his own to the attack position, he readied to strike the unarmed Baron, but stopped short as the shepherd ran through the door, short sword drawn.

"A band of horsemen is on the cliff! At least twenty," he blurted, out of breath. It was just enough of a distraction for Falconi.

"Axe," said Falconi, with a quick flick of his right hand to his side while still watching the Templar.

The man at the side door tossed his battle axe toward his Baron. It turned twice in the air. Falconi caught it by the handle and immediately rotated the axe, the blade facing down.

The axe was an ancient weapon. It was best used in close quarters or in a melee where its short handle was an advantage. Its heavy weight could deliver a killing blow in any direction, but in hand-to-hand combat against a sword, its short handle meant that a skilled swordsman could keep the wielder of the axe at a distance while still being able to strike. In addition, the handle, though made of seasoned hardwood, could not withstand a sharp edge. The only chance a man with an axe had was to get inside the guard of his opponent. Without the use of a shield, that was unlikely against a skilled opponent. The assassin struck, a sweeping blow parallel to the floor and aimed at Falconi's unprotected left side. The Baron jumped back, feeling the blade of the sword pass just under his armpit, scraping the links on the chain mail shirt protecting his torso.

A flash of memory passed before Falconi. The Baron had watched Thomaso, his son, taking instruction in weapons, seeming to know the techniques before they were demonstrated to him. Falconi was good with the axe, but his son was his better even before he had left for France. He envisioned his son executing a perfect parry of a side blow, slipping inside and using the axe's shorter arc to sweep up and deflect the path of the sword. The weapons had been wooden, but the contact and pain had been real nevertheless.

Now Falconi saw the assassin's sword continue past him, its momentum carrying it in an arc parallel to the floor. His axe came up by reflex, catching the leading edge of the sword and deflecting it above the assassin's shoulder. The ringing of metal against metal reverberated off the walls before being deadened by the dirt floor. The assassin's control and strength surprised Falconi, as he was able to stop the blade. Still, it gave the Baron the chance to emulate the technique used by his son in practice. He stepped inside and to the right, letting the blow from the sword deflect the head of the axe downward, using its momentum to sweep it in a tight circle around and upward. The head of the axe struck between the assassin's legs, up under the mail of the Templar' haubergeon. The blow was not hard enough to disembowel the man, but it was enough to emasculate him in his tracks, his sword falling from his hands as he slumped screaming to his knees.

Falconi hesitated not for a moment. Swinging his axe three hundred and sixty degrees around his body, he struck the knight on the temple with its blunt end, metal against metal sparking as it crushed the links of the Templar's coif, past his ear into his brain, killing him instantly.

"To the boats! Quickly!" he yelled as he regained his sword and started for the door of the inn.

CHAPTER TWENTY-THREE

Paris, September, 2000

There were only two ways Leca could get to Audrey's room in the Crillon. The front lobby gave an adequate view of the two elevators that might be used to transport a man with large paintings. Mats stationed Carlo in the waiting area, a large tip in the hand of the bell captain ensuring that if a man with paintings somehow slipped by, he would be alerted. The service area was more of a problem. The back alley was often crowded with delivery vans. He wished he had another besides Mario to watch the alley should Leca arrive there.

Carlo carried a large bouquet of flower and pretended he was looking for someone yet to arrive. Mario had borrowed a dog and was walking it just off the entrance to the alley. Both would stay in their positions until contact was made. Both had cell phones to warn Mats of Leca's arrival. Mats had taken a room at the end of the hall that gave him a sightline to Audrey's room. With his door opened a crack he could view the whole expanse of the hallway and the landing area in front of two of the three elevators.

At exactly ten-fifty, Mario phoned from the alley. His message was brief: a man resembling Leca had passed him driving an unmarked van. Mats watched as three minutes later Leca exited the elevator with three large canvases wrapped individually in brown paper secured with rough twine. It was not lost on Mats that while the paintings were stretched, none were framed, and all looked to be the same size. He knocked on Audrey Kent's door and entered with the paintings. Before the door closed, Mats could hear Audrey's welcome and see the kiss that she planted on the killer's cheek.

The plan was to let Leca exit the building, then capture him if it could be done without causing harm to any spectators. Although both Mario and Carlo were armed and Mats had his sword hidden beneath his shirt, he did not want a fight if there were people around. If that was not possible, then they would follow him until it could be done. Once they had him, they would question him, then phone Inspector Medau and take him to the police. With Leca in custody, they would have Angela, Forget's wife, come forward and testify that Leca had killed her husband. The drugs and the murder of Falconi's father would fall into place.

A half hour later, Leca opened the door. Mats took a deep breath, relieved to see Audrey's red-haired figure standing and laughing in the doorway, safe. Saying goodbye to Audrey, Leca turned toward the elevator. He carried only one of the paintings he had arrived with. Mats smiled to himself; even having been warned of the danger, Audrey was not about to let a bargain slip away.

Mats waited until the elevator door closed before he ran toward the stairs. He texted the group, "Leca is coming down."

"I am in the car, but a truck is between me and Leca's van. It is blocking my way. There is a group of hotel workers taking their lunch around the hotel exit. Do you want me to stop him?" came a return text from Mario.

"No, not if there are people around. There is a possibility that he is armed," Mats texted back.

Mats ran through the lobby to the front of the hotel and found Carlo waiting in the car, the bouquet of flowers thrown on the back seat, the fragrance of the two lilies in the bouquet filling the vehicle. As soon as Mats had closed the door, Carlo took off, speeding to the only exit from the delivery alley.

Mats phoned Mario as Leca pulled out into the street. "We have him! Mario, go to Suzanne at the warehouse." For safety, he had insisted that she leave the hotel and go to the office at the warehouse. "Stay with her and wait for me."

They had no trouble following Leca as he drove straight down the street toward the outskirts of Paris. Mats felt frustrated sitting in the passenger's seat, relying on Carlo to follow the van. He caught himself pressing on a non-existent gas pedal and searching for the brake. This was a deadly game they were playing. If he had to injure or even kill Leca, he would do it. But first Leca would have to stop the car and get out of it long enough for Mats to overcome him.

Mats almost lost sight of the van as it took a sharp right turn into an ancient section of town, actually a small village that had been engulfed by Paris hundreds of years before. Here the roads were narrow and winding, seemingly without purpose or direction. What was Leca doing? It seemed inconsistent that he would pick such a place for his base. For one thing, there were many blind alleys with only two main streets bisecting the center of the area, more or less at ninety-degree angles to each other. Mats had a strong suspicion that he was no longer in control of the situation, and with that realization, anger overcame his frustration.

Leca's van turned off the main road and onto an even narrower street before coming to a stop. Mats watched as the van screeched to a halt. Then he saw the other man. He was standing a few yards away from the van, looking out of place in his dark double-breasted Armani suit.

Mats recognized the man that he had seen at the back of the gallery. The man was slight. Carlo would have no trouble with him should it come to it. As Mats began slowing, the door to the van swung open and Leca stepped out, looking back directly at Mats. A grin spread over his face as the gallery owner moved toward the van with abbreviated steps, his arms moving in exaggerated rhythm.

Carlo stepped on the accelerator, closing the distance rapidly. Leca didn't wait for d'Avignon to reach the car before moving away from the van toward a narrow walkway between the buildings. Leca looked back and smiled again, looking straight at Mats. Then he turned and disappeared. Mats had realized what was happening as soon as he saw the other man, but he was helpless either to stop Leca or to counter what was surely his plan. He turned to Carlo.

"As soon as I get out, I want you to drive to the other side of these buildings. If I am right, you will have to backtrack a considerable distance." Carlo nodded, saying nothing but readying himself to follow directions as soon as Mats jumped out.

"What do you want me to do with the other man?" asked Carlo.

"Nothing. I know where to find him. Just pick me up on the other side."

The void Leca had disappeared into was narrow and dark. Mats hurled himself into its opening, seeing the retreating form of Leca already nearing the other end. It was hard to gauge the distance separating them. Mats was confident he could gain on Leca; he was just not sure if he could gain enough. Leca looked back over his shoulder. As Mats came out of the cleft between the two buildings, he saw Leca stop, reaching into his front pocket and taking out a black fob. A dark blue BMW parked just off the street gave a soft beep as it was unlocked.

Mats saw Leca watching as he ran down the street after him. When he was ten yards away, Leca opened the door and jumped in, locking the door behind him. The car's engine roared to life, but the car didn't move. Mats started to think he might have a chance. He reached the rear of the car, half stumbling to the passenger's side door. He looked inside the car. Leca was sitting with both hands on the wheel, looking straight at him, laughing. Then the car lurched forward, wheels spinning. Mats took his sword from behind his back and swung at the rear tire, watching it bounce off the sidewall, leaving a gash but not penetrating the cord under the black rubber. The car accelerated down the street, across a stone bridge, and out of sight. As Mats stood panting, he recalled the previous night's dream, in which Baron Falconi had sought to trap the priest-assassin but was instead caught in a trap himself. A deep feeling of disquiet came over him, which turned to anger at being played, as he waited for his car.

Minutes later Carlo pulled up next to Mats and got out of the car, letting Mats take the driver's seat, having long since given up on catching Leca. With a two-minute start through this section of Paris, you could lose an elephant.

"I told the driver of the van to stay put. I think he will, signore."

"Let's see if he did." Mats turned the car in a sharp U-turn and headed back. The van was still in place, d'Avignon sitting at the wheel, as they swung back onto the narrow street.

"Get out!" Mats barked. He grabbed the handle and yanked the door open. "Where did Leca go?" he asked as the man hit the pavement.

"Who are you?"

"I'm working with the police," said Mats in perfect French. "Leca is a drug smuggler and a murderer. You are in serious trouble. Now where did he go?"

The gallery owner hesitated before answering. "I was just supposed to wait for him here after he showed some paintings. That was all. I was about to drive back to my gallery, but that man told me to wait." He pointed at

Carlo. "There is only one left, and I don't have the sale money if you intend to rob me."

"We are not here to rob you. How do you contact Leca?"

"I don't. He phones me. He just told me I was to pick up the paintings here and he would phone me tomorrow."

Mats believed the man. It fit with what he knew of Leca. It could be that as far as the gallery owner knew, Leca was a legitimate importer and agent. Nothing would be gained by pushing him now.

"Thank you for waiting," Mats said evenly.

"Wait. There were three paintings. I assume he sold the other two. How will I get my money if he is what you say?"

"You know him better than I. I will come to your gallery tomorrow." Mats and Carlo drove away, moving slowly down the street in silence.

The man watched them drive away and brushed off the sleeve of his suit before turning to the van. "Leca also said to keep the van here and to delay them if possible. Tell them anything they wanted to know," said the man softly as the car disappeared. "I guess you might have liked to know that, too." He brushed the other sleeve of his jacket with the back of his hand. "Ruffians!" he added as he climbed back into his van for the drive back to the gallery.

Mats doubled back on his route twice. His recollection of his ancestor's confrontation with the priest-assassin played over and over in his mind, making him careful now. After losing Leca, he wanted to be sure that he and Carlo were not themselves being followed.

He drove the car slowly, making still another diversion to check for following cars, and then drove to the warehouse. Someone had parked in front of the retractable door, denying him entrance. *The price of driving a car in Paris*, he thought as he drove down the street, looking for a parking spot. He spied a couple with packages who had stopped beside a car and pulled up behind them. It was just his luck that the woman was driving.

"Men get into a car and start it. Women get into a car and apply lipstick and fluff their hair for at least three minutes before turning the key," Mats grumbled to Carlo. This one was no exception. At last she started the car and pulled out. By that time, three cars had backed up behind Mats, trying to intimidate him into moving forward, hoping to get the parking spot for themselves. He didn't budge and was eventually able to pull into the opening. Mats took the oversized gym bag he used to carry his sword out of the trunk, and then he and Carlo walked the block to the warehouse.

Inside, Mats and Carlo moved past Mario's rental car and through the cases of wine. They started to climb the wooden stairs to the office.

Mats paused halfway up the stairs. A puff of breeze carrying the distinctive odor of the Seine caused him to turn. The large sliding door on the ground floor opening to the river landing was opened a crack on its tracks. Through the opening he could see the bow of a sleek motor cruiser tied to the landing, bobbing up and down in the current of the river.

"Call the pol—no, wait. Take down that boat's number, and then call the police. This number." Mats gave Carlo the card from Inspector Medau. They looked at each other, comprehending what had happened. Leca had laid his trap carefully, setting it in a place where Mats would be most at ease, least on guard. It had almost worked. In seconds Mats would have walked through the door to his office and almost certainly had his head blown off.

"Suzanne!" he yelled. "Suzanne, are you all right?" He waited for what seemed an eternity for the answer. It came weakly to him from the other side of the closed door.

"Mats," came a muffled reply, then silence. Mats looked at Carlo, who was putting his phone back in his pocket and shaking his head.

Mats positioned Carlo with his handgun to the right side of the door. Mats tried the handle. It started to turn, unlocked.

"Leca," Mats said softly, his voice just above a whisper. "Leca."

"Come in, Mr. Falcon. I have been waiting for you." Mats heard the voice through the door, accented slightly and almost as soft as his own had been.

"I was thinking that you should come out instead."

"Ah, but that would leave your man, who is bleeding, and this lovely lady all alone, which would be terribly rude of me." Leca's voice had a slight lisp, making him sound as though he were hissing the words.

Mats visualized the small room and its contents. He searched his mind for a way to break the standoff. "I won't come in until you send the man and woman out. If they're not out in three minutes, I'll call the police."

"And then I will kill them both. And still get away. Don't be stupid, Falcon."

"I've seen your boat. You won't get away in that."

An evil laugh sounded through the door. "You fool. I have been following you ever since you arrived from Corsica, you and your inept little group. Don't you think I've planned many ways of eluding you? The boat was merely a way of getting here. I will escape. And if you phone the police, the girl and the man will die before I go. Now come in. I want to talk with you face to face."

"And if I don't?"

"Then I will shoot the lovely young lady. My gun is silenced, but you will be able to tell by her screams. First her kneecaps, then her elbows. She will make a beautiful cripple."

Mats made a decision. He leaned closer to the door and said, "Soon you will be watched from the water. I know Mario is already down. Harm her and you'll be shot."

The picture window occupied almost all the wall facing the Seine. The entire apartment was visible from the river, only a four-foot expanse of wall near the door offering any seclusion. Mats motioned Carlo to get ready to burst into the room with his gun. Then he unzipped the bag that held the sword. There was only a small area where Leca could stand to the side of the door and not be seen from the water. The table at which they had eaten was against the wall. Leca would be on the door side of that. He would not have backed into the corner but would give himself room to move while still being away from the swinging door. That left only about two feet of space.

"Before I come in, I must know if you know of our history," said Mats.

"I know you have talked with Forget's bitch of a wife," came the reply.

Mats gauged the location of the voice, moving to a spot adjacent to where Leca must be standing. He raised the sword high above his head and with both hands thrust it with all his strength through the drywall. The sword sank up to its hilt in the soft plaster board, pausing at the halfway point as it met the resistance of Leca's body on the other side of the wall. Leca screamed in pain as his gun wheezed two sudden rounds through its silencer.

"Go!" shouted Mats as he felt the sword enter flesh. Carlo burst open the door and dove inside the room with the gun pointed directly at the corner. The sword had come through the wall and entered high on Leca's back, passing down and under his right clavicle. His right hand, which held the gun, was dropping slowly, involuntarily, to his side as Carlo fired. The bullet entered Leca's right wrist, shattering bones as it passed through and lodged in the flesh of his buttock. Leca's gun fell to the carpeted floor as Carlo drew his sights on the assassin's forehead.

"I have him, signore!" Carlo shouted as Leca slumped, sliding partially off the blade until it caught, suspending him, half-bent against the wall. Mats rushed into the room; seeing Leca was alone and covered by Carlo, he ran to the others.

Mario was on his back staring at the ceiling, the front of his shirt burnt black around the red hole above his heart, blood pooling beneath him. He was dead.

Mats crossed himself, then moved immediately to Suzanne. She had blood running down the left side of her face from a deep gash somewhere above her hairline. She smiled weakly at him as he removed her gag and lifted her to the couch.

She whispered, "Thank you," and then closed her eyes.

Mats glanced back at Carlo. Seeing him in control, flipped open his phone and called Medau. The call was short: the address given, a man murdered, a woman injured, Leca captured.

"Watch him." Mats said, indicating Leca, and went back outside. He grasped the grip of the sword with both hands and pulled it from the wall. He could faintly hear the sucking sound as it left Leca's body and the thud as the man fell to the floor. He placed the sword back in the bag and quickly descended the stairs, hiding it behind a stack of wine boxes.

CHAPTER TWENTY-FOUR

M ats could tell Carlo was not looking forward to the police arriving, suspecting that in Corsica, the authorities were often on the other side. He had Carlo go down to the warehouse floor and lock the sliding door to the dock, then return with a spool of coarse twine. Keeping the gun on Leca, Mats went to the kitchen drawer and took out the largest carving knife. As Carlo returned, he handed him back the gun and wiped the knife across the wound in Leca's shoulder, covering it with blood.

"Search him and tie him to the chair," said Mats, drawing a thin line of blood with the knife when Leca moved in response to his instructions.

Carlo moved behind the man and grabbed his destroyed hand; looping cord around it, he pulled the left arm behind the man's back, tying the two together tightly. Mats was aware that Carlo did not even try to protect the shattered bones, but Leca did not cry out. Only a slight resistance to the knots being tightened gave any indication that it hurt him at all.

With the assassin's hands secured and Mats with the knife still to his throat, Carlo dropped down to his knees and searched the prisoner, starting below the ankles, taking off his shoes. When Carlo finished the groin, he stood, taking out his knife and cutting Leca's trousers, ripping free a thin six-inch blade that had been taped to the man's thigh. Farther up, under his left armpit, he found a second gun, this one without a silencer. Mats' horror of this man grew with each new discovery. Even when injured and bound, the man was dangerous. His last weapon was a thin wire that had been expertly laid beneath coarse black hair cut fashionably long. Carlo whistled softly when he found it, making Mats wonder if he had missed any other tricks in his search.

Grabbing the man's hands, Carlo pulled him backward to the chair behind Mats' desk, yanking him down onto it. Mats followed, the kitchen knife now pointing at the killer's heart as his head moved back and forth in response to Carlo's work with the cord. In seconds, every extremity was securely tied to the chair. Carlo stood and nodded to Mats, who waited until Carlo had his gun pointed at the murderer's head again before he lowered his knife and went back to Suzanne.

She was unconscious, but her breathing was deep and regular. The gash in her scalp had stopped bleeding, but the dark brick red color of her blouse and skirt attested to the amount of blood she had lost. Mats took her pulse. It was strong and rhythmic. Satisfied that she would be all right, he turned his attention back to Leca.

The man was in the center of the room, tied to the chair, facing the light from the window. Part of him wanted to kill the man as he had killed his father.

"You killed my father." Leca's calmness infuriated Mats.

Leca just smiled at him. "Did he die well? He was nothing to me."

Mats had to hold himself back from striking the bound man.

"I should have shot you as you came out of the alley," Leca spat. "I will not make the same mistake again."

Mats looked into the eyes of this man who had killed his father and Mario, and would surely have killed him if he had walked into the office. Leca returned his stare, showing no remorse, asking no pity. A sardonic smile slowly spread across the man's lips. Then, as if he were playing the child's game of trying to get Mats to look behind him, Leca shifted his gaze past his shoulder. Leca's grin froze, his eyes and mouth open in surprise and fear.

Mats fought the impulse to turn around, to follow Leca's eyes in gazing behind him. Then he heard the window shatter but had no chance to react before the bullet hit. Down flat on the ground next to Carlo, he looked up and saw the small red hole in the center of Leca's forehead, saw the head recoil and slump to his chest, saw the back of his head gone in a spray of blood and brains.

Mats was the first to recover. He crawled quickly to the short windowsill and peeked up over the edge in the direction the shot had come from. Just past the moored speedboat there was another cruiser with a sleek green hull. In the cabin stood a man in a black ski mask, a rifle held to his shoulder. Mats saw the gun move slightly toward him, saw the barrel of the gun kick up, and instinctively pulled his head and shoulders back and to the left. The bullet struck the building below the window in exactly the place where Mats' chest had been an instant before. It plowed through the wood and struck the blade of the knife only inches from Mats' hand. The sound it made— a shrill screech as it ricocheted across the room—would have been comical if it had not been so deadly.

Mats lay on the floor and looked first at Carlo, then at Suzanne. Carlo had pulled her to the ground and tipped over the couch. Both were on the floor, the desk and couch shielding them from the gunman on the boat outside. Mats' hand stung, growing numb from the bullet's impact. He reached for the knife. The bullet had scarred the metal with a diagonal abrasion just below the grip before deflecting into the ceiling. He heard the roar of twin engines as the cruiser outside turned in the current and sped away.

It took fourteen sutures to close the wound on Suzanne's scalp. She was kept for two days at the hospital, not because of the gash but because of the concussion she had received along with the wound.

Mats spent almost all of the two days at the hospital with her. After he was questioned by the police, he paced up and down the corridor outside the ICU area. The nurses quickly got used to his presence in Suzanne's room. They somehow knew the full story of the attack even before the police had taken their report. They knew that Mats had captured the man who had been responsible for his father's death. They knew that he had protected their patient at great risk to his own life and that he had lost a friend in doing so. Part of the story had been pieced together from the doctors' reports, part from eavesdropping on the police, and part from listening to Mats and their patient talking. In the end they knew the whole story and they thought, to a nurse, that it was terribly romantic.

The *San Francisco Chronicle* and the *Marin Independent Journal* ran full-page stories on the murders, mostly comprised of material they had gotten from the police reports, French newspapers, and several phone calls to Paris. Noticeably absent from the articles was any mention of Mats' sword. Leca had been stabbed, according to police reports that were edited by Inspector Medau, by a kitchen knife.

At first the French police thought to tie Mats into a story of a drug deal gone sour. They repeatedly questioned him on the identity of Leca and his murderer, whom they assumed Mats knew. Finally, with Suzanne's testimony, the strength of the fingerprint evidence, the ballistics on the shot that had killed Mario, and the reports on the murder of Marc Forget and Mats' father, Mats and Carlo were cleared. Inspector Medau also supported Mats' account with a firm verification that Mats had come to them not once but three times. Medau concluded it had been Mats' ability to identify Leca that had prompted the attack, not drugs. Medau had become friendly, almost apologetic, to Mats, though less so to Carlo, whose every encounter was tinged with obvious distrust.

Now the police had finished and Mats sat in a chair next to Suzanne's bed, sipping coffee provided by one of the nurses.

"They tell me you will be discharged tomorrow morning," said Mats.

"I guess that two days of waking me up every four hours was enough," said Suzanne with a smile. "In truth I'm happy for the rest. The first day I was not sure of just walking from the bed to the bathroom. They say the concussion is past the critical stage, but I should stay quiet for a few days."

Mats watched Suzanne resting on the pillow beside him. She was so beautiful. She would have to restyle her hair to hide the shaved portion around the sutures, but in time the scar would not show.

Despite his precautions, Mats knew he had almost lost her to Leca's trap. The police had no idea who Leca's murderer was, but whoever it was had tried to kill him as well. Inspector Medau had confided in Mats that Inspector Fuchs, piecing together intelligence, had uncovered evidence that Leca was an underling, an enforcer, in a larger drug organization. In the last year he had begun acting with more autonomy. Beyond that, they had no knowledge as to who the kingpin was. *How could he protect himself or Suzanne from someone unknown, someone who could shoot*

from a moving boat with the accuracy of an Olympic marksman?
Mats asked himself.

Mats was tired. The police interviews as much as the death of Leca had exhausted him. He held Suzanne's hand in his own and closed his eyes.

THE COAST OF FRANCE – August 1329

With two men on either side, the Baron pushed the gray Cat Boat slowly across the pebbles, the grinding of the wood strakes over the knuckle-sized round stones testifying to their effort. The boat moved with increasing speed down the steep incline toward the sea. It was the largest boat on the beach and could easily have held twice their number. Its single mast lay unstepped far forward. Behind them, the sound of men on horseback could be heard, riding down the trail leading to the valley. The Baron looked back as the bow of the boat hit the small waves lapping at the bottom of the rocky shore. The riders were no more than a hundred yards away, perhaps a score, now at a full gallop. The boat veered to the right with their effort to float the vessel, and then the weight of it was fully borne by the water. Falconi's men clambered over the side, hurriedly placing the oars in the locks, and immediately started pulling hard as the boat edged away from the shore.

In the stern, Falconi judged the distance. They were still within bowshot of shore. A skilled archer would have no trouble finding his mark. The four men at the oars were facing aft. They would be easy targets. Falconi urged them to row harder as he stood by the tiller.

Falconi could see the archers. They had dismounted and were now standing on the shore with their bows at the ready, awaiting only the command of the late arriving d'Avignon. Falconi wondered how men could follow someone such as d'Avignon, who would not lead from the front. On the gray craft, Falconi stooped, holding the tiller steady with his leg, and grabbed two spare oars, attaching them to the lose jib sail. He lifted the oars, sticking them one after another, hard between the deck planking and the thwart, their length sticking up and out at a slight angle. As the second oar was wedged into place, the sail, now spread between the two oars, blocked the view of Falconi's men. The men on the beach could launch their arrows, but it would be a blind shot through the sail.

In addition, the slight offshore breeze that filled the jury-rigged canvas helped Falconi's men in their efforts. They rowed, their muscles bulging. The arrows came, but Falconi had placed the eight remaining oars up behind the sail. The first of the arrows found one, and the second. Falconi peeked around the raised jib. He could see discussion between the archers as they pointed to their shafts sticking out of the sail. It had been luck that the first arrows had hit the oars, but the result was that the archers, seeing that their arrows stuck hard in the sail cloth, assumed that a solid barrier had been raised to thwart them and in turn raised their aim high over it, a much more difficult shot and one greatly affected by the wind. Others of d' Avignon's men pushed two of the small boats left along the beach into the water, leaving the archers to their task on the beach, and began rowing in pursuit.

Falconi's men were rapidly pulling the gray boat out of arrow range, but the small boats, filled with men, posed a new and no less real threat.

One of the boats in pursuit had a man in armor standing in the bow. On his shield was the crest of d'Avignon. Falconi's adversary had laid his trap well but seemed to have left an avenue of escape: the sea.

The Baron's sentry had said that the four men in the inn had come ashore in the grey boat. Where had they come from? It could not have been far, given the trouble his own men were having with the craft. Then he understood. The plan to trap him on this isolated stretch of beach had been too well laid for them not to have a ship waiting in case the Templar did not succeed. The mounted column had effectively sealed off any chance of escape by land; the sea was too obvious to leave uncovered. It was predictable that Falconi might seek the freedom of the Mediterranean.

Now out of bowshot, Falconi stood in the stern and scanned the horizon. He saw nothing but blue sea and sky, and far out his own ship, battling against the foul wind. The small pursuit boats would drop back when they reached the open water, where Falconi's craft would have the advantage of size and sail. His eyes left the boats, settling on the high cliff that fell to the sea, effectively cutting off the small village from the rest of the coast to the southeast. A man was standing at the very tip of the promontory waving a full-length shield back and forth in the bright sunlight.

Falconi looked again to sea. Coming around the tip of land to the southeast was a corsair under full sail and crowded with fighting men. Even at a distance, Falconi could see the sunlight reflecting off their mail tunics and swords. They could not return to the beach and could not outrun them under sail. They could only fight.

He could do nothing but postpone the inevitable. He adjusted the tiller, heading straight out to sea, and watched the vessel alter course to intercept him. He moved forward between his men and stepped the mast, setting sail with practiced skill. The wind caught and added more speed to that already achieved by the men. His own ship was tacking back and forth, trying to make way toward the enemy. They were sailing as close to the wind as they could, but it would be a miracle if they were able to arrive in the bay in time to save their leader. Falconi sensed the mood of his men. It was as good as any place to die. He only had two regrets: that he would not put an end to d'Avignon, and that he would leave Lady Le Vere after just finding her love. He ordered his men to rest, letting the sail catch the full wind.

His men had seen the caravel corsair and understood what it meant. They had dedicated their lives to their Baron, and if it came to an end like this, so be it. They would die with their weapons in their hands, and somehow that gave each one of them comfort.

Falconi searched his memory and the memory of his ancestors for a strategy, but he could only envision ways of dying bravely. The thought of Lady Le Vere came to him instead, and with it came a resolve to make his own legend. He would lead the shore boats out to sea, and then, when their return to shore was impossible, he would turn and attack. With luck, he could kill d'Avignon before the corsair could board him.

The men, placing their oars mid-ships, readied their weapons. The archer clutched the quiver between his legs. Falconi saw him count his arrows. He had added the shafts that had stuck in the sail barrier to his own, but still they numbered fewer than twenty.

As the Baron had anticipated, the smaller boats from the shore had lost distance once the shoreline surf was negotiated. Still they followed, spread out, cutting off his escape to the mainland. A third sail came around the headland, closer in than the ship that had brought him to the mainland, which still tacked back and forth against the wind. Falconi shouted a command and swung the tiller hard to port. The craft rocked wildly in the swell as they turned toward the corsair closing in from the southeast. A thrill of impending battle filled Falconi's soul as his archer stood and let the first of his shafts sing through the air.

The first arrow struck home, taking the man at the tiller, causing the corsair to swerve and lose its wind. It was followed by another and yet another before the other vessel could retaliate. When retaliation did come, it was with flaming arrows, two of which struck Falconi's craft. Two of his men rowed, protected by the shields left behind by those killed at the inn. When the arrows hit, they were immediately retrieved before the wood could catch flame. They were passed, still burning, to the archer, who launched them back at the enemy. He aimed high in the sails, out of reach of the men on deck, and he aimed well. Soon there were sparks and bits of burning sailcloth falling among the men-at-arms. The sails of the pursuers were dropped and doused with water, and no more fire arrows were shot.

Falconi laughed out loud, his men echoing his joyfulness. He'd turned their own stratagem against them, literally taking the wind out of their burning sails. He stayed at the helm, protected only by a shield that still left his head and shoulders exposed. Clumsy as his craft was, it was under sail and oar, more maneuverable than the corsair.

The sails of the third ship were fast approaching. Once the ship arrived, Falconi would no longer be able to avoid boarding tactics and sheer numbers would seal their fate. He could hear shouts from the smaller boats approaching from the shore. His eyes fell on the shield of d'Avignon. Before he was trapped, he would fulfill his vendetta, taking the villain with him to eternity.

D'Avignon's boat was much smaller than Falconi's, but it was crowded with eight men-at-arms and four oarsmen. It would be a fight in which Falconi would have a chance.

Falconi jibed, moving his boat away from the becalmed corsair and toward the shore.

Falconi bore down on d'Avignon's small boat with all the speed his men could muster. They had been rowing with only a short rest since they had left the beach and the strain showed on their faces. Not once had they asked their Baron what he was doing; not once had they asked for relief from the strain of the oars. Now he issued a command that gave them new energy.

"Archer, launch at the small boat off our port bow. The rest of you row hard but have your weapons at hand as soon as we touch."

As they neared, Falconi could see that d'Avignon had filled his small boat to the maximum. The men at the oars, not experienced seamen, were sloppy in their strokes, the men-at-arms crowding the man at the stern. It was a small boat without a mast or sail, so even though they had the weather gauge, it would do them no good. D'Avignon had left his archers ashore to launch their shafts at the retreating Falconi, giving his single bowman the advantage now.

Falconi looked back, noting the exact positions of the ships preventing his escape to the sea. Nearest were the two that had been hidden just beyond the head-lands. They were now close enough to identify Duke Colletti's crest on the nearest, but no markings on that of the other. Suddenly it made sense. D'Avignon was no seaman. This trap smelled of one knowledgeable of Falconi's ability and of the sea. This would be Colletti's doing. The Baron from Corsica had placed the two ships blocking Falconi's possible escape by that route. Further out to sea, Falconi's ship had taken advantage of a slight shift in the wind to shorten its final tack and was nearing the headlands, but it was still well out of bowshot of the two enemy vessels.

Falconi steered his boat directly at d'Avignon. Colletti's corsair was in the process of turning, but already the distance between it and Falconi was spreading. The second corsair was still a kilometer away.

Three arrows fell among d'Avignon's men, one deflected by a shield while the other two found their marks. Then two more came, one killing its man, the other finding the flesh of a man's shoulder. Falconi urged his men to give two great pulls as his bow hit the side of d'Avignon's craft, snapping its oars down the port side. The broken handle of an oar hit d'Avignon in the midriff, knocking him off his feet. As the gunwale of d'Avignon's vessel slid down toward the water, Falconi's men were already leaping over the side, weapons in hand, onto the tangle of bodies that had resulted from the collision. Falconi was first over the side, stepping on d'Avignon's throat as he swung his battle axe at the nearest warrior. Where there had been twelve men, in seconds their numbers were reduced to d'Avignon and one man-at-arms, who quickly yielded his sword. Falconi took his foot from his enemy's throat as his men pulled d'Avignon to his feet. There was a strong smell of old fish from the bilge mixing with the copper odor of the spilled blood. A look over his shoulder confirmed that the corsair had completed its turn and was fast bearing down on them.

"I have no time to enjoy a slow revenge," hissed Falconi, passing the razor-sharp edge of the axe up under the mail tunic, catching the flesh of d'Avignon's groin, and continuing until the blade was stopped by a rib.

In terror the Frenchman looked down at his intestines, which spilled to his feet from the gaping wound. His mouth opened. "Colletti will have your head," he whispered with the sound of a death rattle.

"You will not see it! Let the fish feed on your guts!" With those words, Falconi pushed the mortally wounded

Duke of Avignon into the gray-blue Mediterranean. He and his men jumped back into their boat, leaving the remaining man-at-arms alone with the dead and dying. The corsair was almost upon them.

"To oars," Falconi ordered.

The men responded immediately, all placing oars in the starboard lock. The archer had been wounded in the boarding and had only the use of his right arm, but he too pulled. Their effort swung the bow around to port and turned d'Avignon's boat with it. The effect was to put d'Avignon's vessel, as well as the sinking body of d'Avignon wedged on a broken oar, between them and the ship closing on them.

The corsair hit the smaller vessel, crushing the suspended body of d'Avignon between them. Its men poured over the side into d'Avignon's boat, weapons ready. But the collision propelled Falconi's boat an oar length away. Falconi did not even have to issue a command. As soon as there was clearance, two men moved immediately into position and pulled hard, away from the tangle of bodies and oars. Colletti's archers, long frustrated, now took aim and let their shafts fly. Falconi's own bowman, wounded, could not both row and adjust his shield. He took an arrow in the neck and slumped over his oar. Another of his men was hit in the arm but continued pulling. At least four shafts bounced off Falconi's shield into water that was beginning to redden with blood.

They had moved a boat length away from the corsair, enough to prevent being boarded, but not far enough away to avoid becoming targets for the archers. The other boat was almost upon them as well. The sail of Falconi's own ship was now visible close to the headlands of the bay. Soon it would enter the bay, taking advantage of the current, but in all likelihood, it would be too late.

The corsair followed in Falconi's wake. With all of their oars still manned, they made up the distance that Falconi had put between them with each stroke. The archers could now aim down into his open vessel. It was impossible for Falconi's men to maintain their shields in front of them while they pulled.

The two vessels now closed on him. Now all lanes were blocked. Sounds of battle echoed off the water, but it was impossible to distinguish individual commands. The Baron stood at the stern, proud of his life. Now that d'Avignon was dead, his only regret was that he would leave Lady Le Vere and would be the last of his line.

He heard the twang of bowstrings and steeled himself against an impact that never came. Cries erupted from the corsair; confusion filled the deck of the ship above him. Another salvo of arrows and new cries issued from the unmarked ship. Then he saw the ship raise the banner of the Falconi—a ship with Edmund Auvray standing at the helm.

Falconi used the chaos to pull away from Colletti. He looked at his men—one dead, another wounded, and another dying—of no use in combat. Of the two remaining, only Paolo was unscathed. The fight was still not even, but the element of surprise and the skill of the archers on Auvray's ship had done much to even the odds. The two remaining small boats from shore had turned and fled after witnessing the death of d'Avignon.

Colletti's attention was diverted from Falconi onto the sleek sea raider that carried Falconi's colors. Falconi saw the danger in which Auvray had placed his vessel in order to repay the debt of his own life. There was no chance that Falconi could provide support. With only Paolo to help, their effect would hardly be felt and would possibly get them killed in the process.

Falconi recognized the shouted commands he was hearing as coming from Baron Colletti. It would be like the man to join forces with d'Avignon against him. With Falconi dead, Colletti could claim much of Falconi's borderlands. But now he would have to earn his reward, and if Falconi had his wish, that reward would be joining d'Avignon in the sea.

As if he could feel Falconi's hatred, Colletti turned and looked at the gray boat standing still in the swell. New commands were shouted, and Colletti's corsair disengaged from Auvray's and moved toward Falconi, picking up speed as it moved closer.

When Colletti was less than a hundred meters from him, Falconi heard a cry from Colletti's mast. The lookout shouted that Falconi's ship had entered the bay and was approaching at high speed toward the battle. The sleekness of the hull and the skill of the crew identified it as Falconi's even without a crest on the sail. His ship had gained the bay, the battle against the wind finally won. Falconi could see Colletti standing in his stern assessing the newly arriving vessel. It gave him no choice. With a last look at Falconi, Colletti snarled an oath, bringing his ship around, setting sail to the southwest.

CHAPTER TWENTY-FIVE

Paris, September, 2000

Mats answered the knock on the door, knowing that it would be Inspector Medau. A call from the desk had preceded him. The inspector entered, appraising the room. Mats could tell that he was placing a price tag on the accommodation.

"Can I offer you a cup of coffee?"

"That would be most appreciated."

Mats started toward the coffee but Suzanne was faster, reaching the serving tray that had been delivered five minutes ago.

"Just a little cream, thank you," said Medau in response to her raising the silver sugar bowl and looking at him. "I am glad you are feeling better, Mademoiselle."

"Thank you, Inspector. I only wish my hair would grow back as fast as the symptoms of the concussion have disappeared." Suzanne had styled her hair carefully, combing over the shaved portion of her scalp and the sutures that were still present, but without full success.

Mats sat in a chair across from the couch that Medau had taken. Suzanne set coffee in front of them both, then returned with her own and sat next to the policeman.

"I wanted to meet with you for several reasons. First, we are releasing the remains of your man, Mario Guibega, but we have not been able to contact his cousin Carlo. If you would help us with this matter and let us know what the family would like to do with his body, it would be appreciated."

"The body will be flown to Ajaccio for burial," answered Mats. Carlo had been quite insistent that the family would take care of the arrangements. Walking to his desk, Mats took a file with a single page of instructions on it and handed it to Medau.

"There will be some costs involved and releases to be signed."

"On the bottom you will find my credit card information. Use it as necessary. I will have Carlo contact you as next of kin to sign the forms."

"Thank you. On the matter of Leca, we have located a garage he rented with crates for the transportation of paintings. It is as you told us; there were hidden compartments in them and smears of oil paint. We found traces of cocaine in one of the crates and quantities of the drug in the garage. What we haven't found is his supplier. It appears that he was the distribution side of a larger operation. The fact that he is involved with the murder of your father would indicate that it is international in scope. That he was killed in your presence, and shots were taken at you, leads me to believe that you are still at risk."

"And the gallery owner, Jean-Claude?"

"He appears to be innocent, other than having business dealings with Leca in the selling of the paintings that masked the delivery of drugs. He is certainly innocent of the shooting. He has a text on his phone from Leca telling him where to pick up the van, and he was at his gallery when Leca was shot. His finances are in order. I didn't realize there was so much profit in art. Speaking of finances…" Medau looked at Mats with a curious expression, not accusing, but not quite friendly. "You have some recent large deposits and purchases that seemed unaccountable. It was one of the reasons this took so long. We thought they might have been connected with the drugs. We found, however, that they were associated with the sale of some old coins and jewelry." Medau cocked his head.

"Yes, some family heirlooms," said Mats.

"We also found that taxes had not been declared on their sale. You still have several months to do so, but you would not want to fall into disfavor, having just started a business."

"Thank you, Inspector. I have a lot to learn about doing business in France."

"The Crillon coffee is excellent. Thank you for your time. Oh, please tell me if you plan to leave Paris." He placed his cup back in the saucer and moved to the door.

"I will leave Paris and accompany Mario's body to Corsica. I will stay there until the burial," said Mats, shaking hands with the inspector.

"But of course," said Medau, standing in the doorway, cocking his head and looking at the door to the bedroom. "Phone me when you return. I'm sure that I will have some more questions. You should know that the medical examiner reports that neither the knife wound, nor the gunshot to his wrist would not have been fatal, clearing you of any possibility of homicide. He did, however, measure the thickness of the wall with the blood drips from where it was withdrawn and has concluded that the blade was not long enough to go through the wall and still have the necessary depth of penetration." Medau smiled. "So many questions." He turned and walked down the corridor to the elevator.

Mats sank into the brown leather armchair, the largest in the suite, as Carlo emerged from the adjacent bedroom.

"You heard?"

Carlo nodded. "He knows you went after Leca on your own."

"He knows that it was probably not the kitchen knife that made the wound, or at least that Leca was stabbed twice in the same spot. Smart. But I just couldn't let them take the sword for evidence. I might never have gotten it back."

Carlo looked at Mats, impassive, as if he was hearing Mats' words but not fully comprehending them. His normally taciturn personality had turned to sullenness. "There will be five days of mourning for Mario, a ritual afforded any Guibega killed in service to the Falconi," he said. "I will make the arrangements with the police today."

Mats phoned Audrey Kent and asked her to have lunch with him at the warehouse office. He asked Carlo to pick her up at the Crillon. The next day Carlo parked the car inside, rolling the door down behind them, and escorted her to Mats.

The newspapers had been full of the murders, but after two days the stories were relegated to the twelfth page, and now there was nothing. Mats had taken Audrey's calls several times, but as the investigation was still in progress, he could not talk.

"Thanks for coming, Audrey," said Mats, standing to greet her. Suzanne rose to kiss her on the cheek.

"How could I not? Everybody is talking about your bravery in the face of this tragedy."

"Thank you, Audrey, but it was more instinct than bravery. I only had time to react to the circumstances, not think about them. Lunch is almost ready. Will you join us?"

Audrey glanced at the small table that had already been set up for four next to the window, which still had its replacement tag on it. "Of course."

Mats nodded to Carlo, who went to the small kitchen. "You may have wondered," said Mats as he held out her chair, "why you were never contacted. The truth is that I didn't think it was any of the police's business that you had dealt with Leca. I suspect Leca might have used you and other legitimate collectors to hide the money made in his drug deals. It would have been the perfect cover; he was already using the paintings to mask the movement of drugs. There's no way you could have known that, so I saw no reason to involve the legitimate art world in general or you in particular."

Audrey smiled a slow West Texas smile, curling the corners of her mouth. "Why does my old horse-trading instinct tell me there's something more?" she asked, the smile never leaving her face as she shook her red hair—a nervous gesture, Mats thought.

"I do have a couple of questions ... things that are your and my business, not some reporter's or the police's."

"Fair 'nuff. What do you want to know?"

"After we told you about the murder of Marc Forget, you said you knew of the whereabouts of some of his paintings. Whom did you speak to and what exactly did you say?"

"I actually went to two galleries. Both had paintings by Forget. I had seen them the previous week but was not particularly interested in them. Two or three of them were of a quality that might round out a show of his better work. I thought I might get them as a bargain before the inevitable price hike. The Gallery Impressionists had not raised their prices, nor had the Ambrage and I bought both their Forgets. However, my good friend Jean-Claude at the Gallery of the Lilies said he had already removed the price tags. I told him I was trying to parlay a couple into a trade for another piece and offered him the price I remembered from the previous viewing. He laughed and told me that I must know something. Then, in confidence, he told me that he also knew of Forget's death. It seems that his partner, who has a villa on Corsica, phoned him with the news, which is why the prices had been removed. He asked if I had seen Mr. Leca's canvases, and I told him I was going to see them the next day. He asked how I had found out about Forget. There didn't seem any harm in telling him, since he already knew about Forget's death. I mentioned you had just been to Corsica and that we knew each other from Marin. Considering what has happened, I guess there was a great deal of harm in that after all."

"Yes." Mats glanced at Suzanne. "But don't feel bad. If there was a mistake in judgment, it was mine. It's important that you have no further dealings with either of these galleries until this murder of Leca is solved. I didn't mean for you to become involved in what you must now realize is a very dangerous situation. Don't meet with them or talk with them. Use any excuse—health, anything—but text me immediately if either of them contacts you. Think carefully—did you tell anyone else about Forget's death, or that you were meeting Leca?"

"No."

"This is important." Mats watched Audrey carefully. "Did you ever see either Leca or Jean-Claude do anything illegal?"

Audrey squirmed in her seat, struggling with some inner conflict, and finally answering in phrases punctuated by pauses. "Not illegal in a true sense…and certainly not to their advantage. But they did do something that was, shall we say, irregular."

"What was that?"

"Both of them would routinely announce the sale of any painting I bought for thirty to fifty percent more than the actual price. So, if I paid twenty thousand for a piece, the figure announced would be thirty-five thousand or so."

"Explain, please."

"Well, it was very unusual, because of the additional money, which, of course, they would get back. But they would have to pay taxes on it. I thought they were jacking up the prestige of their gallery and Jean-Claude as an agent, with a better sales figure, but it still cost them money in taxes."

"And the advantage to you? I assume you went along with it for a reason."

"I had no choice in the matter of their announcement. The first time they did it, I was very surprised, but I quickly saw that it was to my advantage. I bought a work, and they immediately announced a higher sales value. In effect, I had a thirty percent return on my investment. Paintings tend to sell at a price that reflects that at which they were last sold."

"Anything illegal on your part?" Mats still could not understand why Audrey was reluctant to talk about the arrangement.

"That first year, I declared the price I actually paid for the paintings to the IRS, but as I began to trust Mr. Leca and Jean-Claude to be discreet, I started reporting the selling prices they announced. It gave me a smaller capital gains obligation when I sold or traded the work. If there was ever a hard audit, I guess there could be a significant tax liability—that is, if it could be proven. But with the taxes being paid at Jean-Claude's end, that would seem impossible."

"Both Leca and the gallery had this arrangement with you on purchases?"

"Yes."

"Which of them first inflated the purchase price?" Mats had only known Audrey as a rich—a very rich—lady who collected Impressionist painters. Now he was seeing in her the qualities that made her a force in her field. She tossed her hair again before answering, and Mats thought he detected a slight blush.

"Jean-Claude, probably twenty years ago, on a small Sisley."

"You mentioned that Jean-Claude had a partner in the gallery. Do you know who he is?"

Audrey thought for a moment before answering. Despite her hesitation, Mats felt no sign that she was trying to hide something or edit her answer. He intuited that she was trying to retrieve some lost bit of information from her memory.

"It wasn't Mr. Leca. I think he took in the partner when he opened his second gallery, the one in Paris. It was just about the time I started to look at him seriously as a source for Impressionist work. I bought the Sisley from his Paris gallery shortly after it opened, but I first saw it displayed in Provence."

"And his partner's name?"

"That's what I'm trying to remember. I've never met him, but I saw him once leaving the Paris gallery showroom by the back door. He is dark and overweight, almost as tall as you are, Mats. He had a beard. I remember thinking that he was probably used to looking behind him. I mentioned it to Jean-Claude and he laughed. That was when he told me he was his partner and that his ancestor was the portraitist François Colletti, who painted the king of France five days before the revolution. Somehow the artist escaped the guillotine, while the king did not, but ever since, his family has looked over their shoulders. His name was not Colletti, however, but it was something like it... Collette. That was his name, Collette."

"Colletti! That is the name of the Baron—" Suzanne was stopped by Mats' raised hand. He had told her of the dream he'd had while at her bedside in the hospital.

"Do you know the man?" asked Audrey, picking up on Suzanne's half-remark.

"Like you, I have never met him," answered Mats as he watched Carlo's forearms tighten into strands of hard sinew. "Audrey, how well do you know Jean-Claude?"

"Not well, not personally. He's something of a celebrity in the art field, as he's descended from French nobility. His name is d'Avignon: Jean-Claude d'Avignon."

Mats saw Carlo stiffen at the mention of Collette—just a subtle change, probably only discernible to Mats, as he placed plates of fettuccini and artichoke hearts on the table.

They shared a bottle of tinto from the Guibega vineyards with their meal and sent Carlo down to the warehouse for another as they delighted in his Queen of Nut cake for dessert. After the meal, Mats reminded Audrey not to contact anyone concerning Forget, going as far as to suggest she leave France with her purchases a week early.

Carlo drove Audrey back to her hotel and returned in less than thirty minutes. Mats heard the door roll up, then down, as he looked out the office door to make sure it was Carlo and that he was alone. He and Suzanne had helped themselves to a second slice of cake and had taken care of the dishes.

"I know a Collette," said Carlo as he entered the room. "He owns much land around Porto and Calvi and as far as Bastia. It was he who made the first offer on the land Jennette purchased for you, signore. He is a fat pig."

"It was good that you didn't say anything about that in front of Audrey. There is a great difference between dealing with the underside of the art world and dealing with the violence integral to the trafficking of drugs."

"It wouldn't surprise me if there was a connection there," said Suzanne. "Collette and d'Avignon."

Two very dangerous men, thought Mats. *Leda helped us find one and now we must find the other.*

CHAPTER TWENTY-SIX

Ajexicco, Corsica, September 2000

It took most of Mats' energy to cope with the ritual of mourning the Guibegas observed for Mario. It was not the preparations; the Guibegas took care of all the details, while Mats stayed with Suzanne at the Alta Mira, meeting Guibega after Guibega during the four days. All of them gave him their condolences, when Mats thought it should be the other way around. The burial would be held in a small, private cemetery on the land that Mats had recently purchased. His presence would not be expected there until the day of the funeral.

Nando saw Mats' questioning look on the second day of the ritual. "Only the head of the clan," he explained, "or one who has died in the service of the Falconi is awarded such honors, signore. It takes five days to gather the family. Many of our young men are sent into French military service, or the Merchant Marine. Some are loaned to organizations that are not quite legal. Many of these young men will not be able to attend, but the five days will allow those who can to be here. Those who are here will prepare his body and the site. All will bring gifts."

"Where will he be buried?" asked Suzanne.

"It is good that you had Jennette purchase the land we know as Falcon's Roost. It has a long history with the Falconi. There is a centuries-old cemetery at its edge. Mario will be laid there."

"One of the masons who helped us in Allos visited us yesterday," said Mats. "He mentioned that he had been working on the old keep."

"Yes, Jennette had them start as soon as you signed the papers. They were no longer needed in France once Suzanne left the dig. It is good. To the Guibega, it gives you permanence here in Corsica."

On the day of the funeral, Mats saw the Guibega gathered together in one place for the first time. By mid-morning the cloud cover had broken, leaving the sun to find occasional openings to bathe the mourners in bright light. He had met any number of them, but only once had there been a group of more than thirty, and that had been at the party, where Mats was busy much of the time with Nando in the upper chamber of the hotel uncovering treasure. Mats was surprised to find that the total clan consisted of fewer than a hundred and fifty people, half of whom were over forty years old; only twenty of the remaining were men over eighteen. As non-prolific as the Falconi were, the Guibega were almost as skimpy in producing offspring. Of the twenty men Mats recognized, most had been among the stonemasons whom Nando had brought to France.

The women, even the young girls, were all clad in black ankle-length dresses, their black hair pulled back in severe buns, their dark eyes burning beneath rigidly straight eyebrows. The men all wore black suits with ties and black hats covering their heads. They all nodded in respect as Carlo drove Mats and Suzanne to the cemetery, but none approached or broke the silence.

On the last day before the burial, Nando brought a man to the restaurant and introduced him personally. His name was Ramondo Guibega. Mats guessed his age to be mid-twenties. He was taller than most of the clan but with broad shoulders and muscles that, while not bulky, rippled with even his smallest movements.

"Ramondo can spend only two days. He serves on the French anti-terrorism squad, the FIPN. In the future he will be of great help to you," explained Nando, placing his hand on the taciturn young man's shoulder. "Many young men of our family travel to the mainland for training and work. Ramondo has been particularly well trained. He will take over many of my responsibilities when I am too old."

Now Mats saw the young man standing next to Nando near the grave that had been dug for Mario. At some signal unseen by Mats, each of the Guibegas filed past, placing a stick or two of hardwood on top of Mario's final resting place, an open wooden casket placed in the center of an irregularly shaped hole. The casket was filled with small items that covered every space between Mario's body and the walls. The pit was lined with stone, which itself was laid with cord wood. It was dug seven feet below the surface of the ground. When all had passed, Nando approached Mats with a torch, instructing him to light the pyre that had grown over Mario.

"It is an ancient custom, signore, followed since the first Falconi came to the island."

Mats walked slowly to the grave and touched the torch to the pile of tinder. The dry wood caught immediately, flames reaching high into the air. Up to that point the mood had been grim and somber. With the lighting of the funeral pyre, a cask of wine was brought out and cups filled. In the background Mats heard the sound of guitars, and the Guibega began singing, chanting, in a tongue that was both strange and familiar. He looked at Suzanne at his side. Suzanne listened intently, both taken by the power of the music and the way it enhanced the pagan spectacle of the flames.

"I have never heard this language spoken, let alone sung, but it sounds like the old Nordic that we used when we were translating your ancestor's journal," whispered

Suzanne. "The words are the same. I don't know about the pronunciation; no one living does. Something like 'gone is the warrior. Gone to the gods.' Mats, look what they're doing." Suzanne was watching the Guibega children returning to the fire with more wood. "Did you notice the shape of the grave? I couldn't tell at first, but now, filled with flames, you can see it's in the shape of a hull. All that's missing is the Viking longboat being pushed out to sea."

The hardwood caused almost no smoke, but the flames, as they consumed Mario and the gifts surrounding him, produced a light gray wisp of smoke. Thin as it was, it was soon lost in the light breeze of the early afternoon and was only noticeable by the sent it left behind.

Mats gazed at Suzanne as though his eyes had just been opened. "I had a dream once when I was reading Thomaso's second volume. It was as if I was having his dream—the one he wrote about, his ancestor helping the Pope's legions. Well, in my dream, I saw the sea battle he described. And Suzanne, his ancestor's men had round shields, pointed helmets, jerkins with short swords like mine, and battle axes, rowing a boat with a dragon's head at the bow. I thought nothing of it until now. They were just men dressed in ancient clothing. I placed no significance on it. I hadn't yet come to believe that the dreams reflected reality in all aspects. But it would explain my skill with the sword and axe as well as the Falconis' skill as mariners."

"And your blue eyes." Suzanne reached for Mats' hand and gave it a loving squeeze.

"And other things we're bound to think of tomorrow," said Mats, returning the squeeze. He took a glass of red wine offered by a young Guibega girl and gave it to Suzanne, then took one for himself. The drinking and feasting would go on all night, only the second time he had seen the Guibega overindulge in anything other than their loyalty to the Falconi.

That night Mats and Suzanne made love in the unfinished upper room of the castle. In just nine days the walls had been restored, giving them privacy. There was no roof yet, and the stars shone down on them in the bed Jennette had provided. They made love with an intensity that surprised both of them, as if they meant to replenish the world for the loss of Mario.

The dawn broke without disturbing their sleep. Mats and Suzanne slept until mid-morning inside the cool confines of the stone walls, yet still awoke before any of the Guibegas.

Mats opened his eyes to find Suzanne placing an open palm on his cheek. Filtered light from the small, high openings in the wall filled the enclosure from the sun that had yet to rise over the walls. He closed his eyes as he felt her trace a line down his forehead, past the arch of his brows, past his nose. She stopped at his mouth, moving her finger back and forth over his lips. He went up on his elbow and inclined his head toward her.

"The wine won," he whispered, a smile slowly breaking as his eyes adjusted to the light.

"Oh, I don't know. You were pretty impressive last night."

"Now I remember why I slept so well. I wonder if anything that allows you to sleep so soundly could also be a pleasant way to wake up." He reached over and touched her breast, pleased by the immediate response. The ache in his head was forgotten as Suzanne rolled on top of him and proceeded to answer his question with a slow rhythmic motion of her own.

They dressed and made their way slowly down the stone steps to the courtyard, where they found many of the Guibegas gathered around tables that had been used for dinner and drinks the previous evening. The tables were set for lunch. Jennette had provided the food needed to settle their stomachs. Most of those at the funeral were still there or had come back after sleeping elsewhere. Jennette was helped by several young girls who were serving a pasta rich with cream and butter, along with a large pitcher of ice-cold orange juice. Jennette had set a table for them separate from the others, shaded by the stone wall of the upper floor. They were joined by Nando, Carlo, and Ramondo. The food, along with the view of the island as it fell away toward the Mediterranean, completed the therapy that their lovemaking had started. As the table was cleared, they discussed what they had so steadfastly avoided during the time of mourning for Mario: what to do with their knowledge of the connection between Jean-Claude d'Avignon and Collette.

"If Leca's actions have been directed by another, then my revenge is only half finished," said Mats. "It is a personal matter, a family affair between the two drug dealers and the Falconi."

"I think that it should be left to the authorities," said Suzanne. "I feel you should turn over all our information, both fact and suspicion, to the narcotics agents working on the case both in California and France."

Mats started to object, but she stopped him with a gently raised hand.

"There have already been two deaths. I do not want the next one to be yours, Mats, or for you to be charged with murder. The attitude of Inspector Medau shows they still think you might be connected to a drug deal gone sour. Another death would be hard to explain as a coincidence."

Mats waited until he was sure she had finished her argument and then turned to the Corsicans.

"It is not over, this thing," said Nando, a look of fierce determination on his lined face. "You are right, signore. If Collette was directing Leca's actions, he must be found and vengeance served. As for Mario, his vendetta belongs to the Guibegas. We will honor it with or without the Falconis' help."

In the end, Suzanne had to admit that they had very few hard facts they could take to the police, no evidence that would ensure the conviction of either d'Avignon or Collette. They could go to Medau once they had proof. They could not take the risk of warning their enemies before that time.

Ramondo had kept silent until now. He said in perfect English, "Nando is right. This is not over for the Guibegas. If you wish for vengeance for your father and Mario's deaths, Carlo's time in the Foreign Legion has trained him well to help you in this. I just have two days' leave or I would be with you as well. I will speak to this Inspector Medau, though. I have worked with him before."

This was the first that either Mats or Suzanne had heard of Carlo's past. "It was for the training and experience that I joined the Legion," Carlo put in. "Not for any love of the French."

"With Leca gone, there has to be a destination for the drugs, and I can't believe that d'Avignon is innocent despite what the police say. If Audrey is right, he is money laundering, and drugs are the obvious source," said Mats. "Besides, he is the only starting point we have."

"If you are to watch him, you will need at least five besides you two," said Ramondo, receiving a nod to proceed from Nando. "You two are known to him, so your use is limited. At least one should be a woman."

"Mario's younger brother Luigi will come even if he is not chosen, " said Carlo. "He must be included. And I have a nephew, also named Carlo, who is ready for such a mission."

"I will come, and bring Leda from her shop in Monte Carlo," said Nando. "It is a good mix of seven people for surveillance and enough muscle, should circumstances require it."

Mats thought it would be wise to caution Carlo not to tell Nando that only the young men were to provide the muscle—not if he wished to remain standing.

"Luigi is a good lad with much promise. Young Carlo looks the most French of us all and is second only to me in fighting skills. It is a good group. We should get to the mainland without being noticed," said Carlo, "since Leca said they had us watched as we arrived last time."

At the Alta Mira, five phone calls lined up not only their party but also a powerboat to take them to the mainland. Mats offered to buy a ticket for the boat's owner to fly to Monte Carlo to pick it up, but the offer was refused. The owner owed the Guibega clan a favor and was more than happy to let them use the boat for three weeks. It was a twelve-meter powerboat with a fully enclosed cabin and stateroom. Two days after Mario's funeral, it pulled out of the harbor at Ajaccio before dawn, the group all carrying bags with several changes in clothes, their knives, and an assortment of rifles, ammunition, and handguns. It took only the first command to Carlo, watching two men jump to cast off the bow line, for Mats to christen the second Carlo "Number Two." By the time they had rounded the stone walls of the Citadel and headed north, he had shortened this to merely "Two," the necessity clear as both men jumped to complete any direction given to "Carlo."

Carlo sat in the stern with Two, Nando, and Luigi, who was eight years younger than Mario but looked enough like his dead brother to be mistaken for him at a distance. Mats had spent time with Mario's immediate family and was startled by the degree to which the two brothers not only looked alike but thought alike as well. Despite the difference in age, the same sense of maturity and quiet competence dominated their personalities. The dark hair, broad shoulders, and heavy eyebrows were the same; only a hint of the fire of youth deep in his eyes, coupled with a hardness set by the desire for revenge, marked a difference in Luigi.

A burst of laughter turned Mats' attention to the stern. Carlo was messing up the hair of Two, who was obviously the butt of some joke. Two definitely looked French. He was fair skinned with light brown hair, youthful in appearance except for a scar on his forehead above his right eye. When Mats returned his attention to the helm, he corrected his setting north toward Monte Carlo.

After receiving Mats' phone call at her boutique, Leda had contacted her assistant manager, giving her instructions for staffing the store, and closed the shop. She packed a bag from the clothes in her own racks and drove directly to Avignon to confirm Jean-Claude's presence at his gallery. She had her cousin, a lawyer, meet Mats at the harbor with a rental passenger van.

Attorneys must be the same the world over, thought Mats, as the lawyer handed over the keys and the information he had received from Leda in Avignon in clipped, officious speech.

"Jean-Claude is at his gallery. Leda is watching him and will contact you at the Inn of the Bridge, where she has booked you rooms."

Mats smiled at Leda's efficiency. He suspected the other boutique owners in Monte Carlo would be glad to have her out of the principality for a few days.

It was dark when they arrived in Avignon. Mats winced at the memory of his dreams as they passed the castle on the banks of the Rhône, where he had first dreamed of the conflict between the Falconi and d'Avignon. It was hard not to stop and go through the old building, just to see if its interior was as he remembered it. It would be, of course. He just wished he knew if he was being helped or directed by his Falconi predecessors. His dreams had become more vivid, not deviating from his father's bedtime stories or Thomaso's journal but expounding on the details and sometimes adding new information.

Leda wasn't at the hotel when the six arrived from the coast. Mats saw the rates for the rooms. He would have to sell a few more items from the treasure. Leda had left a note for them to stay at the hotel saying that she would call. They didn't have to wait long.

"I'm watching the gallery from a café across the street. Jean-Claude welcomed a customer at the front door, so I'm pretty sure he is still in the building."

"I'll be right over," said Mats, replacing the phone in its cradle and moving toward the door. Nando and Carlo came with him to meet Leda, leaving Suzanne at the hotel with the two young men.

The vantage point Leda had chosen proved that she was a Guibega, even if she chose to live in the stratified elegance of Monte Carlo and had been given a Greek first name. Her table had a full view of the entire street in front of the gallery, as well as the narrow alley next to it. Furthermore, she herself was partially hidden from view by a vase of flowers placed slightly off center on her table. She had told the waiter she was not sure when her husband was arriving, but he was to meet her shortly before dark. Enough money had been spent on lunch and drinks, many of which she had dumped in the vase, to keep the proprietor away. Still, she was relieved, and the flowers in the vase very happy, when Mats walked up to the table,

319

followed by Carlo and an old man she immediately knew to be Nando. She had not seen the acknowledged head of the Guibegas for over ten years, but he looked the same. She tried to remember some of the tales she had heard as a girl about this man, but she was interrupted in her reverie by Mats asking a question.

"Is he still in the gallery?"

"Yes, as far as I know. There is a back entrance. I can't see both at the same time. He did come to the entrance for a customer at four-fifteen. That was just a little over an hour and a half ago."

"Has the customer left?"

"Yes, about half an hour ago, but I didn't see d'Avignon when he left."

Mats looked at the street of fashionable shops. It was plain that they would be detected if they used the restaurant as their only observation point, and it would be hard to conceal a stakeout for any length of time in any other location. If their surveillance lasted for more than a couple of days, they would be noticed.

"Nando, go around the building and see if you can find a point where the back door can be watched without your being seen. Carlo, you go to the restaurant manager and see if there are any rooms to lease above the restaurant. Tell him you want the room for a month. Don't tell him you need a view of the street, but make sure any room you rent has one."

The two men nodded and left, leaving Mats at the table with Leda. The waiter arrived, standing behind Mats. "Would Monsieur care to order?"

Mats accepted the menu. "Have you eaten yet?" he asked Leda.

"Yes, but you go ahead. I'll have dessert."

Mats ordered, instructing the waiter to add two settings to the table to accommodate the men who would be joining them. He had not eaten, except for a few pastries early on the voyage from Ajaccio, and he was hungry.

He took the opportunity to explain the events of Paris to Leda, who was one of the few Guibega women who had not attended Mario's funeral. "There is a second man besides d'Avignon. His name is Collette. He's from Corsica and he's d'Avignon's partner in the gallery. He was probably also Leca's partner in drug-running, and his murderer."

Mats produced a copy of the sketch he had asked Audrey to do of the of the man she had seen in the back of the gallery. "I suspect he's more dangerous than Leca or d'Avignon."

Carlo suddenly appeared at the table behind Leda. "We have a room. It has little to recommend it, but it has a wonderful view of the street."

Mats started to ask if it had a bed, but his attention was diverted to Nando, who came running with age-stiffened strides around from the back of the gallery. Mats feared he had been seen and was being chased, but instead of crossing the street, Nando turned and went to the front entrance of the gallery, straightened his cap, and rang the bell. Mats watched in wonder as a man answered the bell, engaging Nando in conversation, and then waved his hand for him to enter.

The waiter brought the food and set it down in front of them. Carlo ordered as Mats watched the door that had closed behind Nando. What the old fox was up to could wait, but the food couldn't. They ate, savoring the taste only after their stomachs started to fill.

Mats had ordered calamari stuffed with spinach, tomatoes, and milked bread. It had been baked with white wine and was served with thin slices of tomato and green beans with a dusting of paprika on top. Mats made a mental note to duplicate the dish as one of his specials when he got back to the Seahawk. Usually the only squid you could get in California restaurants was deep fried, but with the trend in favor of healthier foods, this baked version might sell. Suzanne had shown interest in his restaurant, and he thought she would like the dish. Still, he would have to keep the staple foods that had made his restaurant so popular—and deep-fried calamari was a Sausalito staple.

They were almost finished with dessert when Nando stepped out of the archway that contained the front entrance to the gallery. Behind him was a man Mats didn't recognize. "Do you know who that is?"

"No, I have not seen him before," answered Leda.

"I guess we'll have to wait to find out what the wise old goat is up to," said Mats, turning back to his cheesecake.

Five minutes later Nando entered the restaurant, taking a table by himself near his friends but with his back to the street. Carlo shoveled in the last of his dessert and rose to join him. Mats and Leda stayed at their table as the waiter appeared and took Nando's order. After he had gone, Mats and Leda turned their chairs slightly toward Nando, still maintaining their vantage point on the street.

"Why are you grinning like the cat who ate the canary?"

"Because I ate the canary," Nando replied. "You are looking at the new janitor for the Gallery of the Lilies."

"How did you manage that?" asked Leda.

"I was watching the back-loading area from around a corner when the manager, a Monsieur Frank, threw out the old janitor. If he had not been thrown, he would have fallen of his own account. He had been into his wine once too often for his own good. Monsieur Frank fired him, something about spilling wine on a painting. As soon as they closed the door, I ran to the front and applied for the position. He will be checking my references. They will more than satisfy him."

"We saw how you ran," chuckled Carlo in his coarse Corsican dialect. "A sea turtle would have made better time."

Nando waved down the waiter and ordered a bottle of wine with two glasses. He was still grinning.

"I take it there is more to your tale, or has your face frozen in that silly grin?" asked Mats.

"Oh yes, I almost forgot. D'Avignon parks his car in the rear. He is gone for the day."

Nando continued grinning, looking at Mats begging another question.

"And?" asked Mats, when Nando remained silent with an ever-widening smile.

"As janitor, I could not be expected to be at the gallery all the time. It would be suspicious, so when I was being shown my duties, I remarked to Monsieur d'Avignon about the poor lighting on the right side of the gallery. I mentioned that before I lost my job to age, I was a master mason and that my son was with me, also a mason and also available. I told them I could put in two large windows well above ground level that would give the perfect amount of north light to an area much in need of it, and that I would do it for the same eleven euros an hour they are paying me for sweeping."

"You really are an old fox," Mats said affectionately. "I'm sure that you and your son will have to do the majority of work after hours."

"But of course, Signor Falcon." Nando grinned again and held up his glass of wine in a toast. "But of course!"

CHAPTER TWENTY-SEVEN

In the two days that they had set up the watch, Nando and his new son, Two, were in place at the gallery. Carlo was watching the front entrance with Luigi. Mats and Suzanne had moved from the hotel to the room across the street from the gallery. Mats felt good about the surveillance but was starting to worry that d'Avignon was not acting like a crook. He was beginning to wonder if the art dealer was involved in the drug dealing or just laundering the money. He questioned whether they would catch d'Avignon with a shipment of drugs. They would need proof to satisfy the police that perhaps the rest of their suspicions were correct. But d'Avignon knew what Suzanne, Carlo, and Mats looked like, and he could not use Nando or Two away from the building because they were now working in the gallery.

Still, by staying out of sight and following at a distance, they had amassed a great deal of information about d'Avignon in the two days since they had set up their watch. They knew where he lived and the model and license plate number of his car, and they had a reasonably good idea of his routine. Nothing in the man's actions gave a hint that he was a drug dealer or a murderer. He was unmarried, living alone in a house that was both fashionable and expensive. The house was filled with expensive art, Oriental rugs, and sculptures.

Mats decided to search d'Avignon's house on the chance that there might be evidence there that would satisfy their suspicions. It took Carlo less than a minute to bypass the alarms, cameras, and secondary security measures and enter the house with Leda.

"There were no signs of drugs in the house," he told Mats and Suzanne later, in the room above the café. "But there was a locked rifle case with three shotguns and the same number of rifles. There was also a handgun case, but I couldn't see inside, and I was afraid of forcing the lock."

"There was also a set of foils and two full suits and masks," added Leda. "Several awards from competition were on the walls for both the foil and the rifles. It looks like he is an expert in both."

"The house was richly furnished with paintings, rugs, sculptures... It hardly looked lived in. Even his closets were organized," said Carlo, shaking his head. "The clothes were hung neatly, in an obsessive manner—a section for formal clothes, a section for suits, all arranged in the order of the darkness of their fabric, then sports jackets and slacks, also arranged by color. Finally, casual clothes, with shirts and Levis all hung in order. His shoes were also arranged and polished on several racks."

"Was there a sign of anyone else living in the house?"

"No," said Leda "It was very strange. Almost every man I know has some sign of a woman's presence in his home. It is as if we have to stake out their territory. A dress, a bottle of cream left in the bathroom—but there was nothing like that in the house. It was almost as if no one else was allowed inside."

"Was anything else odd?" asked Mats.

"I did find something that I didn't think of until now," said Carlo. "In the second bedroom were more clothes, arranged in the same way as the master bedroom. I thought at first that they were just more of d'Avignon's, but there were fewer of them. They were arranged in the same way, but they were different. They had a different style, showed different tastes. They appeared to be a little smaller than d'Avignon's as well."

"Well, well." Suzanne concluded she had been correct in her evaluation of him. "It seems we have a drug-running, money-laundering art dealer who prefers men."

"Yeah, now all we need is proof. I will ask Nando if he has seen any sign of d'Avignon's companion in the gallery. We don't need to know his sexual preference. It's of no importance. We need to know if he is dealing in drugs."

Being from Sausalito, in close proximity to San Francisco, Mats was accepting of all sexual orientations. He did not care if d'Avignon was gay, but he knew a number of his gay friends did not advertise the fact and felt vulnerable in certain social situations. Dealing in art would not be one of them, but even successful, fastidious gay men could run drugs.

After the third day, they had a routine set in place. Nando was supervising Two as he opened two holes for the installation of skylights eight feet above the ground on the steeply sloping roof. Two arrived at five AM and worked until the gallery opened at ten. Nando arrived at nine and helped his "son" clean up the loose plaster and stone that had fallen past the catch canopy and into the gallery. By the time d'Avignon's manager arrived to open the shop, it was clean. Nando could tell d'Avignon was pleased with the progress, the light that the work admitted, and particularly the cleanliness of the workers. Nando worked until six PM. Two returned at five. Nando would help set up the canopy, give any necessary instructions, and then leave. Two would work as long as the light would permit and then clean up the rough stuff, close off the openings with plastic, and arrive back at the hotel around ten. The first thing he would do when he went back the next morning would be to uncover the openings and walk around the ground level to see if anything had been moved or disturbed.

After three days of work, the openings were complete. Nando and Two started hoisting the windows that d'Avignon had purchased into the holes in the roof they had created. The sealing of the frames would take the longest time, and this was also the area where a master mason would make all the difference, not only in the water tightness of the finished product but also in the aesthetic effect. Nando began spending more time on the scaffold and less on cleaning the gallery below. Instead of complaining, d'Avignon was so pleased with the increased visibility due to the light passing through the windows that he gave the men a pay raise. Nando now made 15 euros an hour. As day after day passed, Mats was becoming convinced that they were looking at the wrong man—that the drugs were being shipped elsewhere.

On the sixth day, Nando was plastering the sill, feathering the mixture to blend with the original coating, when he heard the sliding rear door open. Two was on the outside of the building mortaring the last of the stones around the window frames. Nando instructed him to go over the roof to see what was going on in the back street, but before he could return, d'Avignon had entered the gallery.

"Come down and help with a delivery," he shouted at Nando.

Nando climbed down from the wooden scaffold and went outside, yelling in French for his "son" to come and help him.

The street that backed the gallery was blocked by a medium-sized van with its rear doors already wide open. The driver was standing beside the rear wheel, smoking a cigarette that hung limply from his lower lip. It was obvious from his posture that he had no intention of helping with the unloading if there was any chance that a strong back was available. Nando looked past the man and saw in the rearview mirror the reflection of another man sitting in the passenger's seat. Their eyes met in the mirror. Nando did not know the man but he knew his type: hard and deadly.

"Which crate do you want taken out, Monsieur d'Avignon?" asked Nando as he was joined by Two.

"All of them. Put them in the back room."

Two reached in, grabbing the edges of one of the wooden cases. He pulled, then pulled again, getting little movement of the crate for his effort.

"I'll push from the inside," said Nando, starting to walk around toward the driver's seat.

"No! Stay where you are!" The command was harsh. D'Avignon shouted to the man in the passenger's seat, "Push the boxes out!"

Nando watched as the end of one of the center crates edged out of the truck, allowing Two to get a grip. As the crate swung clear of the tail gate, Nando grabbed the free end and followed Two into the storage area at the back of the gallery.

"Careful." D'Avignon had followed them into the building. "Be careful putting that down."

The two Corsicans obliged, setting the case down lightly on the uncovered cement floor, leaning it against the wall before returning for the rest of the containers. When they were finished, six wooden boxes were stacked against the wall and the van had pulled away almost before the last one was inside.

"Would you like us to take out the paintings?" Nando asked, already knowing the answer. The crates were too heavy to contain only paintings. This was what Mats had instructed them to watch for.

"No. Leave them be."

That evening Nando was told to finish up work early. Unlike most nights, d'Avignon was still at his desk at closing, focusing on paperwork. Nando and Two said goodnight and left, walking three blocks before Two doubled back and silently climbed to the roof, where by stretching himself prone on the outside scaffolding, he could be hidden beneath the plastic tarp.

When Mats received Nando's message that crates had arrived, a wave of relief swept over him. The waiting had been hard on both him and Suzanne. He envied Nando and Two, who were working and occupied. Even Carlo, Luigi, and Leda had been busy, following d'Avignon between the gallery and appointments as he made his daily rounds. Mats and Suzanne, afraid of being recognized, had stayed in the hotel room across the street, their presence redundant while Nando and Two were on duty.

Mats was lying on the bed when he answered Nando's call. The message was brief.

Nando's voice sounded clear over his cell phone. "Six crates have arrived by van, signore. Too heavy for only paintings. D'Avignon is nervous. Did not want us to open them."

It was what they were waiting for. If they could confirm that there were drugs in the crates, they could inform Inspector Medau.

"Leave Two there tonight to watch the building until Carlo can relieve him," Mats told Nando.

"It is already done."

Mats had been moody, lying on the bed and staring at the ceiling ever since breakfast. Now he was sitting on its edge, smiling, his eyes focused out the window on some distant point.

"Who was it?" Suzanne asked as he relaxed.

"Nando. Six crates of paintings have just been delivered to the gallery. Heavy crates that have d'Avignon nervous."

"Shall we call Inspector Medau?"

"No. D'Avignon shows no inclination to open them. He especially didn't want Two or Nando to do it. We have to know for sure that there are drugs, or we will lose even more credibility with Medau."

Mats' cell phone rang. He saw Two's number. Two was whispering. "D'Avignon is just sitting at his desk as if he is waiting for a phone call. I suspect he is waiting until dark when the street is empty to open the crates."

Mats relayed the message to Suzanne. "Then we have nothing to worry about until tonight," she said. He watched as she crossed the room, pulling her loose-fitting cotton pullover over her head.

Her timing had been perfect. Caught by surprise, he found himself leaning forward with a kiss. Suzanne gave a hum of pleasure as he pulled her down to his side.

Mats lay back in sweet contentment. His head rested on the pillow and Suzanne snuggled next to his side, her head on his chest. His eyes closed as he gave in to the sleep of lovers.

He felt himself entering the dream. There was the motion of the boat, the tang of brine in the air, the odor of unwashed bodies at the oars. The sun beat brightly on the cliffs, cut thousands of years ago by the River Rhône.

SOUTH OF FRANCE – August 1329

Baron Falconi felt the reflected heat as his men shipped the sail and rowed up the waterway into the heartland of France. He had followed Colletti's ship after the battle that had seen the Duke of Avignon killed at sea, taking command of the ship that had dropped him on the mainland. In the time it had taken Falconi to board and see to the four men who had served him so well, Colletti had been able to reach the estuary of the Rhône. Instead of landing at the first safe harbor, Colletti had rowed his vessel up the river past the coastal villages.

Falconi's men pulled hard against the current as they tried to make up time on their adversary. Colletti's ship was not in sight, nor had it been since it had turned into the mouth of the river. Still, there was scant underbrush and no tributaries in which to hide a ship. Falconi was sure they had not passed it. He was beginning to worry about the possibility of an ambush. They had traveled far, and the banks of the river were now close enough to each other for bowmen to fire on a vessel from both sides at once. Yet he did not think that ambush from the riverbanks was a strategy Colletti would rely on. There was too great a chance that a party from the boat could storm one bank and, once ashore, be out of range of the archers on the other side. The river would effectively cut off those same archers from offering aid. No, Colletti would try an ambush, but he would not split his troops to do it.

Falconi guided the ship around a bend of the river and saw Colletti's boat tied up on the west bank. A cluster of small huts hugged the shore with a trail switch backing up the side of the cliff to the vineyards above. The sun at its zenith was harsh on the cliff. There was no sign of the crew or men-at-arms in the village or on the trail, but the Baron felt sure that Colletti would plan an ambush somewhere—if not on the trail, then in the fields above.

As they neared Colletti's vessel, Baron Falconi, standing at the tiller, closed his eyes, and a vision swept over his consciousness. He saw cliffs, but they were not the cliffs cut by the Rhône River; rather, they were stark grey rock, foreboding, swept by harsh winds and free of vegetation. The ship he was on was square-rigged with a single mast: smaller and sleeker than the ship he had used in the Mediterranean. In front of him were two rows of warriors clad in rough cloth and animal skins, each gripping a long oar. These were not slaves but fighting men. Most had axes at the ready, although a few had swords and fewer yet, bows and arrows. Hung along the gunwale on the side of the boat were round shields made of wood with layers of animal hide stretched taut over them. Some were studded with iron brads. All were at the ready.

The Baltic Sea – 941 AD

The men were large and most wore full beards. Their eyes were pale, their noses long and straight. Almost all had scars on their faces or arms attesting to previous battles.

Falconi felt a hand on his shoulder. Turning his gaze from the oarsmen, he saw two men dressed like the crew but with eyes that burned with intensity. The men were identical in looks and dress. Both had light blond hair tied with rawhide thongs in the back, and both had full beards and moustaches flecked with patches of golden-red. They were the warriors Thomaso had described in his journal.

The leader looked at the top of the cliff.

"I fear that Eric Redhand will not take defeat so easily, my brother," said one of the men. "Even with your victory luck and my weather luck, it would be wise to beach our boat and attack from this side of the fjord rather than risk the passage up his waterway."

"Jan is right, Jarl," said the other. "We have captured one of his long ships, but he has many left. Most are with his allies and will take days to reach here. He is no longer a threat to us on this stretch of sea. I think the old rascal will line the cliffs of his fjord with his men. They will be strung out well away from his stead. By the time they return, we could burn him out."

Jarl, the leader, looked at one twin and then the other, for the two could only be twins. Even their voices sounded the same as they spoke the strange tongue that Falconi did not know but at the same time could somehow understand. When Jarl gave his answer, it was in the same strange language.

"I agree with your reasoning. Still, I have a premonition that the land attack will be the most dangerous. Eric Redhand has not lived this long by acting like carrion. He is more dangerous now that he has been hurt." Jarl walked to the side of the boat. Three shields were hung next to each other, but unlike the others, they faced inward instead of toward the sea. One had a center plate of polished copper. As Jarl passed, it caught his reflection. Falconi looked at the image through the eyes of a stranger. Jarl was dressed just like the twins and was indeed their brother, their exact duplicate. His face was their face, his eyes their eyes. Only his helmet, which had short rivets protruding from the side, offered a way to tell him apart.

Then Falconi heard it: a voice in his head, belonging to one of the triplets; a voice that was in his awareness without using the spoken word; a voice put in his mind by the Gift.

We should go ashore now before the sentries see us and spread a warning.

Jarl, nodded as if the words had been spoken.

Call your two boats in. He answered his brothers, again without speaking, watching them wave hands to two ships idling just off the starboard rail.

Falconi recognized the precision with which the men at the tillers guided their boats toward the shore. He looked at his brother and then to the steep incline of gravel that would act as their landing area. As they beached on the rough shore, the brother called Kjell jumped onto the gravel and thought back to him. *I will check the trail to make sure we are not taken by surprise with the ship beached too far ashore.* He watched Jan, the other brother, nod and grunt his assent along with Jarl, leaping to the shore and taking the line of his own ship as it beached.

Falconi felt the Gift as the words tumbled into his mind from his ancestor's brother, now on the clifftop above.

The way is clear.

The thought was strong, filling the Baron's mind, more defined than if he had heard it through his ears over the splash of waves against the hull. Falconi wondered if this was the beginning, the birth of his own special abilities. These three brothers, these Viking triplets, shared the Gift as a birthright, a fluke of shared birth. Falconi sensed that they were the first. They were the ones who would pass on to their offspring the ability to see into the mind of a close relation, until the gift reached him, centuries in the future. In his dream state, he wondered if somehow these ancestors were aware of his presence, as he was allowed to view their deeds. If they were, they gave no indication.

As soon as the boats hit the shore, oars were slipped from one side through the boat to the other. Strong men half lifted, half pushed the vessels high up the rocky incline. Moments later the men had retrieved their shields and weapons and stood waiting at the foot of the cliff.

Is the way still clear?

Yes.

Jarl pointed his axe toward the trail and without hesitation or confusion, the combined crews of the three boats started up the trail. There was no sound as they moved, no shouts or battle cries. Those would come later. They were reserved for the enemy—to send chills into their souls, to make them feel fear.

The River Rhône – 1329

Slowly, the onion skin of awareness separated the passing of centuries. Falconi watched the line of tall, silent warriors climb swiftly up the trail, then shook his head and opened his eyes to his own time and the cliffs about the River Rhône. Soon his own men would be climbing that cliff in pursuit of an enemy of a different age.

Baron Falconi brought his ship to the landing with the same maneuver used by the Viking dragon ship. As the ship nestled next to the corsair already secured against the current, the Baron, with the energy of a much younger man, leaped over the rail and onto the deck of the corsair, moving across it in two bounds. He made his way across the stone landing in pursuit of Colletti.

The Baron left four men on the ship. Their instructions were simple. If anyone other than Falconi approached the ship either from land or sea, cast off. Do not let either ship be taken.

CHAPTER TWENTY-EIGHT

Avignon, France, September, 2000

Mats, awakening, felt Suzanne as she kissed his ear before moving to his cheek, neck, and shoulder. She was in the process of retracing her journey when Mats, unable to stay somnolent, stirred. At first irritated at being pulled back to the twenty-first century, he soon became aware that it was Suzanne intruding and let the pleasant sensations she was arousing in him dominate his mind.

She pulled apart far enough to see his eyes open, and then she reapplied her kisses with less tenderness and more passion. They had been asleep for only an hour, but it had been enough. Their earlier lovemaking had released their tension. This time there was no urgency, only the sweet discovery of each other's depth of feeling.

Afterward, Mats lay on his back, his chest glistening with sweat. He looked at Suzanne and smiled before rising and kissing her softly on the lips. "I love you."

"I know."

Mats' phone rang, breaking the magic of the mood. It was Two.

"I am in place. I have installed two mirrors in a section of bent drainpipe. It allows me to see into the back room."

Two was covered partially by a crumpled tarp, and sounds from the gallery could clearly be heard from the open window. "He had a phone call. He did not name the caller, but he said that he would remain in the gallery with Monsieur Frank until the men arrived in the morning, then take the shipment to the rendezvous."

"You've done well," said Mats, emulating Two's whisper. "Stay put and let me know if you see d'Avignon transfer anything into his car or the van."

Mats quit the call and phoned Nando. "Nando, the plan is in place. Have Carlo wait in the car and pick up Two when the drugs are moved. Have Luigi park the car behind my hotel and wait for me. It will probably be in the early morning. When they move out, you follow anyone left at the gallery. If all of them leave, come and stay with Suzanne."

Mats ended the call and turned to Suzanne. "I want you to stay here and act as an information center. I want Leda to watch d'Avignon's house. I don't think he'd risk having drugs brought to his residence, but we can't take the chance."

"I want to come with you," Suzanne protested.

"I'd like to have you near me too, but think about it, please. I need you in a place that has cell service. You have the trust of the Guibega. They will take instructions from you. We need you to act as headquarters in case I'm not available. It has to be you."

"Yes, nice and safe in the hotel."

"Oh, Suzanne. Yes, nice and safe in the hotel. Remember, I'll have Carlo, Two, and Luigi with me. I'll be safe, maybe safer than you."

"You should phone Medau."

"We've discussed this. We can't risk that the drugs are not in the crates. We also don't know who d'Avignon is meeting. Once we have that information, you can call the police."

Leda accepted her assignment but was not happy. "I will watch his house, but if it should prove unnecessary, I will come back and stay with Suzanne," she said.

Mats pulled a chair to the window and waited.

An hour later, Monsieur Frank left the gallery, walking two blocks to a gyro restaurant and bringing back two large rolls stuffed with meat. He and d'Avignon ate their dinner in the small office at the back of the gallery, sharing a bottle of wine. Then they stretched out on the two sofas and went to sleep.

At seven the next morning, a van pulled up to the front entrance and the two men who had delivered the cases stepped out. Mats watched as d'Avignon himself opened the door. He came a few steps out of the gallery, looking up and down the street before closing the door after them. Minutes passed, and Mats' phone rang.

Two, who was still at his vantage point, having slept under the tarp, could see through the open door into the back room. "They've gone directly to the crates," he whispered. "They're opening one after another, removing the paintings and stacking them against the wall. Now they are starting to work on the top, bottom, and unopened sides of the containers."

Several minutes went by. Mats could hear Two's breathing, along with slight scrapes as he adjusted his crude periscope. "Brick-sized bars sealed in some sort of wrapping and painted with bright colors are being removed from the hidden compartments and stacked on a dolly."

Suzanne moved to Mats' shoulder and pressed the speaker icon on his phone.

Five minutes later Two said, "I think all of the bars have been removed. There is a full stack of bars on the dolly."

The scene that Two described, even distorted by his crude periscope, was accurate enough for Mats to decide he had what he wanted. "I think you can call Medau with reasonable assurance that d'Avignon is trafficking in illegal drugs," he told Suzanne.

"I should also phone the local police," said Suzanne.

"Best wait on that until we see whether d'Avignon goes with the drugs. Wait until I see where they're going before you call the locals. We want to catch Collette, not some courier. I don't want a local yahoo tipping our hand." Mats gave Suzanne's hand a squeeze.

As the last crate was emptied, d'Avignon ordered the dolly pushed to the front door, leaving depressions in the lush carpet in the front viewing rooms of the gallery. The unhelpful thug Two had seen the previous day hopped into the van and backed it to the front door of the building.

Mats could not see what was passing between the inside of the building and the van from his window, but Two could, and he described what he saw in an even softer whisper.

"They are placing some the painted bricks in the van. The rest they are placing in a compartment in the wall behind one of the couches. What should I do if they leave?"

"Luigi and I will follow them. If d'Avignon stays, keep a watch on him. If he leaves, Carlo will swing by in his car and pick you up."

As soon as the van was loaded, d'Avignon left the building, trying to hide a rifle along the side of his leg. He put it on the passenger's seat and then jumped into the driver's seat, starting the van. The manager came around and took the other side. The two thugs scrambled into the rear, closing the doors behind them. Even before the rear door shut, d'Avignon had the van moving in the direction of the river.

"The two in the back have rifles," said Two. "I think I saw the manager, Monsieur Frank, take a gun from the desk."

"I'll let you know their route. Use Nando's phone to relay the information to the others," Mats said, kissing Suzanne.

"Mats, be careful. Let the police handle it," cried Suzanne as he left the room. He ran down the stairs to where Luigi waited, the car already running.

The van went directly through the nearly empty streets to the ancient bridge crossing the Rhône. Two and Carlo were just blocks behind Mats. They crossed the Rhône, turning south along the banks of the river. Mats had Luigi keep a distance between their car and the van.

Mats phoned Suzanne. "They have crossed the Rhône and are heading South on Rue de la Justice."

He felt the lack of sleep that his watch on the gallery, and the night with Suzanne, had necessitated. He closed his eyes. The dream came lightly at first, so subtly that he would not have noticed it had he not become so sensitized to the feeling that preceded the Gift. He was again transported back in time to the banks of the Rhône, feeling the strain of his ancestor's climb up the cliff from the jetty below...

The River Rhône – 1329

As Baron Falconi crested the ascent, he saw the trail leading inland through rows of grapevines that covered the rolling hills. There was no sign of Colletti or his men, other than the tracks left in the tilled dirt surrounding the vines. Falconi squinted, resisting an overwhelming desire to close his eyes. Finally, he could resist no longer. He shut his eyes against the glare and opened them to the hard, semi-Arctic light of the Baltic Sea...

❧ ❧ ❧

THE BALTIC SEA – 935

A hand pointed an axe in the direction of Redhand's stead. The trail ran west across treeless hills cut with clefts, as if Odin had tried to tear the land apart.

Brother, is it still clear?

As far as I can see, there is no one.

Jarl Falkhand could see his brother Jan less than a kilometer in front of him, running in a broken pattern, first to one side of the trail and then the other. They had gone three kilometers when Jarl felt the command: *Stop!*

At the same time, he saw in the distance his brother creeping on his stomach up to a small rise in the trail. He watched for several minutes, then waved the band on.

Eric Redhand's farmstead is less than a kilometer away. Everything looks quiet.

Jarl saw Kjell nod, having also received Jan's message. Jarl still felt uneasy. Something was not right, but even with the shared feelings of his brothers and his own victory luck, he could not define the threat he sensed.

His men, three longboats of them, massed below the rise and at his silent command moved as one over the crest, running toward Eric Redhand's farmstead.

A band of warriors emerged from the dwellings. Their numbers equaled Jarl's men, but most were young boys who were probably a year away from going a-Viking or old men, veterans of many battles, past their prime but hoping to die in battle, their weapons in hand, and thus to attain Valhalla. At their head was Redhand.

Jarl brought his band into the fighting formation, the Boar's Snout, distinctive to his family. He took the center of a large V with each flank commanded by one of his brothers. Each brother directed his tusk of the formation in response to the information supplied by the other two. In this way they could take advantage of weak points without fear of leaving a flank exposed. The initial clash of shields was like thunder, the sound of axe and sword reverberating over the desolate landscape. Both Redhand and the Falkhand brothers were known for their ferocity in battle, but the coordination allowed by the use of the Gift gave the brothers a great advantage.

Before many strokes had been made, Redhand's band moved back, and their giant leader stepped forward calling for a halt in the fighting.

"Falkhand, I seek to talk," he shouted above the few sounds of weapons that still rang in the air.

Jarl yelled at his men, "Stop fighting! I seek a truce with Eric Redhand."

Jarl's brothers immediately echoed the command. In the time it took to complete a sword stroke, the sound of weapons clashing had ceased. Jarl stood in front of Eric Redhand and slowly lowered his axe until he was holding it directly in front of him, horizontal with his palms up. Eric did the same with his sword and the two men faced each other.

"Why did you reject our friendship, Redhand? Ours could have been a great alliance."

"I did not want to be subject to your ways."

"Our ways are your ways. Each man is an equal. No one is another's master. Last month we sent a man to propose joining together in a great fleet that would bring many prizes back once spring planting was completed and the fowling done. He did not return."

Watch out behind you! Kjell's words entered his brother's mind, which was already wary as he faced Eric Redhand, a warrior of almost mythic proportions.

Jarl spun and stepped to his right as Kjell's warning reached him. He threw the head of his axe in a short arc over his right shoulder. The weapon came around already carrying the momentum necessary for a killing blow. Its edge connected with the hand that held the sword that would have taken his life. The sword hit the rough ground, leaving a furrow in the dirt, the hand still around its hilt. Jarl guided the momentum of the axe, which had hardly slowed as it went through the limb, around another short arc and had begun a killing blow when Redhand shouted.

"Stop!"

At the same time, Jarl saw his attacker's face. The face was not that of a man but of a boy, no hair yet growing on his chin. Somehow, he willed his axe to stop centimeters from the young man's head. The youth's eyes were wide, gazing at the arrested axe head. His brain had not yet registered the loss of his hand, the pain masked by the adrenaline flowing through arteries that were carrying blood in spurts to the ground at Jarl's feet.

"Hold!" Eric Redhand's voice boomed again over the bare landscape, paralyzing the movement that had already started toward the confrontation. "I have given my word of truce. Let no man under me raise a sword unless I am slain."

"Kjell, bring this lad to our healer." Jarl turned back to Redhand, his axe again held at the ready.

There were murmurs as Kjell led the young man away, a leather thong already tied around his arm to stop the flow of blood from his severed wrist.

"The youth was foolish, but not as foolish as I to let such a one come to battle unprepared. Still, the attack was a good one. The blow should have split your spine. It is true, then, what they say of you and your brothers. You use the black magic!" Redhand's eyes were hard, squinting under heavy lids at Jarl Falkhand.

"Is that what they say?"

"It is said that you are bewitched with the Dark One's power. That you have second sight."

"Is that why we have met such resistance the last two seasons when we have gone a-Viking?"

"There is a saga being told, sent to all by the Dane, Blood Axe. It is said that the darkness killed your mother and claimed you and your brothers at birth. Three years ago, the Angles defeated Olaf Blood Axe on the misty isle, but you, fighting beside him with fewer men, not only escaped but also removed much booty from a second town. The saga tells of the bravery of Blood Axe and the black magic you used to move your ships to the other town. It tells that you have dark powers that spell bad luck for those who sail with you. No Viking chief, hearing that saga, will sail with you or your brothers."

"Blood Axe is a fool. He was crazed with battle lust. He threw his men at the strength of the enemy. I reasoned that so many men could not come from a single village. They must have come from the neighboring ones, leaving them undefended. I tried to counsel with Blood Axe, but he would not hear me."

"And how did you detect the attack to your rear just now?"

"My brother warned me, but it is not the dark power. We have our own language." *Our minds were connected at birth*, he failed to add. "It is a thing not uncommon for brothers who have the same birthday."

"Humph." Redhand's eyes narrowed even further. He had not heard the warning, but the rest of Jarl's words rang true. However, his actions and those of his brothers during the brief fight suggested powers and abilities that could not be understood.

There was a sound of men behind Jarl's band. He turned and saw the main force of Redhand that had indeed lined the edges of the fjord and now had moved to block their retreat. Jarl realized the trap and was about to give his signal to resume fighting when he was stopped by Redhand.

"Hold, Jarl Falkhand. I have given my word and I am never foresworn. You will not be attacked."

"We came because we sought an alliance with you. Sailing together, we could have attracted others, enough to sail deep into the rivers of the southland. When our messenger was killed, we sought to convince you by a show of force. We never wanted to fight Viking against Viking. We did not understand why you met our overtures with such hostility. Now we know. I would hear this saga of Blood Axe's. Do you have a skald, a poet who could recite it?"

"I have a skald," said Redhand. "But your messenger was not killed. He is at my stead, unharmed. We kept him safe when Blood Axe sent a dragon ship just two days after his arrival." Redhand opened the palms of his hands.

"He is alive!" cried Jarl Falkhand. "We do not want to finish this fight. Your death would bring no honor to my family. Instead, we will walk away and pay tribute to your brave fight if you grant us two things." Jarl watched the old warrior to see if his words would be taken as a sign of weakness.

"What two things do you ask of me?"

"One is your counsel. Your wisdom and standing on how to overcome this false saga you speak of. How do we escape being outcasts among our own kind?"

Eric Redhand stared at Jarl a long time before answering. Then, placing the tip of his sword in the dirt, he squatted on his haunches. Without a sitting bench, it was the preferred position for discussion among chiefs. Jarl immediately placed his axe head down in the dirt as well and joined him.

"I grant the first of your demands and will listen to the second. Your terms are accepted."

Jarl followed Redhand's gaze west along the line of jagged cliffs that marked the narrow opening of the fjord. He could now see, against the flat sun of the late summer day, the hurried movement of the last few men racing back to where they stood. Jarl had misjudged the size of Redhand's forces and with the new arrivals, they greatly outnumbered his own men.

"Fear not, Jarl Falkhand," said Redhand. "I will not betray my word of truce or your trust. Listen to the saga and then decide. Tonight we will feast in the great hall. We will see if you drink as well as you fight. You and your men will be safe from all but the effects of the mead. May Thor strike me with his hammer if I am false."

Redhand's great hall was forty strides long and twenty wide. The roof, thatched and covered with turf, provided protection from the winter cold. On either side of the room, above the heads of the revelers, two carved dragon boards hung from the rafters, denoting areas that were sacred to the warriors. Women and children could not pass beneath them. Only serving slaves were allowed to pass under, and then only to provide food and drink for the warriors.

The three brothers Falkhand sat at the head table with Redhand and his captains, all drinking and telling tales of battle that became more exaggerated by the cup. A fire burned in the center of the lodge, providing needed warmth even though the weather was clear and the sun's rays still hit the southern wall. Every so often, a slave would put a wet bough of a fragrant hardwood on the blaze, causing billows of smoke to rise above the flames. He then used a large circular fan to urge the smoke into the reaches of the hall, killing insects and providing a pleasant aroma that partially covered the stench of the men and their habits.

As Redhand's skald began telling the story, an uneasy quiet came over the great hall. Jarl could see that Redhand was wary of how he and his men would react to their first hearing of Blood Axe's saga.

The saga was not long, taking only one hour to tell. The skald was skilled, and he lent his talents to the tale. Some verses he sang, some he spoke, lowering his voice an octave when he became the Dark Spirit advising the Falkhands. His voice was rich and changed with each situation, alive and vibrant when telling of the brave deeds of Blood Axe, dropping in tone and emphasis when telling of Falkhand fleeing the battle. Often the telling of an epic saga took days, but this one, composed primarily to cover up the stupidity of Olaf Blood Axe, was no epic. At its conclusion there was no shouting, no banging of horns on tabletops, as was customary after a good recital. All eyes were on Jarl, his brothers, and their men.

After a period of silence, Redhand said, "Well done, skald," flipping the man a gold coin. Of all those in the hall, the skald was the most nervous, watching the Falkhands carefully. "Go now. It is best that you leave this hall and do not return this night." The story-teller, despite Redhand's words of praise, was more than happy to leave.

Redhand turned to Jarl. "Now you know why you have been shunned."

Jarl felt the amazement of both his brothers in his mind, contemplating the tale and the problems it posed for them.

"A false saga, one that serves Blood Axe well—and one that will bring him death for the dishonor it unjustly visits upon the Falkhand."

"His death is your matter, but you asked for my counsel. Do you still want it?"

"Yes," said Jarl.

"First, you must not sail as brothers," said Redhand. "Each of you must go his own way. The saga states that only when you are linked in battle, as you were at birth, do you succumb to the dark. Chiefs will welcome you as individuals into any alliance."

"Do I have your word that this will not just be a way of dividing us so that we may be defeated?"

"If you accept my counsel, I will form an alliance with each of you. I will even give you my daughter as a hostage. All three of you will be granted my protection. If you agree, then I will take one of your brothers as my second in command. I suggest that your other brother join the Danes to the south. Most have little love for Blood Axe, and with my word as to your brother's loyalty, he will have the status of a chief. You, I suggest, should return to your farmstead and look to the east and the south. The rivers lead deep inland and flow all the way to the lands of the dark-skinned ones, who have many fine things to trade. Each of you will be able to use your luck, but you will no longer be tainted with the specter of the dark."

"I will discuss the saga with my brothers. If we can devise no other way of dispelling its lies, we will separate and welcome your offer of protection."

"What is the second thing that you ask for, Jarl Falkhand?"

"I ask for the young boy who would have taken my life. I will make him my responsibility and train him to use his other hand with weapons. It is my oath."

"I have already given you the youth as your responsibility, but the training will be in more than swordplay. He is a girl. She is my daughter."

❧   ❧   ❧

South of France, August, 2000

Baron Falconi was surprised. Only twenty steps separated his present position from the point on the trail where he had closed his eyes and given in to the dream. So much had transpired in his vision that he'd imagined he must have moved far into the vineyard. He looked around him, knowing for sure now that there was to be an ambush. He believed the dream on that point. The dream had seemed directed by a power beyond himself. He had tried to suspend it once he had learned of the ambush, but he'd been unable to stop the recounting of the event until the conclusion of the council. One thing he was sure would be different. Despite the message of the dream—the peace between the brothers Falkhand and Redhand—there would be no truce between the Falconi and the Colletti.

Deeper into the rolling vineyards they went, three abreast, between rows of vines still burdened with clusters of red grapes growing distended, awaiting harvest. To each side hills sloped steeply upward, the vines only reaching a quarter of the way up the slopes. Only the sound of the snapping of crickets accompanied their movement. Motioning, Falconi sent a man over each of the rises that defined the valley.

"I fear an ambush. Parallel our path and warn me if you see anything."

"Yes, sire," answered both scouts as they began their ascents to the north and south.

Somewhere the valley must intersect the wagon road that paralleled the banks of the Rhône from the coast to Avignon; it was the same route taken by the Baron's wife and Thomaso when they had been murdered by d'Avignon. Already they had lost sight of the river. Only the sound and smell of the rushing water gave away its nearby presence.

The scout came skidding down the slope from the right. "I have been seen. There are men hidden by the ridge to the right."

Falconi turned at the warning and saw the first of the arrows arch over the small hill, still ascending in its arc.

"Cover to the right!" he yelled in time to allow his men to raise their shields, angling them above their heads and shoulders as they knelt.

He was almost too late in kneeling and raising his own shield to his shoulder before five shafts hit. One went all the way through the horse hide and oak, missing the iron studs, and protruded a good hand's width just above his arm. The impact almost knocked him into the row of vines to his left.

Before the last arrow had clattered off their shields, his men were running up the hill, the axe men leading, followed by six bowmen. Falconi watched for the inevitable second volley from Colletti's archers, but it came not as before in a single mass but rather in sporadic shafts, much easier to pick up and avoid in the air. Colletti's bowmen were of such different abilities that they could not load and release together. Still, three more shafts stuck his shield.

Falconi's men were met before they reached the top of the hill. Sounds of steel clashing against steel reverberated through the vineyard. Colletti had chosen his ground well. Falconi's men were caught on the hill, the slope working against them. They were forced to fight defensively against the downward blows of their enemy.

Falconi was still climbing the incline when he saw two of his men fighting side by side at the top. One had an axe, the other a sword. The axe man hit a shield, lodging deep into the wood rim. He pulled hard, exposing the man who was strapped to it to the sword of the man on his right. The opening in the shield wall was brief, but it was enough. The men rushed through the breach and stood back to back, attacking to either side. It took only seconds to destroy the order of Colletti's line and, once that was done, gain the upper hand in the battle. Those who tried to run were brought down by Falconi's bowmen. Those who didn't try to escape either surrendered or were killed.

The Baron scanned the battle for Colletti. He was not in the melee. The battle was finished. Colletti's men were laying down their weapons and begging for mercy.

"Milord!" The shout came from the scout who had warned him of the attack. Falconi ran back to the floor of the valley and up the hill to his left, knocking clusters of grapes to the ground.

"Here."

Falconi looked around him but could not locate his man. Then he saw the feet, twenty paces away just over the ridge, and the scout who had given the warning kneeling at his side.

The man was a Guibega, dead. His body was surrounded by hoof prints in the soft earth. The killing blow had been given by a sword that still stuck straight up from his heart. Both of the Guibega's hands were wrapped around the blade, not as if to pull it from his body but as if to prevent its removal. On the hilt Falconi saw the jewel-encrusted crest of a noble—the crest of Duke Colletti.

He heard the sounds of a horse and looked toward the west. Colletti sat mounted, watching the battle. Falconi had not seen the animal on the ship, but it might have been in the hold or been stolen at the landing. From the height of his perch, Falconi saw the wagon road stretching toward the south and the Mediterranean. In the distance,

Colletti reared his horse, then with a punch of his mailed fist, rode off to the south.

Falconi was infuriated. The trap had been nothing more than a delaying tactic, ensuring that Colletti would get away. He had watched the fighting from a distance on the chance that the ambush might work and Falconi might be killed or injured. The man was a coward, ready to sacrifice his men to ensure his own escape. D'Avignon had been paid in full, yet the vendetta against Colletti would persist. The Baron now saw the powers that had been working against him with clarity: d'Avignon on the mainland and Colletti assisting him with men and information on Corsica. He was now sure that it was Colletti who had recruited the assassin priest. Colletti was noble only in title.

CHAPTER TWENTY-NINE

Avignon, France, September 2000

"Slow down, Luigi," Mats said as he watched the van in the distance. "I know where they're going, and I think they want us to follow them."

The van turned the corner in front of them and was quickly out of sight.

"Okay now, let's see if I'm right."

They turned the corner in time to see the van less than a block and a half in front of them. It drove straight down the street, allowing Luigi to close the gap easily.

"Pretend you're having traffic problems," ordered Mats.

This time the van, which must have been observing them through its blackened rear windows, slowed immediately.

"Pick it up."

As their car started to close on d'Avignon, the van again picked up speed and kept the distance.

Mats smiled at Luigi. "They're going south to the Montfort Vineyard." Then he texted the place where he now knew the van would eventually stop to Suzanne, Carlo, Nando, and Two. He received confirmation from all except Carlo. Worried, he called Two.

"Two, where is Carlo?"

"He picked me up in the car but stopped a block from the gallery, gave me the car, and took a motorcycle. I have not seen him since."

Mats looked at the van maintaining a steady two-hundred-meter lead on their own car. *So, you know we're back here and you want us to follow. You've set up an ambush and I think I know where, but how many men do you have and how many do you think are with me?*

"Suzanne, phone Medau and tell him everything. Tell them to meet us at the Montfort Vineyard, southwest of Avignon," Mats instructed, looking at a map of the area. "Nando, go with Suzanne to the local police. Help her convince them of the urgency of this situation. There are at least three men with d'Avignon and I suspect more at the vineyard. Then try to find Carlo. I can't contact him. He might have been spotted and hurt. They know about us."

Mats rubbed his temples with his fingers before dropping his hands to the sword in his lap. "Take it easy," he told Luigi. "They won't lose you. I need a little time to rest."

Back when he had first had the dream of Thomaso's murder at the hands of d'Avignon, and the subsequent death of his mother, Mats had been curious. When he had stopped at d'Avignon's keep on the other side of the Rhône, he still thought that he was remembering his father's bedtime stories. He had been curious about the location and had looked it up while on the ferry to Ajaccio. It appeared to now be called the Chateau Monfort and was owned by a French company based in Corsica. He was sure that was the van's destination.

Luigi followed his instructions, occasionally looking at Mats, who sat next to him swaying gently with the motion of the car. The route took them through the outskirts of the town of Armon, then southward down a rural road until they entered the highway that was the main connection to Arles, then along the Rhône to the coast. Although it was mid-day, the traffic on the road was steady. They traveled for ten kilometers, never exceeding the speed limit, before the van exited the highway on a road that was unmarked on Mats' map.

The road, ruts and cracks attesting to its sparse use, wound through gentle hills. Once the van was certain that Mats had made the turn, it sped off, leaving a cloud of dust in its wake. After three slow kilometers, they came to a wrought-iron gate spanned by a sign reading "Chateau Montfort."

Two pulled up behind them. The easy pace of the trip from Avignon had allowed him to catch up easily with Luigi and Mats.

Mats got out of the car and walked over to Two. "Carlo assured me you were the best he ever trained. And you'll have to be if I'm going to get out of this alive." Mats gripped Two by the shoulder and looked east toward the river. The landscape was familiar. It was the same place where in his dream he had witnessed Baron Falconi overcome Colletti's ambush over six hundred years before. The centuries had changed the land little; the vines, gnarled and ancient, had been planted first by the Romans.

"We know of at least four men. Two, go to the left. Stay at least fifty meters off the road. I think you'll find someone waiting in ambush on the ridge. Luigi, you take the right. Be careful and come to the road only at my command."

"You will be alone!" said Two, his fear for Mats reflected in his words if not his expression.

"Yes, and that's why I'll be safe. One man with only a sword is not much of a threat these days."

"That is true. You will not be much of a threat. You will also not be much trouble to kill," said Luigi, joining in and echoing Two's concern.

"This has been going on for too long for them to do me in quickly. Collette, if he is here, will want to gloat a bit. Go now. I'll wait exactly ten minutes before I drive to the chateau."

Both men left so quietly that Mats was confident they would perform to Carlo's expectations. "They are the best I have trained," Carlo had said when Mats had asked about their youth. "And they were both close to Mario. They will not mind killing if it should become necessary."

Exactly ten minutes later, Mats slipped back behind the steering wheel and started slowly down the road. The car rounded the first curve, entering a shallow valley that extended six hundred meters toward the Rhône. On either side of the valley ran parallel ridges. They framed the valley rather than enclosed it. On both sides, the slope became so steep that no vines had been planted. The road led down the valley to a manor house of modest proportions. It appeared unoccupied. Weeds were growing in a small fountain in the center of a circular driveway.

Mats' eyes followed the road, past the residence, to a thick-walled barn encroaching on the vines of the vineyard. Unlike the house, the barn had seen recent activity. The doors stood wide open. Inside, despite the darkness, Mats could see the outline of a wine press and a wall of barrels. D'Avignon's van was parked in the large working area in front of the barn. Next to it was a black BMW.

Five men stood at the back of the van, three of them passing painted bricks between the van and the trunk of the car. D'Avignon and another man watched them without speaking. The driver of the black sedan was taller than d'Avignon and overweight, his eyes almost puffed shut in a squint. Carlo's description fit; this was Collette, d'Avignon's mysterious partner.

As Mats pulled his car into full view, the men stopped work but there was no sign of panic. Then they redoubled their efforts, transferring the last of the bricks to the trunk of the BMW.

Mats stopped the car a hundred meters from the barn. He took the key from the ignition and placed it under the seat, well hidden from view. The car did not present much of an obstruction, but the surface of the road was sufficiently raised along its shoulder that anyone leaving would have to pick his point of exit carefully. He swung the door open and stepped out into the hot late afternoon sun. Behind him he pulled the sword of Falconi, a sword that had seen this field of battle before. A warmth spread up his right arm as he extended the blade downward toward the dirt. Then, lowering his left hand to his side, its open palm facing the small group of men, he walked slowly toward them.

After only ten steps Mats felt his phone vibrate once in his pocket, the signal they had agreed upon; it was Two, informing him that he'd found a man set to ambush the meeting from the right ridge and had overcome him. Seconds later, two vibrations told Mats that Luigi was also in position with the same result. He had to trust in the two young men and to Carlo's training.

One of the men loading the BMW took out a .38-caliber Glock and pointed it at Mats' chest.

"Stop there," said d'Avignon as Mats approached. "I was told to allow you to follow us. Why do you want to die?"

"Your man Leca killed my father. I come because you would only send another hired assassin to do your blood work."

"I had nothing to do with your father's death."

"Leca was your man. Now only my grief and the vendetta remain."

"Leca was an artist's agent. I helped him with certain things, but I know nothing about the death of your father. Now put down the sword before you are shot." D'Avignon looked at the man standing next to him and received a nod.

"Cover him!" D'Avignon waved his hand above his head, the signal for the men on the ridge to come down.

The three men who had been loading the Mercedes now all held guns pointed at Mats, who stood still with both arms outstretched, the sword gripped firmly in his right hand.

D'Avignon looked sharply to the right and left towards the sides of the valley. He looked again and dropped his hand. "Disarm him."

The three men moved toward Mats, spreading their ranks as they approached. All were dressed in work clothes, leaving d'Avignon and the fat man at the side of the van. The lead man, slightly taller than the other two, spread his legs, taking a stance as he brought his pistol to firing position.

As the gun started up, the man suddenly went down with the crack of a rifle, his weapon thrown far to one side as he dropped, his kneecap shattered. The other two men looked first at Mats, then at the ridge. One fired off a shot toward the ridge before he was downed, a bullet tearing the flesh from his elbow and another smashing his tibia just below his knee. The third sprang toward Mats, realizing that he would be safer from the unseen marksman with a hostage. He never reached his goal. Mats' sword flicked up, striking his wrist. His gun flew against the side of the BMW even as the sword swung around, slicing both muscles and tendons behind his knee. Mats stepped over him and approached d'Avignon and the fat man, who stared in disbelief at the three men writhing in pain on the bare ground.

"This was supposed to be an easy pickup! You didn't say anything about my men getting killed!" The fat man with the narrow eyes had his hands up. Fear was evident in his face as he spoke in a cracked voice to d'Avignon.

D'Avignon ignored the man, oblivious to all but Mats approaching with the bloodied sword held before him. "How did you know?" he sputtered.

"Six hundred years ago, Colletti planned a similar trap for my ancestor. We keep notes." Mats nodded toward the dark fat man, who was still holding his hands high in a sign of surrender and shaking with the fear that gripped him. "The d'Avignons and Collettes are a treacherous lot, now as well as then."

"My ancestors! They were not my ancestors. We did not hold the title then. My ancestors were wine merchants who acquired the title ten years before the revolution. The d'Avignons failed to produce an heir and my family bought the title. Half of them lost their heads to the guillotine for their bad timing."

"And now you are to suffer a similar fate for your deeds." Mats could feel the energy from the sword pass through his arm into his whole being.

"Why? I have done nothing. I know nothing of your father."

"Luigi, Two, come down here and gather the arms. Keep d'Avignon and Collette covered," shouted Mats. "And you." He turned to the fat man. "Are the Colletti as pure as the driven snow as well?"

"Monsieur, I am innocent. I only came to pick up the shipment," whined the fat man. "My men were on the ridge but only to guard against the police."

Luigi and Two slid, first one and then the other, down the steep inclines. Luigi moved to the fallen men, placing their guns in the chest and side pockets of his jacket, then frisking them as they lay in the dirt. He moved quickly, never lowering his gun. Two came up behind d'Avignon and Collette and quickly ran his hands over them, starting with their ankles and ending with Collette's cap, which he took off and threw to the ground after searching it. Only

Collette was armed. From under the man's belt he drew a long, thin dagger and from his jacket a handgun. As Two finished, Luigi joined him, still guarding the downed men while backing up to his cousin. Watching them work, Mats appreciated the training Carlo had given them.

"Innocent, with a knife and a gun. Now I know the Colletti to be liars as well as cowards."

"Monsieur, on my oath, I am not Collette. My name is Jacques Dahan. I am just here to pick up the shipment."

Mats read the truth of it in the man's face. He was terrified, a drug dealer who had been caught in a situation not of his choosing. His terror was too real to be faked. But the ground was the same, the vineyard the same as the dream. He had been warned. There had to be a connection. If d'Avignon was telling the truth about his family buying the title, and this man was not Collette, then how had this exact spot been chosen?

"Who do you work for?"

The fat man's eyes widened slightly. Still holding his hands up, he jerked a thumb toward the barn. "I work for Marcel Collette."

Mats flinched as if struck in the face. "Move! Now!" he screamed at Two and Luigi.

The shotgun blast echoed from the darkness through the open doors of the barn. Once, twice, in such rapid succession that the sounds became one as they reverberated from inside the stone building. The spread of pellets tore first into Luigi and then past him into Carlo Two. The two men flew into the air, propelled by the narrow scatter of lead that ripped into their flesh. They crumpled to the earth, Luigi on top of Two, their blood mixing before falling to the ground in rivulets.

A wayward pellet had struck d'Avignon in the temple and now a stream of blood flowed through his fingers, which he held cupped tightly over the wound. The man called Dahan, short and thick next to d'Avignon's slender elegance, now had his hands raised straight over his head but was facing the barn, not Mats. Mats heard the click of a gun being reloaded, and then a man stepped through the opening into the sunlight, a shotgun at his hip.

Mats was astounded that he had ever mistaken Dahan for this man. Both were heavy and dark, but the man who emerged from the darkness of the barn exuded pure menace. He had the shape of a fat man, but under the slacks and shirt Mats could see the ripple of hard muscle. His eyes were narrow, dark protruding brows shading them from the afternoon sun. Even in the bright light they did not blink but held Mats in a cold, unyielding stare.

"So, you are Egel Falconi's son." The words were hissed rather than spoken in the Corsican dialect. "My father told me he had missed the opportunity to kill the last Falconi during the war. Now you come to me." A laugh like snakes hissing escaped the man's lips as he walked toward Mats. "Tell me now, is it true that you are the last of the Falconi? No brothers or sisters? No children?" The malignant laugh told Mats that he already knew the answer. "Leca told of the old man he killed in California. He said the old man cursed him in Corsican even as he was shot. Was that your father, Egel Falconi? Is that what started this? How great is fate?"

"The Guibega told me you were a fat pig." Mats stole a look at Luigi and Two.

"They will die, if they are not already dead," said Collette, following Mats' gaze. "Just as you will, with all the rest of the fools. All killed in a drug deal gone sour. How unfortunate." Again the hiss-laugh split the air.

Behind him the wounded men heard Collette's words and looked for the weapons that had been collected by Luigi. One started to crawl toward the car blocking the road, leaving a trail of blood behind him.

"Then d'Avignon is telling the truth. His family bought the title."

"D'Avignon is a fool," said Collette, swinging the barrel of the shotgun quickly toward the gallery owner. "He is useful for the laundering of money and as a way of transporting the drugs. That's all. As for Leca, he was the best man in my organization. I lost my right hand when I had to kill him, but I could not risk him as a captive."

"My father—his death was not planned?" Mats felt his fingers tighten on the sword.

"A fortunate circumstance indeed, but completely unplanned. My father searched for him but could not find where he had gone after he left Corsica like a coward before the war. He came back during the Nazi takeover, but my father was unable to pierce the Guibega network that protected him, not even with the Nazis' help." Collette smiled, showing a row of yellow, uneven teeth. "I did not connect Leca's tale with Egel Falconi until you visited that idiot painter, Forget. Then it all became clear—the Guibegas falling all over themselves to help you. Better to kill you here in France than in America."

Mats started forward but was stopped by the barrel of the shotgun.

"The Falconi have stolen from my family, usurped our lands, killed our men. My father thought you had a sixth sense. Where is it now? I will kill you last. Like a good dessert, the death of the last Falconi after eight hundred years will be sweet and fulfilling." His shotgun swung swiftly away from Mats and blasted Dahan full in the chest at short range. The man flew backwards, dead before he hit the dirt.

D'Avignon's eyes widened as he realized what Collette meant to do. "Don't kill me! I will never tell anyone!"

"My silly little d'Avignon. You were useful when I first set up the network of art galleries. All the art boys were more trusting of you. The money you laundered was necessary in the beginning, but now I have banks that do it in much larger amounts, and much more efficiently as well." He drew a revolver out of his jacket pocket with his free hand as he spoke. "My family tells stories of the old days," he said to Mats. "We have a family history that each boy is made to read when he turns thirteen. This place is fitting for our meeting, don't you think?" Collette pointed the handgun at Mats while keeping the barrel of the shotgun trained on d'Avignon.

The blast caught Mats by surprise. Collette seemed intent on him, not paying attention to d'Avignon. The shot severed d'Avignon's right arm, tearing great gaps out of his neck as well. Blood spurted from his arteries, propelled by his still beating heart. He twitched spastically, his eyes wide with the realization that he was already dead.

Without looking at the man he had just murdered, Collette said, "Now it is just you and me, and soon it will be just me, just the Colletti, after all those generations. It was a nice touch, blocking the road. It will make it easier for the police to explain this mess. No one could have left in a car, with it still on the road. The police will think you killed each other." The laugh hissed out of his mouth, his teeth held together. "The river is such a nice way to travel at dusk, don't you think?" Holding the handgun on Mats, Collette cracked the shotgun open with his right hand and slipped two more shells into it, replacing the spent cartridges while still covering Mats with the handgun. Mats looked at the fat man's hands. They were covered in thin latex gloves and moved like a surgeon's as they went through the task of reloading. The barrel swung up, terminating its arc with a metallic click, now pointing at Mats' chest.

"If you had not moved so quickly when I shot at you in Paris, this entire sham would not have been necessary, and I would still have Dahan and d'Avignon to amuse me. You have cost me part of a shipment and my organization in San Francisco. Your death will be a pleasure."

"Then it was you on the boat who killed Leca." Mats tried to think of some way of keeping the man occupied, trying to stretch the time until his own death.

"Of course." Collette stepped back two paces. Mats saw his finger tighten on the trigger. He hesitated, as if weighing the pain the answer would give Mats against the pleasure of his immediate death.

"Leca killed your man while I watched from the river," said Collette. "But it was my pleasure. He was a Guibega, was he not? He was shot for sport as the Colletti have always hunted the Guibega—for sport."

A vision flashed before Mats' eyes of his first dream, which he had thought was just a recounting of his father's bedtime stories: the killing of Thomaso on this very ground and the escape of his man-at-arms, Carlo. The picture was gone in an instant.

"Your enjoyment of this is rash," said Mats. "You think you've won."

"I have," laughed Collette, leveling the barrel of the shotgun at Mats' chest.

The earth to the right of the barn entrance moved as if an earthquake was rolling the ground, and then it exploded upward, filling the air behind Collette with dirt and dust. A hand shot out from the confusion and grasped the barrel of the shotgun, forcing it upwards and away from Mats. Another arm went around Collette's neck, a long knife held at the man's throat.

"For sport? The Guibegas are no one's sport!" Carlo, dirt caking his sweaty head, drew the knife across Collette's throat.

Collette felt the pressure of the blade against his flesh and jerked the butt of the gun stock back against Carlo's unprotected ribs. He was at least six inches taller than Carlo and outweighed him by eighty pounds. The blow cracked hard against Carlo, forcing the knife deeper into his own flesh, but Mats saw that Collette had turned, ducking his chin, and the edge of Carlo's blade was now cutting fat rather than his windpipe.

Carlo maintained his hold on the barrel but was thrown off balance by the force of the blow. He was in trouble. His body was no longer in contact with Collette. The handgun, still in Collette's left hand, swung toward Carlo as he kicked at the inside of the big man's knee. His blow landed high on the muscles rather than the joint. Mats could see that Carlo had lost. Collette was too strong.

Then, the shotgun still in his grasp, Collette simply deflated, falling in front of Carlo. The handgun dropped from his hand and the shotgun, still clutched against his side, hit the dirt, barrel first, with the full force of the killer's weight on top of it. Two muffled blasts went off, lifting Collette into the air.

Mats stood with the sword of his ancestors held in readiness for another blow should it be needed. The power of the blade ran up his arm and through his being. Collette's back had a deep gash running from the base of his skull past his waist. Mats could see the fresh cut ends of ribs and nerves sticking through the open wound. He stood like a statue, looking down at the man responsible for the death of his father and so many others.

Carlo finally brought him back to reality. "He is dead, signore."

To make sure his words were true, Carlo bent over the form and placed his fingers on the man's neck. No pulse greeted his touch.

Mats had never killed a living being before. Forget had only been injured. Leca, whom he had had reason to kill, had been killed by Collette. In his dreams he had seen the violence of his ancestors, but now he knew the feeling of power, the exhilaration of using a weapon to take a life. The blood lust of a warrior was in him. Still, a feeling he had experienced in the dreams of both Baron Falconi and Jarl Falkhand predominated, a feeling of sadness and despair.

Mats saw Carlo staring at him, his look of admiration reminding him that he was the leader. The Falconi had always been the leaders and this day had not yet come to an end.

"Carlo, look to Luigi and Two."

Mats' head was throbbing with the adrenaline rush that had gripped him in the encounter with Collette. He knelt next to Carlo, who had separated the two young Guibegas and was now compressing the flesh of Luigi's arm just below the shoulder.

"Press here, signore. Both are alive, but barely. I will see to the men they left on the ridge."

Mats took over the task of stemming the flow of blood from the young man's arm and looked at Carlo Two. Blood was oozing from wounds all over his body, but the pellets had not severed a major vessel.

The sound of a police horn entered his consciousness as he looked down at the pale face of the young man. "Hurry, please hurry," he whispered, as if the oncoming ambulance crews could hear him over their sirens. Between his car and the bodies of d'Avignon's men, a helicopter was landing, dirt flying up and obscuring the arrival of the medics.

Chapter Thirty

In the end, only the fact that Carlo had buried himself in the courtyard prior to the arrival of Collette and the van was kept from the police. Medau had arrived with Inspector Fuchs, Suzanne, and a doctor in the helicopter. Mats accompanied Medau as he questioned each individual connected with the case.

"How were these three injured?" Medau asked as they approached the two men on the ground and the one who had crawled some twenty feet away toward the road. Medau walked slowly, surveying the scene with a critical eye. He followed the trail of blood. Mats saw him note that the trail led toward the road, not toward the dead Collette.

Inspector Medau looked at both ridges, the car that still blocked the road, and the placement of the fallen men. Every five paces he turned and looked back at the cluster of three dead men with the van and car behind them, their trunks still open. Mats could see Carlo moving toward the dirty blanket that still lay to the side of the shallow ditch, and he casually moved between Carlo and Medau, pointing toward the injured men in front of them.

"They were about to shoot me. Luigi and Two, that is the younger Carlo, shot them with the rifles they had taken from snipers on the ridge. That man I disarmed with my sword." He pointed at the man who was holding his wrist, blood seeping through his white knuckles. "Luigi and Two collected their weapons before they were shot."

"You will not say anything to them while I question them," said Medau.

The men shot by Luigi and Carlo Two, as well as the one hamstrung by Mats' sword, gave essentially the same account. They had heard Collette and knew they had escaped death at his hands. Pain and fear enhanced some parts of their recollection while clouding others.

The dirty blanket lying near a slight depression to the side of the barn was the only detail overlooked by the investigators. Carlo had picked it up, shaken it, and put it around Suzanne's shoulders. Mats looked past Medau and saw Carlo whisper in her ear. It was not cold, but he knew she would now clutch it, as it helped fight her chills. He knew it would be impossible to explain how Carlo had selected that particular plot of earth to conceal himself prior to the meeting; it would be foolish to explain that seven hundred years before, another Guibega had hidden in the same ground. Fortunately, no one asked.

Carlo then left Suzanne and led a policeman up the ridges, dragging the two snipers, still trussed, down to the ground in front of the barn.

Luigi's captive on the ridge had regained consciousness and squirmed to the crest, and although unable to loosen his bonds, he had witnessed the confrontation between Mats and Collette. Mats listened as he described Collette's killing of Jacques Dahan and d'Avignon to the inspector. His story was even more forceful because it incriminated himself at the same time as it corroborated Mats' account.

Suzanne came to Mats' side as the man described the scene of Collette gunning down his two henchmen and turning the gun on Mats.

"How did you arrive so quickly, and with Medau and the doctor?" asked Mats, turning her away from the man.

"I phoned Inspector Medau, against your wishes, while you slept last night. He stopped in Avignon and allowed me to come with him in the helicopter. We followed the directions you gave me. I'm glad I did. I just wish we had arrived faster."

Medau approached them after seeing the last ambulance away and delegating the crime scene to Fuchs and his second in command, an inspector from the Avignon office. He motioned Mats to the side, out of the hearing of the others.

"My instincts tell me that everyone is telling the truth," said Medau, to Mats' great relief, "but the case is so strange, the events so bizarre, that I still feel there are pieces missing. The elements fit together neatly, but there were just so many coincidences, so many moves that could have gotten you killed. No one is that lucky when drugs and murder are involved."

"I agree," said Mats, "Nothing like this has ever happened to me in America. I've had enough excitement for the rest of my life." He looked around the scene. The injured men had been flown out or taken by the ambulances. Only d'Avignon, Dahan, and the massive Collette remained, waiting for the coroner. Mats' gaze paused on the black BMW, and he thought back to the death of his father and the car that Leca had taken to escape. Irony or destiny? He could not decide which force had brought this story full circle.

Medau looked at Mats, then at Suzanne, wrapped in a blanket with the grubby Corsican standing protectively at her side. "I hope your wish holds true," said Medau, looking at Mats and not smiling. "There is much left for me to understand about this affair."

EPILOGUE

Collette's was the only death connected to the American, but even that was only probable, not certain. The medical examiners reported that the two shotgun blasts that had torn all the organs from Collette's abdomen and chest had taken his life. The slash in his back would probably have been fatal, but he was alive when the shotgun went off. The man with the cut leg confessed that Collette had had a gun on Mats before he was struck down. Medau had to promise a lighter sentence to the other two gunmen in order to coax their full testimony from them. Tests showed that Collette was the only one who had handled the shotgun, and powder marks were still on his gloved hands and his jacket.

Initially, Medau hadn't been able to question either of the two young Corsican cousins who were evacuated in the copter. Luigi was still in intensive care but was now expected to live. The young Carlo was in guarded but serious condition, having taken most of the pellets on the right side of his chest and shoulder. The doctors said it was unlikely he would regain full use of the right arm, but Medau had seen this type of man before. He would recover and so would his arm. In his old age he would be stiff, but he would recover. He would interview Luigi when the doctors gave their permission, but Medau knew instinctively that the story would be identical to that of his friends—a perfect fit.

Mats Falcon would not be charged. It was clear from the testimony that he had been led to the vineyard to be killed. He had only injured a man who had been threatening him with a gun. The other, Collette, had pointed a shotgun at him and had already murdered two men. Falcon explained that he had been carrying the antique sword in his trunk, planning to take it back to America with him as a wall decoration. It had been the only weapon available when he had realized he was in over his head. It seemed reasonable, but Medau wondered why the blade had been sharpened to such a razor's edge.

The press would have a field day: a man killing a drug lord with a fourteenth-century sword, a modern-day Edmond Dantès. For his own part, Inspector Medau was more than happy to hide the use of the antique sword.

Since the event, Inspector Fuchs had uncovered evidence of the scope of Collette's drug operation. For a while at least, the supply of drugs into Provence and the west coast of America would be hampered. Medau was too much of a pragmatist to hope that the change would be permanent. There was always some slime ready to step up and fill the demand. He secretly wished that all dealers could come to such a final and just end. The interview with the injured Corsicans, then one more with Falcon, would be necessary, and then he could close the file.

Mats sat on the veranda of the hotel. Two weeks had passed since the killings. Both Luigi and Carlo Two had gone from critical to intensive care, and then to stable condition. The doctor said that only their superb physical shape, combined with luck, had saved them from death.

Inspector Medau acknowledged that Suzanne's call had undoubtedly saved the men's lives. Her calling him had been a precaution, but Mats realized that after Leca's murder and her previous injury, it had been logical, and his refusal to cooperate unreasonable. Both Luigi and Two would have died if they had been transported by ambulance. Carlo had taken the helicopter back with the two wounded men. Upon being told by Carlo that he and Luigi had the same blood type, the doctor had tapped raw blood directly from Carlo the older to replenish that lost by Luigi. Two, having lost less blood, was placed on a plasma bag. A police sergeant had crowded into the already full helicopter, guarding Carlo while he gave the blood of the Guibega from one generation to another.

The entire group, including Leda, was instructed not to leave France. In his first session with Inspector Medau, Mats had asked that Suzanne be allowed to fly back to Paris before Professor Gilbert managed to forget the origins of the Bougainville find. He was candid with the inspector, who took the time to document Suzanne's credentials before agreeing.

The police had kept his passport but said it was just a formality until they could finally talk to the two injured Guibegas. So Fridays at four, Suzanne would leave the Bibliothèque in Paris and take a taxi to the train station, where she would catch an express train to Avignon. On Monday mornings, she would return to Paris and her books, secure that Mats' love for her would survive during the next week of work.

Mats watched as Suzanne walked across the café toward his table. He rose to hold her chair. He knew she liked this old-fashioned attention, fostered by his father. They had stayed in their room since she had arrived the previous evening. Morning found them still in each other's arms until Mats finally broke away for nourishment. They would visit Two and Luigi and spend time together solving the mysteries of the heritage that had brought them together and molded the events of the past month.

"You look lovely," he said, kissing her behind the ear as she took her seat.

She smiled coyly. "Special?"

"Always," Mats said. "And me?"

"Handsome and special," said Suzanne.

"Special enough to marry? After Luigi and Two are released, I would like to meet your parents and ask for your hand in marriage. Will you marry me?"

"Yes," she answered, a radiant smile spreading across her face. "Of course I'll marry you! But not before breakfast."

As they finished their meal, Suzanne said, "You're very quiet. Is something bothering you?"

"While you've been gone, I've mostly thought about the Gift. I've had time these past weeks to go over Thomaso's writings. Every time I read his last volume, I understand more. Before the business in the vineyard, I read his words, 'a dream in a dream,' and his references to the dreams of the others, and I didn't fully understand their significance."

"But now you do?" asked Suzanne.

"In the room, just after we made love and before d'Avignon left the gallery with the drugs, I had a dream. It started like the others, centered on Baron Falconi. The difference was that I was back in the Baron's time, but he was having a dream of his own, a dream about his ancestors. For the first time, I didn't dream about an event or an encounter of Baron Falconi's. I had a dream about *his* dream. It was like I had been transported through the Baron's mind another four hundred years deeper into the past, into the mind of a Viking."

"A dream within a dream?"

"Yes. The Viking had two identical brothers, triplets. They were born knowing each other's thoughts and experiences. I believe it was the origin of the Gift. Their ability was strong, a condition of their birth. It must have been a tremendous advantage in war before radios and cell phones. Other Vikings denounced the brothers for having this ability, calling it black magic."

"Is that all you know about these Vikings?"

"Just that a Danish chief by the name of Blood Axe spread a saga saying that they used dark powers. A king named Eric Redhand, whom they first fought and then befriended, advised them to split up so they'd be accepted as individuals."

"I've read about him," Suzanne said. "Eric Redhand, if he's the same one and I remember this correctly, was called Redhand the Undefeated. Never lost a battle and died one of the most powerful of the Viking chiefs. I can't recall Blood Axe, but I know where to look. Anything else?"

"Just that I haven't had any dreams since the killings. I think that I might never have another. I think the dreams were meant to protect me, and I no longer need protection. Whatever the reason, they no longer come to me. I can't seem to encourage them when I sleep. They're gone, and it worries me."

"Signor Falcon, Inspector Medau is getting out of his car in front of the hotel," said Carlo, approaching them from where he had been standing on the edge of the veranda.

Medau approached the table. "Ah, Mademoiselle De Lacy, Monsieur Falcon, how lucky I am to find you here together."

"Inspector Medau, would you please join us? We have just ordered coffee. Could we offer you a crêpe?" said

Suzanne, as Carlo moved back to his spot at the edge of the terrace.

"I have already eaten, but I will join you for a cup of coffee, if you would not mind the intrusion."

"No intrusion." Mats waved to the waiter.

"Inspector, are you sure you wouldn't like a crêpe?"

"Ah well, no one would trust a thin Frenchman anyway. Merci, I will join you."

"Make that three orders of the crêpes and more coffee, please," said Mats to the waiter, who had anticipated the summons as Medau sat down.

When the waiter had departed, Inspector Medau began. "This morning I was finally able to talk at length with Luigi Guibega. He is still short of breath. It seems he had placed a handgun in his jacket pocket which protected his heart but not his lungs. The doctors are ready to let him out of the hospital, though."

"He is a fortunate man to have survived the shotgun blast," said Mats. "His condition still concerns me."

"Yes, fortunate and loyal—very loyal. Why do these Corsicans offer you such loyalty? Why is it they would put their lives in peril for you?" asked Medau, his tone penetrating.

Mats stiffened. He felt Suzanne place her hand on his arm in support.

"I am not sure myself, Inspector. Old family ties, I suppose. In part, it has to do with my father…When he left Corsica, he gave the Guibega family part of his land. On the other hand, it might not be loyalty to me so much as hatred for Collette. I honestly don't know. The Guibega family doesn't talk much, as I'm sure you found out, even to me. I do know that I trust them."

Mats looked at Carlo, but he stood stone-faced, ten paces away, looking straight ahead, not responding to the remarks and questions about his family.

"As well you should. I have checked up on them and on you."

"And what did you find?" asked Suzanne.

"The Guibega family was the backbone of the Resistance against the Germans," answered Medau, the edge in his voice softening. "They have put many men into the service of France, and they have always served with distinction. I have even heard the occasional mention of your father, Monsieur Falcon."

Medau turned toward Suzanne. "The minister himself told me you are responsible for the recovery of some of France's most important historical documents. He confirmed that you two met only months ago."

"You seem to have been very thorough, Inspector," Suzanne complimented him.

"Five dead, four others seriously wounded…An American defending himself with an antique sword that belonged to his family for seven hundred years…a sword that is razor sharp and has traces of several different blood types beside that of the two men who were slashed at the scene. Yes, I have tried to be thorough."

Mats heard Medau's voice harden again and saw his eyes narrow, scanning his face for evidence of a lie.

"Some of the stains were old, very old, perhaps even centuries. Evidently your family has used the sword to defend itself before."

"I know nothing of that. Your tests must be quite sophisticated," said Mats.

"Four samples were from our time," continued Medau, ignoring Mats' comment. "One matched the criminal Leca, who we know was shot, but had a stab wound from what you said was a kitchen knife. Another was from Forget, whose murder we know was done by garrote, but he had a healing sutured wound on his bicep. How do you explain these inconsistencies?"

"Does it matter, Inspector? Neither was the cause of death. The blood trace could have been transferred by me in handling the sword."

Medau stared at the American. A minute went by. Carlo remained still, looking out over the street, but tension showed in the muscles of his forearms. Only Suzanne became visibly uncomfortable in the silence, shifting in her seat.

"Inspector," said Mats finally. "Last week you told us that you closed Forget's murder case and found garrotes in Leca's belongings, which had any number of blood traces that you are linking to several unsolved similar murders. You also found the rifle used to kill Leca in Collette's possession, and you have the testimony of several men at the drug transfer who heard Collette admit to killing Leca to silence him. Why would you want to complicate your cases because of minute traces of blood that were most likely transferred by accident?" Mats smiled and held his hands apart in a gesture that offered a truce.

Medau continued to stare at Mats; then, as if accepting the reality that the Guibegas were not the only close-mouthed individuals in this case, and that what the American said was the truth as far as it went, he smiled and sat back in his chair.

"I came to tell you that you are free to leave France. Luigi's story matches exactly with the others. The only thing I need to know before I close the case is if you can account for the money you have spent in France."

"It is money that my father had hidden on Corsica during the German occupation. I didn't know about it before I arrived and was only shown it after I met Carlo and Mario. It wasn't even money, just some old coins and jewelry that had belonged to my family for generations. I have taken your suggestion. I have hired an attorney to make sure all taxes are paid."

"Good. Do this, and I will have no other reason to detain you. But I would ask that you return if you are needed for testimony."

"Certainly, Inspector. What about Carlo and the other Guibegas?"

"They are also free to go with the same provisions. We may need them to testify against Collette's men."

The meal arrived, carried by the waiter, who somehow balanced three cups, a pot of coffee, and three plates of dessert crêpes, managing to place them gracefully in front of first Suzanne, then the inspector, and finally Mats.

When the waiter had left, the inspector turned to Mats, a trace of blueberry on his lower lip. "I don't suppose you would make me happy and tell me what I am missing in this case?"

"I don't know what you mean, Inspector. Missing?"

"I'm a good policeman, Monsieur Falcon. I can see the truth better than most and usually find a way to expose it. In your story and that of the Guibegas, I see truth. I felt before I checked you out that everything you told me would prove true. Yet I also know that I am not being told the whole truth only because I do not know the right questions to ask. You will not volunteer the information. Still, I cannot keep you prisoner to pay for my inadequacies as an inspector. If I felt that these unanswered questions would change the outcome of the case, perhaps I would keep you longer. But I feel in my heart they would not. I thank you for your help in ridding France of the scum Collette, Leca, and Forget. I hope that your business continues to grow and that you will return to France, Monsieur Falcon."

"Falconi," said Mats, smiling. "I've decided to replace the 'i' removed by my father. The Guibega insist on calling me Falconi regardless, and I've become proud of my heritage these past months. What about my passport and my sword?"

Inspector Medau looked toward the alcove and nod-ded. His assistant came out onto the veranda carrying a tennis bag and a large manila envelope.

Mats unzipped the case and withdrew the sword. He hefted it, rejoicing in its familiar weight, and then placed it point down, resting his head against its hilt. His father's ring provided a gold cushion between his forehead and the cold metal of the blade. He closed his eyes and saw Baron Falconi at home on Corsica, the Lady Le Vere hold-ing an infant to her breast. Another vision flashed into his mind: a tall, fair Viking among dark-skinned men. Mats forced his eyes open and smiled at Inspector Medau.

The dreams had returned.

THE END

ACKNOWLEDGMENTS

Any writer draws help and inspiration from many sources. I am no different, and probably more dependent than most.

First on my list would be Audrey Beck, whose encouragement, knowledge and insight into so many of the subjects in this book, from the art world to life on Corsica, kept me on track. I miss you, Audrey.

To Sarah Goss, self-confessed word junkie and English professor at the University of San Francisco, who not only reads and offers suggestions that make the novel a better read but corrects my most obvious mistakes without making me feel inadequate.

To Jennette and Ray Ambrosio, who read my stuff in its raw state and offer advice on all things Italian, cooking, and food.

To Anne Lamott, who first told me to pick up a pen and write.

To Matt Nelson, my oldest son and severest critic, who is quick to point out when something isn't working and why.

To the Mill Valley Library Writers Drop-in Group, especially Bill Mena, who writes beautifully and makes me feel young; Jen Hart, who insists for her readers to expect the unexpected; John Byrne Barry who constantly reminds me that scenes are better for the readers than narration; Barb Elwell, who makes sure my endings are worth the book; Asma Aschen, who makes me realize there are whole worlds of people about whom I have no knowledge; and Kate Moore, English professor supreme, who makes sure that romance lives in the written word, even mine. Those who haven't read her series *The Husband Hunter's Guide to London* are missing a treat. Finally, to John Geoghegan, who writes tremendous non-fiction but loves tales of knights, battles, and vendettas. His suggestions are always spot-on and help me become a better writer.

To Brian Van Camerik, who designs the covers for my novels with such an original and light touch. He is a true artist.

Special thanks to Pat Lyle, whose master's degree in English from Oxford doesn't prevent her from offering help with this bit of fun.

To Josh Freel at Waterside Publications, who shepherds my manuscripts through the final process.

To my agent, Bill Gladstone, who has put up with me on and off for thirty-five years, both on the golf course and as a client. He is simply the best.

Finally, to my wife Kellie, who endures the tippy-tap of keys at odd hours when the creative juices flow. She is my true inspiration.